Courage for
the journey
— Michelle Gregory

Eldala

by

Michelle Gregory

Wildwoman Press

Eldala

Published in the United States of America by Wildwoman Press.

Library of Congress Control Number: 2007929343
ISBN 978-0-6151-4818-2

To my one true Eldala ~

You believed in me,
and it changed everything.

Dear Reader,

If I'd had my way, you wouldn't be reading this.

My original intent in 2005 was to join thousands of other new authors in writing 50,000 words in 30 days for National Novel Writing Month. If I finished, I'd have a story for me and my children.

No one else.

When my husband (the dreamer in the family) suggested self-publishing, I was intrigued – but only because I liked the idea of having *one* printed copy to show that I had written a story.

That was it.

Little did I know that over the course of a year, while I wrote and rewrote and revised – and revised again… and again – that I would unintentionally tell friends and acquaintances I was writing a novel. Before I knew it, *a lot* of people knew I was writing a novel. And they all wanted to read it.

That put me in a difficult position.

Writing the story took most of my courage. *Sharing* the story is taking *all* of it. As I expose my heart, I have to remember that I'm not here to keep anyone happy.

But this is still risky.

So even though the thought of you reading my novel threatens to tie my stomach into knots, I have to remind myself, once again, that I wrote this story for my family. Despite that fact (and considering that you're already holding it in your hands), I hope you like it as well.

~ *Michelle Gregory*

Teleria
Forest of Ithil
Kolachel
Hada Clan
Gedelar
Morigon
Pent
Arath
Merah River
Merah Lake
Agora
Linden Clan
Kofar Clan
Sea of Voronezh
Iligan Mtns.
Orizant
Benda River
Felonia
Barpeta
Korisan
Lenkar
Koslan Mtns.
Maquoya
River
Korisan
Ilich Island
Koridoc
Tyman Clan
Nedebar Clan
Agadir
Toboso
Trevet
Rapid
Nosora
River
Ancala Clan
Kavali
Zaria Mtns.
Pomora
Lonely River
Lake Batna
Kelefar
Temir
Sodoya
Kumai Clan
Map by Brandon, Joshua & Michelle Gregory

Prologue

Arathor's heart thundered as he swung astride his black stallion and strained his eyes for any movement on the road in front of him. It was a moonless night, but he knew King Rahnak's spies were watching him; he'd fought off three of them in Felonia. He couldn't risk engaging anyone in a sword fight again. Speed and cunning were is only protection now.

Before leading his horse out of the ash grove, he unwrapped the bundle he'd fought so fiercely to protect the night before. Aiden was fast asleep, swaddled in a blue woolen blanket, completely unaware of the danger surrounding him.

Arathor grimaced.

"How can I give you up?" he whispered.

He clapped his heels to the horse's flanks. Telegar's strong, confident gait thundered beneath him as they sped towards the next town. Suddenly, his mount let out a shrill whinny, and the hair on Arathor's neck bristled. He looked behind him, taking in the ground they'd just covered.

Five hooded riders, black cloaks flying behind them, were closing in on them.

Fighting his alarm, Arathor shouted the ancient words his father had taught him: "Kel-lema menan-dai kah-gish tehai."

In a split second, a wall of searing red flames, twice Arathor's height, sprang up behind him and engulfed his pursuers. Their tortured screams echoed in his ears as he urged the stallion forward.

Kale lit a candle on his way to answer the urgent knocking. Before he got to the door, his wife Elisa was beside him.

When he opened the door, they both drew in a quick breath. Although the man's face was hidden, Kale recognized him at once. No one else had Arathor's commanding stature.

"What…?" Kale asked.

Arathor stamped the mud from his boots before handing Elisa a bundle. He sat at the table and pulled back his hood. The pale light couldn't hide the concern in his face.

Elisa parted the wool blanket. Her eyes grew larger and she covered her mouth. "Is this… who I think it is?"

"He's in danger," Arathor said. "Will you raise him as your own?"

"Why us?" Kale asked.

Arathor looked at him, but his intense dark eyes were more than Kale could bear. "You've been my smith for many years now and I know I can trust you."

Kale had always lived a quiet, sheltered life. Now Arathor was asking him to risk his security and Elisa's to take in the boy. All the reasons for not doing this flew through his mind in a heartbeat. The only argument he could stammer was, "I'm sure there's someone else more suited for the task."

Arathor's face tightened.

"Then I have no choice?" Kale asked.

Arathor rubbed his brow and his face took on the haggard features of a warrior too long in battle. "No, I'd never force this on you." He shifted his weight. "But I need an answer now."

Kale glanced at his wife. Elisa never asked for much, but her eyes were pleading with him now. The haunting sadness in her face extinguished his arguments.

"All right, we'll do what you ask."

Arathor glanced at the door, as if expecting someone to burst through it at any moment. "I have to warn you – if you take him in, you'll be in as much danger as he is."

Kale tried to stifle his mounting fear. "We'll move away as soon as we can."

Arathor smiled grimly and handed Kale a rolled parchment. "You can tell him he was adopted, but nothing more. When he's twenty-one, give him this letter." He pulled up his hood and put a hand on the smith's shoulder. "Kale, I know you can do this."

Arathor walked towards the door and then stopped. "There's one more thing." He pulled a battered scabbard out of his cloak. The flickering candle light danced on the sword's hilt.

"After he reads the scroll, give him this. It may help him accept the truth."

Grief lined his face as he put his hand on the child's head and kissed his brow. “Grow well, Aiden.” He bowed to the couple and went out into the night.

Elisa looked at her husband and smiled. “I never thought this day would come.”

“A son,” Kale said, half hearing his wife.

How will I be able to do this? he wondered.

Elisa moved closer to Kale and handed him the child. “Aiden.”

Kale put his fingers to her lips and lowered his voice. “We can never speak that word again.”

The boy needed a strong name, one that would give him the courage he needed to face his destiny, yet not reveal the nature of his birth. After a long silence Kale said, “His name will be Kieran.”

Chapter 1

Twenty years later…

Kieran woke up, his heart racing and his clothes drenched in sweat. It wasn't unusual for him to have strange dreams, but this one had been the most terrifying of all.

He'd been walking with his mother and father near the sea. Suddenly, a sword sprang from the waves and flew into his hand. Elisa's face froze in horror and Kale stepped in to defend her. Before Kieran could stop himself, he'd killed both of them. Their blood covered the sword and his cries of despair woke him up.

Still shaken, Kieran walked to the kitchen and washed his face. Normally he would have eaten a quick breakfast, but the dream had stolen his appetite. Frustrated, he returned to his room, put on a clean shirt, and headed for town.

With his long stride, it took him only a few minutes to walk from his home near the shore to the smithy near the center of Pent. On his way, he passed several low-roofed cottages, each with a small garden plot and racks of drying white-fish. Turning to the left, he noticed the familiar odor of wet clay coming from Jelcahd's pottery shop, and the mouth-watering aroma of fresh bread coming from Helgar's bakery. The sun was just coming up as he jumped over the fence around the cooper's yard and walked into his father's smithy.

Kieran had learned his father's trade quickly. By the time he was seventeen, people said he was the best smith in northern Teleria. While Kale forged the ordinary, Kieran preferred embellishing the ordinary and creating the extraordinary. When he walked through Pent, he could see his handiwork – ornate door handles, hinges with intricate flower motifs, and gates that looked like they could grace the castle at Korisan.

Today he had to settle for making ladles.

Walking past the racks of tools, he pulled off his shirt and was about to put on his leather tunic when he heard a disturbance. A cluster of unmarried women had gathered at the door. They came every day and tried to get his attention. Despite their obvious beauty, none of them caught his eye. There was only one woman for him. He just had to find her again.

Now Kieran turned his back on them and quickly put on his tunic.

When his father joined him, Kieran donned his leather apron and stoked the fire.

"Do you have that order ready for the cooper?" Kale asked.

"It's over in the corner," Kieran said, pointing to a pile of iron barrel hoops. "I made two extra for the children."

Kieran loved having children in the shop. Kale was always worried that one of them might get hurt, but Kieran invited them in anyway. He enjoyed making things for them, and their favorite toys were the iron hoops. When the children raced the hoops in the street, Kieran always stopped to watch. This had been his favorite game as a child, and the only game where he could beat his cousin.

As if on cue, his cousin entered the shop and stood to one side.

"I see your adoring throng is here today," said Gilrain.

"I'm sure you'll be happy to take them off my hands," Kieran muttered.

"Maybe later. What are you working on today?"

"Are you offering to help?"

If Gilrain saw that Kieran was annoyed, he ignored it. "Hunting's been slow this week. I thought you could use a hand."

Gilrain was the best archer in the area, usually bringing home the largest deer and wild boar. Although he hadn't taken up sword smithing like his father, he knew how to keep the fire going, and was an excellent striker. It was too bad he was so unreliable.

"I'm working on ladles, for Lord Destra's cook."

While Gilrain moved over to the fire, Kieran picked out an iron bar and brought it to the anvil. Using a hammer and chisel, he cut the bar to the proper length and then began the process of heating and hammering the metal, stretching out the handle, and forming a small bowl. When he'd finished shaping and smoothing it, he repeatedly plunged it into the slack tub to harden it.

Kieran looked up to ask Gilrain to get another tool. Gilrain was in the corner, flirting with a blond who'd made it past the door.

Kale shook his head.

Kieran swore under his breath.

Gilrain's careless attitude toward finishing his work was one of his *least* annoying traits. He charged headlong into fights without thinking, was openly affectionate with unmarried women, and gambled at dice and cards whenever he had the chance.

Still irritated, Kieran turned his attention to the next ladle and imagined it was Gilrain.

While he worked, a crowd started to gather inside the shop. It wasn't unusual for people to meet in the smithy to discuss the latest news, and Kieran had learned to keep one ear on the banter while he worked. This afternoon they were heatedly discussing the way Lord Destra had treated a man who couldn't pay his taxes.

"I heard he had the man and his whole family sent to the dungeon in Korisan."

Gilrain abandoned the blond and moved closer to the discussion.

"That's the last time we'll see Becknar."

Gilrain looked over at Kieran. "Somebody should do something."

Why was Gilrain looking at him that way? Kieran walked to the forge and waited for the bowl of the ladle to reheat.

His blood boiled every time he heard about the way Lord Destra mistreated the townspeople. It seemed the nobility felt it was their sole purpose in life to make everyone in Teleria miserable. They charged too much for taxes, demanded that the peasants produce superior products – despite the poor soil and scarcity of materials – and when foreign marauders or gangs roamed through the towns, they did nothing to stop them, despite having legions of soldiers at their command.

Kieran had never spoken of rebellion himself; his father had taught him to avoid trouble. But if he were a lord or a king, he would use his position to help people. Then he'd remind himself that he was a just a blacksmith, and all he wanted in life was to have his own smithy, marry, and have a dozen children.

"You know Rahnak set up all the liege lords in Teleria," someone said. "If you cross them, you're crossing him."

"I think it's about time someone crossed him."

When Kieran returned to the anvil, Gilrain nudged his arm. "Are you paying attention to this?" he asked.

"It's nothing new."

Gilrain took the hammer out of Kieran's hand.

Kieran moved to take it back. "Some of us have work to do."

Gilrain let go and lowered his voice. "*You* could do something."

Kieran continued to pound at the metal. “If you want swords for a revolt, go talk to your father. I already have too much work to do.”

“That’s not what I meant.”

Kieran stopped in mid-swing. “Then what *did* you mean?”

“They haven’t told you yet?”

Kieran grabbed Gilrain’s arm to take him outside. Gilrain tried to wrench himself away but Kieran persisted. When they were outside, Gilrain broke free of Kieran’s iron grip.

“What are you talking about?” Kieran asked.

Gilrain looked confused and then started to chuckle. “How ironic. All these years and they never told you who you really are.”

Chapter 2

Nothing could calm the tempest swirling in Kieran's gut.

After trying and failing to get more information out of Gilrain, he'd returned to the smithy to finish Destra's ladles. When he finished, all he had to show for his impatience were three ruined ladles. Disgusted with himself for wasting the metal, he threw them into the fire and grumbled all the way home.

When he reached the door, he noted that another of Teleria's infamous storms was fast approaching. How fitting that the weather mirrored his mood. As much as he hated confrontation, he had to know the truth. He didn't want to hurt his parents, but he couldn't go on without having an answer to this riddle.

Kieran was just about to go inside when he saw Gilrain and his parents walking down the path.

How could he have forgotten? Today was his twentieth birthday, and his mother had planned a special celebration as she did every year. And she always invited Loric, Sorina, and Gilrain. Having them here would complicate things. If he were lucky, they would leave early, and he could talk with his father privately.

Family celebrations were usually happy times, and although Kieran didn't share his mother's opinion that birthdays were sacred occasions, he enjoyed spending time with his aunt and uncle. Loric always made the conversation livelier and Aunt Sorina always brought him an apple pie. Gilrain was usually on his best behavior. However, as the evening progressed, Kieran's impatience was turning a pleasant evening into an impending shipwreck.

Just as he was thinking of a way to get them out of the house, he overheard words that grabbed his attention: "He looks more like Arathor every day."

Kieran exploded from his chair, catching the edge of the table and sending his plate to the floor. His mother jumped and his aunt let out a gasp. Surprised by his own outburst, Kieran stooped to pick up the broken dishes. When he stood, he tried to keep his tone even. "What did you mean just now, Aunt Sorina?"

His aunt shot a worried look at Kieran's parents. "I'm sorry. I shouldn't have – "

His father interrupted her. "No, Sorina. We should have told him sooner."

"Told me what?"

Pale and tight-lipped, Kale walked across the room to Elisa's cedar trunk. Kieran remembered watching his father buy the trunk in Felonia. It had cost him a month's wages, but Kale had been so proud of himself for choosing just the right piece for his wife.

His father opened the trunk and removed the contents. Turning it over, he located a hidden drawer and pulled out a yellowed parchment. He handed it to Kieran.

"You'd better read this," he said.

Kieran took the parchment and walked to the hearth. As he unrolled it a musty odor made him sneeze. The lettering was elegant, like none he'd ever seen before. At the bottom, there was a blue wax seal, imprinted with an eagle.

"Dear Son…"

Kieran narrowed his eyes as he looked up at his father. "Did you write this?"

Kale leaned against the stone work and stared into the fire. "Just keep reading."

Kieran looked at the parchment again.

Now that you are twenty-one, it is time to tell you about the circumstances of your birth. Twenty-two years ago, when your mother Annalisa was with child, my chief steward usurped the throne and threatened your life. In order to protect you and your mother, we left Teleria and went to live on Ilich Island. When you were born, I brought you to Kale and Elisa. By right of birth, you are Aiden, prince of Teleria.

Kieran swallowed hard to fight the nausea churning in him and continued to read.

You now have a choice, and it will take great courage to choose the right. From this moment on, you will be walking the path between who you are now and who you were born to be. All I am asking you to do is let yourself make the journey. Just remember that courage is not the lack of fear, but instead it is the decision that something else is more important than your fear.

"I am sure you will have many questions for me. When you are ready, you can find me in Koridoc. – Arathor.

Arathor was the name of the previous king. He'd ruled Teleria for only a few years before unexpectedly disappearing, leaving Rahnak to assume the throne. Telerians' opinions regarding Arathor's disappearance ranged from cowardice to outright abandonment. While some spoke of his return – always in hushed tones lest they be put in prison – others said they preferred Rahnak and Ciara.

Kieran rolled up the parchment and fixed his eyes on the man he'd called father for twenty years. "What's going on?"

"You'd probably better sit down to hear this."

Kieran crossed his arms and stayed on his feet.

His father ran his hand through his graying black hair. "We would have told you sooner, but Arathor said to wait until you were twenty-one."

"Do you mean King Arathor?"

Kale nodded. Kieran felt as if a crashing wave had hit him full force. This couldn't be happening.

He'd known since he was five that his parents had adopted him and it never bothered him. Once in a while, he wondered about his birth parents, but most of the time he was content to be the son of Kale the blacksmith.

When Kieran had regained his composure, he looked at his mother. "So you didn't tell me because Arathor told you to wait?"

Elisa's face was full of pain. "He must have had his reasons."

"But you told *them*?" Kieran said, gesturing towards his aunt and uncle.

His father answered. "The day after we took you in, we started to pack up and when Loric asked why, I had to tell him."

"And how did Gilrain find out?"

The question seemed to catch his parents by surprise. They looked at Aunt Sorina. Her face was red and Kieran knew from experience she was just as likely to defend herself as she was to run out of the room. Gilrain spoke before she could do either.

"She was angry about moving from Morigon, and when I asked her why, she told me everything."

Kieran looked at all the faces in the room, faces of the people he trusted. Impossible as this story was, it seemed even more impossible that his family had intentionally lied to him.

Unless they'd all been fooled, and the man who abandoned him wasn't really King Arathor. Or maybe someone had dropped him into one of his nightmares and he would wake up at any minute.

Whatever the answer was, he didn't want to be anywhere near his family right now. He turned to walk out the door but his father stopped him.

"There was one more thing Arathor wanted you to have." Kale left the room and when he returned, he laid a battered wooden scabbard on the table. "He hoped this would help you believe our story."

Kieran picked up the scabbard and withdrew the sword.

The highly polished steel blade was half his height and bore intricate engravings. The gold hilt fit his hand perfectly. He held it up and sliced through the air, feeling its grace and balance. It felt like the sword a prince would use.

An uncomfortable feeling twisted in his gut. This was the sword from his dream. In revulsion, he threw it to the ground and went out to face the storm.

Chapter 3

Kale watched his son rush out of the house. Kieran usually kept himself under control, but the look on his face when he'd left said he was ready to explode. Not that Kale could blame him. He probably would have reacted the same way if *he'd* been the one to learn he was a prince. Still, Kale wondered again if he and Elisa should have told Kieran the truth sooner. If they had, maybe Kieran wouldn't be so angry right now.

Only once before in his twenty years as Kieran's father had he seen his son this upset.

When Kieran was ten, he'd raced into the smithy, gasping for breath and yelling something about slave traders and rescuing a girl. On the one hand, Kale wanted to help, but on the other hand, he knew he couldn't let Kieran pursue the girl; it could bring dangerous attention to the family.

As gently as he could, he told Kieran there was nothing they could do.

A mixture of anger and disappointment filled Kieran's eyes. He beat his fists on Kale's chest and pleaded with him to help. When Kale refused, Kieran ran off, presumably back to the forest. Kale hoped his son would see how foolish it was to go after the girl. He waited up all night for Kieran, and when he finally returned the next morning, Kale was more relieved than angry.

Before Kale could ask him where he'd been, Kieran speared Kale with a hurt look. His chin trembled when he said, "My real father would have gone after her."

The words hit Kale like a sledge hammer.

After that day, they never spoke of it.

Kale picked up the sword. In all the years he'd kept it for Kieran, he'd never looked at it. Now he ran his fingers across the intricate leaf and vine pattern. Although sword smithing was his brother's specialty, Kale appreciated the fine craftsmanship that had gone into the weapon.

He suddenly drew in a quick breath.

This had to be Restamar, the sword from the stories his father had told him. Carefully, Kale returned the sword to its scabbard and put it in Kieran's room. In the morning, Kieran might be more willing to listen to their story.

Elisa walked in behind him. "Did we do the wrong thing, holding back the truth from him?"

Kale sat on Kieran's bed and Elisa sat next to him. He pushed a wisp of her hair behind her ear and stroked her cheek. Her clear green eyes sparkled and her honey-brown hair, now streaked with strands of silver, fell over her shoulders. She was as beautiful as the day he had proposed to her.

"It probably wasn't the best way to tell him," he said.

"Sorina feels awful."

Kale exhaled slowly. Sorina was usually careful about what she said around Kieran. They all were. "No, it's my fault. My instincts said to tell him when he was younger, but I wanted to honor Arathor."

He ran his calloused fingers through his hair. "I shouldn't have held him back."

Elisa took his hand and traced the back of it with her delicate fingers. She smiled at him. "You were only trying to protect him."

Kale shook his head. "By teaching him to avoid trouble, I haven't prepared him at all."

"Kale, we did the best we could. I know Arathor didn't make a mistake in choosing you to be his father." She leaned over and gave him a tender kiss. "And what's done is done. Now he's going to need your help to get through this."

Chapter 4

Kieran stood on the shore and put his hands on his knees, panting for breath, ignoring the rain soaking into his clothes. He looked out over the churning waves. The light from the storm had turned them an unnatural shade of green. He'd seen storms like this before but had never felt like one was inside him.

This was his favorite place to come when the cares of life weighed him down. He could depend on the ocean to calm him and help him think. But now he couldn't even depend on that. His world had been turned upside down. He didn't know who he was, he wasn't sure he could trust his parents, and if they were telling the truth, he didn't want to believe their story. More agitated than ever, he anchored his feet and let the storm buffet him from all sides.

Whenever there was a problem no one else could solve, he solved it. When things were difficult he always found a way around them. How was he going to get himself out of this?

What if the man who had said he was Arathor had tried to deceive them for some reason? How could he test his parents' story? He ran his hand across the back of his neck, trying to ease the tension creeping across his shoulders and into his head. What could he do? If he'd been Gilrain, he would have charged ahead and embraced the news. But he wasn't Gilrain. He was Kieran – cautious to the end.

This dilemma would have to wait. The storm was getting stronger. His parents' home was in danger and he knew he should go home to help. When he arrived, his uncle and father were boarding up the windows, and his mother and aunt were sand-bagging the foundation. Gilrain was in the barn, taking care of the livestock.

Kieran went to help Gilrain and saw that all the chickens had escaped. He called to his cousin and the two of them ran through the yard to catch the unruly fowl. Soon his uncle and father came to help.

Despite Kieran's frustration with the recent news, he had to laugh. The bedraggled birds weren't cooperating, darting here and there, squawking and fluttering about. When he thought he had one hen cornered, it flew into his face, making him land on his backside. Gilrain saw him and let out a loud guffaw. Kieran responded with his own chuckle when Gilrain lunged after one and slipped in the mud, falling flat on his face. His father and uncle weren't doing much better. Although they each had two chickens, the birds wriggled free when they tried to put them in the barn.

Just as Gilrain caught the last one, Kieran's mother and aunt showed up.

"You'd think four grown men could catch a handful of chickens," said his aunt.

"I think they just enjoy playing in the mud."

When the men walked towards the house, Kieran's mother put up her hands. "If you think you're going to come into my house, you're wrong"

Kieran looked down at his clothes. He was covered in mud, head to toe. His fellow chicken wranglers didn't look much better.

"I think they need to spend the night in the barn," said his aunt.

His father gave his mother a half pleading look. "Turned out of my own home."

With a flip of her skirt, Elisa turned toward the house. "We'll see you in the morning, when you've dried out," she said over her shoulder.

Inside the barn, Kieran's father lit a lantern and hung it on a hook. Kieran made sure the chickens were settled and his uncle tried to calm the old draft horse. The two pigs slept, and the goat was happily chewing its cud.

A cold gust of air blew into the barn and made Kieran shiver. He rubbed his arms and blew warm air on his fingers. Gilrain closed the barn door.

"So what do we do now?" Gilrain asked.

"Wait until we've dried out," said Loric.

"I can't believe Aunt Elisa wouldn't let us come in," said Gilrain.

"Well, it *is* her house," said Kale.

"I wouldn't let my wife treat me like that," said Gilrain.

Kieran hung his shirt over a rafter to dry and imagined Gilrain lording it over his wife – that is, if he could choose one from among the ever-widening circle of women who seemed to throw themselves at him.

The idea made him chuckle, until Gilrain interrupted his thoughts. "What will you do now that you know you're a prince?"

Kieran jerked his head around to look at Gilrain. If this was going to turn into another challenge, Kieran didn't want to argue with Gilrain here.

"You're not going to do anything, are you?"

Kieran noted the obvious disdain in Gilrain's voice and moved towards the door. And then stopped. Which would be worse – leaving the barn to face the storm outside or staying to face the storm in here? He knew his cousin. Gilrain could be like a hunting dog on the trail of its quarry. If Kieran didn't settle this now, Gilrain would hound him until he did.

He turned around, all the while trying to sound as if none of this mattered. "I don't know if any of this is true, so just let it go."

"What do you mean, you don't know if it's true?" asked his father.

"How can you not believe it?" asked Gilrain. "You saw the letter and the sword. How do you explain those?"

"Maybe the man was just a beggar and the sword was stolen." He looked at his father. "How did you know it was Arathor?"

"Arathor is built just like you, and despite the way he was dressed, there was no mistaking him."

"So the sword training was all because of this?" Kieran asked.

His father shrugged. "I thought it would be good for you to know how to fight."

Kieran shook his head and laughed. "Except for swords, you *never* let me fight. It was always, 'Kieran, don't draw attention to yourself' or 'Kieran, let someone else fight.'"

"I was doing what I thought was right. If you had stood out, Rahnak might have found you and then…" His voice trailed off.

Kieran pulled his damp shirt from the rafter and lifted it over his head, feeling the familiar hostility churning inside him. He knew that if the conversation continued, he'd say something he'd regret. As much as he resented Kale's efforts to keep him safe, he didn't want to hurt him or embarrass him, especially not in front of Gilrain and Loric.

He opened the door, then turned to Kale. "Father, I'm – "

"Sorry" is what he should have said, but he wasn't exactly sorry. He wasn't quite sure how he felt. "Let's talk about this another time."

A biting wind hit him in the face as he charged into the storm.

Chapter 5

"What am I supposed to do with this?" Kieran muttered.

The sword lay on a chair next to Kieran's bed, right where he'd left it after sneaking into his bed last night. How could such a simple thing be so repulsive? And why had he dreamed of *this* sword?

He started to reach for it and then drew back.

"It's a fine weapon."

Kieran looked up to see his father. "I suppose it is."

"Aren't you going to look at it?"

"Why should I?"

"Because it belongs to you."

"It belongs to Arathor," said Kieran, stamping his foot into his boot.

"He gave it to *you*."

Kieran pulled on a shirt, rolled up his sleeves, and tied back his hair with a leather strip. "I need to start repairs on the house."

His father put a hand on his shoulder. "Why are you having such a hard time believing this?"

Because if I believe it, Kieran thought, *I have to give up the life I have now.*

"What did the letter say?" Kale asked.

"Read it for yourself," Kieran said as he brushed past him to go to the kitchen.

When he got there, his mother was ladling corn meal into an earthen bowl for him. He added honey and cream, and moved to the table. This was his favorite breakfast and his favorite time of day. Early morning was the only time in his otherwise noisy life when he could enjoy a small measure of peace. He just hoped his parents wouldn't interrupt it with pointless questions.

Downing a mug of pear cider, he was just rising to leave when his mother drew up a chair beside him and offered him a warm roll. How could he resist that? He took it and drizzled more honey over the top of it. His mother pulled her purple woolen shawl around her shoulders and carefully broke the roll in half before eating it like a lady in the king's court. How many times had he looked at her and not noticed how elegant she was?

"What have you decided?" she asked.

"I don't know."

"Did you look at the sword?"

His father walked into the room and kissed his mother on the cheek. "He said he didn't have time for it."

Kieran shot his father a warning glance.

"How will you know the truth if you don't look at it?" Elisa asked.

"Why would looking at the sword make any difference?"

"Because," said his father, "it's a special sword."

Kieran took a bite from the roll. "What do you mean?"

"I'll show you," said Kale, gesturing towards Kieran's room.

While Kieran leaned against the doorframe, Kale and Elisa sat on the bed.

"The sword you don't have time to look at is called Restamar. The stories say that the great warrior Alardin used it to defeat an evil queen."

"Do you mean the same Alardin who agreed to help Kieran the Valiant?"

Kale nodded.

Of all the stories Kale had told Kieran over the years, this was Kieran's favorite.

An ancient people lived under the curse of a terrible queen. A man named Kieran decided something should be done, so he left his family to search for a great warrior who would help them. Kieran traveled hundreds of miles, across oceans and kingdoms, until he came to the kingdom of Benalia. It was in this kingdom he found a man named Alardin. Alardin was the third son of a king, and instead of waiting for an inheritance, he became a warrior. Now he was the leader of the Benalian army. When he heard Kieran's story, Alardin and half the army agreed to go with Kieran to fight against the queen and her forces.

When they arrived in Kieran's homeland, Alardin and Kieran fought side by side. Just before Alardin defeated the queen, her general dealt Kieran a death blow. During his funeral, the newly appointed King Alardin decreed that his comrade would always be known as Kieran the Valiant.

"I thought those were just stories," said Kieran.

His father rubbed his stubbled chin. "So did I."

"How do you know that this is Alardin's sword?"

Kale took the weapon and gave it to Kieran. "Look at the design on the blade."

Kieran ran his fingers over the cold metal. The pattern he'd seen last night was gold inlay. It was the most intricate work Kieran had ever seen.

"If I'm right, you should be able to see Alardin's name on the other side."

Kieran turned the blade over. The inscription was wearing away, as if someone had run their fingers across it many times. He could just make out the names Alardin, Dalamar, Jendric, Egron, Aeron, Duncan, and Arathor.

A chill went up Kieran's back when he read the rest of the inscription.

"When the line of kings is broken, and an evil ruler takes the throne, a child will arise to end her reign; a child will arise to break her curse."

"What does it say?" asked his mother.

Kieran was too dumbfounded to speak and handed it to her.

"I don't see anything," she said, and then gave it to Kale.

His face fell. "There's nothing here," he said. "I was sure this was Restamar."

Kieran took it back. "There it is. Can't you see it?"

His father's face went pale. "Why can you see it when we can't?"

"That doesn't matter now," said his mother. "What does it say?"

Kieran repeated the words. They were so unbelievable he almost thought someone else was saying them.

"I don't understand," said his father. "Rahnak must be the evil ruler, but what does it mean about ending *her* reign and breaking *her* curse?"

"Why would it matter?" Kieran burst out. "None of this is true."

His parents looked up at him in apparent shock. Before they could say another word, he put the sword in its scabbard and left.

When Kieran reached the shore, he wished his mind were as clear as his surroundings. The rising sun had burned off the morning fog and now the sky was as blue as Kieran had ever seen it. The waves thundered against the rocks, and in the distance, flocks of gulls pestered the fishermen for scraps. Piles of rotting seaweed, swarming with black gnats, lay on the beach where the storm had thrown them. Shells of every color adorned the gray sand like jewels in a king's raiment.

Kieran knelt down and scooped up a handful of tiny moon shells. As he stirred them around with his finger, he knew that if someone were to see a grown man kneeling in the sand, playing with sea shells, they would probably think it strange. He didn't care; shells had always fascinated him.

He dropped the white shells and moved down the shore to see what other treasures the storm had brought. A purple glint caught his eye. He picked up the shell and rubbed the grit from it. He'd seen a shell like this before. When they'd lived in Ithil, his father took him to the shore when he was nine and he found two pieces of a purple and pink shell. His father said they were from an abalone.

They were a perfectly matched set of jewels from the sea – until the day he gave one away to the girl.

The first time Kieran had seen the girl, he was ten. He and Gilrain were setting rabbit snares in the forest and stopped by a stream to get a drink. As Kieran leaned down to scoop up some water, he sensed someone watching him. He cautiously stood and looked around. At first, he saw no one, but after scanning the trees, he noticed a girl, maybe eight years old. She sat in the branches of a gnarled oak tree.

Surrounded by black boulders, the tree was taller than fifteen men. Kieran and Gilrain had named it "The Old Man" because it looked like the oldest tree in the forest. A single trunk split into two parts; from these two smaller trunks, more branches than Kieran could number reached to the sky, like gnarled fingers trying to grab the clouds. The rough gray bark was perfect for helping them climb, and the two cousins clambered up the tree almost every day.

Kieran scrambled up in a flash and sat next to the trespasser. "My name is Kieran and that's Gilrain," he said, pointing to his cousin. "And this is our tree."

She looked at him, unblinking. Kieran thought she might put up her fists at any moment.

"I come here all the time," she said bluntly.

Kieran usually ignored girls, but this one had his attention. Her cinnamon-colored hair grew to her waist and her eyes were black. He'd never seen anyone with black eyes. They were mesmerizing – even to a ten-year-old boy. It took him a moment to give her an answer. "We're *older.* It's *our* tree."

She moved closer to him and the pitch of her voice went up. "My family has lived here much longer than *you* have, so it's *my* tree."

Kieran had never met a girl like this one. He was enjoying himself.

"The three of us could share," he suggested.

Now she was in his face. "I don't share anything."

"Maybe someone needs to teach you how."

Gilrain tried to stifle a laugh. "How long are you two going to keep this up?"

The girl started to giggle and Kieran couldn't help but laugh with her. Before they knew it, they were all on the ground, rolling with laughter. Tears streamed down their faces and Kieran's sides ached. When they finally stopped, the girl looked at Kieran again.

"I still say it's my tree, but I'll let you climb it."

"Do you always get your way?" Kieran asked.

She was about to answer, but turned at the sound of someone calling her.

"I have to go," she said, lowering her voice. "I'm really not supposed to be talking to you." But there was something in her eyes that said, "Let's be friends."

She'd almost disappeared into the forest when he felt the pieces of shell in his pocket. He called out to her to stop. When he reached her, he gave her one of the pieces. She took it and smiled.

"What's your name?" he asked, a little breathless.

Her eyes sparkled with mischief and she leaned closer, cupping his ear with her hand. "Jessara," she whispered.

Then she was gone.

Kieran put the shells in his pocket and pushed away the memory. It was time to do what he'd come here to do.

He sat on a boulder and unsheathed the sword. When he looked more closely at the inscription, he saw another name, more deeply etched than the others: Aiden. He lost his grip on the sword and dropped to his hands and knees, doubling over as a sea of nausea swirled around him.

Chapter 6

Heavy drops pelted Kieran's face as he trudged through the muddy lanes of Pent. When he entered the smithy, he stamped the mud from his boots and moved next to the forge. Putting his stiff fingers near the coals, he looked around his father's shop.

This was the only life he'd known. His father had put him to work from the time he was seven – chopping wood, making coal, stoking the fire, pumping the bellows, and cleaning out the forge. It was hard work, but Kieran relished every minute of it and longed for the day when he could be an apprentice. Even at seven, all he'd wanted was to be a smith, like his father.

Like my father, he thought.

For the last two months, he'd wrestled with the possibility that he had *two* fathers.

Kale was a good man, and although he and Kieran had their differences, Kieran was grateful for all his father had taught him. What he appreciated most was that his father had always been honest with him – until now.

Kieran blew out a frustrated breath. Was holding back part of the truth a lie, or just a way to protect him? Did it really matter? Either way, it left Kieran feeling used and betrayed. All he wanted to do was find the man claiming to be Arathor and expose him as a fraud.

What was he thinking? He couldn't leave now. There was too much to do. Farmers needed their tools repaired before the harvest, Lord Destra needed a new gate, and Kieran and his father were making special items to sell at the spring festival in Felonia. No, finding Arathor would have to wait.

He pushed his tangled thoughts away and threw himself into his day's work – a set of tools for his uncle. It was easy to lose himself while he focused on the steady rhythm of the hammer on the metal. If only it could take away the memory of last night's dream.

Despite the horror of watching himself kill his family, he was learning to put the dreams aside and forget them. But he couldn't ignore last night's dream; it was the most terrifying he'd had yet. In last night's dream, he killed Jessara. It was more terrifying than when he had actually lost her.

After his first encounter with Jessara, they'd met in the forest every day and spent their time building forts out of dead branches, making leaf boats to race down the stream, and climbing the tree. It continued that way for several months, and although he couldn't explain it, the longer he knew her, the more he felt connected to her. No matter how hard his ten-year-old self tried to deny it, he thought he might love her. Only as a friend of course, but it was something he'd never felt for anyone.

She was the first thing on his mind when he woke up and the last thing he thought about before falling asleep. And between waking and sleeping, he could hardly concentrate on his chores for thinking of her. He hoped they would remain friends forever.

All it took was one horrible event to shatter his hopes.

It started like any other day. Kieran reached the tree ahead of Jessara and while he waited, he sat on a lower branch and carved their names into the bark. After a few minute, he heard her coming.

Just before she reached him, six of the dirtiest, most roughly-garbed men Kieran had ever seen came up behind her and tried to grab her. Kieran yelled for Jessara to climb up the tree, but she couldn't reach it. Kieran jumped from the branch with the knife still in his hands. Jabbing at one of the men, he told Jessara to run home. The man hit Kieran across the face with a knotted fist and knocked him down. Kieran recovered and drove his knife into the man's foot. The man dropped to the ground, screaming in agony, while another grabbed Kieran from behind and held him fast with arms like iron bands. Jessara screamed for help as two others chased after her.

A blond-headed boy ran towards her, yelling for the men to stop.

"Stefan," she yelled. Before she could reach him, the two men caught her and dragged her by her hair back to the tree. Stefan ran after them, but a third man wrestled him down and drove a boot heel into his back.

When the slave traders reached their horses, they bound Jessara's hands and feet, stuffed a rag in her mouth, and tied her to a saddle. Before joining their comrades, the men holding Kieran and Stefan let them go, warning them not to follow. Stefan ran one way and Kieran ran home.

And when he asked Kale for help, his father had done nothing. That was the night he started dreaming about her.

For Jessara to be in *this* dream, and to see himself killing her with the sword was unbearable. More than anything else that had happened, it made him want to get rid of the cursed thing.

Kieran threw himself into the day's work, fighting against the guilt he felt not only for losing her, but for not being able to stop himself from killing her in the dream. He knew it didn't make sense to blame himself for either one, but he couldn't shake the feeling that he was somehow responsible for all of it.

By late evening, a chill wind replaced the rain. Leaving his father's shop, Kieran lowered his head and walked through Pent towards home. He was just coming to the western edge of town when he heard a cry for help. One of Destra's soldiers was attacking a young woman.

Not this, he thought.

Kieran looked around for help. Seeing he had no choice, he aproached the attacker from behind and threw him to the ground. Recovering from the shock, the soldier got up and charged at Kieran. Kieran met his attack and hit him in the ribs. A cracking noise echoed between the buildings.

In a drunken rage, the man hit Kieran in the jaw and briefly stunned him. Kieran shook his head and drove his fist into the man's stomach. The blow sent the soldier flying into the stone wall. For a moment, the man's face took on the appearance of one of Jessara's abductors and Kieran found himself beating the soldier repeatedly. He stopped when the man fell limp to the ground.

Kieran spit the blood from his mouth and extended his hand to the woman.

"Thank you," she said grimly.

"Are you all right?"

She looked up at Kieran. "I will be. But I think he's dead."

To Kieran's surprise, the man lay in a pool of blood. What had he done? How could he have lost control so easily?

Suddenly, Kieran heard a crowd approaching.

"You'd better get out of here," he said to the woman.

He watched her go and then ducked into the trees, running towards home. He was shaking when he went through the door. His mother looked up. Kieran studied her face. She looked so peaceful and content. How could he tell her he'd just killed a man?

Before he said anything, alarm was in her eyes. "What happened?"

Kieran paced the room, briefly explaining what he'd done. His mother pursed her lips. "You did the right thing."

He *had* done the right thing. Why did he feel so guilty?

Just then his father walked in the door. When his mother told him what had happened, his face tightened and he looked at Kieran. "It seems circumstances have forced your hand."

"What are you talking about?"

"Destra will put a price on your head and then he'll have you sent to Korisan."

"But the man was attacking an innocent woman."

"Destra won't care."

"Where will I go?"

"Maybe you should go to Koridoc, to find Arathor."

Suddenly, Kieran's painstakingly ordered life was slipping from his grasp. How could he get out of this? "There's too much work. You can't do it alone."

Kale gave him a grim smile. "I appreciate the concern, but I'm sure Loric can help." He put his hand on Kieran's shoulder. "I've protected you for as long as I can. I can't protect you anymore."

Chapter 7

Kieran gave the house a final look. A blue vase filled with autumn roses sat on the table. His father had picked the roses for his mother just yesterday. A trio of iron lilies Kieran had made when he was seventeen rested by the fireplace. His mother's embroidery work hung over the back of a green chair.

Then his eyes rested on his family. Would he ever see them again?

His mother smiled sadly and smoothed a loose hair into place. Aunt Sorina tried to compose herself, but her face was red from crying. Loric stood next to Gilrain. If only Kieran were as eager as his cousin to leave. At least with him along, Kieran wouldn't go hungry on the way to Koridoc.

His mother pressed her hand to his face and reached up to kiss him. He kissed her cheek and then Aunt Sorina's. Loric shook his hand. "I hope you find the answers you need," he said.

His father embraced him and looked him in the eye. "Good luck," was all he could muster.

By the time the cousins made camp it was evening of the next day. Unlike Gilrain, who seemed to be enjoying himself, Kieran had spent the day imagining a soldier behind every tree. Any noise or crack of a twig set his heart racing. More than once, his hand went to the hilt of his sword. Now he was exhausted, but his sleep brought no relief; he dreamed about killing Jessara all night long.

By noon of the second day, they came to a narrow stream and were about to cross when Kieran heard someone crying. He turned around and went to investigate. Just down the bank, he saw a small child. Her dress was torn and her hair was matted and filled with cockleburs.

He tried asking the child where her parents were, but she just stared at him with wide, fearful eyes. He picked her up and carried her back to where Gilrain waited.

"I'm not sure what to do with her," Kieran said.

"Did you see any adults?"

"No."

The girl tried to break free, but Kieran tightened his arms around her and held her close.

"She's obviously very frightened," said Gilrain.

"We can't take her with us."

"Orizant is just down the road."

Kieran trudged ahead, dodging the girl's fists and ignoring her screams. By the time they reached the village, the sun was almost down.

Orizant was half the size of Pent and consisted of small cottages. Most of them were crumbling with age, their thatched roofs falling in on themselves. The few people they saw scurried into their homes like frightened animals.

After knocking on several doors, someone finally opened to them. An old woman with a face covered in wrinkles peered out. When she saw they had the girl, she smiled.

"I'm Corinna. Please come in."

Kieran put the girl down and she fled to the woman. "We found this girl by the stream," he said.

"Do you know her?" Gilrain asked.

"She's from the Linden Baraca clan."

"Can you get her back there?"

"I visit them often. And Sheena is usually the reason." Effortlessly, Corinna took the girl into her arms and carried her to a rocking chair near the fireplace. "She's always running away."

"Thank you for your help," Gilrain said.

Kieran looked around. Although the outside of Corinna's cottage needed more repair than the others in town, the inside was more carefully kept than his mother's home. A loom and spinning wheel stood in one corner. A low table and chair under the window looked as if they had been lovingly polished.

"Can I offer you a bed for the night?" Corinna asked.

"I'm afraid we have to be going," said Gilrain.

The woman's face darkened. "There are several Baraca gangs on the road. You shouldn't travel in the evening."

Kieran looked at his cousin. "What do you think?"

"It depends on how anxious you are to get to Koridoc."

"We have nothing to give you in exchange for your hospitality," Kieran said.

Corinna smiled. "You look like strong young men. I'm sure I can find something around here for you to do."

The early morning was thick with fog when Kieran and Gilrain went outside. Corinna had given them several chores: repairing the thatched roof, chopping wood, and chinking the walls of her waddle and daub cottage against the coming winter. When they were finished, it was well past sundown. After a simple meal of lentil soup, Kieran was glad to finally drop onto the straw pallet in the back corner of the house.

When they took their leave of her the next day, she repeated her warning about the Baraca gangs. Kieran thanked her and shook her hand. As they were going out the door, she said, "The gangs aren't the only danger on the road."

Gilrain gave her a puzzled look.

She leaned closer and whispered. "You have to watch out for the gurithents."

Chapter 8

A day later, having narrowly escaped an encounter with the local militia in the sea port of Lenkar, the cousins continued towards Koridoc. They'd walked a few miles when Gilrain stopped and told Kieran to look at the sky. Boiling black clouds were forming over the sea. Lightning flashed and they heard the thunder almost immediately. To their right, the sea began to pitch. To their left, sheer cliffs rose up, at least two hundred feet from the ground. They managed to duck inside a small cave, just avoiding the rain that poured down in sheets.

The howling wind blew through the rain and Kieran shivered. He dropped to his hands and knees, feeling for anything to use for a torch. When he found a large stick, he ripped a piece off of his cloak and wrapped the cloth around the stick. Gilrain made another torch and the two of them searched for wood.

When they'd found enough fuel for a small fire, Kieran pulled his cloak more tightly around his shoulders and wished he were in his home instead of this dismal cave. He cursed the bad luck that had forced him to start this journey during the rainy season instead of in the summer.

For that matter, he cursed the bad luck that had put him in this position in the first place. How could he have been so careless as to put his family and himself in danger?

But then he remembered the woman's screams and realized he'd done the only thing possible.

Gilrain sat next to the fire and folded his arms. Kieran kicked several stones out of the way and tried to get comfortable on the uneven floor.

"I still can't believe you don't want to be a prince," said Gilrain.

"And I suppose you would?"

"If I had a chance to make a difference – "

"I'm not you," Kieran growled.

"No, you're not. You were always the first to walk away from a fight." Gilrain shifted and exhaled sharply. "When Kale told us you'd killed that soldier, I didn't believe him at first."

"I couldn't let him hurt that woman… and I didn't mean to kill him."

"At least you did something."

"Look where it got me – on the run from Destra."

Gilrain chuckled.

"What's so funny?" Kieran asked.

"I was just thinking – as long as you're an outlaw, you might as well go up against Rahnak."

Kieran gritted his teeth and turned away from his cousin. "I'm done talking about this."

The words were barely out of his mouth when a high-pitched shriek pierced the darkness. In a flash, the cousins were on their feet, drawing their swords. A creature with black feathers and a large sharp beak entered the cave and seemed to fill the space. Kieran shrank back. Gilrain stabbed at it, but the blade couldn't penetrate the creature's armored chest.

Seeing no way to defeat it, Kieran grabbed Gilrain and tried to pull him out of the cave, but it was too late. The creature struck at Gilrain's shoulder with its beak. Gilrain yelled out. Kieran moved towards the opening, but the creature blocked his path.

Kieran maneuvered around and struck at the monster's bird-like legs. The black beast lunged. Kieran ducked, saving his head from its beak. He made one more wild stroke and cut through the leg. The creature fell to the ground, its severed leg oozing gray blood.

Gilrain collapsed. Kieran helped him up, grabbed their swords and provisions, and made a dash for the opening.

Kieran looked at Gilrain's shoulder and drew in a quick breath. The twilight revealed that it was turning a sickly green.

"What was that?" he asked, hoping Gilrain could hear him.

Gilrain managed to say just one word before he passed out: "Gurithent."

Kieran caught him just before he hit the ground. He hoisted Gilrain over his shoulder and started down the road.

The only thing he knew about gurithents was that if the victim didn't get help within three days, he would go mad and die. Kieran quickened his pace and hoped they would come to a town soon. By the time they reached a small cottage, it was well past midnight and Kieran was exhausted. He was just able to knock on the door before he dropped Gilrain on the front step and passed out.

A light breeze, smelling of salt air, came in through an open window, and a pale morning sun barely lit up a small room. An older woman stood in the corner. Kieran tried to sit up to look for Gilrain, but his throbbing head forced him back into the bed.

"You need to rest," the woman said.

"Who are you?"

"My name is Gisela."

"Where's Gilrain?"

"Your friend?"

"Yes, he needs someone who knows how to cure the bite of a gurithent."

"The Healer has already taken care of him."

That was odd. What were the chances that he'd accidentally stumbled upon someone who could help Gilrain?

Gisela walked over to his bed. "How are you feeling this morning?"

"I'll feel better once I've eaten."

"I have just the thing," she said.

He tried standing, but decided it was better to sit.

"Let me bring it to you."

Kieran got a better look at her. A black apron covered most of her green woolen dress. She wore her hair in a loose knot on the back of her head. When she looked up at him, he saw a delicate fringe of white hair framing her surprisingly girlish face.

She brought his meal to him, along with a cup of tea. The eggs were the most delicious he'd ever eaten. The bacon was perfectly salted and smoked. This was better than the meals he got at home.

When he'd finished, he stood up slowly, steadied himself against a chair, and walked over to Gilrain's bed.

His cousin was asleep. The green in his shoulder had vanished. The mysterious healer had saved Gilrain's life.

"Where can I find our host?"

"He's out fishing this morning."

Kieran found his cloak and went outside. The late morning sun sparkled on the water. He walked down a worn path to the shore. It was nothing like the shore near home. So many round, small stones covered it that he couldn't see the sand. Grass-covered cliffs rose to his left, and the azure plain of the sea stretched in front of him.

He found a dry spot on the rocks and sat while he waited for the healer, whoever he was. He closed his eyes, listening to the steady sound of the waves on the rocks and the crying of the gulls, enjoying a moment of peace. He put his hand up to his brow to block the sun and looked up and down the beach.

Someone was coming towards him, confidently making his way over the stones.

At six feet tall, he looked to be a little older than Kieran's father. His brown hair was short and his face was clean shaven. A coarse cloak hung loosely on his broad shoulders, and over one arm he carried a gray fishing net.

Kieran stood, extended his hand in greeting, and introduced himself.

The man shook Kieran's hand and his deeply weathered face broke into a warm smile. "Everyone around here calls me the Healer."

"Then I have you to thank for helping my cousin?"

"I did all I could. He should rest for a week before traveling."

Another delay.

"Will that be a problem?" the man asked.

"I'm trying to get to Koridoc. I'm supposed to meet someone there."

The man shook his head. "He really should stay here."

Having nothing more to say to each other, the fisherman continued along the shore. Kieran went back to the cottage, checked on Gilrain, and grabbed some clean clothes from his pack After locating a secluded cove and discarding his clothes, he plunged into the icy water and let the familiar rhythm of the waves wash over him, removing the grime of travel. While he dressed, he whistled a familiar tune – a tune Jessara had taught him.

Jessara loved to sing. During their time together in the forest, she taught him the melody to her favorite song. After a little practice, Kieran knew it perfectly. Later, she taught him a folk dance that went with the song. Soon they were dancing and laughing.

Now he had to dance with her in his dreams.

Chapter 9

Kieran watched wide-eyed as Gisela and the fisherman brought platter after platter of food to the low wooden table. Kieran ate fish all the time, but here were fish he'd never seen before. Only his host's explanations told him what he was eating: herring, salmon, eel, flounder, whiting, and cod. If that weren't enough, Gisela brought platters laden with several varieties of fruit, along with three kinds of bread and four kinds of wine for washing down their meal.

"Where did all this food come from?" Kieran asked.

The man gave him a curious smile. "I have certain enchantments I can use. It's how I saved Gilrain."

"Who are you?"

"It depends. To some, I'm the healer, and to others, I'm the hermit fisherman."

More riddles. This was exasperating.

"Where are we?"

"Koridoc."

Kieran's stomach tightened and he put down his food. It just couldn't be. He was almost afraid to ask the next question, but knew that he must. "Are you the man who gave a child to a blacksmith twenty years ago?"

The man nodded. Kieran resisted the sudden impulse to hit him across the jaw. If this was his chance to ask the questions that had pressed in on him for the last few weeks, why was he having such a violent reaction?

"Tell me your name," Kieran said.

"Arathor."

Now that Kieran had found him, he didn't know quite what to say. He didn't want to insult his host but he needed to have his questions answered.

"You look skeptical," said Arathor.

Skeptical? That was an understatement. "My parents may have believed you, but that doesn't mean I do."

"Haven't you noticed the resemblance between us?"

Arathor's statement caught Kieran off-guard. Kieran didn't look at himself often, and he hadn't really considered that he might look anything like this fisherman. Now he focused on the man's facial features and build. Perhaps they did share a few characteristics, but that wasn't enough to convince him.

"Maybe if I told you what happened," Arathor said, "I could put your doubts to rest."

Kieran thought for a moment. As long as he was here, he should get as much information as possible. "All right," he said through tight lips. "What happened that night?"

Arathor rested his elbows on the table. "The story you need to hear goes back further than that night." He cleared his throat and began. "I was twenty-three and had just married your mother, Annalisa. A few days after our wedding, my parents disappeared and the crown fell to me. Soon after I became king, I appointed a man named Rahnak as my chief steward. My father had warned me about him, but I was young and inexperienced. If I'd known that Rahnak would try to take over the kingdom…" His words trailed off, as if he were reliving his mistake

"Things went well until Rahnak married a Zagoran named Ciara. Somehow she convinced him that once I was gone, he would be the king."

"Didn't he know you'd have an heir?"

"For four years, it seemed that Annalisa would never bear a child. The longer it took, the more Rahnak believed that he would inherit the kingdom from me. If I'd known how incensed he would be when he learned of your coming birth, I would have banished both of them. But I didn't."

Arathor shook his head. "The whole kingdom rejoiced when they heard we'd have a child. Except Rahnak. He went wild with rage and envy. He ranted that he was destined to be the next king and that he would destroy anyone who stood in his way. That's when Annalisa and I realized your life was in danger. We left Korisan and fled to Ilich Island. After your birth, I traveled to Maquoya and gave you to Kale and Elisa."

"And what happened to Annalisa?"

"Giving up her only son was too much to bear. She died a few days after I returned to the island."

Kieran could see that Arathor was trying to hide his emotions, but he couldn't mask his grief. If Kieran weren't so irritated with him in the first place, he might have felt more compassionate. But there were still unanswered questions. "Why didn't you stay and fight for your kingdom?"

Arathor let out a slow, even breath. "A Baraca mystic came to me and said she'd had a vision of our family dying if I tried to take Rahnak off the throne."

Kieran had heard of the Baraca mystics. People said they had visions of the future. Most Telerians looked on them with suspicion. "You left because of someone's vision?"

For the first time since meeting Arathor, Kieran saw signs of impatience on his face. "If you knew Dorinda, you wouldn't say that."

"Then giving me up was the only way to save my life?"

"Yes."

The conversation wasn't going in the direction Kieran had hoped. While he searched his mind for a better approach, Arathor interrupted him. "I've answered your questions. Now I think I should ask you a few."

Kieran hadn't expected this, but the man was right. "Fair enough."

"Why did you come here?"

"My father gave me the letter and I wanted to prove you were a fraud."

Gisela had just come into the room with tea. Her eyes widened and the teapot and cups crashed to the floor. Arathor was at her side in a moment and helped her pick up the broken dishes.

When they were seated, Arathor continued to press Kieran. "Why do you think I'm a fraud?"

Because if you're a fraud, Kieran thought, *I can go back to my old life.* But what kind of life would he go back to? He couldn't return to Pent. By now, Destra would have spread word of his crime through all of western Teleria. Kieran wouldn't be safe anywhere. And he didn't want to end up in Korisan. Men who went there never returned.

"I'm just cautious."

Gisela shook her head and sighed. Kieran just wished she would leave. It was difficult enough talking to Arathor without having another person in the room. As if sensing Kieran's dilemma, Arathor suggested that they continue their conversation outside.

As the two strangers walked along the shore, the only sounds were the waves lapping the rocky beach, the flapping of their cloaks in the breeze, and the pounding of Kieran's pulse in his ears.

It was several minutes before Arathor said anything.

"I think if I hadn't been a king, I would have been a fisherman."

The comment caught Kieran off guard. He'd expected Arathor to continue his arguments. "Why is that?"

"I love the sea. When I was seven, my father took me to Lenkar when he went to inspect the new ships."

Their mutual love of the sea made Kieran let down his guard for just a moment.

"I first saw the sea when I was nine, when my father took me to Kolachel. I can't think of a better place to be."

Arathor stooped to pick up a white and black speckled rock. Kieran looked between the rocks for shells. All he found were broken remnants.

"Why are you having such a hard time believing the facts?" Arathor asked, rubbing the sand from the rock.

Kieran's guard went back up. "What facts?"

"The letter, for one. I sealed it with this ring." Arathor stood. He removed a gold ring from his right middle finger and handed it to Kieran. Kieran looked at it closely. It bore the raised image of an eagle, perfectly matching the seal on the letter.

Kieran returned it. "You could have stolen it."

"All right. What about the sword?"

"You could have stolen that too."

Arathor gave him a wry smile. "So you think I went to all that trouble to give you the false hope that you were a prince, hoping you'd never find out you were merely a smith?"

Arathor's answers were washing away Kieran's arguments, like the sand castles he used to build when he was a boy. Once the tide started to come in, there was nothing he could do to save them.

Kieran picked up a black stone and threw it into the water, watching it sink to the bottom. How could he admit to this stranger what he was really thinking?

"Why does it matter if I believe it or not?"

Arathor's dark eyes seemed to bore into Kieran's. "Do you remember the words on the sword?"

Kieran tried half-heartedly to remember. Before he said anything, Arathor recited them. "When the line of kings is broken, and an evil ruler takes the throne, a child will arise to end her reign; a child will arise to break her curse."

Arathor waited for his response. When Kieran remained silent, Arathor said, "Aren't you the least bit curious about what that means?"

"I suppose."

Kieran thought Arathor might lose his temper at this point, but the man remained annoyingly calm. "And didn't you wonder why you could read the sword when Kale and Elisa couldn't?"

There was no avoiding this. "All right, tell me."

"When the Hada Baraca first engraved Restamar, Alardin placed a spell over it so that only his descendants and the Baraca could read it."

Despite his skepticism, Kieran couldn't overcome his curiosity. "Why?"

"So that if it ever fell into Leandra's hands, she wouldn't discover the prophecy."

Too many questions swirled in Kieran's head. How could ask them all? The only comment he could conjure was, "I didn't think Alardin was real."

Arathor half smiled. "It's unfortunate that history has become legend. Will you let me set the record straight?"

Pushing aside his doubts, Kieran listened while Arathor briefly told him about Alardin. Kieran knew the first part – it went along with the story of Kieran the Valiant. What he didn't know was that the land was Teleria; the people who'd been enslaved were the Baraca; the queen's name was Leandra; and after Alardin defeated her, she swore she would come back and have her revenge on the Baraca, and on the descendants of Alardin.

"What does that have to do with the curse?" Kieran asked.

"The curse is upon us now. It began the moment Rahnak took the throne."

"Are you saying Ciara and Leandra are the same person?"

"After consulting with the Baraca elders, I believe so."

Kieran shivered, but it wasn't from the chilling wind blowing across the water. Still, he pulled his cloak closer to his chest. "How can that be possible?"

"Leandra is an enchantress with many powers. When she was first here, she ruled for a hundred years. It's not impossible to think she could still be alive."

"I don't see how – "

"If it's not her, it's one of her descendants. Either way, she's fulfilling her vow to have her revenge. Her reign must end. And her curse must be broken."

A curse I'll have to break if any of this is true. Kieran pushed the thought away.

"And what *is* the curse?"

"It would be easier to explain what life was like before the curse. Alardin came from a line of enchanted kings. When the Baraca asked him to become their ruler, he pronounced a blessing over Teleria. The blessing turned Teleria's desolation to abundance. But more than that, it helped the Baraca work side by side with the Benalian soldiers and their families."

"Benalian soldiers? Do you mean they stayed?"

"They sent for their families and settled here."

"And called themselves Telerians?"

Arathor nodded. "At first, the Telerians and the Baraca didn't get along. When their disagreements began to escalate, Alardin pronounced the blessing."

"So things haven't always been like this?"

"For a hundred and fifty-three years, the people lived under Alardin's blessing."

On the one hand, Kieran couldn't imagine how any of Arathor's story could be true. But on the other hand, he knew from living in Pent that beggars roamed the streets, that the nobles were abusive, and that most encounters between Telerians and Baraca did not end well.

"You're going to have to make a choice soon, Kieran. Ciara cannot be allowed to continue."

Arathor went into the hut, leaving Kieran to face the storm brewing inside. He walked around aimlessly and breathed in the cold night air. Memories from his childhood churned in his head and before long, he remembered how he'd wanted to save the world and how he'd wanted to save Jessara from the slave traders.

It was too late for Jessara, but was it too late for Teleria? Was this the chance he'd been looking for? If he were honest with himself, he would have to admit that he wanted to be the hero in Kale's stories.

Kieran raised his face to the clouded sky. He was just an ordinary blacksmith, not some prince who was supposed to depose a false king and end a curse. Arathor's story was too incredible. It would take more than tales of blessings and curses to change his mind.

Chapter 10

A cloaked figure sat on the step outside Arathor's cottage. When the figure stood and pulled back the hood, Kieran was shocked to see that she was Baraca.

She extended a hand and said, "I've been looking for you, Aiden son of Arathor."

It seemed like an eternity before Kieran could find his voice. "I beg your pardon."

"I said that I have been looking for you."

"Who *are* you?"

"My name is Dorinda, and I am a mystic from the Hada Baraca clan."

Kieran eyed her suspiciously. "Did Arathor put you up to this?"

She gave him a curious smile. "No one controls me. I came here because I knew you needed me."

Once he'd recovered from the shock, Kieran invited the woman inside. The house was quiet; only the hiss of an occasional raindrop hitting the fire's embers greeted them. Kieran hung their cloaks by the door and led the woman to a chair near the hearth. After bringing two cups from the sideboard, he poured some tea for both of them.

Kieran swirled the tea and then took a sip. Dorinda inhaled the steam from her cup. "I have waited twenty-two years to see you," she said.

Kieran dropped the cup and let out a cry of exasperation as the tea spilled all over his clothes and the cup shattered on the flagstone floor. Before he could stop her, Dorinda scooped up the fragments and, after setting the pieces on the sideboard, returned with another cup and poured more tea for him.

"What did you mean just now?" he asked as he took the cup.

"When a new Telerian king takes the throne, my kinsmen engrave the king's name on the sword and then present it to him. When it was Arathor's time, I had a vision of Arathor and Annalisa having a male child, so I told the engraver to add the name Aiden to the sword."

Kieran felt his throat tighten. "Are you the mystic who told Arathor to leave the throne?"

She paused and contemplated her tea. "It was the hardest thing I have ever had to tell anyone. And it was the hardest thing Arathor ever had to do."

"And now you've come to warn me?"

"Just before your birth, I had another vision."

Kieran's throat tightened.

"I knew you would be the one to fulfill the prophecy."

He'd heard enough and stood to leave, but Dorinda grabbed his arm and by a force unknown, held him in place. "You must see what I have seen," she said. Almost instantly, a series of images raced through Kieran's mind.

A man on a black horse, looking over his shoulder to see a wall of flame separating him from his pursuers; the same man handing an infant to a man and woman and then leaving with a heavy heart; the woman smiling with joy as the man pronounced the name Kieran over the child; a young Kieran crying out over the loss of Jessara; Kieran grimacing in his smithy as he heard of Becknar's plight; Kieran in the heat of battle, surrounded by unfamiliar comrades; Kieran seated on a throne draped in blue velvet, the sword across his lap and a simple gold crown on his head.

Dorinda released her grip, and the throbbing in Kieran's arm jolted him back to his surroundings. The fire had died down to just a few glowing embers. Kieran stared at them, his mind stunned by the vivid images. He knew it wasn't logically possible, but he was sure he'd seen *his* life, past and future. How had she done it?

More confusing was what he had experienced – Arathor's anguish at giving him up, his father's pride and his mother's joy at having a son. And his own emotions had been magnified – the anguish of losing Jessara, the rage over Becknar's punishment, the consuming rush of power from killing his enemies, and the absolute confidence needed for being king.

"This is my future?" he asked.

Dorinda was seated now and spoke with great effort. "I have seen your life up until this moment, with all of its possibilities. What you saw is what has already happened and what could happen if you choose to walk in the truth."

His mind felt like a tangled knot of what he thought he knew and what he'd just seen.

"And if I don't choose it?"

She let out a heavy sigh. "If you wish, I can show you what could happen if you do not."

"I wouldn't ask you to do that. What you showed me before seems to have taken your strength."

She gave him a weak smile. "I came here to help you. My well-being is a small thing, and I would not be doing my duty if I did not give you a chance to see Teleria as it might be."

Kieran wrestled with the idea of seeing an alternate future. Did he really want to see it? A mysterious compulsion moved him to kneel beside the mystic. Gently, she placed her trembling hand over his heart and closed her eyes.

The scene before him was as real as one of his dreams.

Kale and Elisa working in Rahnak's gold mine; Gilrain hanging on a gallows; Arathor dying from a wound to the heart; Jessara rotting in a dungeon; Teleria dying under a curse; an old man, hammering at his anvil, grieving the life he could have had, and the loss of all he loved.

Kieran reeled, and Dorinda collapsed to the floor in exhaustion. He carried her to his bed and watched her shallow breathing. Her wrinkled face was wet with tears. He knelt beside her, unusually overcome with emotion. Before long, he was grieving all the loss he'd known, and the pain he would cause if he ran away from the truth.

He could see only two choices ahead of him: He could go back to his carefully ordered life, condemning everyone he knew to live under the curse, or he could walk into the life he had dreamed of as a boy. All he knew for certain was that he was tired of being cautious, tired of running away. It was time to listen to Arathor.

A woodpecker's morning staccato woke Kieran. He stood and stretched, stiff from sleeping in a chair all night. He glanced at his bed. The mystic was already gone. Had she really been there last night?

Three cups, one of them broken, rested on the sideboard. A stain from the tea Kieran had spilled was on his shirt and breeches. And the visions Dorinda had shown him still haunted him.

After changing his clothes, he went outside and let the new sun warm his stiff muscles. He was surprised to see Arathor working through a series of complicated sword exercises. He was more surprised to see Arathor using Restamar. As much as Kieran detested the weapon, it bothered him to see someone else wielding it.

"What have you decided?" Arathor asked, still concentrating on his forms.

"I'm staying to learn what I can from you."

"Then you believe you're my son?"

"Yes."

Arathor stopped and turned to face him. "May I ask what made you change your mind?"

Kieran held his piercing gaze. "Dorinda was here last night."

"I thought I heard her voice," the king said, returning to his exercises.

"She showed me… things about myself."

"Disturbing, isn't it, having someone else show you your life?"

Kieran shivered involuntarily.

After a few moments of silence, Arathor went into the hut, and when he returned, he held two wooden swords. He tossed one to Kieran and cast aside his cloak.

The last time Kieran had held a wooden sword was when he was a boy. At first, he was excited about learning the art of sword fight-ing. He'd seen Loric practice with other blade smiths who came to town, and secretly hoped to fight as well as his uncle. But when Gilrain knocked him down again and again during their sparring matches, he realized he would never be as good as his cousin. From then on he approached his lessons half-heartedly.

Arathor sliced through the air a few times and then faced Kieran. Without any effort, the king began to attack Kieran with his sword. Caught off his guard by Arathor's speed, Kieran tried to block. Arathor's sword went to his throat. Kieran pushed him away and thrust at him. He was using all he could remember from his uncle's training, but it wasn't enough.

"I can see we have a lot of work to do," said Arathor. "Did you pay attention when Loric was teaching you?"

"I gave up the sword when I was thirteen."

"Why?"

"I was tired of having Gilrain humiliate me."

"So you quit?"

"I put my efforts into being the best smith in Teleria."

"Now you need to put your efforts into this."

Kieran swore under his breath. He was not looking forward to looking foolish.

Arathor faced him again. "Let's start from the beginning."

Kieran threw off his shirt and prepared to defend himself.

The king made the first thrust. Kieran blocked. They continued on, Arathor thrusting, Kieran blocking. After being smacked across the arms and chest several times with Arathor's sword, Kieran threw down his sword. The weapon clattered on the rocky ground. He grabbed his shirt and headed for the sea. In a few moments, Arathor was beside him.

"What happened back there?" Arathor asked.

Kieran put on his shirt and looked out over the unsettled sea.

"Did you think this would be easy?"

Kieran fixed his eyes on the waves. They weren't the only things churning. "I don't know what I thought."

"It takes most men years to become proficient swordsmen."

"Most men? What does that mean?"

"You're not 'most men.' The blood of Alardin flows through you. It fills every part of you."

Kieran wiped the sweat from his face and looked at Arathor, his eyes narrowing.

"Haven't you ever wondered why you're an exceptional blacksmith, even better than Kale?"

"Once in a while."

"It's the blessing of Alardin, giving you greater abilities than other men."

"How does being Alardin's descendant give me special abilities?"

"Because Alardin came from a line of enchanted kings."

"It just seems too fantastic that anyone could be enchanted or have special powers."

Arathor stood up and said, "Kel-lema menan-dai kah-gish tehai." Kieran jumped as a wall of flames hotter than his forge rose up around them. The sweat poured from his face, down his neck, and over his chest. Kieran looked at Arathor but he did nothing.

Kieran was no stranger to fire, but this fire was different. He had no control over it.

The flames grew in height and intensity. Kieran winced as a tongue of flame licked his shoulder. His nose wrinkled at the familiar odor of singed hair. He didn't think he could take much more. Finally, Arathor said, "Kel-lema menan-dai mah-rog." Immediately the flames died, leaving a ring of scorched stones around them. Kieran let out the breath he'd unknowingly held in.

Arathor mopped his brow and sat down. Kieran washed his face in the waves and then returned to the king. It took him a few minutes to express his thoughts. "That was… I've never seen anything like that."

"I only use it when necessary."

Standing this close to Arathor, Kieran noticed a blue light glowing through Arathor's shirt.

"What's that?" he asked, pointing.

Arathor pushed back his collar so Kieran could get a better look. "It's my Keldar stone. Alardin brought several of these from the volcanic mountains of Keldar in Benalia."

The flat, round stone was silvery-blue and moved with Arathor's skin. Kieran couldn't help but touch it. A strange warmth flowed out of it and up Kieran's arm. Kieran pulled his hand away.

Arathor pulled something out of his pocket and gave it to Kieran. Kieran saw a round blue stone on the end of an intricately woven but heavy silver chain. "This is *your* Keldar stone. I've been saving it for you. If you wear it, it will enhance your abilities, and you'll be able to speak with me over long distances. If you choose to make it part of yourself, it cannot be removed."

Kieran held the stone up to the light. He could just make out something that looked like a small flame burning inside of it. He put the stone in his pocket. He would have to think about wearing it.

Chapter 11

Arathor smiled as he watched Kieran and Gilrain sparring under a warm spring sun. During the long months of training, there had been many times when Arathor had thought that Kieran would give up entirely; it was one of the most frustrating things Arathor had ever endured. Now, as he watched the two combatants, he knew the hard work had been worth the effort. Kieran could match Gilrain's strokes, and more often than not, he was the victor in their hour-long sparring matches.

Kieran ignored the sweat trickling into his eyes and positioned himself to bring the match to an end. Gilrain wouldn't make it easy – he never did. When they'd first started training, Gilrain had been a formidable opponent, even while recovering from the gurithent bite. But for the last few days, Kieran had been a confident, unstoppable force.

The newly-conditioned muscles in Kieran's left arm flexed as he twirled Restamar and came in for the killing stroke, stopping just short of Gilrain's abdomen. Seeing no way out, Gilrain dropped his sword and put up his hands in defeat. "I never thought you'd make it this far," Gilrain said, "but you've been full of surprises lately."

Gilrain was right. When Kieran had first introduced himself last fall – it seemed so long ago and yet almost as if it were yesterday – he'd been a cautious blacksmith. Now Kieran was closer to being a king than ever before.

Besides his knowledge of swordsmanship, he knew almost as much as Arathor did when it came to Telerian and Baraca history, matters of court etiquette, how to govern a nation, and how to use his powers of enchantment. With the help of his Keldar stone, Kieran could control the elements, heal wounds, and sense the presence of danger.

Kieran shook Gilrain's hand and wiped the sweat from his face. Just yesterday, Kieran had cut his long hair and shaved off the scraggly beard that had grown to his chest. Now his reddish-blond hair was short against his head, and his clean-shaven face revealed old scars from working in the smithy and new scars gained from nicks with the sword. His arms and chest bore more of the same. Several marks obtained from a recent match with Arathor had already healed, and

Kieran would have another due to a frustrated stroke from Gilrain today.

Now Kieran ran his hand over the cut and said, "Jedza mar kaa-vah." The stripe of coagulating blood disappeared, replaced by tender new skin.

While Kieran and Gilrain changed clothes, Arathor contemplated the best way to tell his son it was time for him to leave.

It wasn't an easy thing for Arathor to tell him, and Arathor knew it wouldn't be an easy thing for Kieran to hear. The two of them had grown closer than Arathor had expected – certainly closer than he sensed Kieran expected.

Most likely Kieran would balk. Staying here was easier, and mentioning Kieran's destiny still brought occasional protests. It seemed the only person under Arathor's roof who didn't think Kieran was ready to rule was Kieran. Arathor knew this was the push Kieran needed to walk into the role of ruling a kingdom and ending the reign of an evil ruler.

Unfortunately, Arathor had learned that removing Ciara entailed more than just killing her.

Only a few weeks ago, a Tyman Baraca spy had fled from the castle to Arathor's hut, bringing news that Ciara had called for the Zagoran army and that she was planning to bring Teleria to its knees. Upon hearing this, Arathor had made his way to the Tyman camp to consult with their council. They weren't as surprised as he'd expected them to be.

On the same night that the spy had come to Koridoc, one of the Tyman mystics had seen warriors entering Teleria from the sea, bringing death and destruction. The mystic wasn't sure when they would come, but was certain they would be in Teleria within eighteen months.

When Kieran and Gilrain came to the table, Gisela set out a simple mid-day meal of corn bread, ham, and beans. After gulping it down, Kieran flashed an expectant smile at Gisela, probably hoping for her apple cobbler. She smiled back and brought a steaming dish to the table. The stimulating scent of cinnamon and other spices filled the room. Arathor served Kieran and Gilrain and waited for them to finish before sharing the difficult news.

Gilrain leaned back in his chair and stretched. "I don't think I've ever eaten as well as I have here," he said lazily.

"The time is coming," Arathor began, "when the two of you won't eat like this for a long time."

Gilrain's chair came forward with a thud, and Kieran's brow furrowed. "You're going to tell us it's time to go," Kieran said.

Arathor nodded.

Kieran looked as if he would protest and then stopped, fingering the blue stone around his neck.

"If I had my choice," said Arathor, "I'd tell you to stay for another six months. But I've received disturbing news from the Tyman council."

Both men arched their brows in surprise. Arathor related the story the spy and the mystic had told him. "Having to deal with Ciara's army complicates ending her reign."

Kieran looked grave. "I was wondering when we would discuss the prophecy."

Up until now, the two of them had avoided the subject. "This would be as good a time as any," said Arathor. "I've discussed this with several of the Baraca leaders. We think the only way to end her reign is to kill her. But now you will also have to raise an army to defeat the Zagorans."

Arathor recognized the signs of Kieran's agitation – the twitching in his mouth, the clenching of his teeth, the shadow crossing his face. He watched Kieran with restraint, waiting for him to make the decision to go or stay. He let out a silent sigh of relief when Kieran remained in his chair.

"How do I raise an army?" Kieran asked. "No one knows me, and as you've said, most people have forgotten you."

"You'll have to travel throughout Teleria and show people who you are. I think many of them are getting tired of living under the curse. If they see there is someone willing to fight for them, they may join your army."

"How much traveling?

"You may have to go through all of Teleria."

Kieran closed his eyes and rubbed his temple.

"You should make the journey anyway," said Arathor. "You'll become better acquainted with Telerians, and it will give you a chance to meet the people. Only they can tell you how difficult their lives really are."

"And the curse – what about that?" Kieran asked.

"That's a question I've thought about for a long time. The Tyman council and I believe it involves you and a Baraca woman."

Kieran clenched his jaw. "As in *marry* a Baraca woman?"

Arathor exhaled his impatience. "We still don't know what it means. But I doubt it involves marriage. Besides, as I told you before, you're already betrothed to Lucia."

Kieran pressed his lips into a thin line. "The daughter of your third cousin Mardok."

There was silence among the men for a few moments and then Kieran let out a heavy sigh. "When do we leave?"

With a mixture of anticipation and sorrow, Arathor stood above his kneeling son. Arathor had already given Kieran a small iron chest full of coins, a map of Teleria, an eyeglass, and a spare Keldar stone. Now Arathor cleared his throat and placed his hands on Kieran's shoulders as he prepared to give Kieran his final gift.

"Aiden, my son. I loved you when you were born and I love you still. Nothing will change that. I've seen your strength grow over the past several months, and I've taught you as much as I can in this short time. The path you will walk is yours alone. You will carry on the line of kings, not only because you are of royal blood, but because you are now a man. Your only weakness is your desire to quit when the circumstances are difficult, and the only one who underestimates your importance is you. You must decide now to set your face like iron and persevere. If you do, no force in Teleria can stop you.

"Over the coming months, you will find that strength of arms will not be enough, so learn to trust your wisdom and your understanding heart. They are your greatest weapons.

"Remember that I love you because you're my son. That love is not dependent on what you do or whether or not you are successful. With all my being, I believe you will succeed. But if you do not, come to me here and we will leave Teleria together."

Arathor paused and removed his signet ring. He raised Kieran up and looked him in the eye. "Now my task is finished. I will diminish so you may increase." He placed the ring on Kieran's right hand and said, "There are many who will know this ring and respect it. I now give it to you, hereby transferring all of my authority and power to you. You are the only one I trust to free my beloved Teleria and its peoples."

A look of shock and painful acceptance filled Kieran's face as Arathor knelt before him, kissing the ring. "I bow my knee and swear fealty to the new and only legitimate ruler of Teleria. Hail Aiden, king of Teleria."

Chapter 12

As Kieran and Gilrain walked through the forest on their way to Trevet, Kieran noticed something disturbing. There should have been green buds on the oaks and maples. These trees were bare. He should have heard the buzzing of bees and the songs of birds. The air was thick with silence and there was no activity at all. It was as if someone or something had shrouded the forest in death.

As they descended from the dusty hills, Kieran looked out over the city and noticed the same thing. Farms and cropland bordered one edge. The fields should have shown some indication of new growth but they were empty, all lying fallow. On the other side of the city, a deep gorge marked the path of a once mighty river. Now a muddy stream oozed its way to the sea through a weed-choked channel.

Had it been this bad when he and Gilrain had reached Koridoc? Or was this a sign of Ciara tightening her noose around Teleria? If she could starve the people, and dishearten them, they would be much easier to defeat.

Kieran stopped to lean against a tree. *Damn Ciara and her curse.* What could he do against such a powerful enchantress? His anger grew, and just when he thought he would burst, he felt a warm tingling flowing from the stone, through his arm, and into the tree.

Kieran and Gilrain stared in amazement as green buds poked out from the lower branches and changed into mature leaves. How had he done that? He knew no words to do this. Was it just a result of his frustration? If that was all it took, what else could he do just because he was angry?

By the time they reached the entrance to the city, it was almost noon. The noise was worse than the din from Kale's smithy. Goats, chickens, pigs, and dogs roamed the streets. Potters, leather workers, and mercers called out to draw attention to their wares. Two men stood side by side, locked into the stockade, and the gallows stood ready for the next hanging. The memory of seeing condemned men twitching at the end of a rope in Felonia made Kieran shudder.

Arathor had told them to look for Toren the sword smith. After making a few inquiries, they found his shop near the center of town. Upon entering the blade smith's shop, Kieran called out Toren's name. While they waited, Kieran took stock of the room. It was twice as large as Loric's smithy and must have had three times as many tools. As the building was made completely of stone, there were no goat skins hanging from the ceiling to protect the thatch from errant sparks. The floor was clean and all of the tools were neatly stored in racks around the room.

Windows twice as tall as Kieran let in the afternoon light, but could be shuttered at any time. A gleaming copper chimney rose from the forge all the way to the ceiling, and Kieran could barely smell the normal odors of charcoal and heated iron.

After a few moments, an older man with short gray hair poked his head out from an adjacent room. A closely cropped salt-and-pepper moustache and beard covered the bottom half of his angular face.

"Can I help you?" he asked in a gravely voice.

"I'm Kieran and this is my cousin Gilrain. We've just come from Koridoc."

"There aren't many who come looking for me. Why are you here?"

"Arathor sent me."

The man's eyes lit up. He wiped his hands on his soot-stained apron and bowed. "I can see the resemblance, your Highness."

Kieran's throat tightened. He pushed the uncomfortable feeling away and continued. "He said you could complete my training."

Toren smiled. "I can still remember teaching him when he was just nine. It was amazing how fast he took to it. Most men take years, but it only took him a few months to master the sword." He removed his apron. "When would you like to start?"

"We didn't get much sleep last night," Gilrain said. "Is there someplace we could rest?"

"Of course. I live in a room behind the shop. You can stay with me as long as you like."

The room was sparsely furnished, with just a table and two chairs. There were sleeping mats in one corner. In another corner there was a fireplace with another gleaming metal chimney. Swords of various sizes and shapes leaned against one wall. Kieran flung his pack into the corner and laid down on one of the mats. Although he knew he was to stay here for a month and receive more training, he was anxious to start his journey through Teleria. But one thing at a time. He lay down, closed his eyes, and tried to ignore Gilrain's snoring.

He rolled over and thought back to his time with Arathor. Things certainly hadn't turned out as Kieran had expected. He hadn't expected to be proven wrong, and he certainly hadn't expected to forge a relationship with Arathor.

Watching his father Arathor kneel before him had sent chills of astonishment through him. It had taken all of his resolve not to run away. The only thing that kept him there was Dorinda's vision.

It still haunted him.

If he did nothing, his family would suffer at Ciara's hands and Teleria would be lost.

The familiar ringing of metal on metal brought Kieran's thoughts back to the present. Curious, Kieran returned to the smithy to see what Toren was doing. The man was just putting the finishing touches on a sword with a gold hilt, humming to himself.

"Who do you make these for?" Kieran asked.

"Arathor. He's preparing for war."

Kieran picked up a hammer. For five months, his mind had dwelt on history and his arms had been occupied with sword fighting. Until now he hadn't realized how much he missed being a smith.

"Could you use some help?" he asked.

The next two weeks were a blur as Kieran and Gilrain helped Toren with his swords and Toren gave them more instruction in the use of the swords in combat. There wasn't a moment when they weren't forging or training. Kieran thought that Arathor had taught him all he needed to know, but Toren surprised him with more complex forms and a more disciplined way of fighting.

Just when he thought he couldn't learn any more, Toren declared there was one more thing Kieran needed to know before going into battle. And only members of the Tyman Baraca clan could teach him.

Chapter 13

Under cover of night, Kieran, Gilrain, and Toren left Trevet and journeyed to the Tyman Baraca camp. Just before sunrise, three clansmen met them in a clearing of oak trees.

On the few occasions when Kieran had encountered Baraca, he had regarded them with polite detachment. No one really knew anything about them except that they kept to themselves. Of course, there were rumors that they did all kinds of bizarre things. Most Telerians held them responsible for anything bad – high taxes, poor crops, and foul weather, among other things. Kieran knew those were only rumors.

Two months ago, he'd learned that *he* was Baraca.

Arathor had told him that when Alardin had defeated Leandra, the Hada Baraca were so grateful they offered one of their women to be his wife. At hearing the news that his ancient grandmother was Baraca, Kieran had been surprised to say the least. It had been only slightly less shocking than finding out he was a prince. Until this moment, he'd put it out of his mind.

As the Baraca approached, he felt the familiar tension working its way up his neck. Even if they knew Kieran was one of them, would they accept him?

At a signal from the leader, the three Baraca led them through the forest to a thickly wooded area. When they reached an apparent dead end, the leader turned quickly to his left and led them through a hidden opening off to the side, just a crevice in a wall. Emerging from a thirty foot passage-way, Kieran stopped.

The pale morning light revealed that the curse hadn't touched this stronghold. Signs of spring were everywhere. Aspen and beech leaves reflected the light, making them look like living gold coins. A thick carpet of green, dotted here and there with white and yellow flowers, stretched as far as he could see. Cardinals and wrens called out their morning songs. Taken all together, the scene made Kieran feel more alive and hopeful than he had in many weeks.

Once they were safely inside the Tyman stronghold, the leader stopped and turned to them, inclining his head and extending his right hand. Toren clasped hands with the man and then turned to Gilrain and Kieran.

"This is Braeden of the Tyman Baraca clan."

Kieran extended his hand in greeting.

Then Braeden said, "The council will meet at noon. Until then, please accept our hospitality."

While Braeden led them through the forest, a few clansmen, dressed in soft leather tunics, greeted them with curious stares, but said nothing. Soon, the three companions stood in front of a small L-shaped house. It sat high in the trees and was supported by narrow poles set every three feet underneath a thin platform. At each corner of the platform hung a delicately wrought lantern.

As they ascended the wooden steps that spiraled up one of the supporting trees, Kieran marveled that anyone could build such an elegant structure. He was even more astounded when they reached the front door and he saw the intricate details carved into the wooden panels making up the walls. All around the house, a series of recessed pointed arches framed scenes depicting horses and their riders. The eaves of the house, as well as the door and windows, mimicked these arches.

Braeden motioned for the three men to go inside. Kieran swung open the door and noted the intricately carved bedsteads along one wall. In one corner, a stool stood in front of a small writing desk. Two lanterns hung from the ceiling, casting a warm, orange light into the room.

Braeden led them around the corner to the back of the house. The small room was a storage area, but it also held a narrow wash stand with a gold basin. A gold pitcher sat to one side of the basin and three linen towels hung on gold hooks.

Once more, Braeden inclined his head. "When you have eaten your morning meal and washed up, I will take you to speak with the council."

At noon, Braeden led them through the forest to another set of houses supported by four large oak trees. Two banners hung on poles, each bearing the image of a rearing horse. Instead of a spiral, the staircase was a gently sloping incline that began a good distance from the main tree and stopped at the door to the council chambers.

Upon entering, Toren bowed and placed his left hand across his chest. "May I introduce Gilrain, son of Loric of Pent, and King Aiden, son of Arathor?"

As they bowed, Kieran realized that being introduced as the king would take some getting used to. Gilrain just gave Kieran a sideways smile.

After a moment, the council members seated themselves. One remained standing. "I am Calafar Mahon, chief of the Tyman Baraca, and this is the Tyman Baraca council. We do not wish to be impolite, my lord, but do you have some proof that you are now the king?"

Kieran had been wearing the signet ring on a chain underneath his shirt. It wasn't that he was ashamed to wear it, but there was no point in drawing unnecessary attention to himself, and so he'd kept it hidden. Now he withdrew it, and after slipping it off the silver chain, he handed it to Mahon. Mahon passed it among the council members, and each one inclined his head towards Kieran. When Mahon returned it to him, Kieran placed it on his right ring finger.

"Please excuse our requesting proof, your Majesty, but we have to be careful."

"I understand," said Kieran.

"We welcome you to our humble fortress."

Kieran thought the fortress was anything but humble.

The calafar gestured for Kieran and his companions to be seated. After seating himself, he spoke to Toren. "Your timing is impeccable, friend sword smith. We were just preparing to discuss the state of relations between Telerians and Baraca. Perhaps you would be kind enough to share your thoughts on the subject."

Toren cleared his throat. "I fear that relations have only deteriorated in the past few months. There is a growing hatred towards your people. The Baraca gangs are making the situation worse."

Kieran leaned forward in his chair. Several men on the council murmured and shook their heads.

"We had heard rumors," Mahon said, "but we did not know it was this bad."

"I do not think the gangs do half as much as Telerians say, but they still raid farms and cause trouble. Some of them start fights. I have heard that things are worse near the Ancala clan's fortress."

"Yes, the Ancala provide refuge for the gangs."

"Who are these gangs?" Kieran asked.

Mahon shook his head. "They are young Baraca men who have left their clans. They think we are not doing anything to make life better. They do not understand that this is the state of things all over Teleria."

"Why don't you stop them?" Gilrain asked.

"We have tried everything," said Mahon, "but they will not listen. In the end, it has been easier to let them go."

"Don't they realize," asked Kieran, "that all of this is a result of Ciara's curse and not the clan leaders' fault?"

"Most of them do not believe in the curse."

"What if they could put their anger to better use?" asked Kieran.

"What do you have in mind?"

"Arathor has given me the task of raising an army to defeat the Zagorans. What if the Baraca joined a Telerian army?"

Mahon and several others laughed quietly.

"I know that the two nations don't get along like they once did," said Kieran. "But couldn't the Baraca clans put aside their differences for a common goal?"

Mahon looked thoughtful. "Did King Arathor tell you the history of the Baraca and the Telerians?"

Kieran nodded.

"Then you know that the two peoples began to work together only after Alardin's blessing. When King Arathor went into exile, the blessing ended, and the tension between Telerians and Baraca has steadily increased. Even if you could get all of the Baraca clans to put aside their resentment of Telerians, we do not believe the Telerians could put aside their resentment of the Baraca."

Kieran suppressed a groan. "Will it not help your people to know that I'm Baraca?"

"We know of your heritage, my lord. Most of the Baraca elders remember that Alardin took a Baraca woman as his queen. To some your Baraca heritage will be a good thing. To others it will not."

"Is there nothing that can be done to get the Baraca and the Telerians to work together?"

"There may be something," one council member said, "but the probability that it will work is quite small."

Mahon cleared his throat and Kieran expected the calafar to explain further. Instead, he said, "The council and I will discuss the solution at length before we give you any more information." Then he dismissed them.

When Toren announced that they were to begin riding lessons, Kieran did all he could to hide his anxiety. He'd fallen off a horse when he was younger, and had almost been trampled under its sharp hooves. When patrons wanted their horses shod, Kieran always let Kale take the role of farrier. And he made sure he was nowhere near Kale when he did.

Kieran knew his fears were irrational, and he understood how important it was to learn how to ride. But the closer he got to the stables, the more he wanted to turn back.

Upon reaching the stables, Braeden introduced them to Jorek. The stable master bowed and Kieran nodded.

"We need two of your finest horses for the king and his cousin," said Braeden.

"Have you ever ridden before, my lord?" Jorek asked.

Kieran tensed his jaw. "No, I'm afraid I haven't."

Jorek went into the stables and returned with two dapple gray horses. "From the time of Alardin, the Tyman Baraca have provided and trained all of the horses for the royal household," Jorek said.

"You are both in excellent hands," said Braeden.

"We have been saving this one in particular for you, Majesty," said Jorek. "His name is Fallon, offspring of Arathor's horse Telegar."

The larger and darker of the two animals snorted and pawed the ground. All of Kieran's old fears came rushing to the front of his mind. What was he getting himself into?

"How long will it take to learn?" Kieran asked.

"I want you to stay for a month," said Toren. "Once you've learned to ride, I will instruct you and Gilrain in the use of swords from atop your mounts."

Gilrain seemed eager to start. Kieran cringed silently.

Before teaching them to ride, Jorek showed them how to care for their horses and how to put on the saddle and reins. Kieran was all thumbs as he tried imitate Jorek's deft movements with the tack.

As Kieran put his foot in the stirrup and hoisted himself up onto Fallon, the new leather creaked under Kieran's weight, and the horse tossed its head impatiently.

Jorek explained how to get the horses moving, how to make them turn, and how to make them stop. Kieran hesitantly followed his instruction, still not sure that he wanted to entrust his safety to the powerful beast moving beneath him.

"Fallon can sense your apprehension," Jorek said, smiling slightly. "You have to remain calm and let him know that you are in command, my lord."

Gilrain, as always, looked confident. Kieran gritted his teeth and tried to relax.

Over the course of the next two hours, Kieran felt himself settle into Fallon's powerful cadence. He had never realized what magnificent animals horses really were. Now he regretted that he hadn't ridden one sooner. When the day's lesson was finished, he was reluctant to dismount.

"You will be glad we finished when we did, your Majesty," Jorek said. "Tomorrow it may not be so easy to ride."

Kieran led Fallon to the barn, pondering Jorek's' statement. Now that he'd experienced Fallon's power and grace, he couldn't imagine not wanting to ride.

After the lesson, Braeden led Kieran and Gilrain to his home in the trees. It was twice as large as Kieran and Gilrain's quarters, but just as sparsely furnished. Braeden motioned for them to be seated at a low table with three chairs. A woman soon entered the main room, bearing platters of food Kieran had never seen before. Kieran started to introduce himself, but the woman scurried out of sight.

Braeden introduced the woman as his sister Hala.

"It is our custom that unmarried women do not speak with men outside of their family, especially Telerian men."

"Are there any other customs we should know about?" Gilrain asked.

"Many. After we have dined, I will instruct both of you in those customs. It would be unfortunate if you were to offend the Baraca by your lack of knowledge regarding matters of etiquette."

"Why didn't you tell us before we met with the council?" Gilrain asked.

Kieran gave Gilrain a sharp look.

"Forgive me, gentlemen," said Braeden, "but there was not time to fully explain our customs before the meeting."

"Of course," said Kieran.

Gilrain just blew out a frustrated breath.

After the meal, Braeden took out a pipe and lit it, inhaling deeply and blowing smoke rings into the air. Kieran studied the Baraca while he waited for him to speak. His shoulder length black hair was pulled back into a knot. He had a squarish face, a strong jaw, a wide nose, and dark bushy eyebrows that shadowed his deep-set black eyes. Kieran had noticed that all the Tyman Baraca he'd met had black eyes.

It made him wonder about Jessara and *her* black eyes.

After Braeden worked his pipe for several moments, he leaned forward in his chair to speak. "For the next few days, I will instruct you in matters of Baraca custom."

He began by explaining the formalities of Baraca hierarchy. The Hada clan was the original clan, and had come to Teleria three hundred years ago. Out of this clan, fifteen others had emerged. Each clan's importance was determined by how closely it was related to the Hada. The eldest members of the clans were the most honored and were addressed with the title of Cala. A chief ruled each clan and was addressed as Calafar.

Kieran was surprised when Braeden told them that married women were more highly regarded than unmarried women. Married women could be distinguished from unmarried women by their two coiled braids. Unmarried women wore their hair in a single braid.

"A Baraca woman's most glorious feature is her hair," Braeden said, "and the longer her hair, the more honor she holds. It is for this reason that only a Baraca woman's husband may see her with her hair unbound."

"And why do unmarried Baraca women not speak with men?" Kieran asked.

Braeden looked serious when he answered. "They are the most treasured members of our families, and only the woman's father, brother, or Eldala may speak to her and for her. It is how we protect them from improper advances."

At that, Kieran couldn't help but wonder how many women would have been saved from Gilrain's improper advances if Telerians followed this Baraca custom.

The rest of Braeden's instructions included the proper way to speak with Baraca – much more formally than when speaking with Telerians – and how to greet a male Baraca by inclining the head, clasping right arms up to the elbow.

When approaching a married woman, one waited for the woman to speak first and then addressed the woman with the title of Mara. Braeden also explained that when Kieran stood before a Baraca council, the greeting was more formal: He was to give a full bow at the waist while placing his left hand across his chest. Also, he was not to speak until the council gave him permission.

After two hours of instruction, Kieran's head was spinning.

On the day Toren declared Kieran and Gilrain proficient at fighting from horseback, Calafar Mahon invited the three companions to a formal meal in Kieran's honor.

A blazing bonfire crackled in the center of a large stone pit. The Baraca women wore their finest doeskin dresses and the men wore elaborate deer skin tunics. A score of wooden tables held more of the unusual food Kieran and Gilrain had come to enjoy – unrecognizable birds, some kind of large game animal, and a wide range of fruits and vegetables.

When the meal ended, four couples went to the middle of the circle and began to dance.

Kieran nearly choked.

The couples were dancing to the tune of Jessara's song. And their dance was Jessara's dance.

Kieran leaned sideways and whispered to Braeden. "What is this?"

"It is a traditional Baraca dance. All of the clans use it during the Eldalafar ceremony."

"Eldalafar ceremony?"

"A bonding ritual between a Baraca boy and girl."

When the couples left the circle, Calafar Mahon stood and bowed to Kieran. "Will you please join me for a private meeting, your Majesty?"

Kieran stood. "I would be honored."

In the council chambers, the calafar poured the traditional cup of tea that he and Kieran had shared on many nights. As they sat facing each other, Mahon sipped from his cup and then set it on the table between them.

"When you first came to us," said Mahon, "you asked me how you could get the Telerians and Baraca to work together."

"Yes I did."

"Do you know the story of the Malazia?"

"No, I am afraid I do not."

"In every other generation of Hada Baraca, a Hada mystic chooses a child from the clan. We call that child the 'Malazia,' which means 'one who is set apart.' When the child turns eighteen, he becomes the leader of all the Baraca until the next child is chosen. In every instance, except one, the child has been a male Baraca. However, the most recent Malazia was a girl. We realized she was destined for a great purpose. But when she was eight, slave traders stole her from the Forest of Ithil."

An unexpected nausea filled Kieran's stomach. "How long ago did they take her?"

"Ten years ago. And the Hada have never found her."

The nausea flared. Certainly, the girl they were discussing couldn't be his friend. It wasn't possible.

"What was her name?"

"Only her clan knows. Before ruling, the Hada present the Malazia to the other Baraca councils in Agora. Then they reveal the Malazia's name."

"What does this have to do with uniting the country?"

"If you could find her and take her back to her clan, it might help to restore the Baraca's confidence in Telerians."

"Do you know where she is?"

"I am afraid not."

"Then how am I supposed to find her?"

"You must begin by speaking with the Hada council. They could tell you where they have already looked. But I must warn you that the

Hada clan is the most traditional of the Baraca clans. Entering their realm is a dangerous endeavor. And speaking to them about the Malazia borders on sedition."

"How will we find them?"

"We will send Braeden with you. He should be able to intercede with their council on your behalf."

"And what will your clan do?"

Mahon smiled wryly. "The Tyman clan will give you all the support you need."

That night, Kieran had a new dream. While he held up the sword, everything went dark and he saw Baraca fighting with Telerians. Just when it looked as if the Telerians would prevail, a young woman walked onto the battle field. Everyone stopped to look at her. She lifted up her hands and Kieran sensed she wanted to say something, but no words came out. Kieran couldn't see her face, but he knew she was distraught. He tried to reach out and call to her, but he couldn't move his legs or his lips. She looked towards him and mouthed the words, "Help me."

It was Jessara.

Chapter 14

An unseasonably cold wind met Kieran, Gilrain, Toren, and Braeden as they left the Tyman fortress. Kieran reined in Fallon and took out his cloak, wrapping it closely around himself. It seemed the curse was worsening.

When they came to Trevet, the companions split up. Hopefully, when Kieran saw Toren and Braeden again, they would have members of the southwestern Baraca clans with them.

A day later, having reached the Rapid River, Kieran and Gilrain dismounted and let their horses drink. Just on the other side of the river, Kieran saw Nosora rising from a harsh, uneven desert. Only small clumps of tough grass broke up the miles of sand and rock.

As they rode through town, the few people they saw avoided looking at them. Eventually they came to a young man on horseback. His armor looked as if it had never seen battle. His gleaming sword hung naked on his belt.

Kieran extended a hand in greeting. The man's gray eyes were as cold as stone. "There aren't many who come to Nosora anymore," he said.

"We're travelers, exploring the country," Gilrain said.

"You'll find nothing of interest here," the man said. "You should keep going."

"Do you know of a place where we could spend the night?" Kieran asked.

"The one inn closed years ago." He frowned and then looked as if he were arguing with himself. Kieran was surprised when he said, "You can stay with me."

Kieran and Gilrain followed him through dusty streets. Darkened windows stared lifelessly out of broken-down homes. Before long, they dismounted outside a half-burned out cottage. The door creaked on its rusting hinges as the man pushed it open.

"It isn't much," he said, "but it keeps the rain off."

Within seconds of his words, the air crackled around them and lightning hit just a few yards away. "What do we do with the horses?" Gilrain asked, keeping one hand on the horse's neck to calm it.

"There's a barn out back," the man said.

After stabling their horses and shaking the rain off, Kieran introduced himself and Gilrain. Their host called himself Riordan.

"What's happened to Nosora?" Gilrain asked. "I'd heard it was a thriving town."

Riordan spat in disgust. "It was. When I came back from Korisan, it was like this."

"You've been to Korisan?" Kieran asked.

"I lived there for three years as a palace guard. Disgusting place. Filth and disease everywhere. You'd think that since it's the royal city, Rahnak would clean it up. But it's just as bad as everywhere else and getting worse."

"Why did you leave?" Gilrain asked.

Riordan looked him square in the eye. "I went to Korisan thinking I could make a difference – fighting off invading armies, protecting people." His jaw tightened and started to twitch. "But they put me in the castle, guarding the gate from no one. Every day, I watched Rahnak and Ciara invite lord after lord after lord, letting them feast for days while the people outside the castle starved. I couldn't stand it, so I left."

"And what will you do now?" Kieran asked.

"There's nothing in Nosora for me. I've been here two weeks. I would've left sooner, but I'm not sure where to go."

"How would you like to come with us?" Gilrain asked.

Riordan gave him a puzzled look. "Why?

"Do you know your way around this part of Teleria?"

"Yes."

Kieran pulled Gilrain aside. "Do you think we can trust him?"

"It sounds like he hates Rahnak and Ciara."

Kieran turned around. Riordan stood there, waiting indifferently.

"How badly do you want to see Rahnak and Ciara taken off the throne?" Kieran asked, trying to read the man's intentions.

Riordan's eyes flared. "I can taste it."

"If you're willing you could come with us. I'm looking for men who will fight Ciara's army from Zagora."

"Why?"

"So I can win back my kingdom."

"What are you talking about?"

Kieran showed him the signet ring. "I'm the rightful king of Teleria."

Riordan came closer and examined the ring. "I wouldn't flash that around if I were you."

"I'm not going to hide who I am. Now, will you join me?"

Riordan remained silent, as if he were trying to measure his words carefully. "Only if you'll accept my challenge to a sword fight."

"Why?"

"I refuse to serve under a man who can't hold his own in a fight."

Kieran and Riordan faced each other in the gray morning light. Kieran's goal was to finish this as quickly as possible without seriously wounding his opponent.

Kieran swung his sword around, and Riordan's blade crashed against Restamar. Kieran let himself feel the rhythm of the fight and the quivering of his weapon as it clashed with Riordan's, trusting his muscles to remember their training. Despite Riordan's bragging the night before, Kieran knew after a few moments he was the better swordsman. But as he went in for the final blow, Riordan surprised him with an elbow strike to his jaw.

When Riordan came in for another thrust, Kieran kicked him to the ground and tried to stab at him, but Riordan rolled away and slashed at Kieran's feet. Kieran jumped up to avoid the blade and in an instant had his blade at Riordan's throat.

Riordan dropped his sword and put up his hands. Kieran reached down to help him up.

"I'll go with you," said Riordan. "But don't ask me to call you your Majesty."

After traveling south for several hours Kieran, Gilrain, and Riordan came upon a peddler who was traveling in the same direction. The two-wheeled wagon over-flowed with pans, utensils, and other oddments. The man stopped his ox and removed his sagging straw hat. As he wiped his brow, he introduced himself as Bonifar.

"Why do you travel alone?" Gilrain asked. "We've heard it isn't safe on the roads."

"It didn't used to be this way," said Bonifar. "It's only in the last twenty years I've had to start traveling with a caravan. This time, no one was going this way, and I have business in Sodoya. I'll gladly travel with you."

By nightfall they were still some distance from Sodoya, so they found a sheltered grove of ash trees. Resting next to the campfire, Kieran leaned back on his elbows and spoke to Bonifar. "Do you have many stories from your travels?"

Bonifar smiled. "I do. But people usually get tired of hearing them."

"I'd be interested to hear them."

"So would I," Gilrain said.

Bonifar settled back against a log, lit an intricately carved pipe, and began to share. "My father was a peddler and I started traveling with him when I was just a lad. When he died, I took over his work. I've been to almost every village or town in Teleria."

"Have you seen things change much?" Kieran asked.

The peddler shook his head. "This used to be a beautiful country, and the land was rich. But now – now it's dying. Farmers and craftsmen used to send their surplus goods to countries across the sea. Now we have to depend on those countries to get the things we need. And very few people are buying what I have to sell. Either they just don't have anything to trade, or they don't have the money."

Riordan gave Kieran a sideways glance, as if to say, "I told you it was bad."

Kieran cautiously asked the next question. "And what do the people think of Rahnak and Ciara?"

"Some are content with the way things are, but I think it's because they don't see any other way to live. And others want to do something, but feel helpless. If someone came along to challenge Rahnak, I think there'd be people who would follow him."

A strange tingling went up Kieran's back. This time Gilrain gave him a sideways glance.

"And where do you stand?" Gilrain asked Bonifar.

The peddler rubbed his chin. "If there was such a man – I'd leave my travels and join him." He shook his head. "But I just don't see anyone to do that."

"I'm going to do it," said Kieran.

The peddler raised a skeptical eyebrow. "You, sir?"

Kieran gave him a grim smile. "When you travel through Teleria, tell the people the son of Arathor is raising an army to bring down Rahnak and Ciara."

Gray clouds, heavy with rain, threatened to drench them as they parted company with Bonifar and made their way to the southern edge of Sodoya. The village consisted of a few farms, most of them lying fallow, and an apple orchard, neglected and ragged. The men set up camp in a clearing, and waited a day for Toren and Braeden.

It was late in the afternoon when Kieran heard someone approaching. His heart sank when he saw that Toren was alone.

"What news?" Kieran asked.

Toren looked as ragged as the apple trees. "We have council members from four clans, and they want us to meet them south of here, at the Kumai camp."

Riordan frowned. "You didn't tell me anything about meeting with Baraca."

"Does it matter?" Kieran asked.

"In Nosora they told me Baraca gangs murdered my parents."

Kieran let out a heavy sigh. He could understand Riordan's reluctance. But if he couldn't convince one man to overlook his prejudices, how would he get whole armies to work together?

Kieran's heart fell when they reached the Kumai camp. He had hoped for the grace and beauty of the Tyman camp. Instead, smoky torches revealed small, mud-covered structures haphazardly built one on top of another, spread out over a rocky plain. A young boy led them to the largest building and told them to tie up their horses. As they dismounted, Kieran cautiously looked around. The Kumai clansmen he saw looked as apprehensive as Riordan.

The boy led them inside a low-ceilinged building. Kieran and Gilrain had to duck to avoid hitting their heads on the doorframe. Riordan's hand went to his sword. Kieran put a hand on his arm.

"Careful. We don't want to start anything here."

At least fifty Baraca sat on the dirt floor. Probably a hundred more stood against the walls. As Braeden had instructed, Kieran gave the proper greeting and waited for permission to speak. Gilrain, Toren, and Braeden greeted the council in a similar manner, and Riordan moved to the edge of the room.

A man seated in the center of the circle spoke. "I am Calafar Falbard. Please be seated and state your business, son of Arathor."

Kieran sat, and after folding his legs into a rather uncomfortable position, asked, "Did Braeden already tell you part of my story?"

"Enough to make us decide to let you into our camp," Falbard said.

"But has he told you I am Baraca?"

"That is why we let you in."

"You know I am the son of Arathor, but Arathor has given me his authority, and now I am the rightful king of Teleria. My plan is to raise an army to defeat the Zagorans and remove Ciara and Rahnak from the throne. I do not believe Telerians alone can defeat the Zagorans. I need the Baraca's help."

A sea of murmurs flooded the room. Falbard looked grave. Kieran continued. "The Tyman clan has already agreed to support me."

"And did the Tyman clan have a plan for convincing the more hesitant clans to help?" asked Falbard.

Kieran quickly explained Mahon's plan.

"The Hada clan has used the Malazia to control us for more than a hundred years," said Falbard. "We and a few of the other clans will not be ruled by the Hada. Whether you find the Malazia or not, the Kumai clan will help you because you are Alardin's descendant, and because we believe you alone can defeat Ciara and her Zagoran army."

Several men nodded their heads. "It seems that the leaders of the Zumat, Abacar, Dathar, and Miri clans agree," said Falbard. "Unfortunately, among our five clans, there are barely two thousand people, and not all of us can fight. The Tyman clan is large and can provide many warriors. But you should also try to get the support of the Nedebar, Linden, and Kofar."

"And the Hada," someone else said. "They have the largest clan in the country."

"From what Mahon told me," Kieran said, "I should not count on their help."

Falbard nodded. "They are so proud of the fact that they have nothing to do with Telerians, it would be hard to believe they would agree, even if you found the Malazia."

"But they will know I am Baraca."

"Your Baraca blood will not be enough to get an audience with their council."

"And why is that?"

"To them you are just a despised Telerian."

"Then the fact that one of their own was my ancestor will make no difference?"

"They will deny that they ever let Jessara marry Alardin."

"Jessara?"

"Yes, Jessara. She was the first female Malazia and Alardin's queen."

There she was again. Would there ever be a moment when something wasn't reminding Kieran of Jessara – and the guilt of failing her?

"Do the other clans feel this way?" Gilrain asked.

"Some of them do. But most of the hostility comes from the Baraca gangs."

"Calafar Mahon mentioned that they blame the clans for their problems," Kieran said.

"But they also blame Telerians," said Falbard.

"And Telerians blame Baraca for their problems," said Toren.

A man from the back of the room spoke up. "I am from the Zumat clan. The gangs have attacked the villagers in Agadir and the villagers blame us for not keeping our young men under control. Now the villagers have started to retaliate."

"Is there any way to make the gangs stop?" Kieran asked. "Could their anger be put to better use?"

"We have no way of meeting with them," said Falbard. "They come and go in the night."

Another man stepped forward. “My name is Nevan. I was once part of a Baraca gang.”

Everyone turned around with shocked looks on their faces. “Please continue,” said Falbard.

“I left the gangs when I saw how pointless it was.”

“Do you think they would fight against the Zagorans?” Kieran asked.

“You would have to ask their leaders,” said Nevan.

“And where would I find them?”

“I can take you to them.”

Chapter 15

After two days of travel, Kieran and his companions reached the village of Pomora. They were just about to set up camp when an unexpected thunderstorm began pelting them with heavy drops. They spurred their horses towards a grove of scrawny trees while Riordan rode ahead to find shelter. After a few minutes, he returned with good news.

"I found a farmer who will take us in," he said.

After caring for the horses, they went into the wood-framed house and introduced themselves to the farmer. He looked to be a man in his forties. He was tall and muscular, matching Kieran in size and probably in strength, Kieran thought. He called himself Brecken.

"Our horses need to rest for a few days," Kieran said. "We can pay you for your trouble."

"That would be fine – and any news from other parts of Teleria you could give us. We don't get many visitors."

In a few minutes, a work-hardened woman came into the room. She gave Brecken a sharp glance. "Who are these men?"

"Mariel, these are travelers who need shelter," Brecken said.

"We don't have enough food for ourselves." She motioned towards Braeden and Nevan. "And we certainly can't feed any Baraca."

Brecken walked over to her and gently put his hand on her shoulder. "Mariel, everyone deserves our hospitality, even the Baraca."

"No. After what they did to Liam…"

"This man says they can pay us."

She bit her lip and looked at her husband. "Just tell them to stay out of my way."

Gilrain spoke up. "If it's an inconvenience – "

Brecken put his hand up. "No, it's all right. Liam was our oldest son. He was killed in a skirmish with the Ancala Baraca. But we're learning to put that aside."

Nevan spoke up. "We are sorry for your loss, mistress. If there were some way to make it up – "

"You can't, so don't try." She stormed out of the room towards the kitchen and started to prepare a mid-day meal.

Kieran wished there was some way to diffuse her anger and moved to help her, but Brecken motioned for him to stop.

"We lost Liam six months ago. Mariel hasn't recovered."

"Do you have any other children?" Kieran asked.

"Five, but none of them are old enough to help in the fields. Liam was fifteen and the strongest of them. The youngest one is two."

As he spoke, children of varying sizes ran into the room and nearly knocked the farmer over. The smallest one climbed him like he was a tree. "This is Liza," he said, wrapping his arms around her.

Kieran felt an unexpected lump in his throat. This was one of the things he'd wanted out of life – plenty of children. Would he ever have this kind of simple life? A wave of regret settled on him and stayed for the rest of the day.

The next morning, Brecken and the others were already outside when Kieran woke up. A crusty loaf of dark bread was on the table, alongside a bowl of white cheese curds. Mariel sat by the fire mending clothes.

Kieran knelt beside her. "I'm sorry for your loss."

She kept her eyes on her mending, but Kieran sensed her sorrow. "Nothing can bring him back, but thank you for your concern."

He was about to leave when he noticed another presence, faint but separate from Mariel's.

"Please pardon my asking, but are you with child?"

The farmer's wife looked alarmed and quickly put her hand to her belly. "Yes, but I haven't told anyone. How did you know?"

"It runs in my family." Then he reached his hand towards her. "May I?" he asked.

Shyly, she took Kieran's hand and placed it over the unborn child. With a sense of wonder, Kieran closed his eyes and saw images of a man giving orders to many people. "Your son will grow strong and be a great man," Kieran said.

Mariel looked surprised but pleased.

Still marveling at what had just happened, Kieran took the bread and went outside to see if he could help Brecken. When he reached the barn, he found the farmer sharpening his small collection of tools, all badly in need of repair.

Kieran ran his fingers over a rusting cultivator. "I could fix these for you," he said.

Brecken turned to him. "I wondered if you were a blacksmith."

"Is there a smithy in the village?"

"Yes, but it's been vacant for years."

"Is there anyone else around here who needs their tools repaired?"

"Three other farmers and I work Lord Rafer's land and our own small plots. We could all use the help."

While Kieran and Gilrain gathered up the tools, Brecken and Riordan went to the other farms to tell the people there was a blacksmith in the town for a few days.

When they reached the smithy, a line of people stretched around the building almost twice. Kieran realized that if he was going to help a few, he would have to help everyone. By the end of the day, they'd repaired or forged a little bit of everything – pitchforks, hoes, fire hooks, hay rakes, and a few horseshoes. It was dark when Braeden finally covered the coals.

Kieran and his friends spent the next few days working in the smithy. In the evenings, they returned to Brecken's house, to share a meal and news from northern and western Teleria. Even Mariel seemed to enjoy their conversations, and Kieran appreciated Brecken's stories.

On the sixth night of their stay, Brecken invited the other farmers and some of the well-respected villagers to his home so Kieran could hear their stories. Brecken introduced Melvek, and the man started the story, while the others added to it as they felt the need.

"Back when my father started our farm, the land belonged to us, not some uppity liege lord. The land gave us everything we needed – food, seeds for new crops, and excess to sell throughout the area. The sheaves of wheat were as bright and heavy as gold, corn grew up over our heads, bending with the weight of the ears, and the barley was the best in Teleria."

Melvek paused.

"That was twenty years ago. Now we break our backs and have so little to show for it. If that wasn't bad enough, Lord Rafer moved here and declared all the land belongs to him. He said he'd let us work it in exchange for his protection."

Someone in the group snorted at the word.

"We can barely feed ourselves with each harvest, but we still have to pay our taxes. Rafer expects a fifth of whatever we harvest, and taxes whatever we sell. He's threatened more than once to have us all thrown into the dungeon in Korisan if we don't pay."

Another farmer spoke up. "We're staking our futures on this one last crop. If this fails, we'll all be in prison."

Riordan interrupted. "Now do you see what I mean, Kieran?"

"What are you talking about?" Brecken asked.

"I told Kieran I left my post in Korisan because I was tired of seeing the lords feast while the people starved."

"Then you've seen Rahnak?" Brecken asked.

"I've seen him and the waste that follows him. He and Ciara act like everything belongs to them and they can use it however they please. They only care about themselves."

"What can we do?" Mariel asked.

Gilrain and Riordan looked at Kieran.

It had been one thing for Kieran to reveal who he was to the Tyman clan and to Riordan. Why was it so difficult to tell these simple farmers? And when he did, would they accept the truth? Would they be willing to follow an unproven twenty-year-old blacksmith from a sea village?

All of his doubts threatened to swallow him up right there, but he pushed down the fear as best he could. "What would you do if there was someone who could do something?"

"We'd join him."

"At what cost? Would you leave your farms and your families? Would you give your lives to get rid of the king and queen?"

Brecken looked thoughtful. "I've pondered that question for years." He looked up at Kieran. "If there was someone like that, we'd follow him anywhere."

"Do you know of such a man?" Mariel asked.

Kieran took a deep breath. "I'm that man."

A murmur went through the crowd.

"But you're just a blacksmith," Brecken said.

"An extraordinary one at that," someone else added. "But still..."

Kieran absently twirled the signet ring. Most of the time he hardly noticed it. But when he did, the shocking memory of Arathor putting it on his finger and declaring him the king of Teleria hit him full force. "Once I thought that being a smith was all there was to my life. But several months ago, I learned that I am Aiden, son of King Arathor."

Their eyes grew wide, and the only sound in the room was the thundering of Kieran's heartbeat in his ears. And then the urgent knocking at the door.

Brecken hurried to answer it. A young boy ran inside, panting hard. "They're attacking the village!" he cried.

"The Ancala?" Brecken asked.

The boy nodded.

"Is there anything we can do to help?" Gilrain asked.

"All we can hope to do is drive them away," said Brecken.

Kieran and his companions grabbed their cloaks and swords, and followed Brecken and the others out the door. Kieran was surprised when the women followed.

Mariel responded to his shock. "Anyone who can wield a sword or a pitchfork fights in this village. Lord Rafer's troops are pitiful and he won't send them to fight anyway."

"But your unborn child…"

"He'll have no home to come into if I don't fight."

Part of Kieran wanted to protest, but he knew she was right. Keeping his arguments to himself, he followed Brecken into town. When they arrived, flames engulfed several of the buildings, and others had already burned to the ground. Kieran stifled a cry at the destruction.

"Why are they doing this?" he asked Braeden.

"Hatred for Telerians," Braeden said. "The Ancala are the most violent of the clans. That must be why they harbor the gangs."

"Can they be stopped?"

"They will only bend their knee to the true king of Teleria."

"And how will I prove that?"

"It will depend on how you wield the sword. Only a descendant of Alardin will be able to defeat one of them in a sword match."

How many times do I have to prove myself? Kieran wondered.

The farmers and their wives had entered the fray, pitchforks and hay rakes flying at the attackers. Kieran and his companions stepped in to help. He hoped he wouldn't have to kill any of the Ancala; it wouldn't be the best way to introduce himself to this clan.

Just as he was about to strike one down, all of the Ancala stopped to look at him. One of them stepped forward. In the light of the dying flames, Kieran saw he was taller than the rest, almost as tall as himself. The man threw back his cloak, and his sword glinted in the light of the fire.

"Why do you carry that sword, Telerian?" he asked.

"Because it belongs to me."

"I am Avareth," said the warrior. "I challenge you to prove your worth to carry the sword of Alardin."

Kieran exhaled his annoyance and handed his cloak to Toren.

"Strike first and strike hard," Toren whispered. "His arrogance will be his weakness."

Avareth stood ready with his sword. As Kieran approached, Avareth drew his dagger. Kieran responded by drawing his own dagger, and the crashing of steel on steel began. Avareth slashed at Kieran's head, but Kieran spun to avoid the blade. Kieran thrust at Avareth's middle and missed. After a few minutes of thrusting and missing each other, both men were breathing hard. Avareth spun around, and the clanking of numerous blocks carried over the sound of the burning buildings.

Kieran was starting to think he might have met his match. He answered his thoughts by redoubling his efforts.

Backing Avareth into a wall, Kieran lunged, but Avareth put up his sword and dagger to block, pushing Kieran away with his foot. Kieran started to fall backwards, and before he knew it, Avareth had him up against a wall. Kieran looked down and saw that their hilts had locked. He gave Avareth a crooked smile and hit him in the jaw, jumping on top of him before he could get up. Kieran finished the fight with another hit to the jaw.

Before Avareth could recover, more Ancala surrounded the two men, and for a nerve-wracking moment, Kieran wondered if they would yield or kill him.

Chapter 16

That night, Avareth led Kieran, Braeden, and Nevan to the Ancala camp. The Ancala held their council in a goat skin tent. Ten men sat cross-legged on a tightly woven rug. Kieran bowed before them and waited for permission to speak. When they said nothing, he rested on his knees and returned their fierce stares. The last two times he had faced a Baraca council, he'd been nervous. Now he was just angry.

After a lengthy silence, he decided to speak first. "Why were you in Pomora?"

"Is it really any of your business?"

Kieran tried to restrain himself. Losing his temper wouldn't help his cause. "I am Aiden, the rightful king of Teleria. Anything that happens to my people is my business. You cost the villagers of Pomora their livelihood. It will take them months to rebuild."

"Why should that matter to us?"

"You are acting just like Rahnak and his liege lords – no concern for the people around you. You bring suffering wherever you go."

His accusation was met with blank stares.

"And because Telerians do not see any difference between one clan and another, what you do affects all the other clans. All they want to do is live here in peace. You are making that impossible."

Some of the men shifted positions and looked away.

The discomfort was working. "Do you really want to be as bad as your enemy?"

They all looked at the floor – except for one. A gray-haired man held Kieran's gaze. His grizzled face bristled, and his black eyes were full of pride.

"Are you the calafar?" Kieran asked him.

"We don't use those formalities here," the man said. "But yes, I'm Sahjahn, the leader of the Ancala."

"Do my words carry any weight with you?"

"Let's speak privately in my tent."

Sahjahn dismissed the rest of the council and motioned for someone to take care of Nevan and Braeden.

Sahjahn's deer-skin tent held only a sleeping mat, two folding stools, a short folding table, and a fire brazier. The man sat cross-legged on a bearskin rug and motioned for Kieran to join him. He took a pair of tin cups from a wooden cupboard and filled them with a steaming brew from a copper kettle sitting on the brazier.

Kieran took one cup from him. As he brought it to his lips, he recognized a familiar, yet elusive scent. "What is this?" he asked.

"An ancient Baraca tea made from cascabel flowers. It helps to clear the mind."

Sahjahn looked at his cup as he swirled the liquid around and around. "I'm old and tired of fighting."

"Then why don't you stop?"

"The other council members and the clan – they expect it."

"If you're the leader, you can tell them it's over."

"As far as they're concerned, it will never be over until the Baraca rule Teleria."

Now Kieran swirled the tea in his cup and watched the white foam dance over the pale liquid. "I'm surprised you gave me an audience."

The chief looked up from his tea. "No one has ever defeated Avareth in a sword match."

Kieran let himself bask in the glow of his success for just a moment. "Still," he said, "from what the Kumai told me, your clan is the most reclusive, even more so than the Hada."

"The Hada!" Sahjahn swore out loud. "Those sons and daughters of dogs. At least the Ancala still keep their promise to serve the house of Alardin."

"Do you think you're serving Alardin by harboring the gangs?"

Sahjahn's face was severe. "They have nowhere else to go. If we don't give them a place to stay – "

"And yet you must have some influence over them."

"And what would I tell them to do? Return to their clans, clans that do nothing to make things better?" He threw back his arms and upset the tea kettle. Hot liquid flew everywhere, some of it hitting him in the face. He stifled a cry and stood to clean up the mess.

Kieran watched the proud warrior reduce himself to the role of a servant, getting down on his knees to sop up the tea from the bearskin. When he finished, he sat cross-legged again.

"Forgive me," he said, inclining his head. "I'm not usually this way."

Kieran took another sip of tea. "Couldn't the gangs put their hatred to better use?"

"What do you mean?"

"Would they consider helping me overthrow Ciara and Rahnak?"

Sahjahn added more water and herbs to the tea kettle. "Only with the right incentive."

"And what would that be?"

"If a Baraca woman were to be the queen."

Kieran felt his heart drop into his stomach. "You mean a marriage of alliance?"

Sahjahn nodded.

"I'm afraid I'm already promised to a distant cousin."

"You must find a way out of your betrothal."

"Is it that important?"

"Yes, and you'll have to force the issue with the Hada."

"Why the Hada?"

"Because the only Baraca woman the clans would ever accept as queen is the Malazia."

Without warning, Kieran dropped his cup and watched the tea soak into the dirt. There was that word again. What was it about the Malazia that mysteriously tied her to him?

He felt as if he were in a boat with no rudder, being swept away on a raging river towards a destination not of his choosing. And there was nothing he could do about it.

Later in the evening, Sahjahn invited Kieran, Braeden, and Nevan to join in one of the Ancala's spring celebrations. The whole clan gathered under the stars around a blazing bonfire. Several tables held various kinds of game: deer, goat, boar, wild sheep, pheasant, swan, goose, and duck. As there were no trenchers or plates, Kieran took what he wanted right from the platters. Large wooden barrels formed a circle around the feast, and several people already showed signs of drinking too much wine.

When the feasting ended, three young women gathered in a cluster and started to dance to the haunting music of flutes and lyres. Their dark hair and black eyes were mesmerizing and made Kieran think of Jessara – again.

The dancers left the circle and an old woman stood in the center of the gathering. In a clear voice, she began to speak. “First, we wish to welcome Aiden, son of Arathor, into our midst.”

Some Ancala murmured their approval, and others glared.

“It is an honor to have a descendant of Alardin here with us.”

The crowd responded. “Hail to King Alardin.”

Kieran dipped his head.

“We honor our guest by allowing him to witness the Eldalafar, a ceremony no Telerian has ever seen.”

A boy and a girl stepped into the circle, followed by four adults.

“Each girl in our clan is betrothed to the proper boy at the age of eight. The two families hold a bonding ceremony called the Eldalafar. When they are finished, the children will share Eldala, a heart connection.”

Kieran watched intently as the boy handed the girl a piece of wood, carved in the shape of a heart. The girl handed him a cloth with an embroidered heart. Then the two children embraced and vowed to remain friends.

“Now they will grow together in mind and heart, and they will see each other in their dreams. When they are married, their bond will be complete and only death will end it.”

Kieran leaned over to Braeden and whispered, “Could this happen between a Telerian and a Baraca?”

Braeden smiled. “No, it is only possible between Baraca.”

An unexpected rush of adrenaline went through Kieran’s body.

He and Jessara had exchanged gifts; he’d given her the shell, and she’d given him a perfect white stone. They had vowed to remain friends. And he was Baraca.

Now the evidence seemed to suggest that *she* was Baraca.

She had black eyes, just like every Baraca he’d met. The melody and the dance she’d taught him were from the Baraca’s Eldalafar. And she shared the name of an ancient Baraca queen, a queen who was once the Malazia – which could be purely coincidental. Or not.

Hadn’t Mahon’s story of the Malazia been similar to Jessara’s? The girl had been taken at the age of eight, just like his Jessara. And it had happened ten years ago. Their stories were too similar to be coincidence.

Now Kieran knew why he was seeing Jessara in his dreams – and it had nothing to do with failing to rescue her.

If the old woman was correct, then he and Jessara shared a bond that would become stronger. Whether she was the Malazia or not, he had to marry her. She was the one woman he was meant to be with for the rest of his life.

He only hoped she was still alive.

Two days later, Kieran and Braeden returned to Brecken's farm. The weary farmer and his wife came out to meet them, but Mariel's smile faded when she saw the group of Ancala Baraca following Kieran.

"What are they doing here?" she asked.

Kieran dismounted and greeted the couple. "They've agreed to help restore your village."

Mariel gave him a sour look and went into the house.

"I don't know how the other villagers will feel about this," Brecken said.

"I know this won't be easy," said Kieran, "but cooperation between Baraca and Telerians has to start somewhere."

Brecken arched a bushy eyebrow. "If that's your wish."

Kieran was surprised at the sarcasm in the farmer's voice. "I'm not giving a command, Brecken. But I urge you and the others to try. I think it would go a long way towards building a foundation of peace between your village and the Ancala."

After a long pause, Brecken said, "Most men wouldn't try to get Baraca and Telerians to work together."

"I told you before I left – I'm the king of Teleria. I have to try."

"I didn't believe you then."

"And now?"

"I'm still not sure. But whether you are or not, you're a good man – and you care about Teleria. When the time comes, send word and we'll fight for you."

Chapter 17

Kieran's heart felt as heavy as the sinking sun as they approached the village of Kelefar. It had been difficult for him to leave Brecken and Mariel. After spending just a few days with them, he'd grown quite fond of the farmer and his wife. In fact, he had come to appreciate all the villagers he met there. He admired the way they maintained the joy of life while eking out a living in such harsh conditions. He hoped they could put aside their hatred of the Ancala and work with them to rebuild the village.

He let out a sigh and looked across the barren plain, up into the foothills of the Zaria Mountains. Only a few small buildings indicated they'd reached Kelefar. While Gilrain tried to secure shelter, the rest of their companions watered their horses.

After a moment, a woman came out of a nearby cottage. Her golden hair flew behind her in the wind, and her green peasant dress accentuated a very fine figure. Kieran couldn't take his eyes off of her. When three giggling children came out of the house and clustered around her, she lifted one of them up and spun around, joining in their laughter. He felt his face flush when she looked up at him and caught him staring at her.

"Can I help you?" she asked.

It took Kieran a moment to find his voice. "I'm sorry. We came from Pomora and we're looking for shelter."

"My home is crowded, but if you don't mind the small space, you and your friends are welcome to stay here."

Kieran dismounted and introduced himself and the others.

"My name is Lucia," she said with a winsome smile.

Kieran felt like he might choke. Could this be the Lucia he was supposed to marry? He ignored his racing heart and followed her into the house.

Before long, the travelers sat around a small table, sharing a meal. Kieran had insisted on sharing their provisions and Lucia graciously accepted. As he ate some vegetable stew, Kieran looked around the small room. Shelves of beautifully crafted pottery lined one wall.

"Who makes these?" Kieran asked.

"My husband and I," she said, smiling.

In fact, she hadn't stopped smiling since he'd met her. Nothing seemed to bother her – not her children's cries for more food nor the youngest child spilling her cider on the dirt floor. She took everything in stride. He had never met a woman like this.

"Where is your husband?" Riordan asked.

Now Lucia's face darkened. "He's in Lord Gorideri's quarry in Temir."

"What happened?" Kieran asked.

"He couldn't pay the taxes when he sold our pottery there. He didn't even get to come home. He had to send a message to me."

"How long ago was that?" Gilrain asked.

"Six months."

"And you've been living here all this time?" Toren asked.

"I can't leave my home, no matter what they've done to Adamar. And I know he'll be back soon."

"How do you know?" Riordan asked.

She looked at him, her eyes brimming with tears. "Because if I believe anything else, I'll die."

She wiped her eyes with the palm of her hand and after a few moments, her smile returned. "I try not to think about it. There's a man who comes by here every month to take the pottery to Pomora and Sodoya. We don't get much, but it's enough to feed us."

Kieran walked over to the shelf. The pottery was some of the finest he'd ever seen. "Who taught you how to do this?" he asked, turning to her.

She joined him. Just being near her made Kieran think thoughts he'd rather not. She was a married woman, for goodness' sake.

"I've always known how to do this. I think it's because I'm a descendant of Alardin."

She could have dropped a trunk on him and he wouldn't have felt any different than he did at that moment.

"Are you all right?" she asked.

He sat down and put up a hand. "I'll be fine in a minute." Now he knew he had to talk to her. He just didn't know how he would approach the subject.

By midnight, Kieran was tired of tossing and turning. When he stepped into the night air, he heard a whirring noise and went to investigate.

Lucia was in a shack behind the house, sitting at a potter's wheel. Kieran watched with fascination as she shaped the formless lump of clay into a slender-necked pitcher. It reminded him of watching Jelcahd in Pent, except that when Lucia worked, it was with a grace and ease that Jelcahd never showed.

"I have trouble sleeping, too," she said.

Kieran jumped at the sound of her voice. "I'm sorry. I haven't watched anyone throw on the wheel for a long time."

"It helps me relax."

She worked at the wheel for several minutes before speaking again. "You look familiar to me."

"I'm sure we've never met. I grew up in northern Teleria."

"You remind me of someone."

Kieran swallowed hard. Arathor had said that he'd met Lucia once, when she was fourteen.

"You're Aiden, aren't you?"

He put his hands behind his back. "I am."

She stopped the wheel and wiped her hands on her apron. Looking up at him, she said. "I'm sorry I didn't wait." There was sadness in her voice. "I had no way of knowing if you were alive. And when Adamar came along – I couldn't wait any longer." She laughed. "It made my father so angry when I ran away. I think Father wanted me to be queen more than I did. It was never very appealing to me."

"It's all right, Lucia. I don't think it was meant to be."

She gestured towards the wheel. "Would you like to try?"

"I'm a smith. I don't think I have the patience to work with clay."

"Being a descendant of Alardin, you should be able to do anything," she said, smiling.

Kieran had to admit he'd always wanted to try. "All right," he said, moving to sit on the stool.

Lucia removed the pitcher she'd made and placed a new lump of clay on the wheel. After showing him how to get the wheel moving with his feet, she wet his hands and placed them over the clay. He felt her warm breath on the back of his neck and shivered.

"Lucia, I don't think – "

"Let yourself feel the clay and imagine what you want it to be."

Kieran tried to concentrate on the slippery clay, but he had never been this close to a woman before, particularly one who was so attractive and alive. When she reached around him, putting her hands on his, her hair brushed against his cheek. He was nearly overwhelmed by the urge to kiss her.

He stopped the wheel and stood, almost knocking her to the ground. "I'm sorry, Lucia. I shouldn't be here," he said and ran back into the house.

When Kieran woke up, Lucia stood in front of the hearth, stirring something in an iron kettle. He watched her for a few minutes and then moved behind her and cleared his throat. When she looked up, her eyes were misty and her face was covered with red blotches, as if she had been crying for a long time.

"What's wrong?" Kieran asked.

"I'm sorry about last night. I shouldn't have asked…"

"No Lucia, I shouldn't have sat at the wheel."

She turned back to the fire and continued stirring. "I didn't realize until last night how much I miss Adamar."

Kieran started to put his arm around her to comfort her, but he stopped himself. It only would ignite feelings he didn't want ignited. Before he could think of something else to say, he heard someone walk up behind him. He turned around to find Gilrain. How long had he been listening?

"Are you the Lucia that Kieran was supposed to marry?" Gilrain asked.

Kieran felt the heat of embarrassment creep up his neck and into his cheeks. Lucia blushed too, but recovered quickly and answered. "Yes, I am. I know it seems ridiculous. I could have been queen, but I didn't want that life, so I married a potter."

"Would you like us to try to help Adamar escape?" Gilrain asked.

"How could you do that?" asked Lucia.

"That's what I'd like to know," Kieran said through clenched teeth.

By now Toren, Riordan, and Braeden were awake and listening. "Perhaps we should discuss this somewhere else," suggested Toren.

When they were outside, Kieran let out the question he'd held in for Lucia's sake. "What were you thinking? How could you volunteer to rescue Adamar without asking the rest of us – without asking me?"

Gilrain shrugged his shoulders. "How hard could it be?"

Why did Gilrain have to be so reckless? Kieran was about to tell his cousin exactly how difficult it would be when Toren interrupted. "If I may, Sire?"

"By all means. Maybe you can talk some sense into him."

"Gilrain, I must remind you that we should avoid drawing unwanted attention to ourselves. Rescuing Adamar would draw a great deal of attention."

Gilrain's brow furrowed. "The woman is obviously distraught over her husband's captivity. How can we stand by when we could help?"

Kieran blew out his frustration while he paced in front of the door. How could Gilrain ask him to endanger himself like this? "It won't do Teleria any good if her king is captured on a fool's errand."

Gilrain looked over at Riordan. Riordan gave him a sly smile. "Let the two of us go," Riordan said. "We have to go past Temir anyway, and we could get him at night."

"It won't do *me* any good if we have to rescue you and Gilrain," said Kieran.

"We won't be captured."

Under a moonless sky, Kieran, Toren, and Braeden waited in the hills outside Temir, listening for Gilrain and Riordan to return. Even though Gilrain and Riordan had scouted the quarry earlier in the day and had reported that there was only one guard at night, Kieran continued to argue against this rescue. And Gilrain had insisted it could be done.

Now, Kieran hoped his cousin and friend wouldn't be the newest additions to Lord Gorideri's quarry.

After waiting for what seemed an eternity, Kieran finally heard the crunching of footsteps on the rocky ground. Having escaped under the fence surrounding Lake Batna, all three men were soaked and shivered in the night air. Kieran led them to the fire, and Toren and Braeden put blankets around them. Kieran offered them hot tea which they accepted wordlessly.

While he waited for them to dry out, Kieran studied Adamar. Six months in the quarry had taken their toll. Adamar's clothes were in tatters, and his eyes were sunken in. His red hair was in knots, and his beard grew down onto his chest. When he raised a hand to stifle a cough, Kieran saw blood-soaked rags around his palm.

A few minutes later, Adamar was able to speak in a rasping whisper. "Who are you?"

"Your wife Lucia was kind enough to offer us shelter," Kieran said.

The man's eyes lit up. "How is she? And the children?"

"They're all well."

"How long was I in there?"

"Six months," said Gilrain.

Tears began to streak Adamar's careworn face. "I can never repay you for getting me out."

"No payment is necessary," said Kieran. "It's enough to know that Lucia will have her husband again."

~

After a short night of rest, the travelers shared a light breakfast of hard rolls and cheese with Adamar. It didn't take long for the color to come back into his face. When he spoke again, his voice sounded stronger.

"I insist on repaying you," he said.

Before Kieran could refuse, Riordan answered. "When Kieran fights against Rahnak and Ciara, you should join him."

Kieran snorted and walked away. He'd hoped Adamar wouldn't discover his identity until he reached home.

"Why would he do that?" Adamar asked.

"Because he's the king of Teleria."

Adamar's jaw went slack and he looked over at Kieran.

"Then you and Lucia…"

"Yes, I'm the one she was supposed to marry. But that's the past."

"You won't take her from me, will you?"

"I wouldn't do something like that. I respect her reason for marrying you and wish both of you a long and happy life."

Unexpectedly, Adamar went to his knees. "Thank you, King Aiden. Call when you need me and I will come."

Chapter 18

The Nedebar Baraca fortress rose from the foothills of the Koslan Mountains. On the other side lay Korisan.

Kieran had never been this close to Korisan, and although the Koslan Mountains were the tallest in the country, it set him on edge to be this close to his enemies' home.

As they approached the fortress gates, three sentries greeted them warmly and led them to the citadel. Two boys took their horses and another led them up the stairs to the council chambers. Kieran was getting tired of council chambers. Thankfully, only one person was in the room, and he said he would wait until Kieran had rested overnight before asking him his business.

When the gray light of morning woke Kieran, he rolled onto his back and looked at the ceiling while he tried to wake up. It was a type of alabaster, carved with battle scenes all around the edge. In the middle of the ceiling was a relief of a crown and a throne. He wasn't sure how he knew it, but it had to be the throne in Korisan. His throne.

Kieran's throat tightened and his heart felt trapped in his chest. A weight, heavier than he'd ever felt, rested on him and wouldn't let him breathe.

Why was it so hard to accept that he was the rightful king of Teleria? He knew it in his head, and there were times when he truly believed it. But it was still odd to introduce himself as the king. If only people wouldn't bow when they found out. It always made him terribly uncomfortable. Despite knowing that it was part of being king, he wasn't sure he would ever get used to it.

Kieran got up and rested the sword on his knees. The light was dim, but he saw the words again and ran his fingers over them, as if touching them might make him believe them. He spoke them out loud and remembered the nausea and fear that had swept over him when he had first read these words. They didn't turn his stomach now, but it was still hard to believe he was the one.

A small part of him wanted to turn his back on everything; the larger part wanted to free Teleria from Ciara's evil grip. Which part of him would win? Would it always be a struggle? He knew that if this was going to work, the part of him that wanted to run would have to be put down once and for all.

He got up, dressed, and walked to the council chambers. Five arched windows let the pale light into a round room. Walnut benches sat in rows in front of a massive rectangular table. Kieran ran his fingers over the dark wood, appreciating the rich color and smoothness of it. Then he glanced at the walls.

Intricately carved wooden panels lined the room. Kieran walked up to one of them to get a better look. The one closest to him depicted a man on horseback. His sword pointed to the figure of a woman crouching in fear.

"Alardin and Leandra," Kieran said out loud.

"You're right."

Kieran turned quickly. Here was the man he'd seen in this room last night.

"I didn't mean to startle you," the man said. "My name is Sahbél. I'm the leader of the Nedebar."

He was a head shorter than Kieran and couldn't have been much older than twenty-five. His black hair reached past his shoulders, and his dark clothing showed no sign of his rank.

Kieran reached out a hand and introduced himself.

Sahbél clasped his hand. "It's an honor to meet the son of Arathor."

"How do you know me?"

"You look like your father."

Kieran half laughed. There was no escaping his heritage.

"If you know who I am, then you know what I'm doing," Kieran said.

"Yes, and the Nedebar will join your fight… with as many people as we can spare."

"How many will that be?"

"It will depend on whether or not we're fighting off the Esgharites. We never know when they're going to attack."

Kieran had heard of the Esgharites. They lived on the other side of Teleria's eastern border and had a reputation for raiding the nearby cities and villages.

"I suppose Rahnak does nothing to stop them," Kieran said.

Sahbél looked disgusted. "I think he actually encourages them. I almost wonder if he wants other kingdoms to take over Teleria."

"And the Telerians here – do they help you?"

"Here on the eastern frontier, we work as closely as we can with Telerians. It's the only way we can survive. If we hear that they're being attacked in Kavali or Barpeta, we send troops. And if they hear that we're being attacked, they send troops."

"How long have the attacks been going on?"

"Since about the time Rahnak took the throne."

Kieran slapped his hand to the table in frustration. The force of the blow stung his palm, and the sound echoed through the room.

Sahbél moved over to the wall nearest the table. "Quite impressive work, don't you think?"

"I was admiring the carvings before you came in." Kieran moved closer. "I work with metal, but I can appreciate the skill that went into these."

"Our craftsmen started carving them when Alardin's son sat on the throne."

Kieran ran his hand over the relief of Leandra.

"There's one panel for each king."

Kieran walked around the room, studying each one in turn. He stopped short when he reached the seventh panel.

It was Arathor. He was giving a child to a man and woman.

Sahbél stood next to him. "This was Arathor's great deed – walking away from his kingdom and giving up his only son."

Kieran ran his hand over the faces and then over the child. There was such a look of sorrow on the king's face and such a look of joy on the woman's. With keen awareness, Kieran remembered Dorinda's vision. His hand dropped to his side and he hung his head, letting Arathor's grief pour through him. It took a few moments before it passed.

Sahbél led him to the next panel. It was blank.

"This one is for you."

Kieran stared at the empty panel, and again felt the weight that had pressed down on him earlier. How could he bear this burden? If only there were someone who could help him carry it.

Suddenly, he sensed a deep compassion surrounding him and realized it was coming from Sahbél.

So right there, Kieran found himself telling Sahbél the details of his life, including losing Jessara, meeting Arathor, and learning that to secure a Baraca alliance, he would have to marry the Malazia. When he was finished, almost two hours later, the burden seemed lighter.

"Will the prophecy come true?" Kieran asked. "Will I be able to rid Teleria of the evil rulers?"

Sahbél looked thoughtful. "I don't claim to have the foresight of the Baraca mystics." He paused and ran his fingers over the table. "I suppose it will depend on what you decide to do. Will you choose to walk the path in front of you or will you hide? That's a decision only you can make."

Chapter 19

Ciara sat in the highest tower of the castle and drummed her long, slender fingers on the windowsill. Having just dismissed Davina, the head servant, she was trying to decide what to do about her latest problem.

She had always known Kieran would have to be stopped, but up until a few months ago, she had ignored him. As long as he had hidden in his smithy, he had been no threat. Now he was traveling through Teleria with a sense of purpose and determination. What could she do to stop him?

As she started to pace the room, she caught a glimpse of herself in the mirror and stopped to study her reflection. Wrinkles were starting to show around her cold green eyes. She was usually able to hide them with her powers, but not now.

"I blame Kieran for this," she muttered.

When she could maintain the enchantments, she was the most beautiful woman in Teleria. She had been the most beautiful woman in Zagora. Back then, it had been easier to keep her youthfulness intact. Zagora was her home country, and that had been more than two hundred years ago.

She moved her head back and forth, trying to find her best side. Her black hair was now silver, and a silver crown, crafted in the shape of a dragon, rested on her head, staring back at her with ruby eyes. Ciara's mouth, usually held in a cruel smile, had little lines around it. Still, for a woman of her age, an age she couldn't even remember, she was charming to look at.

Her thoughts were interrupted by Elath, one of the pages. The teenage boy bowed to her, fear in his eyes. She loved her ability to instill fear in the servants.

"What is it?" she snapped.

"Begging your pardon, your Majesty, but the king wanted me to tell you he will be traveling to Felonia and won't be back for several days."

"Is that all?"

She waved her hand and Elath backed out of the room.

Why did it matter to her where Rahnak went? Now that they had a child and ruled the kingdom, she didn't need him.

He was such a weasel of a man. She had fawned over him like a slave, and had only used a few of her charms to get his proposal of marriage. The thought of it still made her sick. If it hadn't been the only way to get Arathor out of the way, she never would have done it. It was only her desire to have revenge on the descendants of Alardin and the Baraca that had overcome her sense of pride.

When she'd first come to Teleria, looking for a kingdom of her own, the Baraca barely tolerated her. Still, she took care of them, in her own way. But they hadn't appreciated her. Idiots. Why had they interfered and called on that man to get her out of the way? Didn't they know she would never admit defeat?

She walked down the spiral stairs to the lowest level of her tower, the clicking of her heels echoing off the polished stone walls. This was where she kept her potions and instruments of enchantment. When she reached the heavy wooden door, carved with mythical beasts, she spoke the words, "Jeskenah mortula, sedrala harkesh." The door opened silently and light from a green crystal illuminated the room.

Cold stone walls, draped in red velvet, sunk below the foundation of the castle. Half-melted candles stood in tall candelabras. A full length mirror hung on the wall, and there were several plush velvet chairs in the room. A round bed, covered in fur, lounged to the side.

This was her private sanctuary, and no one was allowed to come in except by her invitation. Rahnak had tried once and had been struck by a shock of lightning when he touched the door. She only let Sharaq, her bodyguard and consort, come down here.

Her consort. She laughed. Sharaq had the chiseled body of a warrior and was her willing servant, giving her anything she desired. Rahnak knew about their trysts, but it didn't matter. Ciara allowed him to have his own affairs. She was sure that was his reason for going to Felonia. He probably had more than one woman in every city in Teleria, and several in Korisan. Some of them were servants in the castle. Who knew how many illegitimate children he had?

It didn't matter. There was only one true heir to their throne, their daughter Delaine. And soon Ciara would introduce her daughter to the delights of dark spells and enchantments. Very soon, Delaine would share the secrets Ciara had kept for so long.

Now she walked over to a silver basin. It was carved with gurithents and dragons. She poured water from a silver pitcher into the basin, uttered more incantations, and waited for the water to still. When it was as calm as glass, she looked into it.

"I know you're close, son of Arathor. But where?"

She waited, holding her breath so as not to disturb the mirror of water. After a few moments, an image came to the surface. Her eyes traveled down the slope of a snowcapped mountain and into the fortress of the Nedebar Baraca. There he was, sitting at a long wooden table, engaged in deep conversation with a dark-haired man.

"So close. So close." She tapped her finger on her chin. "What can I do to discourage you, or at least slow you down?"

She couldn't get into his mind, not without exerting more power than she could afford right now. She would have to be content with putting obstacles in front of him. For now, she would start small. Controlling nature was easier than controlling people, and she had to conserve her powers.

A cruel smile of pleasure curled over her lips as she cast her spell.

Chapter 20

"This is Ciara's doing."

Toren was the first to put words to what Kieran had been thinking for the last few days. Despite the fact that it was almost summer, snow had been coming down for days. At first, they'd all thought it was a surprise storm. But now it was apparent that this was probably an enchanted blizzard.

"If it keeps up," said Riordan, "we won't be able to get to Barpeta until next month."

"I think Kieran could do something about it," said Gilrain.

Starting small fires and causing a tree to bud were one thing. But what Gilrain was suggesting was beyond Kieran's abilities. And besides, he hadn't practiced using his enchantments since leaving Koridoc.

Rather than argue with Gilrain, Kieran went outside. Many of the drifts came up to his waist. As he stood looking over the endless field of white, fears he didn't want to admit swirled in his head like snow flurries.

He wasn't thinking about Arathor, but suddenly his father was in his mind, once again sensing his thoughts

You knew this kind of thing could happen. When you walk in who you are, you* will *be opposed.

I just didn't expect it to come so soon.

You'll have to be on your guard from now on.

I've never done anything this big.

The spell you'll have to use will take more than your natural abilities. You'll have to absorb the Keldar stone.

Most of the time Kieran ignored the Keldar stone, just like the ring. He had never quite decided if he wanted to make it part of himself. He knew that if he did, he could never go back to his old life. Becoming one with the stone would change him forever.

Sitting in Sahbél's chambers, Kieran appreciated the rich furnishings. His bare feet sank into a thick woven rug. Leather sofas and

chairs were casually arranged around the room, and a fire crackled in a stone fireplace.

Sahbél poured wine from a crystal decanter into two clear goblets and handed one to Kieran. A comfortable silence settled between them as they sipped the berry wine and watched the fire.

"What can I do for you?" Sahbél finally asked.

"Arathor knows I can stop the storm. But I have to absorb the Keldar stone to do it."

"Then what's the problem?"

Before meeting Sahbél, Kieran would have worried about looking weak in front of the calafar. Now, having spoken with him countless times over the last few days, he didn't feel the need to hide. "I'm afraid I'll lose who I am if I take it."

"And who do you think you are?"

It wasn't a question Kieran had ever considered. Sahbél waited patiently while Kieran took his time with the answer.

"You know my history," Kieran said, "who I was – a boy who wanted to save the world. Over time, I became a teenager who gave up, and a blacksmith who became very good at what he did."

"And you always took the safe road."

"Something Kale taught me."

"But you also learned how to overcome that when you stayed with Arathor."

Kieran recalled Arathor's words: "*Your only weakness is your desire to quit when the circumstances are difficult, and the only one who underestimates your importance is you. You must decide now to set your face like iron and persevere. If you do, no force in Teleria can stop you.*"

A wisdom and peace beyond his years filled Sahbél's face. Kieran envied his friend. "I wasn't asking who you were," said Sahbél. "I want to know: Who are you now?"

Kieran put down his goblet and thought again about Sahbél's question. After several minutes, he answered. "I'm Kieran, son of Kale, but I'm also Aiden, son of Arathor. My country is in ruins, but just as I've forged shapeless pieces of iron into objects of beauty, I'll restore Teleria to a nation of beauty."

"And what will you do about the stone?"

Kieran knelt before Sahbél, honoring the man who had so quickly become his friend and mentor. He took the chain from around his neck and removed the Keldar stone from its setting. As he gave it to Sahbél he said, "I'll need your help."

Sahbél took the stone and nodded in understanding. After Kieran had removed his shirt, Sahbél placed the stone over Kieran's heart. Both men watched in surprise as Kieran's body absorbed the blue gem. Then a searing pain, hotter than any forge fire Kieran had ever felt, began at the stone and spread through his limbs, causing him to collapse to the floor.

When he woke up, he was in Sahbél's bed. His head throbbed and the skin around the stone was tender to the touch. A young woman came into the room to attend him. Chagrined at his half-dressed state, Kieran pulled the blankets over himself. He would have thanked the woman, but he remembered the Baraca customs and nodded his appreciation. When she left, Sahbél entered and sat next to the bed.

"I count it a privilege to have witnessed a part of your transformation into king," he said.

"Thank you for your help. I couldn't have done that alone."

"Now there's one more thing you must do before you meet the Hada."

Kieran winced as he tried to sit up. "What's that?"

"You must acknowledge your Baraca heritage and take the mark of your clan."

"What does that mean?"

"When a clan member reaches the age of thirteen, he takes a tattoo marking him forever as Baraca."

Kieran found the thought of letting someone pierce his skin repeatedly repulsive. "Will it help my position with the Hada?"

Sahbél smiled. "Does it really matter?"

"Yes."

"You'll have to stand before them one way or another. Whether or not they accept the mark is one thing. But it may help the other clans accept you because they'll know that *this* clan accepted you."

Kieran considered the consequences of taking the Hada mark. Yes, it might help him when encountering Baraca, but what would Telerians do if they saw it? Kieran repeated his misgivings to Sahbél.

Sahbél folded his hands and waited a moment. He pushed back the sleeve of his robe and let Kieran look at his mark.

"Why a bear claw?" Kieran asked.

"Living on the frontier, we've become a clan of fierce warriors." Sahbél ran his fingers over the mark. "Most of us wear it on the wrist so other clan members can see it. If I were you, I would wear it more discreetly, on your upper arm perhaps."

Kieran smiled ruefully. "So I can show it when I choose. Is that what you're saying?

Sahbél returned his smile and nodded.

Knowing he should take the mark of his clan hadn't made enduring the abuse to his body any easier. But Kieran had allowed the seemingly endless piercing without flinching. When the tattooist finished, Gilrain helped him to his room where Kieran collapsed onto his bed in a flood of pain and nausea. At the time, he was tempted to speak the words of healing, but knew that enduring the pain would strengthen his bond with his Baraca kinsmen.

So he waited, drifting in and out of consciousness, vaguely aware of someone coming into his room to rub a salve into his left bicep. On the second morning after taking the mark, he'd recovered enough to be aware of the deep throbbing in his arm and chest. He rose from his bed and went to the mirror to get a better look at what he'd done to himself.

It was difficult to see past the redness and swelling, but Sahbél had said that the mark was a perfect blue replica of an oak tree, except that the branches and roots joined to form a woven circle around the outside of the tree. Sahbél called it "The Tree of Life." It symbolized the fact that the Hada clan was the first Baraca clan, out of which all the other clans had come. The only difference with his mark was that the tattoo artist had added a crown above the tree as a sign of Kieran's royal heritage.

Kieran's eyes traveled to the Keldar stone. The spherical gem had become a silvery blue circle on his chest. It too was surrounded by red, swollen skin. When he touched it, he flinched.

He returned to his bed, letting himself regain his strength. Tomorrow he would face Ciara's enchantments and end the storm.

Ciara awoke in a sweat. Someone was interrupting her spell. She grabbed her black silk robe and flung it over her slender shoulders. Racing down the stairs, she hissed the words to open the door and nearly broke the door off its hinges before it opened.

She poured the water, cast the spell, and waited for the water to still. A shooting pain went through her heart when she saw what had happened.

Kieran had stopped the snow and cleared the road.

She paced the floor, uttering every foul curse she could think of and some she made up. After several minutes, she grew faint from the anxiety and went to lie down on the bed. An hour later, she was finally able to calm herself and think rationally.

"There has to be something that will stop you, son of my enemy. But what is it?"

There was an impatient knock at the door. Who could be knocking at this time of night? Everyone in the palace knew not to disturb her, especially here. She flew to the door, ready to strike whoever was standing there.

She stumbled backwards when she saw it was Delaine.

"What are you doing here?" Ciara asked.

The girl was in a rage. Her raven hair, usually so perfect, was disheveled and tangled.

"What happened?" Ciara had never been involved in her daughter's life. That's what Delaine's nanny was for. Now Ciara felt something unfamiliar, something like concern. The feeling made her shudder.

"Father said I won't be going to Felonia for the summer festival." The girl paced the floor, her arms flailing and her hair whipping around her pale face. "I always go to Felonia."

"Did he tell you why?"

"No, but it's probably because he's going to be there."

Ciara exhaled annoyance. It didn't matter to her if Delaine saw her father in Felonia. Then she smiled. "Stop fussing. You'll go to Felonia. And tonight I'll give you your first lesson on enchantments."

Chapter 21

Gilrain took a long look at his cousin and shook his head. Kieran wasn't the same man who had left Pent last fall. And it wasn't just his outward appearance that had changed, although there *was* a marked difference in the way he looked. His jaw was hardened, his face was lean, and his eyes had turned from dark brown to black. He continued to wear his hair short and his face beardless.

Still, there was more to it than that.

Kieran had begun to take on the countenance of royalty when he left Koridoc. But since absorbing the stone and wearing his clan's mark, his whole attitude had changed. The fear was gone, replaced by a confidence Gilrain had never seen before. He saw it in the way Kieran carried himself – shoulders thrown back, head held high – and in his voice, strong and commanding.

He'd never imagined that his cousin could change so much in six months. The man who left home with the intent of refuting his heritage had grown into a king.

Gilrain pulled his cloak around his shoulders, wishing that Kieran had had enough strength to stop the rain that had come after the snow – a rain that had turned a simple journey to Barpeta into a two-day ordeal. Everything was damp – clothing, saddles, provisions, blankets, and their spirits – and mud stuck to everything. Each man kept his thoughts to himself, and even the horses looked miserable.

When they reached the edge of Barpeta, they met an old woman gathering sticks. Kieran dismounted and went to help her. She looked up and smiled at him as he took her bundle. She stood and stretched while Kieran gathered more sticks for her.

Still humble despite his rank, thought Gilrain.

"There aren't many around here who would stop to help an old woman gather wood for her fire," she said.

Following Kieran's lead, Gilrain and Braeden dismounted to help gather more sticks while Toren and Riordan held the horses' reins.

"It's too cold for you to be out here," Kieran said.

"The sticks won't gather themselves," the woman replied with a crackling laugh. "Neither will the goat milk itself nor the food cook itself. If I don't do it, no one will."

"Isn't there anyone in town who will help an old woman?" Toren asked.

"There are fewer than a hundred people in the village and they have to take care of themselves."

"May we carry these to your home?" Kieran asked.

The woman's face spread into a huge smile. "That would be fine."

As they walked, she introduced herself. "My name is Neera. I've lived in Barpeta all my life."

Kieran introduced the others. "Do you have any family here?"

"Many years ago, I had a grand-daughter who lived with me. But slave traders took her when she was eight."

Kieran looked as if he would choke.

"Where would they have taken her?" Gilrain asked. And then wondered why he'd asked.

The woman's eyes were misty. "The largest slave market is in Korisan. I've thought many times about going to look for her, but I can't make the journey. I'm much too old now."

They stepped inside the decaying cottage and put down the sticks. Neera threw some of them on a pile of ashes in the corner of the dark room. Immediately, the fire sprang to life, but it still provided little heat. Cobwebs hung from the ceiling, and a broken spinning wheel stood in the corner.

Presently, Neera invited them to sup with her, and Gilrain was surprised at how she took the simple dried meats and cheeses Kieran gave her and combined them with dried vegetables and spices from her garden to make a mouth-watering stew.

"We'll be near Korisan," Gilrain said. "Maybe we could look for your grand-daughter."

Kieran shot him a warning glance and shook his head.

Gilrain ignored him. "What was her name?"

"Sienna."

Sienna. What a lovely name, he thought, noting Kieran's growing agitation. "Can you describe her?"

Neera began to clear the table. "She had golden hair and blue eyes like robin's eggs."

Gilrain's anticipation was growing. He didn't know why, but everything in him wanted to find Sienna and restore her to her grandmother. "If we find her, we'll bring her back to you."

Neera's eyes lit up and then she frowned. "I wouldn't look too hard. I've heard that girls don't last very long as slaves, especially in Korisan. Most of them are sold as prostitutes, and those who aren't usually end up in the castle as King Rahnak's slaves. If she's in the castle, you'd never get her out."

The next morning, Gilrain repeated his promise to try to find the girl.

A sad smile spread across Neera's restored face. "I've decided to leave my home and I'll be traveling to Agora with a caravan next month. If you find her, bring her there."

As the companions rode towards their next destination, Kieran looked back at his cousin. He'd never seen Gilrain look this determined. Gilrain caught his eye and moved closer. Kieran tried to keep his temper when he said, "Wasn't it enough that you risked our safety to rescue Adamar? Now you've promised to find this girl?"

"I just want to help."

Kieran laughed bitterly. "You've never cared about anyone but yourself."

"You've changed. Maybe I have too."

"I don't think you've changed at all. I think you're looking for glory. And maybe in this case it's about a pretty girl."

"It's not about glory, Kieran. It's about doing the right thing." Then Gilrain spurred his horse forward and rode alone.

Determined and headstrong – Gilrain had always been that way. At times Kieran had envied him. Part of him envied Gilrain now. At least he knew where to start looking for this girl. Where was Kieran supposed to look for Jessara?

When they made camp, Gilrain remained silent. One part of Kieran wanted to leave him to himself. The other part knew that if he didn't clear the air between them, it would be a long ride tomorrow. Gilrain crouched next to the fire. Kieran sat next to him.

"I'm sorry I was so harsh with you this morning," Kieran began.

"At least you could try to understand."

"I do understand."

Gilrain turned to him sharply. “You do?”

“Yes. There’s someone I have to rescue, too.”

“What are you talking about?”

Kieran motioned for Gilrain to follow him into a thicket so they could talk alone.

“Did I ever tell you what happened to that girl in Ithil?”

“No, you didn’t. We saw her once but after that – ”

“I went back there every day for several months. She was my best friend.”

Gilrain half laughed. “I thought I was your best friend.”

“You’re my cousin, Gilrain. And this was different.”

“How?”

Kieran closed his eyes for a moment. “We had a connection – I can’t explain it. But one day slave traders took her and I couldn’t do a thing about it.”

“And you’ve blamed yourself for it all this time?”

“Yes.”

“That’s too much of a burden for any boy to carry. Or for any man.”

“Just when I think I’ve forgiven myself, something comes up to remind me of my failure.”

“Neera’s story?”

“This time. First it was finding the Baraca girl in Orizant and then it was Mahon’s story of the stolen Malazia.”

“You don’t think the girl from Ithil was the Malazia?”

“The story is amazingly similar. But it might just be coincidence.”

Gilrain stopped. “You told me that Sahjahn said you should marry the Malazia.”

“Whether Jessara is the Malazia or not, I have to find her, Gilrain.”

“Why?”

“We share Eldala.”

“What does that mean?”

“When a Baraca boy and girl are betrothed to each other, they’re connected by heart. Somehow Jessara and I became Eldala.”

“Then you and Jessara – ”

“She’s the one person in Teleria I have to marry. And after hearing Neera’s story about Sienna, I think she’s in Korisan.”

Chapter 22

As the road took them closer to Korisan, Kieran had the awful feeling Ciara was looking at him and that he couldn't escape her gaze. He wondered what obstacle she would throw at him next. His jaw tightened at the thought of it.

At least they didn't have to go into Korisan yet. Despite Gilrain's eagerness to find Sienna, and Kieran's hunch that Jessara might be there, they were traveling to the Kofar fortress to meet Arathor. Since none of them knew a faster cross-country route, they'd agreed to take the road through Felonia.

There was only one problem with that: There was something about Felonia that Kieran wanted to avoid. He just didn't know what it was.

A day later, Felonia lay before them. Kieran had been here twice with his father, both times to sell some of their finer pieces. Kale had told him that although Felonia had two or three blacksmiths, their work couldn't compare to Kieran's, and that nobles and merchants from around Teleria would be eager to buy Kieran's work. Both times, Kieran had been fascinated by all the colors and smells and craftsmen in the market square. But he had also kept his eye out for Jessara.

On the slim chance he was wrong about finding her in Korisan, he scanned the crowds for her now.

The crowds weren't making it easy. Jugglers and dancers moved in front of his horse, vendors called out to sell their wares, and music from a flute filled the air. More than once, painted women propositioned him. He pressed forward, just wanting to get to the other side of town. He was relieved when they made it through the market and into another section of the city, reserved for the craftsmen.

The companions passed shops for potters, coopers, book makers, candle makers, and tailors. Kieran wasn't sure why, but he stopped when they came to the glass blower's shop. Fallon whickered nervously and planted his hooves in staunch refusal. Kieran kicked his horse forward, surprised at Fallon's reluctance to approach the shop.

When Fallon continued to stand his ground, Kieran dismounted and dragged him towards the hitching post. Without waiting for the others, he went inside.

The heat from the man's furnace was at least equal to Kieran's forge. Fascinated, Kieran watched the craftsman take a lump of molten glass on the end of a pipe and begin to blow. Soon, a small bubble had formed on one end, and the glass blower worked the bubble back and forth until he made a perfect blue sphere.

A woman with an enticing aroma stood at Kieran's elbow. "Beautiful," she said.

Kieran glanced at her and swallowed down his surprise. *Just the word I was looking for*, he thought.

The scoop neckline of her purple dress revealed more skin than Kieran had ever seen on a woman. A belt of gold links hung around her delicate waist, and a waterfall of black hair flowed over her shoulders. Her skin was fair and fragile, like the glass being worked in front of them.

"He's making it for me," she said.

Kieran just nodded.

He tried to look back at the glass blower, but his eyes had a mind of their own and kept returning to the woman's face. The way she returned his stares should have made him uncomfortable, but he found he rather enjoyed it.

"I've never seen you before," she said.

"I'm just passing through."

A voice behind him made him jump. "It's time to go."

It was Toren.

Now that Kieran was here, standing next to this elegant creature, he didn't want to leave. Toren put a hand on his shoulder. "We really must be going, sir."

Reluctantly, he turned towards the door. The woman caught his hand before he could leave. As she rubbed her thumb over the back of his hand, he felt a tingling spread across his hand and into his arm.

"Will you be going to the festival tonight?" she asked.

"Are you inviting me?"

"I have no one to escort me."

Toren cleared his throat. Kieran bowed and exited the shop.

The company made its way to the northeast side of the city. Toren and the others had picked up plenty of provisions and were anxious to reach Agora. Riordan even suggested they travel through the night so they would be as far away from Felonia as possible. They all looked shocked when Kieran told them they would stay outside the city for the night.

"Are you sure that's a good idea?" Toren asked.

"The horses need a rest and so do I," Kieran said irritably. "I've never commanded anything, but we're staying here for the night."

As they silently made camp, Toren came up beside him. "You should be careful," he said.

"And why is that?" Kieran asked, rubbing the spot where the woman's thumb had touched him.

"When Riordan was in town, he heard them talking about the summer festival."

The spot on Kieran's hand was turning red. What had she done to him?

"I've heard that the Princess Delaine always attends that festival."

Kieran bristled. "What are you trying to say?"

"That may have been her in the glass blower's shop. I've heard descriptions of her and that woman was very similar." Toren paused, watching Kieran's response. "If a man weren't careful – "

"I can take care of myself."

"I've sworn an oath to protect the house of Alardin. I would be remiss in my duties if I didn't remind you that your life is no longer your own. It belongs to the people."

"You've fulfilled your duty. That will be all."

Where had that come from? He never talked to his companions like this, particularly not Toren. But even if Toren were right, Kieran was the king – he could do whatever he pleased. And tonight he would do just that.

While the rest of the companions slept, Kieran left the camp and walked towards Felonia. A stick snapped behind him. When he turned around, he saw no one.

After he entered the city, it wasn't difficult to find the celebration. All he had to do was follow the sound of flutes and mandolins, and the scent of incense, fire, and too much wine. He drew closer to the crowd. The music had slowed, and one person was dancing in the center.

This time the woman wore a red dress that moved with her as she swayed to the music. She stopped and looked straight at him. Before he knew it, he was answering her invitation to dance. He let himself follow her slow, rhythmic movements. It was all he could do to breathe as she brushed up against him. When his eyes swept over her body, he forgot to breathe entirely.

She put her hands on his shoulders and pulled him closer, whetting his appetite for more. When she put her lips to his, she tasted like perfectly aged wine. It only increased his hunger.

"Who are you?" he whispered.

"Who do you want me to be?" she purred.

Jessara. He clamped his lips shut before he could say her name.

"Let me be the woman in your dreams." Her eyes were half-closed, and her full lips were parted, inviting him to have another taste. He was about to escort her to a secluded spot for the next course when he heard someone behind him.

"Kieran!"

He snapped out of his trance and turned around. Gilrain stood next to him.

Kieran had never seen his cousin this angry. And was that a look of disapproval on his face? Or just envy?

"Is this why we stayed?" Gilrain asked.

Kieran wanted to knock Gilrain to the ground. When he turned to face the woman, she was gone. A string of curses spewed out of his mouth.

The two men walked back to the camp in angry silence. Closing his eyes to sleep, Kieran's lips still relished her taste. When he dreamed, he dined with a green-eyed, black-haired woman. Jessara was nowhere to be seen.

Ciara smiled satisfactorily and rolled over. Tonight she would sleep better than she had in weeks.

Chapter 23

It felt like the longest ride Kieran had ever taken. Traveling to the Kofar fortress was only supposed to take half a day; Kieran's pounding head told him it had taken three days.

Whatever the woman had put on his hand made his ears sensitive to every sound – the clop, clop of the horses' hooves on stone, the cracking of every twig, and every word between his companions. All he wanted to do now was crawl into bed and sleep for a week.

Arathor waited for him at the gate.

Kieran dismounted and murmured a quick greeting, leaving Fallon with a young groomsman. Another boy stood ready to take him to his quarters. Before Kieran could follow, Arathor put a hand to his shoulder. "I need to talk to you."

That was the last thing Kieran wanted. He grunted something about being tired and followed the boy. When he reached his room, he dropped into the feather bed without removing his traveling clothes.

On the morning of the second day, someone opened the shutters. Blazing light shattered his sleep and sent a stabbing pain through his head. Kieran rolled over and covered himself with the blankets. Whoever was in the room with him pulled them off.

Kieran was about to bellow his disapproval when a familiar voice stopped him. "Good morning, your Majesty."

Damn. It was Arathor.

"I want to see how your skills have improved. Get dressed and meet me in the practice arena."

An awful taste in Kieran's mouth stopped him from saying anything. When he stood to get a drink, his spinning head pushed him back into bed. He hadn't felt this way since he'd had too much to drink at the Ancala camp.

After dressing and washing his face, Kieran slowly made his way to the center building of the fortress. Each step was torture to his throbbing head.

Arathor was methodically going through his practice forms. It reminded Kieran of the first time the two of them had sparred. Back then, Kieran was a poor excuse for a swordsman. Now he considered himself at least equal with Arathor. He hoped Arathor would notice.

Kieran rolled up his sleeves and sliced through the air.

With no warning, Arathor lunged. "What happened in Felonia?"

Kieran recovered quickly and took a defensive posture. "Nothing."

Arathor swiped at Kieran's abdomen. "I heard that a beautiful woman turned your head."

Kieran evaded and thrust at Arathor's arm. *Yes, and she was delicious.* "So what if she did?"

Arathor circled patiently, biding his time to find a weakness. Kieran kept up his guard, ready to dodge at any second.

"Women can be dangerous," said Arathor. "They can easily distract you from your call. And that woman in particular could have easily destroyed you."

Kieran lunged at Arathor. This was ridiculous.

Arathor blocked. "Did you have any idea who she was? Even a page could have seen that trap."

Kieran let the insult pass and parried. "Haven't you ever turned to look at a beautiful woman?"

Arathor stepped up the tempo of the match. "Yes, but it never went beyond looking."

Kieran moved to get the upper hand. "As the king, I can have whoever I want."

Arathor answered Kieran move for move. "Yes, you're the king and you can use your subjects as you choose, but you must decide now if you will be a good king and give more to your people than you take from them. If you don't, you'll be just like Rahnak."

How dare Arathor insult him like this? Using every technique he could think of, and a few he made up on the spot, Kieran doggedly tried to get past Arathor's defenses. Arathor calmly blocked every stroke. After several minutes of futile attempts on Kieran's part, Arathor announced the match was over. Kieran persisted, despite the escalating pain in his head. He wasn't going to surrender now.

With effortless precision, Arathor struck the skin between Kieran's thumb and hand with the pommel of his sword. Kieran immediately lost his grip on Restamar and cried out, more from anger than from pain.

Arathor took advantage and put the tip of his sword up to Kieran's neck. "Will you yield?"

Kieran's eyes shot daggers. "I am at a disadvantage, sir."

"Yes you are, but only one of your own making. Perhaps next time, you'll keep yourself under better control and you'll be able to win. For now, you are disarmed."

Arathor shook his head as he watched Kieran leave the room. It would have been easy to be disappointed with his son. After the snowstorm at the Nedebar fortress, Arathor thought Kieran would have been on his guard for something like this. Instead, he had come dangerously close to losing everything because of one foolish act. Still, Arathor knew he'd had his own share of mistakes – least of all being that he'd allowed Rahnak to remain his advisor despite his father's warnings. Now all of Arathor's hopes – all of Teleria's hopes – rested with Kieran.

Arathor picked up Kieran's sword and continued his practice forms. He had to admit he was proud of how much Kieran had improved. He was stronger, more flexible, and had amazing endurance and lightning-quick reflexes. If Kieran hadn't lost control of his emotions, he could have easily beaten Arathor. Yes, Kieran had learned well. The only teacher who could improve his skills now was experience.

When Kieran's bruised hand had mended, Arathor would give him a chance for a rematch. He only hoped Kieran's bruised ego would be mended by then.

Muttering loudly enough that anyone could hear him, Kieran strode to the stable to saddle Fallon. A long ride might be just the thing to clear his head. Gilrain was there, grooming his horse. Wordlessly, Kieran brushed shoulders with his cousin, found his tack, and put it on the dapple gray. After leaving the fortress, he clapped his heels to the horse's flanks and Fallon exploded into a full gallop, churning up mud clods from the rain-saturated road. It didn't take long for Kieran to get into the rhythm of Fallon's pace, and soon it felt as if they were one being.

Arathor had been completely unreasonable to expect that Kieran would recognize Delaine – if that's who she was. All Arathor had were Toren and Gilrain's descriptions. And that must have been who had told him. He would tell them to be more discreet next time.

Why did it matter anyway? Kieran had been completely in control the whole time. He would have made sure that nothing came of it. Besides, what was the harm in using his position to get what he wanted?

For the next two days, nothing was right. None of the food placed before Kieran was to his liking. It was too hot, too cold, or too bland. Practicing his forms was an exercise in futility. No matter how hard he tried, his uninjured left arm refused to remember its training. Riding Fallon did nothing to improve his humor. The horse seemed to sense his frustrations, and instead of cooperating, he threw Kieran to the ground every time he tried to get on.

On the third day, Kieran's family arrived.

He'd just returned from a morning ride – a ride that thankfully hadn't ended in being thrown – when he recognized Kale's voice. He quickly handed Fallon off to a groomsman and made his way to a knot of people. Moving past Arathor and Gilrain, Kieran clapped Kale on the back. The look on Kale's face was one of true surprise.

"Kieran?"

"Yes, it's me."

When the shock had passed, Kale shook his hand and then embraced him as only a smith could.

"What are you doing here?" Kieran asked.

"When you left, Destra suspected we were hiding you. His soldiers searched all of Pent, three times, harassing everyone. When they stopped, we thought Destra had given up, but then Rahnak's agents came a few months later and started the search all over. Wanted posters were everywhere. It was getting ugly. Some of the villagers made it very clear they wanted us to leave so the soldiers would leave."

Rahnak. That arrogant bastard.

"How did you get here?" Kieran asked.

"We came across some of the Linden Baraca. They'd heard Arathor was here, and they knew the Kofar could hide us."

"Is Mother here?"

"She and Sorina were in the kitchen the last time I saw them."

"My mother and father came with you?" Gilrain asked.

"Yes. You should go find them. Your mother's been beside herself with worry about you."

Gilrain left, and Kale broke away from the group. Arathor caught Kieran's eye for just a moment. Kieran ignored him.

When they reached the kitchen, his mother's eyes lit up, and without wiping her hands, she ran to him and put her arms around him. After a moment, she looked to search his face. "You look different."

He reached over and kissed her cheek. "I am different."

"Tell us everything that's happened to you," she said.

Where to start? As briefly as he could, Kieran recounted his time with Arathor, training with Toren, finding out he was Baraca, and meeting Baraca and others in his travels. He avoided the subjects of becoming king and meeting Delaine altogether.

At dinner, every face was familiar – his parents, his aunt and uncle, his cousin and traveling companions, and Arathor. The conversation was unremarkable and Kieran did his best to play the part of gracious host, but inside he was steaming. Thankfully, no one mentioned the incident in Felonia, and although his companions were polite to him, they were also playing their part. Underneath their pleasant façade, Kieran knew that at least two of them still weren't happy with him.

As king, it wasn't his duty to keep everyone happy. If they didn't like the decisions he made, there was nothing he could do about it.

Lost in his thoughts, Kieran ran his finger over the rim of his goblet, swallowed down his wine, and was about to leave the table when

Kale raised his goblet for a toast.

"To good friends," he said.

"To good friends," everyone replied.

"And good health to his Majesty, King Arathor," added Loric.

Arathor nodded. "Thank you Loric, but you're speaking to the wrong person."

Kieran's family all had blank expressions on their faces. Before Kieran could say anything, Arathor raised his glass and dipped his head in polite respect. "Good health to his Majesty, King *Aiden.*"

Elisa's eyes went wide, Kale's jaw dropped, and Loric and Sorina looked dumbfounded. Kieran exhaled loudly through his teeth. This was not how he wanted his family to find out.

"I thought Kieran would have told you by now," said Arathor. " I transferred all of my authority to Kieran before he left Koridoc."

When the shock had passed, his family echoed Arathor's toast. Kieran's companions said nothing as they raised their glasses. Were they *all* angry with him?

Quietly furious, Kieran left the table and went outside. A sliver of moon cast dim light on the ground. Had he really behaved so badly that all of them were still holding a grudge? Why couldn't they just let it go?

Kale walked up behind him. "Come with me," he said.

The two men strode in silence. When they reached the smithy, they changed into the rough tunics hanging on the wall closest to the door. Kieran took a deep breath and let the familiar odors fill his head. He had stayed away from his first love too long.

After putting on his leather apron, Kieran tried to pick up a hammer and let it drop.

"What happened to your hand?" Kale asked.

"Arathor."

"From what he told me, you're better with the sword than he is."

"I wasn't good enough the other day. He kept goading me and I got so angry with him I lost control. He disabled me with a hit to my hand."

"Well, if you can't strike, at least you can work the bellows."

Kieran hadn't worked the bellows since he was a boy. Grudgingly, he started to pump air over the coals.

"I can remember when working the bellows was all I'd let you do," said Kale. "You were so eager to learn how to use the hammer, and when you finally did, it took a lot of practice for you to gain your skills. You made a lot of mistakes before you were able to make anything decent."

Kieran kept his eye on the fire, feeling his anger boil inside him.

"Looks like it's going to take a lot of practice to be king."

"Apparently my companions don't think I'm doing so well."

"Do you want to tell me more about that?"

Kieran stood and started pacing the room. "Arathor thinks I met Rahnak's daughter in Felonia."

"And what do you think?"

"Toren said she looked like Delaine, but he could've been wrong."

"Did you have any control over meeting her?"

"Not the first time. She was in the glass blower's shop, and when I turned to leave, she invited me to be her escort for the spring festival that night."

"Is that when Toren warned you?"

"He didn't say anything until we reached the outskirts of Felonia."

Kale stopped hammering. "And you went back anyway?"

Kieran narrowed his eyes. Hadn't it been enough that Arathor had prodded at him? "I was curious about the festival."

Kale shook his head and returned to his work. "Sounds like you fell pretty hard."

"It was just a kiss. To hear Arathor tell it, you'd think I almost lost the kingdom."

"Sometimes a kiss is all it takes, son. Question is, are you going to learn from this mistake?"

Without a word, Kieran charged out of the smithy and went to find his horse.

Chapter 24

A long, hard ride ended at the western edge of Lake Merah. Kieran dismounted and looked out over the sun-dappled water. Fallon shook his head and grazed on the tender grass. A flock of small, black ducks paddled near the shore. Just as they took off, a dark blur dove out of the sky, and there was an explosion of feathers in the midst of the flock. As the last feather fell to the lake, Kieran realized a peregrine falcon had taken one of the ducks. The bird never knew what had hit it.

If only they'd been more cautious, Kieran thought. *Didn't they know there would be predators?*

Then a thought hit him with as much force as the diving falcon.

Stupid. That was the only word for it. He should have seen it coming. He *had* seen it coming before they'd entered Felonia. But then he'd ignored his own premonitions. He'd ignored Toren's warning. *Fire and torment.* He'd even ignored *Fallon's* warning.

How humiliating to realize he didn't have the sense of a horse.

One bad decision, one moment of selfishness had endangered his companions and his whole reason for existence. The fact that he had used his position to get what he wanted – just like Rahnak – was the worst part, especially considering he'd fought so hard to deny he was a prince in the first place. What had Delaine done to get him to act like such an ass?

It galled Kieran to think he was just a pawn to Ciara. He would have to be more careful next time. In fact there wouldn't be a time when he could let his guard down, not for a moment. He was sure Ciara would use Delaine again, and next time, Delaine would probably try to use more than a kiss to ensnare him.

Upon returning to the fortress. Kieran gathered Kale, Loric, Arathor, and his friends around him to admit his blunder and ask for their forgiveness. It was humbling to hear them pardon him.

"I'm sure it's a mistake you will not make again, Sire," said Toren.

"I appreciate your wisdom, Toren, and from now on I will listen to your counsel." When he looked each man in the eye, he realized that he needed every man here. These men would watch his back and keep him alive. They would keep him from stumbling and pick him up when he did. And they would help him see his course to the end.

For five days, Kale watched his son throw himself into his work, as he never had before. Every morning, he found Kieran outside, practicing his forms with both hands. After breakfast, Kieran worked with Kale, Loric, and Toren in the smithy, making the necessary tools for war. In the afternoon, Kieran and Gilrain practiced using their swords from horseback. And in the evenings, Kieran worked on using his enchantments, something Kale never imagined his son would be able to do.

On the afternoon of the sixth day, Arathor challenged Kieran to a rematch.

Kieran's family and companions gathered in the practice arena to watch the match. The two kings faced each other. Arathor looked tense. Kieran looked stalwart.

Arathor put up his sword and said, "Defend yourself."

As soon as Kieran's sword went up, Arathor attacked with a high slash to the right and then a high slash to the left.

Kieran blocked each stroke with ease.

Arathor spun around and made another high cut to the right and then a thrust to Kieran's stomach. Kieran parried. Arathor spun to his left and made a cut low to the left and then low to the right.

Kieran again blocked effortlessly.

Kale had seen other sword matches, but nothing like this. He was surprised at how quick and agile his son had become; it seemed Kieran could anticipate Arathor's every move.

Up until now, Kieran had only reacted to Arathor's movements. Now with a playful smirk, he went on the attack. Arathor had to back up to absorb the energy of the blows.

The older king wiped the sweat from his eyes and attacked with another thrust. Kieran deflected the blade and stepped sideways, spinning around to face Arathor's back. Arathor turned suddenly with a sweeping slash to Kieran's midsection. Kieran blocked with little effort and began a series of high and low strokes. Arathor moved back a few steps to regain his footing.

It appeared Arathor was having difficulty matching Kieran's speed. Sweat trickled from his face and soaked his white linen shirt.

In an effort to distract Kieran, Arathor began to spin his blade in his hand, but Kieran ignored the ploy and kept his eyes on Arathor, making a series of high and midsection cuts. Arathor parried, but with great effort.

Arathor thrust towards Kieran's midsection. Kieran quickly sidestepped, deflected the blade to his right, spun to his left, and tapped Arathor on the right shoulder with the hilt of his sword. In a desperate attempt, Arathor made a sweeping slice towards Kieran, but Kieran hooked Arathor's blade with the cross piece of his pommel and twisted Arathor's sword from his hand, causing him to yield.

Kale had never felt such pride.

The next day, all of Kieran's family and companions gathered in the Kofar Baraca's great hall. The pride Kale had felt at watching Kieran defeat Arathor was nothing compared to the pride he felt now as he watched Arathor bestow his blessing on Kieran.

His son stood before Arathor in armor the Kofar smiths had custom-made for him. Light from the afternoon sun drifted through the stained-glass windows and glinted off of the gold chest piece which bore Alardin's crest – an eagle with a serpent in its claws. Matching gold vambraces protected Kieran's wrists, and gold greaves covered the front of his black boots. The sword Restamar now had a gold scabbard.

How could it be that the infant he and Elisa had adopted twenty years ago was now being proclaimed the king of Teleria? Kale was not a man prone to emotion, but as Arathor bowed to Kieran, he couldn't help but let the tears come. The day he'd hoped would come was here, and he was privileged enough to witness it.

One by one, each person in the room followed Arathor's lead by bowing to their new king and shouting, "Hail Aiden, king of Teleria."

With overwhelming wonder and humility, Kieran watched and listened as each of his companions and family members bowed before him. Although it was difficult, he kept his composure as each of them gave their oaths of fealty. It wasn't until his father Kale went to his knees to give his oath that Kieran felt his throat tighten.

"By this oath, I, Kale, son of Elkar, do swear to do all that is in my power to aid the kingdom of Teleria; to trust the judgment of my king; to place my body, mind, and heart at the defense of Teleria in times of war and ill fortune, with courage and prowess; to protect and defend all other subjects of Teleria as commanded by my king. This I swear until my king releases me, or death takes me, or the world ends."

It didn't seem right that his father was calling him "my king" and swearing fealty to him. It took Kieran a moment to find his voice and speak the proper response: "I accept your oath with greatest thanks and I will hold you to your promise until I release you, or death takes you, or the world ends. I shall reward your fealty and your deeds with honor for as long as I shall hold the throne of Teleria. This I swear as your king."

Chapter 25

Kieran looked up at the clouded skies. He and his company, which now included Kale, had traveled for three days under the same dark curtain. As much as he didn't want to face the Hada Baraca, he was relieved when they reached the edge of their encampment.

When Kieran saw Dorinda, he dismounted and went to greet her. "This is unexpected," he said.

"I knew that if I did not come, the Hada council would not give you an audience."

As the travelers made camp, Dorinda took Kieran aside. "You still carry a heavy burden," she said.

"Burden?"

"I sense that you still hold yourself responsible for Jessara's capture."

Kieran hadn't thought about losing Jessara for several days now.

"It is time to lay the burden down and ask for forgiveness," she said.

"Who would I ask? I can't go to Jessara."

The mystic smiled. "No, you cannot. But you can go to her mother."

Kieran felt his heart drop into his stomach. "Her mother is here?"

"Yes, Tiana is here, and she also carries a great burden. Neither of you will find healing until you meet."

Kieran thought he'd gotten past the guilt of losing Jessara, but now he realized it still gnawed at him, like a worm working its way inside an apple. Facing Jessara's mother might stop the worm, but the thought of meeting her made his head pound.

"When can I meet her?"

"I will take you to her tonight. Tomorrow morning, I will take you to the council."

Long after midnight, Dorinda led Kieran to meet Tiana. As they walked, Kieran tried to settle his nerves and think of what he might say to her. After walking for several minutes, Dorinda stopped at a clearing in the forest. A woman cloaked in black waited there.

Dorinda embraced the woman. “Thank you for coming, Tiana.”
The woman remained silent.

Dorinda gestured towards Kieran. “This young man has something that he wishes to tell you. Hear him out before you make any judgments.”

Tiana nodded. As was Baraca custom, Kieran waited for her to speak first. His own anxiety kept him from sensing anything from her and he wished he could see her face. Did she know who he was? If she did, was she holding a grudge against him?

“What do you wish to tell me?” she asked.

Kieran took a few deep breaths and plunged in. “Mara Tiana, my name is Kieran. When I was ten, I met your daughter Jessara in this forest.”

Tiana covered her mouth, but couldn’t stifle a gasp. “You are the one,” she whispered.

“Do you know me?”

“I know that my daughter found ways to leave her family’s protection every day. She never told us where she went, but I suspected she had found a friend outside of the clan.”

The woman leaned against a tree and put her head in her hand. “I have never been able to forgive myself for not finding a way to keep her from going.”

“And I have wrestled with the guilt of not being able to stop the slave traders from taking her.”

Tiana sniffed away a tear. “Jessara hated being confined. If she had not met you, she would have found some other reason to leave.”

“If I had known that meeting with her would end in her being captured, I never would have encouraged her. Please forgive me.”

Tiana put her hand on Kieran’s face. “There have been times when I blamed you for giving her a reason to go. But in my heart I know she was a child who needed freedom. You did nothing wrong.”

Kieran didn’t know how it was possible, but hearing Tiana’s words caused a great weight to be lifted from him. Now what could he do to help Tiana?

“Mara Tiana, if Jessara could not be confined, then you must not blame yourself that she found ways to get away. You must forgive yourself, as I must forgive myself.”

"It is not only for this that I bear a burden," she said. "I blame myself for not going with her father to look for her. The council would not send a search party, and so her father decided to go. I refused to leave my home."

How often had Kieran felt the sorrow and regret that he now sensed from Tiana?

"Devan searched for a year. The last letter I received from him said that he thought she was in Korisan. Then I heard no more from him and counted him lost."

"Your husband was doing what any good father would do. And if you had gone with him, you might have suffered the same fate. Then Jessara would have no one to come home to."

"No one to come home to?"

"I believe that Jessara is alive."

The emerging dawn revealed the shock on Tiana's face.

"How could you know that?"

"Because we share Eldala. If she were dead, I think I would know it."

Dorinda had been standing off to the side to give them privacy. Now she moved closer and said, "Kieran is right. Your daughter is alive and in Korisan."

Tiana stood. "Why did you not tell me sooner, Dorinda?"

Kieran wondered the same thing.

"Because I knew that this meeting had to take place first."

Then Tiana turned to Kieran. "How is it possible that you share Eldala with my daughter? You are not Baraca."

Kieran stood. "But I am, Mara Tiana. I am a descendant of Alardin and Jessara."

Tiana looked as if she would faint. Both Kieran and Dorinda moved to catch her.

"Now do you know who this is?" the mystic asked.

"It cannot be," said Tiana when she had recovered. "You cannot be the son of ..."

Kieran expected Tiana to say "Arathor." When she didn't, he felt something else coming from her. It was regret, but not the same regret and guilt she felt for losing her daughter. And the pain was more deeply etched into her face.

"I *am* the son of Arathor. And once I find your daughter I will bring her here. Then I plan to marry my Eldala."

Tiana's brows knit together. "You honor Jessara and myself with your intentions, but marrying my daughter is out of the question."

"Why?"

"The council will not allow it."

"Why would they have anything to say about it?"

Tiana looked at the mystic. "Dorinda, did you not tell him?"

Dorinda shook her head. "It was not the right time."

This was exasperating. "What were you supposed to tell me?"

"When my daughter was three years old, the council chose her to be – "

Kieran felt his knees go weak. "The Malazia?"

Kieran returned to his companions and ate a quick morning meal. While he shaved his beard off, he tried to unravel Tiana's revelation that Jessara was the Malazia.

It was one thing to have suspected Jessara was the Malazia, but to have Tiana confirm it had shocked Kieran more than he'd expected. And knowing that many of the clans would agree to fight for him if he married the Malazia gave him one more reason to marry Jessara – as if he needed any other reason beyond the one he already had. Ironically, though, it placed another obstacle in his path.

How was he going to convince the Hada council that it was in everyone's best interest for him to marry their Malazia?

Once Kieran had finished cleaning up and changing clothes, he followed Dorinda to the fortress. He had thought that the Tyman stronghold was impressive, but this was majestic. Everything he saw spoke of the ancient history that resided here.

They stood at the edge of a large circle paved with large, flat stones, now covered in moss. In the center of the circle, water from a fountain bathed four stone swans. Four towers, filled with blue windows and topped with blue scalloped shingles, stood watch over the circle.

Dorinda led him across the circle to a fortress with stone walls and the same blue shingles. Several women stared at them from gracefully arched balconies. After walking down a long passageway, Dorinda and Kieran entered a well-lit room, occupied by seven men. All of them were grim-faced and seated at a rectangular, black marble table.

Kieran stiffened. The animosity coming from the men was as thick as molten metal. If he had been the old Kieran, he would have looked away from their stares. Now he returned them. After a moment, he gave the proper bow and waited for permission to speak.

While he waited in uncomfortable silence, he wondered why he was here. Now that Dorinda had revealed Jessara's whereabouts, he didn't have to ask the council where they thought she was. And he certainly didn't need their persmission to search for her.

However, charging ahead without telling the Hada council his intentions could widen the rift between himself and the Hada, something he wanted to avoid if at all possible – especially since his entire reason for coming here was to enlist the Hada's help in fighting the upcoming war with the Zagorans. And the way he had hoped to get that help was by telling them he would find their Malazia.

At least he knew where to start his search.

After a time, the man seated in the center stood and surveyed Kieran. By the way he carried himself, Kieran saw that this was a man who held a high position and was accustomed to getting whatever he wanted. When he spoke, his voice was strong and commanding. "I am Calafar Galen. How did you find your way to our camp?"

"I brought him here," said Dorinda.

Galen raised an eyebrow. "You did so without our permission."

Dorinda held his gaze. "I knew that you would never give your permission, Galen, not that I needed it. Being a mystic gives me authority here. Your father was wise enough to listen to my counsel. Perhaps you should do the same."

Galen sat and pressed his fingers together. "Why did you feel the need to bring him here, Dorinda?"

"Because he has come to ask for your help."

The calafar looked at Kieran. "Why would a Telerian ask for our help?"

Kieran had never heard the word Telerian spoken in quite that way. It reminded him of the way some Telerians said the word "Baraca" – with superiority and prejudice. He'd heard that the Hada were proud that they didn't associate with Telerians, but he hadn't expected them to regard him with such disdain. This would be more difficult than he'd first thought. How could he approach this in a way that wouldn't make them think he was an arrogant Telerian?

"I am Aiden, son of Arathor, and I have come to ask for the Hada clan's help in fighting against Ciara's Zagoran army."

There were several murmurs among the council members.

"That is quite a claim, sir," said Galen. "Do you have any proof?"

Kieran was tempted to pull back his sleeve and show them the mark, but decided to wait. Instead, he drew Restamar from his belt and laid it on the table. "The sword of Alardin, engraved by your own smiths and presented to Arathor before my birth."

Galen took the sword and examined it. Then he passed it to the others and cast his piercing eyes on Kieran. Kieran held his gaze, while remaining fully aware of which man currently held the sword. When it appeared that the council was satisfied, Galen set Restamar on the table. Kieran left it there for the moment.

"Is there any other proof?" Galen asked.

Kieran removed the signet ring. Again, it was passed from man to man. Again there were murmurs. Although Kieran sensed their doubt was waning, he also sensed they were becoming more agitated.

When Galen returned Kieran's ring, Kieran put it on and looked at each council member in turn. "You have seen the sword and the ring. What is your answer?"

"You have provided considerable proof of your claim, but the Baraca no longer have dealings with Telerians."

"Some of the other calafars warned me that you would respond this way."

Galen's eyebrows flew up in surprise. "Which calafars?"

"Mahon of the Tyman and Sahbél of the Nedebar."

"I would have expected this from Sahbél, but not from Mahon. Did they give you an explanation?"

"I suspect it has something to do with losing Jessara."

Galen's mouth dropped open and his face turned a blotchy red. "What do you know of the Malazia? And how is it that you know her name?"

"I met her when I was ten, and she told me her name. I only learned last night that she is your Malazia."

The rest of the council members stood as one and slapped their hands on the table in disapproval. "No one speaks the Malazia's name other than the council, her parents, and her Eldala," said Galen. "It goes against all of our sacred traditions for you to know it, let alone speak her name aloud. I could have you banished from our presence this instant."

Despite Galen's threats, Kieran maintained his composure and then gave a sly smile. "Your threat is premature. I have broken no traditions."

"How can you say that?"

"*I* am Jessara's Eldala."

The pounding on the table resumed, and many of the men raised their fists in protest.

"This is not possible."

"I told you that I met her when I was ten. We became friends and exchanged gifts."

"But only Baraca can share Eldala."

"If you remember your history, then you know I am Baraca. I can trace my lineage back to the first Jessara, the woman your clan gave to Alardin when he drove Leandra out of Teleria and freed the Baraca."

"That is something we would rather forget," someone murmured.

Kieran was losing patience. "Four other calafars have accepted my claims," he said through his teeth. "Why do *you* have trouble accepting that I am part of this clan?"

Galen flashed a wicked smile. "How could you be part of the Hada if you do not wear the mark?"

Kieran narrowed his eyes, rolled up his sleeve, and slowly walked along the front of the table so each council member could get a good look at the tattoo. The reactions were varied, from jaws dropping open to hissing through teeth to stares of utter disbelief and shaking of heads.

Galen's voice trembled just under the surface when he spoke "Do you think that because you are her Eldala you now have the right to marry her?"

"Yes, I do."

Kieran had never seen anyone come as undone as this man. If it hadn't been so maddening, it almost would have been amusing.

"The Hada council is the final authority in matters concerning the Malazia," said Galen, "and it was our intent before she was taken that she be joined with her cousin Stefan."

Kieran remembered hearing Jessara call that name when she was captured.

"We will not let an accidental meeting of two children interfere with our plans for the Malazia. You will have to give up any claim to marrying Jessara."

Kieran clenched his jaw and knotted his fists against his legs. He'd had enough of Galen's arrogance, of Galen's arguments, of Galen himself. And he saw that his attempts to get their cooperation were futile at best. He might as well have tried convincing Ciara to give up her plans to destroy Teleria.

"Gentlemen," he said – realizing that the word was too good for these arrogant bastards – "I did not come here to seek your permission or to beg your pardon. My intention in coming here was to enlist your help. I had hoped that my plan to restore your Malazia would cause you to put aside your obvious disdain for Telerians in order to secure the greater good and stand against Leandra's threat to enslave Telerians and Baraca. I do not ask your permission now when I tell you that I will find Jessara and restore her to you. As to my marrying her, I will let her decide."

Kieran paused. "If you cannot put aside your prejudice, then you are truly lost."

Galen and the council looked at Kieran, their eyes full of hatred. Kieran sensed that Galen was trying to keep his temper.

"Whether you find her or not," Galen said, "we will never help you."

Up until now, Kieran had kept himself under control, but hearing these last words from Galen fanned the coals of frustration into a bonfire. In a fit of anger, Kieran picked up Restamar and held it above his head. Galen froze in fear while Kieran brought the sword down on the table. The two halves collapsed in on each other with a thud that echoed through the whole room.

"I will keep my word to restore your Malazia. When I do, I will give you another chance to join the battle. If you will not join us, I will consider the Hada clan cut off from the rest of Teleria. When the Zagorans try to invade your fortress, I only hope I can defend it."

Chapter 26

Kieran's arms and legs shook from fatigue. His confrontation with the Hada council had taken more out of him than he'd anticipated. Now he stood outside the fortress and breathed in the warm summer air. As he walked towards camp to find something to eat, Gilrain walked up to him and asked about the meeting.

"They're as arrogant as Mahon and Sahbél said they'd be. I'm almost ashamed to think I'm part of their clan."

"Did you mention you want to marry their Malazia?"

Kieran laughed. "The subject came up, but I said I'd leave it up to Jessara."

"And how did they take that news?"

"About like you'd expect. They think they can tell everyone what to do. They're almost as bad as Rahnak."

As they prepared to leave, a lone rider came from the direction of the fortress. His blond hair was tied back, and his black eyes stared out from a hardened face. There was something familiar about him.

Braeden nodded at him. Gilrain and Riordan started to draw their swords. Kieran motioned for them to wait.

"What can I do for you, sir?" Kieran asked.

"I am here to join the search for my cousin."

"Your cousin?" Kieran asked.

"The Malazia."

Kieran bristled. "Are you Stefan?"

"How do you know my name?"

"The council mentioned you. Why do you want to come with us?"

"I watched the slave traders take her ten years ago, and I swore that I would find her. When I heard that you were going to look for her, I knew I had to accompany you. I am not going to trust a Telerian to find her."

As they traveled towards Gedelar, Kieran realized that he needed to find some solace from the only place that could give it. He just wondered how he could convince his companions that it was in his best interest to visit the sea.

Surprisingly, Gilrain, Toren, and Braeden agreed that it *would* be in his best interest – as long as at least one of them went with him. Kale was the only one to protest. But when Gilrain agreed to be Kieran's escort, Kale relented. They agreed to meet in Agora in five days, recruiting men and supplies for the war as they traveled.

As the cousins led their horses, Gilrain asked, "Can you believe Stefan's attitude? Why did you let him come along?"

"I think it's a Hada trait – to be as arrogant as possible. But I don't see that we really had a choice. He has just as much reason to find her as I do. I'm just not sure what will happen when he finds out that he probably won't be marrying her."

By sundown, Kieran and Gilrain had reached Kolachel, a small town on the northern shore of Teleria. Kieran had visited this town with his father when he was young. It was on this shore that he'd found the purple shell he'd given to Jessara.

Now that he was here, he tried to empty his mind, letting the sound of the wind and the waves wash away the burden of his many tasks. Until this moment, he hadn't realized how much he missed the shore. It was the one place that could help him work through his problems and put everything into perspective.

While Gilrain tethered the horses, Kieran went to look for driftwood for a small fire. As he bent down, he sensed something behind him. When he turned around, the creature was upon him before he could draw his sword. In an instant, it had him by the shoulder and all he felt was the searing fire of the poison spreading through him. Then his world went dark.

Fading in and out of consciousness, Kieran was vaguely aware of what was happening to him. He thought he remembered hearing Gilrain cry out, and then he felt himself being flung into a carriage with no windows.

His mind told him to fight, but his body wouldn't cooperate. He didn't know if it was day or night. The only thing he could be certain of was the intense pain in his left shoulder and the throbbing in his head. More than once he heard himself cry out, but no one came to his aid.

They traveled without stopping for what seemed like weeks until Kieran sensed they'd come to a city. The horses' hooves clopped on cobblestone streets, and the smell of human waste, rotting vegetables, and rancid meat swirled around in the carriage. The intensity of the smell and the constant swaying motion of the carriage made him throw up more than once.

He was relieved when the street smells dissipated and he felt the carriage being pulled up a ramp. They must have reached some kind of courtyard because he heard the horses' steps echoing off stone walls. They stopped and someone said, "We have him."

A stern voice instructed his captors to take him to the guest quarters. Someone opened the carriage door, pulled him out, and carried him by his arms and legs through several passages and doors. The chill air hit his sweating skin, making him shake uncontrollably. When the men carrying him stopped, he was in a dark room. They dropped Kieran into a bed, and he fell into a fitful sleep.

Gilrain growled at himself again as he handed the two horses off to a stable boy and went to find Arathor. He had ridden from Kolachel to Agora in two days, stopping only to eat. Now he was exhausted, but this was no time for sleep. When he reached the living quarters, Arathor and the other companions were studying a map of Teleria. Arathor turned to look at Gilrain as he entered.

"Where's Kieran?" Arathor asked.

"He was captured two days ago," Gilrain said.

Kale's face turned ash gray.

Hurriedly, Gilrain explained the situation.

"I knew something like this would happen," said Kale.

"And you think they took him to Korisan?" Toren asked.

"Where else would they take him?" Gilrain said.

"Well, if he's there," said Riordan, "don't expect to see him a-gain."

"Why not?" asked Braeden.

"The whole city is like a fortress, with the castle at its heart. Get-ting him out would be next to impossible." Riordan shook his head. "And if we were caught, we'd be thrown into the dungeon or sent to the gold mine."

Gilrain slammed his hand into the table. "I'm not going to just abandon him. Who knows what Ciara will do to him."

"And do not forget we need to look for my cousin as well," said Stefan.

Gilrain turned to Stefan, trying to keep his temper under control. "Right now, finding Kieran is our first priority."

"You're both right," said Arathor. "You can go as soon as I can confirm where he is."

"How will you do that?" Gilrain asked.

"I have my sources."

Chapter 27

The same vivid dream had kept Jessa up three nights in a row, and now she was exhausted. She'd seen a man walking on the beach to gather wood. All of a sudden, a gurithent came up behind him and attacked him. When the man fell to the ground, her sobs woke her up.

Before she could get back to sleep, Elath burst into the servants' tower.

"What is it?" Jessa groaned.

"Davina says you must come to the guest quarters."

Davina was the chatelaine, and although Jessa was a slave in the castle, she sometimes felt that Davina singled her out from the other servants and made her life particularly difficult. One of Davina's favorite ways to hound Jessa was to tell her to "come this instant" when there was never any reason for the hurry.

Jessa pulled a blue smock over her cotton shift, braided her hair, and made her way down the stairs to the back of the great hall, letting out a sigh. Her steps echoed through the enormous room, despite the tapestries lining the walls.

There were two places where guests stayed when they visited the castle. One was in the tower just east of the servants' tower. It was reserved for the various lords and ladies who came to visit the king. The other was a large, but seldom-used room near the princess's chambers, reserved for the king's most honored guests.

Once in the courtyard, Jessa hurried to the other side of the castle where the royal family lived. She never liked coming to this part of the castle. Ciara made it clear that she disliked Jessa, and Jessa tried to stay out of her way. But occasionally, Davina called her here for one chore or another, or to help with Princess Delaine.

She was curious as to why Davina would summon her to the guest's chambers now.

A guard in full chain mail leered at her, then opened one of the large mahogany doors, and let her in. Jessa dropped the required curtsy for Davina and moved next to her.

"He was bitten by a gurithent," Davina said.

Jessa brushed past Davina, threw open the curtains, and approached the man in the bed. Her stomach fluttered and she drew in a quick breath. There was something vaguely familiar about the color of his hair, the shape of his face, and the set of his jaw. Where had she seen him before?

Davina cleared her throat, calling Jessa back to the task at hand. Jessa's hand went to his head. "He's burning up with fever," she said. "I'm too late."

As she turned to go, Davina called her back with a familiar sharp tone. "He is Prince Aiden of Benalia, and a guest of the king and queen. You must do everything you can to help him."

Benalia? That was a country only reached by crossing the Sea of Voronezh. What would he be doing in Korisan?

Biting her tongue, Jessa hurried across the courtyard to the other side of the castle and climbed the stairs to the herb pantry. Most of the herbs were for seasoning the king's food, but the cook allowed her one corner in the upper tower for medicinal herbs. She surveyed her collection. There, on the topmost shelf, sat a jar of crushed petals from the cascabel flower, the one flower in Teleria that could draw out the poison of a gurithent.

Jessa had to admit she was proud of her knowledge of herbs. Her friend Samuel, the local apothecary, had once told her that she was the best herbalist in the city, even the district. She'd learned everything she knew about herbs from Samuel and considered him a master. To have him tell her that she had surpassed his skills was surprising and humbling.

She gathered everything she needed – a few clean cloths, a basin, the jar of cascabel, and a kettle of boiling water. Going back across the courtyard, she ducked under the porch just as it started to rain.

When she reached the room, she pushed past the doorman, put everything down, and looked at the prince. He looked worse than when she'd left him. She knew she had to bring down the fever, and that would mean removing his shirt.

Jessa had seen some of the male servants half-clothed, and had nursed numerous soldiers back to health. Why did the thought of taking *this* man's shirt off send a shiver of anticipation tripping through her?

She pushed the unexpected feeling away, unbuttoned his white linen shirt, and lifted it over his head.

Magnificent. That was the only word for him.

His musculature was perfectly proportioned and defined. If it hadn't been for the erratic rise and fall of his ribcage and the reddish hair covering his chest, she would have thought he was sculpted from marble. A flutter danced in her stomach and moved down her legs.

She took a deep breath and tried to concentrate on her work. This man was royalty and a guest of the king. If she didn't attend to him quickly, he would be lost. Still, it would take all of her resolve to keep her thoughts under control.

She left the room to get some cold rain water for his fever and when she returned, she looked at the site of the wound and stifled a gasp. She'd never seen a wound this bad. From the place where the creature had bitten him, she saw green, web-like streaks going past his elbow, and up into his shoulder, neck, and cheek. The skin around the site of the wound was blackening.

Jessa dipped a linen towel in the rain water and was about to place it over Aiden's chest to bring down the fever when she noticed something odd. Just over his heart was a silvery blue circle. If she hadn't known better, she would have thought it was some kind of stone. She was about to touch it, and then stopped. What was she thinking?

She scolded herself and quickly covered his chest with the cold cloth. As she took another cloth to clean the wound, she noticed something else.

Just below the gurithent bite was a tattoo, still healing. She'd seen this mark before. If he was the prince of a distant land, why did he have the mark of her clan? It didn't make any sense.

Aiden shuddered and let out a moan. Whatever the answer was to this mystery, she would have to solve it later.

While she worked on the cascabel poultice, it didn't take long for another sensation to sweep through her. It was like a long-forgotten melody, buried deep in her heart, now pushing its way to the surface. It only came to her when she thought about her best friend. How could she feel this way about a complete stranger?

She put her hand against her stomach to still the rush of song settling there and placed the poultice on the gurithent bite. The flower's sweet fragrance filled the room. It was her favorite smell, heavier than roses but lighter than jasmine. She had little reason to use it and always regretted that most of the time it was for cases like this.

As far along as this victim was, Jessa was afraid it would take longer than the usual one day to draw out the poison. She'd have to use all of her skills as a healer to help him.

After a long day of bringing down the prince's fever and changing the cascabel poultices, Jessa realized she hadn't eaten anything at all. She was just about to leave to go to the kitchen when someone startled her from behind. She dropped to her knees when she saw it was the king.

She knew he was leering at her just like the guards. A sickening discord replaced the sweet song that had stayed with her all day. She held her breath, waiting to hear what he might say.

Jessa stiffened when Rahnak took her hand and raised her up, tilting her chin so she had to look into his pallid face with its sickly green eyes and patchy black beard and moustache. His breath reeked of old wine and meat. She quickly looked away.

He fondled her imprisoned hand while he spoke. "Dear Jessa. I'm so glad I found you." He laughed. "I was looking for you and here you are, attending to Prince Aiden."

Jessa swallowed the bile rising into her throat.

"You will move into his quarters and be his personal healer and attendant."

The discordance spread from her stomach to her head and legs, threatening to drown her. Being this close to the king's quarters was the last thing she wanted.

"Your Majesty..." she started to protest.

"It will make things much easier to have you close."

When he left, Jessa felt the air rush back into her lungs.

Chapter 28

Feeling nauseated from her encounter with the king, Jessa raced from the prince's room to the servants' tower. Without lighting a torch, she fell into her bed. After a few moments, she heard Sienna come into the room.

Jessa and Sienna had been sold to the king on the same day by the same slave traders. At the time, both girls were only eight years old. Back then, neither one of them had really understood what had happened to them. But over the years they pieced together that they had both been stolen from their families by the Esgharites. When the two factions joined up on the road to Korisan, the girls became friends and took care of each other along the way. By some twist of good fortune, Davina purchased both of them to work in the castle. Since that time, they'd done everything together.

"Where have you been all day?" Sienna asked.

"Taking care of the king's guest."

"All the servants were talking about him. They say he was bitten by a gurithent."

Jessa shuddered. "It was horrible. I've never seen a wound that bad." *Or a man that handsome,* she thought. Where had that come from?

"How long did you stay?" asked Sienna.

"I just returned. And I'll have to move to his quarters tomorrow."

Despite being unable to see her friend in the darkness, Jessa knew Sienna was drawing her face into that funny little frown she always had when she was perplexed. "Why?"

"The king said it was his idea."

Sienna let out a groan.

Both women knew the king's reputation for seducing women. Everyone in the castle knew about it. How could they not when he made a point of bragging about the number of women he had taken to his bed?

"Of course it was his idea," said Sienna. "He's had his eye on you since you turned sixteen."

Jessa sat up and pulled the braid out of her hair. There were times when she wished she was still fifteen. At that age, no one had noticed her, least of all the king. But when she turned sixteen, she'd changed from girl to woman. At the time, she was pleased. It was difficult watching the other servant girls blossom into women. Joining their company was a relief.

Now, the figure she'd longed for was nothing but trouble. Every guard in the palace stared at her like she was a piece of meat. And now the king had his eye on her.

Jessa ran her fingers through her thick hair and lay down again. She would miss being with Sienna. In the morning, she would move her few belongings into Prince Aiden's room. For now, she just wanted to sleep. Sienna went to her own bed, and Jessa let her exhaustion finally overtake her.

The rest she longed for didn't come. Instead, images of the gurithent attacking the man haunted her dreams. Only this time, someone was trying to stop the gurithent. Before he could, though, the gurithent struck back. And this time, five men in hooded cloaks caught the man and put him in a black carriage.

When she woke up, she knew beyond any doubt that on the first night of the dream, she'd witnessed the attack on Prince Aiden. She only wondered why the king's men were waiting to catch him. And who was the man who tried to help him?

With her stomach complaining loudly, Jessa snuck into the kitchen to find some breakfast. It was still dark, but Halda was already preparing the morning meal for the royal family.

This was one of Jessa's favorite rooms in the castle. Herbs and flowers Jessa had picked hung from their strings on either side of the enormous fireplace. Several black pots hung over the coals, their contents bubbling and steaming. The smell made Jessa's mouth water.

She sat next to the hearth and Halda approached. Her kind, blue eyes smiled out of a face that reminded Jessa of fresh dumplings. The woman patted Jessa's cheek and sat next to her.

"How is our prince this morning?"

"I haven't been to his quarters yet."

The portly woman reached into her pocket and handed Jessa a small, warm loaf of bread. Jessa eagerly took it and broke it apart, savoring the rich flavor of the yeast.

"You know what Davina will say if she finds out you gave me fresh bread."

The cook chuckled. "Davina won't find out. It won't hurt the king one bit if you have some real food instead of that dry bread and hard cheese you usually get."

As Jessa continued to eat, Halda brought her a mug of cider.

"I hear the prince is a handsome one," Halda said.

Jessa felt the heat rising into her cheeks. "I suppose."

"Don't be getting any ideas, Miss Jessa."

Jessa snapped her head around in surprise. "Halda, he's a prince and I'm a slave. What kind of ideas could I possibly have about him?"

Halda shook her finger at Jessa. "Slave or not, you're a young woman. Don't be getting any romantic notions."

Jessa finished the cider and ran out of the kitchen before her face could give her away. Why would the cook think such a thing about her? Besides, the idea that a prince would see her at all was impossible. The nobility never paid attention to servants. As far as they were concerned, servants were like furniture – functional and necessary.

If only Rahnak would think of her as a footstool.

When she reached her quarters, she half-heartedly began to gather her things. The only advantages to being in the prince's quarters were that she would be right there if his condition worsened, and she would get to sleep on a feather bed in a warm room. It wasn't that she minded sleeping on straw, but even on the warmest nights, she was always cold in the stone tower.

As she put her things in the willow basket, she thought again about Halda's warning. It was ridiculous. Or not. Hadn't she felt something stir in her yesterday?

Stop it. He's a prince, you're a slave.

She had to banish thoughts like this to the farthest corner of her mind and lock them up. Anyway, he was probably like other men she knew – unreliable. Her father had doted on her and called her a princess before she'd been chosen. In the end, when it really counted, he never came. Her cousin would be old enough by now to come for her, and yet he hadn't come.

Kieran hadn't come.

Kieran. She hadn't thought of him for several months now.

Jessa let out a heavy sigh and carried the basket across the courtyard towards Prince Aiden's room. It was deathly quiet, save for the sound of the prince's labored breathing. When she reached him, she let out a cry and dropped the basket. Her possessions scattered across the blue carpet.

The green streaks had spread across his chest and into his right arm. She'd thought that he would have improved just a little. How could this have happened?

Rahnak smiled to himself. When Ciara had first mentioned that she would incapacitate Arathor's son and bring him to the castle, Rahnak was skeptical and more than a little anxious. Did he really want his enemy's son under his roof? Despite all of Ciara's assurances that it was the only way to help Rahnak keep the throne, he'd only agreed because he knew he could get Jessa to care for him.

This was working out better than he could have hoped. It wouldn't be long before Jessa was coming to him.

When Jessa had first come to the castle, he hadn't paid much attention to her. But two years ago she'd turned into a woman, almost overnight, and there was something about her that made him want her like he had wanted no other woman. It wasn't because of her full, blossoming figure or her cinnamon tresses. It wasn't even that she would be the only slave he'd taken to his chambers.

She was Baraca, and that meant Ciara hated her more than any other woman he'd taken.

And he'd taken so many that he'd lost count over the years. In the beginning, he felt some remorse, but what was he supposed to do? After giving Rahnak his only heir, Ciara had moved into her tower in the northwest corner of the castle and had brought in a consort. How was a man supposed to get any satisfaction if his wife didn't provide it? It was almost as if Ciara had forced him into the arms of other women.

Jessa would be different. She was already subservient, but he didn't want to use his power or position to get her into his chambers; he wanted her to come willingly to his bed. He would have to find ways to make Jessa think it was her idea, and to show her he wanted her as more than a mistress. And when she finally came, he would have to find a way to banish Ciara and Delaine from the kingdom.

Chapter 29

Arathor watched Gilrain pace the room like a caged animal. Patience was not Gilrain's strong suit, and although Kale and Riordan preferred to plan every detail, Arathor knew Gilrain would rather make his plans on the spot.

Arathor couldn't blame him. But he'd wanted to be cautious. Sending out search parties across Teleria would have been a waste of time and man power. Now that he was sure of his son's whereabouts, he called Kieran's companions around him.

"I've just received a message from Dorinda, a mystic from the Hada clan," he said. "She said that Kieran is in the castle – and Jessara is there with him."

Both Gilrain and Stefan looked relieved.

"There's something else you should know," said Arathor. "The poison will suppress his memories. Right now Kieran could be more dangerous to you than Rahnak or Ciara."

Gilrain walked to the other side of the room. "Surely he'll know *me*."

Arathor put a hand to Gilrain's shoulder. "I know it's hard to believe, but he wouldn't know Kale."

Kale blew out a frustrated breath.

Gilrain's face tightened in resolve. "So when do we leave?"

"Tonight."

After the others had left the room, Arathor took Gilrain aside. "I have something for you."

"What?"

Arathor pulled a Keldar stone necklace out of his pocket. "When you find Jessara, make sure you give this to her, so I can talk with her."

"I know you trust Dorinda, but how can you be sure this is the right woman?"

Arathor could understand Gilrain's doubt, but he knew from experience that Dorinda was never wrong. And when she'd explained that this Jessara shared a heart connection with Kieran, Arathor knew that he had to speak with her.

"All I can do is hope," said Arathor. "If she's not his Jessara, Kieran will never completely recover."

Jessa recognized the smell of lentil stew just as Sienna came into the room. “How is he?” Sienna asked.

“Worse. I don’t understand it.”

Sienna approached and gave Jessa a sideways smile. “How can you look at him all day?”

It was a good question. The prince was hard to ignore. Besides his muscular frame – which Jessa had thankfully covered just this morning – there was his striking face with its high cheekbones and his square jaw, most of it covered with the same reddish hair that was on his chest. She hoped he would recover quickly so she could move out of his chambers.

“I brought you something to eat.”

Sweet Sienna. Jessa hadn’t eaten a bite since breakfast. She took the bowl and quickly finished all of the stew. Sienna sat next to her on the prince’s bed and put her hand on Jessa’s face. “You look terrible. Why don’t you let me watch him for a little while so you can get some rest?”

Jessa yawned and walked to her small bedchamber which, thankfully, had a door so she could have a little privacy. Before lying down, she lit a candle and looked at her things. They seemed out of place in this setting, just like her. Now they rested on a shelf next to the bed. Of her few possessions – a small book of charcoal drawings, a silver key, a blue jay feather, and a dried rose – the object she treasured most was her small silver box.

Bairn, the castle’s sword smith, had given her the box when she was ten and had lined it with black velvet. Jessa ran her fingers over the clasp and smiled. She’d always hidden it from Davina. The woman would never have let Jessa have something so costly. She opened it and took out her treasure. The candlelight danced on the iridescent shell fragment, reminding her of the day when Kieran had given it to her. It seemed so long ago. It was all she had left of her old life, and all she had left of him.

Sometime in the night, Jessa woke to the sound of someone moving in the prince's room. Quietly, she opened her door and peered into the dimly lit room. What was Ciara doing here? And in the middle of the night? The queen never came out of her tower, not even when Rahnak entertained Teleria's lords and ladies.

Jessa ducked behind the door and watched Ciara lean over Aiden. When she poured something onto his shoulder, the prince let out a moan and then stiffened. After whispering something Jessa couldn't understand, the queen turned and walked towards the outer door.

As Ciara strode past her, Jessa pressed herself against the wall and held her breath. Thankfully, the queen was too preoccupied to notice her. It wasn't until Ciara had closed the door and Jessa could no longer hear her footsteps that she finally started to breathe again.

She looked towards Aiden. He was moaning and thrashing around. Before Jessa could restrain him, he rolled out of bed. If he stayed on the floor, his condition would worsen.

Putting her arms around his torso, she ignored the romantic ideas crashing around in her head, and pulled him into the bed. Then she put his legs up and covered him with a blanket. He was burning up from the fever again. She lifted his shirt over his head and couldn't believe what she saw.

The candlelight revealed that the poison was spreading. The green streaks now covered his entire chest and both of his arms. Some had even spread up into his face. His breathing was shallow and his heart was racing.

She rubbed the sleep from her eyes and made a new cascabel poultice to draw out more of the venom. How could he be getting worse? She should have seen some improvement by now. It was as if he'd been bitten again.

Ciara.

Jessa's mind flashed back to the image of Ciara sitting next to him, pouring something on his shoulder. If Aiden was a guest, why would Ciara continue to poison him? It would only result in the loss of all his memories.

Unless that was Ciara's intent all along. Maybe that explained why she'd seen cloaked men waiting for Aiden in her dream. Ciara had sent them, knowing the gurithent would attack him. And maybe she'd sent the gurithent in the first place.

Jessa shook the thought from her head. It was too impossible. Ciara was one of the most cruel, unpleasant people Jessa had ever met, but what reason would she have for making the prince forget who he was?

Right now it didn't matter. Despite Jessa's fatigue, she had to get the poison out of his system before it spread to his whole body. She had never tried this before, but she knew that poison could be drawn out by sucking it from the wound. It sounded ridiculous, and she would have to be careful not to swallow it, but she had to try.

She took a basin from the dressing table and put it on the floor next to the bed. Then, pushing her loose hair aside, she moved to Aiden's left side and put her mouth to the wound.

This was the first time her face had been this close to his skin. For a moment, she stopped and inhaled. What was that smell? There was the aroma of cascabel, and there was Aiden's sweat from the fever. But there was something else, something like smoke and metal, a scent she'd only smelled on Bairn. Why would Prince Aiden smell like a smith?

It was another mystery that would have to wait, just like the stone and the tattoo. She had to get the poison out of his body. Carefully, she put her lips to the wound and began to work her cheeks and tongue to draw the poison from his shoulder into her mouth. As soon as the poison hit her tongue, she recoiled. It was the most awful thing she'd ever tasted – more bitter than cinnamon and more sour than lemons. As quickly as she could, she spit it into the basin. Over and over, for more than half an hour, she repeated the process until her cheeks ached and her tongue couldn't move. She only hoped it was enough.

In her exhaustion, she didn't care where she slept. She rolled Aiden on his side, curled up next to him, pulled the quilt up over the two of them, and drifted off to sleep.

Chapter 30

Jessa pushed herself out of bed, shocked that she was sleeping next to the prince. And why was her jaw so sore? Then she remembered drawing the poison out of Aiden. When she looked at his shoulder, she decided it looked better than it had last night. Now she had to wait to see if his fever broke today. If it didn't, she wasn't sure what she could do for him.

Knowing she wouldn't get back to sleep, she pulled the quilt back over Aiden and went to her room to dress. As she braided her hair, she thought about the dream she'd had last night.

It had been her dream from childhood – except that it wasn't *her* dream exactly. And she hadn't had the dream about meeting Kieran in the forest for many years. In this dream, she was in the forest, but she was looking at a girl with long, cinnamon brown hair and black eyes. Why would she be dreaming about a girl?

As she thought of it, she drew in a quick breath. What if it hadn't been her dream? What if it had been the prince's dream? No, it wasn't possible. She knew that two people could never share dreams. Not unless they were Eldala. And she didn't have an Eldala.

Just as she was leaving to get some breakfast, King Rahnak burst into her room and closed the door. Panic raced through her and her heart pounded like a thousand drums. The king pushed her to the bed, staggering as he did. Although he was only slightly more in command of his lust when he was sober, being drunk made him lose all self-control.

Jessa looked around. In this small space, she couldn't hope to escape. And there was no one, except maybe a guard at the door, who would hear her cries for help. Not that anyone would help her anyway. Rahnak was the king, and everyone, including Ciara, looked the other way.

As he drew closer, she was just able to roll away from him when he sat on her bed. He looked oddly peaceful. The familiar leer in his eyes wasn't there. He moved to stroke her face and stopped just in front of her lips.

"Beautiful Jessa."

She inched away. He moved closer.

"You don't have to be afraid of me."

His face was in hers. He reeked of ale. Between the odor and her predicament, and possibly swallowing some of the gurithent poison, her stomach churned. Under normal circumstances she would have tried to hold it in, but now she wondered if it would be enough to stop the king's advances, so she let herself throw up all over the bed, just missing the king's face.

Rahnak exploded in a tirade of unkingly insults and ran from the room.

It was past midnight when Toren led Gilrain and the others to the home of a friend, just on the outskirts of Korisan. The woman who opened the door looked surprised, but welcomed them in. Toren apologized for waking her and quickly explained that they needed shelter.

The woman scurried around, finding places for them to sleep. Toren took the horses to the stable out back. When he came in, he introduced the companions to the woman. She frowned when she saw Stefan. "Baraca," she said with a sniff.

Stefan scowled and looked as if he might say something. One look from Gilrain silenced him. Grudgingly, Stefan went to a corner and unrolled his pack.

There were times when Gilrain wished Stefan hadn't come with them. He was pompous and overbearing, and had nothing good to say about Telerians. In fact, on their first night of travel, after Stefan spent all day complaining about Gilrain's decisions and saying how he should have been the leader, Gilrain took Stefan aside and told him that Arathor had put him in charge, and if Stefan didn't like it, he could go back to the Hada. From then on, Stefan kept his opinions to himself.

In the morning, Gilrain woke to the smell of ham cooking on the hearth. As he walked into the kitchen, he saw that Toren was already talking with the woman. When Toren saw Gilrain and the others, he said, "My friend died several years ago. But his widow says there are people in town who will help us. We'll have to be careful. In this town, there are many spies for King Rahnak."

Stefan joined them. The bitterness he'd displayed last night seemed to be under control. The woman looked at him. "Yes, and you'd better not let anyone know you're Baraca," she said. "Not in this city anyway."

After breakfast, the woman told them where to find two people who might be able to tell them if Kieran was in Korisan. Toren and Kale went to talk with Petra the blacksmith, while Riordan went to look at the castle gate, hoping to find a hidden way in. Gilrain and Stefan headed for the apothecary's shop. Gilrain hoped Stefan wouldn't do anything to jeopardize their mission.

As they walked through the streets, the first thing that struck Gilrain was the stench – garbage, human waste, smoke, and dust all mixed together to make an offensive smell that sent his head reeling. Korisan must have been a glorious place at one time, but now dingy gray houses and shops, one on top of another, towered on either side of them. Tattered blue and red awnings blocked any light that might have reached the narrow streets, and in the back alleys, the poor sheltered themselves or begged for money.

When they reached the center of town, they came to a clearing. Gilrain looked up and let out a low whistle.

The street they were on gave him a clear view of the castle. The massive gray structure sat on the highest hill and looked down over the city. Intimidating marble spires and domes reached towards the clouds.

And Riordan was right when he'd said it was the heart of the fortress. It was a fortress itself. Gilrain shook his head. How would they ever get inside?

Presently, they found the apothecary's shop. A bell rang as they opened the door, and while they waited for someone to help them, Gilrain noted the countless shelves lining the walls, each one laden with labeled jars and earthen containers. Soon a short, balding man came out to greet them.

"Welcome, strangers," he said. "I'm Samuel. How can I help you?"

Gilrain looked around to make sure no one else was in the shop. "We're friends of Toren the sword smith."

Samuel led them to another room. "How is my old friend?"
"Quite well," Gilrain said. "But he needs your help."
Samuel's eyebrows went up in a question.
"King Arathor's son was captured several days ago," Gilrain said. "And he was bitten by a gurithent."
Gilrain noticed two young women had come in. One had dark brown hair, drawn into a long braid. The other had golden hair, loose over her shoulders.
She was the most beautiful woman he'd ever seen, which surprised him since he'd seen quite a few beautiful women. But there was something about her... What was he thinking? He didn't have time for this. He turned his attention back to Samuel.
"If he's in the castle, only one person would be able to take care of him."
"Do you know her?" Stefan asked.
"She just walked in the door."
Stefan spun around and stared at the women. He flashed a smile and moved towards them. Clasping the hands of the dark-haired one, he let out a cry of joy. The woman pushed him away, the shock evident on her face.
"Do you not recognize me, cousin?" he asked.
"No. Should I?"
Stefan took her by the arm and led her to a corner. Gilrain strained to hear the muted conversation. "Jessara, I am Stefan, your cousin."
Jessara? Kieran's Eldala...
Gilrain ran his hand through his hair. Arathor had said Jessara was here. At the time, it hadn't seemed possible. Now it looked like the mystic was right again. Or maybe it was just good luck.
The woman quickly looked to her companion, her eyes pleading for help. When she mouthed the word, "Sienna," Gilrain's jaw dropped.
Kieran believed in fate and Gilrain had always scoffed at the idea – until now. To have found Jessara in Korisan was one thing, but to find Sienna here as well... What were the chances of that?
Whether it was fate or just more good luck, he would have to think about it later. All that mattered now was saving Kieran.
As he walked over to the women, he caught the eye of the golden-haired beauty. Her face changed to a pleasing shade of pink, and

Gilrain had trouble finding his words. What was wrong with him? Women never made him tongue-tied.

"Please excuse me, ladies, but we really can't waste any time. My name is Gilrain and I'm looking for my cousin. He was captured in Kolachel and we believe he was brought to the castle."

The dark-haired woman looked surprised. "The newest arrival to the castle is Prince Aiden."

Aiden? Of course. "Yes that would be him." Gilrain put his hand above his head. "He's about this tall, has reddish-blond hair, and has a blue stone in his chest."

The woman's jaw dropped. She broke free of Stefan's grasp and motioned for the men to join her behind the curtain. "Prince Aiden is your cousin?"

Sienna interrupted. "Jessa, we really have to get back to the castle." She glanced at Gilrain with her blue eyes. Was he just imagining it or was there a hint of a smile on her face?

"I'm sorry," Jessa said. "My friend is right."

Samuel entered with two containers. "Here you are, Jessa – more cascabel."

Jessa gave them all a tight smile and dropped a curtsy. "We really must be going."

Before they left, Gilrain took her arm. "Jessa, will you please help us get Kieran out of the castle?"

Jessa's face went pale. "Kieran? I thought you said his name was Aiden."

"It is. But we call him Kieran."

Chapter 31

The jars fell from Jessa's hands and shattered on the flagstones. Her knees buckled from underneath her and she dropped to the floor. She looked up at everyone and blinked.

The man calling himself Stefan put out his hand to help her up. Reluctantly, she took it, avoiding his black eyes. When she looked at Sienna, she knew her friend was as surprised as she was. As Jessa rubbed her backside, all she could think was that she wanted to run from the room, back to the castle where at least she knew who she was and had some measure of control over her world. Her legs just wouldn't cooperate.

She took a deep breath of the spilled cascabel. It calmed her only a little. "Please forgive me, gentlemen," she stammered. "I'm afraid this is all a bit too much to take in."

While Samuel cleaned up the broken jars, Stefan led her to a cushioned chair. Jessa eased into it and winced. Sienna came to her and put a hand on Jessa's shoulder.

"We really have to go," Sienna said.

Gilrin looked at them hard. "We need your help, ladies. Arathor said Kieran was in danger."

"I'll think about it," Jessa finally managed.

As she rose from the chair, Gilrain took her arm again and pulled her to one side. "Is your name Jessara?"

First Stefan and now Gilrain. "Why do you need to know?"

"If it is, I have something for you." He pulled a small package from his cloak and handed it to her.

She took it from his hand without answering and put it in her apron. Gilrain's eyes met hers. "You must choose quickly, Jessa. My cousin's life depends on it."

Going to Samuel's shop was supposed to be pleasant. The aroma alone beckoned Jessa to stay. But more than that, she enjoyed Samuel's company. Each time she visited the herbalist, he showed her some new plant he'd found, or shared a new way to treat one illness or another. Jessa's encounter with Gilrain and Stefan had made it anything but pleasant. They had turned her world upside-down.

Sienna interrupted her thoughts. "Will you help them?"

"What?" Jessa asked, still reeling.

"Will you help them?"

Jessa stopped and turned to her friend. "Sienna, I don't know if I believe them."

The two walked the rest of the way in silence. When Jessa reached her room, she closed the door and sat on the bed. The package rustled in her apron. She pulled it out and looked at it. What could a stranger have possibly given to her? And how had he known her name?

Besides Sienna and her parents, only a handful of people knew her real name. One of them was Kieran.

From the moment she'd argued with Kieran about the tree, she knew that they would become fast friends. It was the reason she told him her real name that first day. She knew she shouldn't have – only her parents and her Eldala were supposed to speak her name. It hadn't mattered. She wanted to share something precious with him.

What was the use of thinking of him? There was no way she would ever see him again – unless Gilrain was telling the truth and the man in the other room was Kieran. She shook her head at the absurdity of it. There wasn't any chance that her childhood friend had wandered into her world under such extraordinary circumstances.

But Gilrain's description had been perfect, right down to the blue stone in the prince's chest.

Jessa stood up, hung her cloak next to her dress, and put the package on the bed. When she tore off the brown paper wrapping, something fell to her bed with a soft thud. It was a blue stone hanging from a delicate silver chain. When she held it up to the light, she thought she saw a small flame inside of it. It was beautiful. Why would Gilrain give her this?

She put the necklace over her head and went to check the prince's condition. She put her hand to his head. The fever was gone, and the green streaks had disappeared. When she turned to leave, the stone around her neck felt strangely warm. She put her hand to it and felt herself being pulled down a tunnel of light. A man in peasant garb stood there, holding out his hand in greeting.

"Who are you?" she asked.

"I'm Arathor."

"Arathor? I heard someone say that name today – Gilrain, I think."

"Yes, Gilrain gave you the blue Keldar stone."

"What's a Keldar stone?"

"A stone my ancestor brought from his homeland. It helps us converse over long distances. Kieran already has one, embedded into his chest. And now you have one as well."

Well, that explained one mystery.

"How did Gilrain know to give it to me?"

"Because I told him to."

"How do you know me?"

"Dorinda, from the Hada clan, told me you were in the castle. I knew you were the only one who could take care of my son."

"Why me?"

"Because you are my son's Eldala."

Jessa's heart froze. "That can't be right. I don't have an Eldala."

"My son is Baraca, and Dorinda said that the two of you exchanged gifts when you were children."

"Then Prince Aiden is Kieran?"

"Yes, but when he wakes up, he won't know who he is."

Jessa took a few deep breaths. "I still don't know how I can help him."

"He was born to take back Teleria. If you don't help him recover his memories, he won't be able to walk in his destiny."

Jessa sank into a chair and put her head in her hands, feeling as if all the air in her chest had been pressed out of her, leaving her gasping for breath, and giving her the feeling that the room was twirling in some kind of mad dance around her.

I have an Eldala? Kieran *is my Eldala.*

She turned to look at the man in the bed, and all the crushing feelings of abandonment came rushing in. Up until a few years ago, some part of her had held onto the hope that he of all people *might* come. But then she'd realized it was a ridiculous dream and she'd told herself that by now he'd probably forgotten her, and was happily married, working in his own smithy, just like his father. It was that realization that made her bury the part of her that longed to be rescued.

Now he was here – and it appeared she was his only hope.

From what she'd read about gurithent poison, she knew that the victim would go mad and die unless treated quickly. But after the initial recovery, all of the personal details of his life would be gone – unless he was Baraca and had an Eldala. There was something about the heart connection that helped the victim remember.

Absently, she put her hand over Kieran's heart and felt an instant connection. It wasn't strong, but it was there. Why hadn't she felt it before? Now it trickled through her and danced in her head – and it sounded like the lilting melody she had once shared with Kieran.

Then a dark presence entered the room and shattered the connection. The click of heels and hiss of skirts made Jessa turn and drop a hurried curtsy for the Princess Delaine.

"How is my prince?" Delaine asked.

Jessa started to answer and then realized that the darkness was coming from the princess. Delaine was annoying and arrogant like her parents, but Jessa had never sensed evil from her before. She wondered if it had something to do with wearing the Keldar stone.

"The fever has broken, Highness, and I expect he'll wake up today."

Delaine sat on the bed next to him, running her hand over Kieran's chest. Jessa bit her lip and tried to push down an unexpected twinge of jealousy.

"He's more handsome than I'd imagined," said the princess.

"Yes he is," Jessa murmured.

Delaine jerked her head grabbed Jessa's arm. "Mind your place, Jessa. He's here to marry me."

Delaine loosened her grip and Jessa felt the full weight of her words sinking in. When they did, she had to fight the urge to shout that it wasn't true, that Kieran was hers, and that Delaine couldn't have him.

Delaine picked up one of Kieran's hands and then recoiled. "I want you to make his hands as smooth as silk. And have Marcus measure him for new clothes. I want him resplendent when he attends the betrothal banquet."

"My lady, it will take him at least two weeks to have the strength to walk."

The princess shot her an imperious glance, and surprisingly, Jessa felt the full hatred Delaine directed at her. "If he is not able to attend, the blame will be placed entirely upon you."

Jessa could only blink as the princess lifted her skirts and brushed past her towards the door. It wasn't until she was gone that Jessa sank back into the chair. How could she help him gain his strength?

She pushed the thought away and tried to concentrate on her immediate task.

Until now, Jessa hadn't paid attention to the prince's hands; they were the last thing she'd been looking at. Now she traced the veins along the back of his hand, noticing how freckled it was. When she turned his hand over, she saw why the princess had recoiled. It was rough and calloused, like Bairn's hands – blacksmith hands.

When Jessa returned from retrieving a jar of lanolin from the kitchen, Marcus was bent over Kieran, muttering. She set the jar on a stand next to the bed and cleared her throat. Marcus turned around, his usually unflustered face pale with surprise. The moment passed and the familiar wrinkled brow looked peaceful.

She was always surprised that a tailor could be so unkempt. His gray and white hair sat in ringlets on top of his head. His white shirt was partially untucked, and several silver pins stuck out of his collar.

Marcus had been like a father to her when she first came to Korisan. He and Bairn took it upon themselves to protect her from Davina and Ciara whenever they could. Bairn secretly taught her to read, and Marcus taught her how to work with numbers. She tried to escape into Marcus's quarters or Bairn's smithy any time she could.

Marcus rubbed his stubbled chin. "It will be difficult to measure him while he's sleeping, but I'll do what I can. Perhaps I have something he can wear until I can make him a more fitting wardrobe."

Jessa laughed. If she knew Marcus, it would take only a few days to complete the prince's wardrobe. He had numerous seamstresses at his disposal, women whose only function in the castle was to make sure that the royal family was well-clothed.

Marcus began to measure, and Jessa took the lanolin and sat next to Kieran. She put his right hand in her lap and took a handful of the soothing mixture. Before massaging it into his hand, she noticed a ring on his finger. Marcus drew in a quick breath.

"That's Arathor's ring," he said.

"You know Arathor?"

"I worked for him before he and Annalisa left the castle. We've remained in contact over the years."

"Do you mean Arathor is a king?"

"*Was* the king. If Aiden is wearing Arathor's signet ring, it means Arathor passed the title to his son."

"I spoke with Arathor in a vision. He said that Kieran was born to regain Teleria. He just didn't mention that his son was the king now."

"Don't tell anyone you've have spoken with Arathor, or that we had this conversation. I'll speak with Bairn, and then we must find a way to get Kieran out of Korisan."

"Get him out of Korisan? Why?"

The tailor lowered his voice. "He's in grave danger here."

"Do you mean he's not here to marry Delaine?"

"No. But if he's forgotten who he is, they'll try to get him to marry her so they can rule the kingdom through him. We have to find some way to help him remember who he is."

Jessa put her head in her hands. This was all too much to take in.

Marcus finished measuring and left. Jessa began to work the lanolin into Kieran's hand. Her mind drifted back to the times when she'd held a ten-year-old boy's hand. Back then, their hands had fit together easily. Now it took two of her hands to hold one of his.

She shook the memory away. Thinking about the past was a waste of time. Her childhood friend was gone, replaced by a man who wouldn't know her when he woke up. How was she supposed to help him if he didn't remember her?

Chapter 32

Kieran woke up. A horrible spinning sensation made him want to go back to sleep. He tried to put his hand to his head to stop the dizziness, but someone held his hand. When he opened his eyes, a woman was sitting on his bed, working some kind of ointment into his palm. Why would a woman be in his bedroom?

A horrible thought crossed his mind. Had he gotten drunk and spent the night with a harlot? He didn't remember doing anything like that, but now that he concentrated, he couldn't remember anything at all.

When he tried to speak, his words came out in a whisper and made the woman jump back from the bed.

"You're awake."

"Where am I?" he finally managed.

"In King Rahnak's castle in Korisan."

Rahnak? Korisan? None of this sounded familiar.

"Do you know who you are?" she asked.

Kieran tried to sit up but the dizziness returned. He searched the darkest corners of his mind for any clue as to who he was, but nothing surfaced. "I'm afraid not," he said. "Do you know who I am?"

The woman sat on his bed and continued to rub the oil into his hand. The smell and the motion were soothing and made the dizziness subside.

"It depends on who you ask," she said, avoiding his eyes. "The Princess Delaine said you were Prince Aiden from Benalia, and that you're here to marry her."

"Marry the princess?"

The woman frowned. "But according to your cousin Gilrain and a man named Arathor, your name is Kieran, and you're the king of Teleria."

His stomach growled. "And how long have I been asleep?"

"Six days, my lord."

Kieran shook his head. This was too much to take in at once – princess, king, marriage, Teleria – the worst part was that none of it was familiar, except for the woman sitting next to him. She was probably seventeen or eighteen. Her blue dress and white apron were smudged and frayed. Her reddish-brown hair was pulled back into a braid, although some of it had escaped, giving her a girlish, unkempt look. He knew he'd seen her before, and just recently he thought. But if he had been asleep for six days, he knew that was impossible. Still, he had to ask.

"Have we met before?"

She stopped and put his hand down. Her eyes were wide, as if his question had caught her off guard. She started to speak, then paused and finally said, "The king bought me when I was eight. And I don't think you've ever been to Korisan before…"

"You seem very familiar."

She wiped her hands on her apron and busied herself with tidying the room. "Perhaps I remind you of someone."

He lifted his hand to rub his forehead – with great effort he noted – and frowned. "I suppose you're right. What's your name?"

"Jessa."

"Well Jessa, when can I get something to eat?"

"It's late sir, but I'll see what I can bring from the kitchen."

While he waited for Jessa to return, he looked around his quarters. The light from the black marble fireplace was dim, but he could still make out his surroundings. He lay in an overstuffed feather bed in one corner of the room. Near the fireplace, two blue sofas faced each other. A rectangular table sat between them. A gilded mirror and dressing screen stood in another corner, and plush blue carpet covered most of the black stone floor.

His stomach growled again, making him acutely aware of just how hungry he was. He couldn't be sure, but he didn't think he'd ever felt this hungry in his life. While he waited, he tried to get up, but the dizziness kept him in bed. He rubbed his stomach and his hand went up to his chest. He felt something hard and circular under his shirt.

There was a hand mirror on the dressing table across the room, but he knew he shouldn't attempt to retrieve it. He would have to wait until the servant came back to find out what it was. He dropped his head back onto the pillow and waited for her to return.

A few moments later, he heard the door to his room open. Jessa carried a small tray with a bowl and a mug.

"I've brought chicken broth," she said.

"I was hoping for something more."

"My lord, you haven't eaten in six days. Your stomach has to adjust to solid foods."

Kieran blew out a frustrated breath and motioned for her to put the tray near his bed. When he tried to feed himself, he spilled the whole spoonful on the quilt. Without speaking, Jessa sat on the bed, took the spoon, and started to feed him.

"This must be difficult for you," she said as she dabbed at his face with a napkin.

He swallowed. "I hate being helpless. And I hate not remembering."

She continued to feed him and frowned. "After all you've been through, you should be grateful to be alive and awake."

He tilted his head. "What have I been through?"

She stopped spooning and looked at him soberly. "You were bitten by a gurithent. When they brought you to the castle, the poison had spread so much that I didn't think I could help you."

He was about to ask her what a gurithent was, but decided he would rather not know.

She continued to feed him the soup, but after just a few more spoonfuls, his stomach started to protest.

"I think I've had enough for now," he said.

She put down the spoon and brought a cup to his lips.

"This drink tastes familiar," he said. "What is it?"

"A tea made from the cascabel flower," she said, putting the cup on the tray. "It will help you remember."

"Cascabel."

Jessa's eyes lit up. "Have you heard that word before?"

"I really don't know, and my head is starting to hurt."

Jessa stood and picked up the tray. "Will there be anything else?"

"Can you tell me what this is on my chest?" he asked, pointing to the spot.

She pulled a chain with a blue stone from inside her dress and showed it to him. "Arathor told me in a vision that these are Keldar stones. They must be for speaking over long distances. He said that you'd taken yours into your body."

He lifted his shirt to look, but still couldn't see it. Jessa's face turned pink. Then she walked across the room and brought back the hand mirror. In the glass he saw a round, silvery blue stone that had somehow become part of him.

When he touched it, he saw a boy, sitting in a huge oak tree, carving something into it. Then a young girl with dark hair and black eyes approached. Just as she was about to climb into the tree with him, several men tried to grab her. He shouted for her to run, but before he could help her, one of the men threw him to the ground while two others caught the girl. They bound her hands and threw her onto the back of a horse.

Jessa gasped and ran from the room.

Jessa flattened herself against the wall outside of Kieran's room. Her breath came in short gasps and her heart drummed in her throat. She slid down the wall and sat with her head on her knees.

She hadn't remembered the circumstances of her capture. Seeing it through Kieran's eyes had been overwhelming.

It had started out as a wonderful day, and it had ended as the worst day of her life, being ripped away from her family and her best friend. For ten years now, she'd lived as a slave in Rahnak's castle. Ten awful years.

How could she have seen it? Kieran had been awake, but he touched the stone, and at the same time, her stone warmed against her skin. Would this happen every time he touched his stone? And if she used hers, would he see her memories? She didn't know if she wanted him inside her head like that. It had been strange enough having Arathor there, but to have Kieran wandering through her mind –

The king's approach jolted her out of her thoughts.

"Come with me to my quarters," he said.

Not this. Jessa stood and muttered a quick, "Yes, your Majesty."

Rahnak had never called her to his chambers before. She hoped he just wanted to talk to her. If he wanted anything else, she was in no position to refuse, and she didn't think she could muster another vomiting incident.

"Arathor," she pleaded inwardly. "If only you could do something to stop this." All she heard was the frantic beating of her own heart.

A fire crackled in the great stone fireplace, casting bizarre shadows on the walls and furnishings. From somewhere in the room, the heady aroma of jasmine wafted towards the ceiling, making her nose wrinkle.

Rahnak gestured for her to sit on the satin divan in the center of the room. “You must know,” he said as he sat next to her, “you’re the loveliest woman I’ve ever seen.”

She swallowed hard and stared at her lap.

He moved close enough that she could feel his hot breath on her neck. His beard almost brushed against her face. “I especially love those black Baraca eyes of yours.”

Jessa pressed her hands against her chest to make contact with the Keldar stone. “Arathor, please help,” she murmured, shifting in her seat.

Rahnak’s eyes flashed in anger. “What did you say?”

“Nothing, my lord.”

“I thought I heard you say Arathor. Speaking his name is forbidden in this place.”

“Please forgive me. It won’t happen again.” She pressed her hand against her chest again. If Rahnak found the stone, who knew what he would do to her. She felt the stone warming against her hand and knew Arathor was with her. She knew he couldn’t protect her, but maybe he could still her mind so she could find a way of escape.

Just as Rahnak put his hand on hers, Jessa felt Arathor’s presence in her mind.

Please help me, she thought.

I’m right here, Jessara. Put your mind at rest. I’ll do what I can.

Jessa tried to slow her breathing and calm herself. But then Rahnak moved closer. “I have something important to tell you.”

“What?”

“I’m looking for a new queen.”

Jessa drew in a quick breath. “Sire, surely you aren’t considering me.”

He brushed his lips against her earlobe. “I’ve never wanted any woman like I want you.”

She pulled away and walked towards the door. “There are other women, more worthy of your attentions.”

He followed her. "No, Jessa. I want you. If you will give me an heir, I'll make you my queen."

A sudden lurching in her stomach caught Jessa off guard and she closed her eyes. *Please, Arathor*, she thought. *Do something.*

"You have a queen, Sire. And it's no secret she hates me. If she discovers your plans, she'll have me killed."

Rahnak raised his voice. "I'm the king. I can have any woman I want." As he kissed her neck, he whispered, "But I want you." He was starting to lower her sleeve from her shoulder when a page burst into the room.

Rahnak snapped his head around. "How dare you enter my chambers!"

The page dropped to the floor. "Please forgive me, your Majesty. There is something that requires your immediate attention."

The king exhaled loudly. He strode towards the door and then stopped. "You can leave, Jessa. I'll have to finish this later."

Jessa let out a long sigh of relief. It took her a moment to find the strength to move, but when she did, she flew from Rahnak's apartments, across the courtyard and into the servants' tower. In the dark, she stumbled over Sienna. Without apology, she lay down on her straw pallet, pulled the woolen blanket over her head, and closed her eyes, hoping she would be lucky enough to dream of absolutely nothing.

Chapter 33

What was the point of sleeping, Kieran wondered, if he didn't feel rested when he woke up? Once again, his sleep had been plagued with painful dreams. Now his heart wouldn't stop hammering. With all of his strength, he raised himself to a sitting position, only to have to lie down and let the dizziness pass before trying to stand.

He needed to relieve himself and couldn't wait around for Jessa or anyone else to help him. When he finally stood, the dizziness returned, and he thought he might black out. But he steadied himself and when the feeling passed, he inched his way across the room to find the garderobe.

By the time he returned to his bed, sweat poured from his face, arms, and chest. How long would it be before he could walk across the room without exhausting himself?

He lay back on the pillows and let his mind drift, trying to recall anything about his life. He looked down at his arms. There were small white scars on them, almost as if they'd been burned by tiny sparks. Both of his hands, although somewhat softened by Jessa's lanolin, were rough and calloused. What kind of a man had hands like this? Certainly not a king. They looked more like the hands of a tradesman, maybe a carpenter or a blacksmith.

As he looked once more at his arms, his hand traveled to the gurithent bite. The spot was still tender, and his arm hurt when he used it. As his hand went down his arm, he noticed something rough just below his shoulder. He craned his head around to look and was surprised to see a tattoo of a tree, ringed with braided roots and branches. And there was a small crown over the top of it.

So many mysteries. Maybe it was time to use the stone to speak with Arathor.

He put his hand over the stone and, for want of anything better to do, spoke the man's name out loud. He was surprised when he felt himself being pulled down a tunnel of light. At the end of the tunnel was a tall man with a weary face.

"Kieran," the man said.

"Arathor?"

"Yes."

"I have questions for you."

"Of course you do."

"Who are you?"

"I'm your father, and the former king of Teleria."

"And who am I?"

"You are Aiden, king of Teleria. But you're also Kieran, a blacksmith from Pent."

"None of this is familiar. The only thing I can remember is a name – Jessara."

The man smiled. "That's a good name to remember."

"Who is she?"

"She is your Eldala, the heart of your heart. Only she can help you remember." Arathor looked grave. "And you must remember soon. You have a task to complete, but you won't be able to do it if you stay in Korisan. Ciara has plans for you, and she must not succeed."

Kieran was about to ask what the plans were – until he heard the rustling of skirts. When he looked to see who was coming, the answers he'd just heard from Arathor left his mind and he couldn't think of one intelligent thing to say.

The woman was draped in red silk, the sleeves of her dress just resting on her porcelain shoulders. A scoop neckline and a long, silver necklace drew Kieran's eyes to places where he knew he really shouldn't be looking. Her perfectly placed hair tumbled over her shoulders and down her back in waves of black. Her green eyes seemed to bore right through him.

He could hardly catch his breath when she put her hand on his. "I'm so glad to see you're awake, Prince Aiden."

"Princess Delaine?" he asked when he'd found his voice again.

She smiled sweetly. "Yes, darling. Does this mean your memories have returned?"

"No, but Jessa told me about you."

The princess's face wrinkled in scorn. "Jessa was supposed to tell me when you woke up. That disobedient wretch will feel my wrath."

How could a woman so beautiful become so ugly in just a matter of seconds?

She looked at him again and her face softened. Still, there was something dark in her that Kieran couldn't put his finger on. But he would have to ponder this later because Delaine started stroking his beard and she seemed to enjoy it.

He was surprised when she said, "I've never really liked beards. I'll tell Jessa to shave it off."

And just as Delaine said her name, Jessa walked into the room. Delaine stood and slapped Jessa's cheek.

"That's for not telling me the prince was awake," Delaine growled.

Kieran flinched. Jessa's stepped back in surprise and then murmured her apology.

"Now, get the razor and shave off Prince Aiden's beard."

Jessa nodded and left. Delaine returned to Kieran's bedside and took his hand.

"I think you were too harsh with Jessa," he said.

Delaine laughed. "She's just a Baraca slave – and she deserved it."

When Jessa returned, her face was tight and weary. The princess stood, kissed Kieran's hand, and scowled at Jessa before she left.

Jessa laid a towel across Kieran's chest and started to sharpen the razor, muttering under her breath. It sounded like she said, "It's not right."

"What?"

"It was nothing, sir."

"Tell me what you said."

She stepped away, but Kieran had just enough strength to grab her arm and pull her back. "I want to know what you said."

Her face flushed. "I think you should decide what to do with your beard."

Kieran released her arm. "And what do *you* think I should do with it?"

"Me, sir? No one ever asks me what *I* think."

"Well, I'm asking you, as my personal attendant. Which would *you* prefer?"

And then he wished he hadn't asked because she looked uneasy and her eyes went to the floor.

"I'm sorry, I didn't mean to make you uncomfortable," he said.

When her chin came up and she looked at him, he saw a glimpse of something different in her black eyes, the woman she might have been if she wasn't a servant. "You'll think me forward."

"You've already been forward."

She closed her eyes and swallowed. "I think you look handsome just the way you are."

Then the resolve in her face was gone and she was just a servant again, avoiding his eyes. But her words had sent a flood of warmth through him. What had just happened?

"All right," he said, "just trim the beard and shave my neck."

After lathering up his neck, Jessa tipped his chin back and ran the razor across his skin, making it impossible to ignore her breath on his face or the rose scent surrounding her. Between the gentleness of her touch and her closeness, he wasn't surprised that his heartbeat quickened, and he became aware of feelings he didn't expect.

She was just a servant and he was a king. Besides, the woman he was supposed to marry was the most stunning woman he could remember. Why would he feel anything for a servant?

He swallowed hard and tried to distract himself with conversation. "You look tired."

She grimaced. "I didn't get much sleep last night."

"Neither did I."

"Why is that?"

"I had disturbing dreams."

Her eyes flicked up to his and then back to his neck. "Disturbing in what way?"

"The first one was like a vision I had yesterday, when I touched the stone."

Jessa drew in a quick breath. "What did you see?"

"Men capturing a girl in a forest."

She dropped the razor onto his chest and slumped onto the edge of his bed. There was pain in her eyes. "Did you recognize her?"

"I think she was a childhood friend. But then I saw her at a slave market. And I felt her shame and embarrassment when someone inspected her."

Now Jessa's breath came in short gasps, and her hand went to her mouth. As if by reflex, he put his hand on her cheek, then took it away when he realized he was being too familiar with a servant. "What is it, Jessa?"

She stood and wiped the lather from his face with a warm, damp cloth. "It's nothing, sir." When she took out the scissors to trim his beard, her face was expressionless.

After she finished, she held up the mirror and asked, "Would you like to see yourself?"

Kieran sat up and took the mirror from her. This was the first time he had looked into a mirror since waking up, and he hoped that looking at his own face would jog his memory. Unfortunately, a stranger stared back at him.

He ran his hand over the reddish-blond beard, the cheeks, the forehead. Nothing looked familiar except the black eyes, but not because they were his. They were the girl's eyes.

"So this is Kieran," he said, half to himself.

"Yes, my lord," Jessa murmured. "Will there be anything else before I have someone draw a bath for you?"

He put down the mirror and looked up at her. "Why did you run out of the room last night?" Her eyes widened in surprise and then she looked off to one side, apparently trying to avoid looking at him altogether. "And don't say it was nothing, Jessa. I know there was something wrong."

No one had ever unnerved Jessa like this, not even Rahnak. Now she just wanted to blend in with the furniture. But if she said nothing, she would be missing a chance to help Kieran remember something of his old life.

It wasn't like she expected him to remember her. Or maybe she did. She wasn't sure. What would she do if he did remember her? Or worse, what would she do if he didn't?

She walked around the room, absently rearranging pillows and straightening the furniture.

"You didn't answer my question," he said, surprising her with the commanding tone of his voice.

She sat on the couch facing his bed. "When you touched your Keldar stone yesterday, I saw what you saw."

And now she felt completely exposed and vulnerable, as if she had taken her heart out and handed it to him.

"Did you recognize her?" Kieran asked.

The urge to run was overpowering; only Arathor's words compelled her to stay. *"You must help my son."*

"It was me."

Kieran pulled himself up and sat on the edge of his bed. She felt his surprise and confusion. Could he feel her desire to run as far away from him as possible? If he did, he didn't show it. Instead, he tried to stand, and when he did, his legs buckled. She was at his side in a heartbeat and braced herself under his arm to help him back into bed.

He leaned on her for a moment, and when he looked into her eyes, it took all of her resolve to not melt right there. Before she could stop herself, her mind sent out the word "Eldala." He blinked, but said nothing about hearing it.

"You shouldn't try to walk by yourself," she said.

"I can't stay in bed forever. And I won't be coddled."

The harshness of his tone was like slap across her face, reminding her that he was a king and he didn't know her. The hope that had started to bloom drew itself back into a tight bud, and her heart told her he would never see her as anything but a servant.

Chapter 34

Getting work in the castle was the best news Gilrain had had in days. It was only last night that Sienna had come with word that she and Jessa would help rescue Kieran.

Now Gilrain stood in his cousin's lavishly furnished room, waiting for Marcus to come with Kieran's clothes. Kieran was in the bathtub, grumbling about the way everyone fussed over him. Gilrain could understand his frustration. It must have been maddening and embarrassing to have someone help you cross the room and then strip off your clothes and help you into a bathtub.

Despite what Jessa had said about Kieran's weakness, Gilrain was surprised at how weak he really looked. It was disheartening to see that his strong, self-sufficient cousin had to be helped. Kieran retained his large, muscular frame, but he was thin and haggard. All of his ribs showed, and there wasn't an ounce of fat on him. Was this the man who had bested him with a sword just a few weeks ago in practice?

The shock at seeing his condition had been almost as surprising as seeing Kieran's blank expression when Gilrain had introduced himself. It had been difficult for Gilrain to hide his dismay. He'd half-hoped that of all the people Kieran might remember, it would be him. Now he realized that with Kieran's physical weakness and buried memories, it would take longer to get him out of Korisan than they had hoped.

Kieran tipped his head back and let another servant wash his hair and back. Gilrain poured more hot water into the porcelain tub. While the steam billowed into the room, Marcus peered around the dressing screen, announcing that he had the first pieces of Kieran's new wardrobe. Kieran clenched his jaw, and Gilrain offered his arm to help Kieran get up, while the servant wrapped a towel around Kieran's waist.

Steadying himself, Kieran pushed away from Gilrain and slowly walked to one of the sofas. Just the effort of walking a few feet drained all of his energy and he collapsed, breathing heavily as he rested his head on the sofa's back.

"Forgive me, sir," said Marcus. "Not having the benefit of measuring you while you were awake, I can't guarantee that any of these clothes will fit, but I can measure you now, if you'd like."

Kieran scowled but agreed to stand so Marcus could take his measurements. After just a few seconds, his face was pale and beads of sweat formed on his face and chest. Gilrain moved to hold him up and Marcus hurried to finish. When he did, Kieran returned to the sofa and let Gilrain and Marcus dress him.

Gilrain laughed to himself. He'd never seen his cousin look so ridiculous. Kieran looked up at him and cocked a brow.

"Would you care to tell me what you find so amusing?" Kieran asked.

Gilrain cleared his throat and tried to think of something benign to say. All he could come up with was, "I'm sorry sir, it won't happen again."

Having two strangers bathe and dress him had been one of the most humiliating things Kieran could have possibly imagined. But if he were a king, or even a prince, wasn't that something he was accustomed to? Whether he was or not, it made him uncomfortable now, and once he regained any strength at all, he would insist on taking care of himself.

Marcus dismissed Gilrain and looked Kieran over carefully.

"Are these clothes to your liking, sir?"

Kieran made his way to the mirror and steadied himself with the back of a chair while he surveyed his reflection. Now he saw why Gilrain had laughed. The white silk shirt wore more ruffles than a woman's skirts, and the green satin vest was embroidered with leaves and flowers.

"It's too elaborate. Do you have anything more… simple?"

Marcus stood behind him, brushing the wrinkles out of Kieran's sleeves. "I'll make something more suited to your tastes today. But the princess will expect you to wear something like this to the banquet next week."

"Banquet?"

"I thought Jessa would have told you. The king and queen are holding a banquet to announce your betrothal to Princess Delaine. They've invited all of the lords and ladies of Teleria."

Suddenly Kieran felt his knees weaken, and he asked Marcus to help him back to the sofa. Why was he feeling so panicked about marrying Delaine? She was beautiful and charming. What man wouldn't want to marry her?

"Of course," said Marcus, lowering his voice, "you could tell them you're not going to marry Delaine."

"Why would I say that?"

"Because you shouldn't marry her."

Kieran drummed his fingers on the arm of the sofa. "Why?"

Marcus frowned and looked into his eyes. "It would help if you truly knew who you were. Have you remembered anything of your old life, sir?"

Kieran shook his head. "Just the name Jessara."

The tailor's brow furrowed. "Jessara?"

"Do you know the name?"

The tailor nodded.

"Where can I find her?"

Marcus folded his hands in his lap. "I'm sorry, sir, but she was an ancient queen. She's been dead for more than a hundred years."

Jessa and Sienna sat in the branches of a towering oak tree, almost as large as Kieran's Old Man of the Forest. How many hours had she and Sienna spent in this tree?

Jessa ran her hands over the rough bark and then stopped. The words she'd carved when she was nine had hardened and distorted over the years, but she knew what they said – "Jessara and Kieran."

She looked out over the garden as her hand ran over the spot again and again. Then she closed her eyes, feeling the warm sun on her face, a whisper of breeze playing on her skin. The aroma of fresh earth and lilacs wafted to her nose. This was her favorite place, and the one place where she could forget who she was.

"Jessa?"

Marcus stood beneath her, staring up at her with a fatherly scowl. "Come down and help me with something."

Jessa and Sienna slid from the tree and followed Marcus down a mossy stone pathway that lead to an ancient keep. The tall, round tower had only two windows and several slits at the top for archers. When Jessa had first seen it as a girl, it had been frightening, and she had imagined it was full of ghosts. Just last month she and Sienna had worked up the courage to finally unlock the door and go inside.

The heavy wooden door moved back slowly as the two women peered in. At this time of day, the keep lost it's menacing aura. Still, Jessa was glad Marcus was with them.

The lower floor housed the kitchen and a small dining area. Marcus had told her that the keep was sufficient for the first king and his small family. It had been his son who had started building the castle that Rahnak and Ciara now lived in.

Jessa ran her hands along the stone walls as they climbed up the spiral staircase to the top floor. How many people had climbed these stairs, and what were they like? she wondered.

When they reached the top, Jessa took in another deep breath and wrinkled her nose. The air was still and musty. She removed her shoes and stockings, and let her bare feet sink into a thick, cream carpet, edged with roses. The round room was at least ten paces across. Golden candelabrum covered in intricately worked vines were spaced every few feet on walls draped in pale blue velvet. Between each set of candles, someone had hung portraits as tall as Jessa.

Light streamed in through the round stained glass window above them. Jessa had seen other windows in the castle, usually depicting battles, but none were like this. At five feet across, the entire window was filled with red roses – one large rose in the middle, surrounded by smaller roses and trailing vines.

"Get a cloth and help me dust these," Marcus said, motioning towards the portraits.

Jessa had never paid attention to the portraits before, but now she felt the people looking down at her, not in an imperious way, but with solemn, noble faces. She stood on a padded bench beneath the portrait nearest the stairs and started to dust. Then she stopped.

A brown-haired, dark-eyed man looked back at her, piercing her soul. There was no way to forget that face. Without looking at the nameplate underneath the painting, she knew his name was Arathor. Seated in front of him was a woman with kind eyes and a winsome smile. Eventually, Jessa's eyes drifted to the bottom edge of the gilded frame. The gold nameplate said, "King Arathor and Queen Annalisa."

Jessa's heart felt like it had moved into her throat. She sat down on the bench and tried to catch her breath.

Sienna was the first to notice that Jessa had stopped working. When she looked at the painting, she put her hand over her mouth. "He looks just like Kieran."

"I know," Jessa said. "But that's his father, Arathor."

Now Marcus stood with them. "The resemblance is amazing."

"Yes it is," said Jessa.

"Did you know him?" asked Sienna.

"I did," said Marcus.

"Why did they leave?" asked Sienna.

Marcus sat next to Jessa. "When Arathor announced that the queen would have a son, Rahnak threatened to kill all of them. Their only hope for saving their son Aiden was to flee to Ilich Island."

Jessa turned to him. "And why didn't Ciara try to kill Kieran when he was a child?"

"Because he wasn't a threat to her before. Once he started to walk in his destiny, she knew she had to stop him."

"Why?" asked Sienna.

"When Rahnak took the throne, Ciara placed a curse over the kingdom. Aiden – Kieran – is the one person in Teleria who can stop her."

Suddenly the room had grown unbearably hot, and a frenzied sensation settled in Jessa's middle, like a hive of bees preparing to swarm. Now she saw Ciara's plan. If Kieran married Delaine…

It was as if fate had taken Jessa from her family and best friend, put her into a horrid life, and then said, "This is why you are here; you were made for this moment." It was something only she could do.

No, she couldn't do it. She wasn't brave enough.

Absently, she fingered the stone around her neck, and suddenly, in her mind, she stood next to Arathor.

"I can't do what you're asking," she said.

"You must be a resourceful woman, to have survived this long in Rahnak's castle."

"I can keep myself alive. I don't think I can do anything for your son."

"Make him notice you."

"Notice me? I've spent my life trying not to be noticed."

"You're a beautiful, intelligent woman. I'm sure you can find a way."

Jessa would admit she was intelligent, but beautiful? He must have been describing someone else. Delaine and Sienna were beautiful; Jessa was as plain as a daisy. How could she get Kieran to notice her with an exquisite rose like Delaine around?

"You can't afford to be timid now," said Arathor. "I'm depending on you to help my son."

"And if I don't?"

"Then Teleria remains enslaved to Ciara and her curse."

Jessa screwed her eyes shut and clenched her fists. It wasn't fair. She hadn't asked for this. Why did the fate of Teleria rest on her?

As if sensing her doubts, Arathor touched her shoulder and said, "Jessara, this is what will happen if you don't help him."

She saw everyone she loved bound in chains and working in Rahnak's gold mine. It made Jessa drop to her knees, and it felt like the hive of bees in her stomach was ready to explode into the room.

Whether she wanted to admit it or not, it was clear that the fate of the kingdom *did* rest on her. If Kieran succumbed to Ciara and Delaine's treachery, it would mean death for him and Jessa and all of Teleria. Whether he remembered her or not, she had to rescue him. She had to help Kieran remember.

Suddenly, a cry from Sienna jolted her out of her trance.

Jessa blinked and looked at Sienna. Her friend stood under one of the portraits, staring at it as if she had seen a ghost. Jessa moved next to her. The man and woman in the painting had the most regal bearing of all the couples.

"She could be you," Sienna whispered.

"And look at the names," said Marcus. "King Alardin and Queen Jessara."

"Why would a Telerian queen have your name, or your face?" Sienna asked.

"She wasn't just a Telerian queen."

Sienna's eyebrows flew up. "What do you mean?"

"She was Baraca, and the first female Malazia. When my parents gave me her name, they never told me she'd married the first Telerian king."

Marcus peered over his spectacles at her. "When Kieran mentioned that he remembered the name Jessara, I told him she was an ancient queen. But that wouldn't explain why he knows the name, would it?"

"I'm the Jessara he remembers."

"Why Jessa?" he asked.

"Because I'm the heart of his heart."

"You mean his Eldala?" Sienna asked.

Jessa nodded.

"I've heard of that. I just didn't think it was possible."

"I didn't know we shared Eldala until Arathor told me," said Jessa.

"Why haven't you told Kieran?" asked Marcus.

She looked at her hands, resting in her lap. How could she admit this to anyone, especially to Marcus?

"Jessa," said Sienna, "you have to tell him."

Jessa looked up at Sienna, then at Marcus. "I'm afraid he won't believe me."

Chapter 35

Kieran smiled in his sleep. The girl from the forest was a woman now and she was dancing alone. When she tipped her head back, her hair almost touched the ground. A circle of gold crowned her head and her blue satin dress flowed over her like wine. Her arms moved to a song Kieran couldn't hear. When she looked at him, she locked her black eyes onto his and wouldn't let go. He was welded into place, waiting for her to come to him. When she finally reached him, he started to breathe, and when she took his hand, they moved together in a glorious dance.

Unlike any of the other dreams, he felt the delicate skin of her hand in his, smelled the scent of roses in her hair, and heard her melodic laughter. Her eyes sparkled, and her engaging smile made him want to stay with her.

Then he woke up and realized it had been a dream and nothing more.

And why was he dreaming about Jessa?

He walked to the window and pressed his head against the glass, growling his frustration through his teeth. Here he was stuck in his room because he was too weak to get out. If only he could leave his room and walk around.

Fatigue threatened to overwhelm him, but he gripped the window frame and clenched his jaw until it passed. As he stood there, he thought about the frustrating day he'd had yesterday.

It had been difficult enough to hear from Marcus that Jessara was a dead queen, but then Delaine had come to visit him. From the moment she walked in, wearing a green satin dress and a gold chain that drew his eyes to her plunging neckline, everything Marcus and Arathor had warned him about dissolved into nothing. When he asked her about their betrothal, she swore that he was Prince Aiden of Benalia, and that their parents had betrothed her to him from the moment of her birth.

Kieran slammed his hand against the wall and swore out loud. What was he supposed to do? How could he reconcile the two stories? Either he was the king of Teleria or the prince of Benalia. Who could tell him the truth?

Of the people he knew, Jessa and Gilrain seemed to be the most trustworthy. And they seemed to have the least to gain by lying to him. He would have to speak with them as soon as possible.

A knock at the door startled him. He motioned for a page to open the door, and in waltzed the princess. Why did she keep wearing these dresses that made him want to take her to bed? He slowly made his way across the room and collapsed into the sofa. She sat across from him and clapped her hands for the servants. Kieran was surprised when Jessa and Gilrain entered with platters of food.

"I thought we could eat breakfast together," she said, flashing that sultry smile that made it clear she had one thing on her mind.

Jessa and Gilrain put the platters on the table between the sofas and Jessa flicked a glance at Kieran before moving to one side with her hands behind her back.

"Serve us the first course," Delaine said.

Gilrain poured apple cider into golden goblets and set the food in front of them. Kieran took a sip. A tingling sensation filled his throat. When he looked up, the room seemed darker. He put the cup down and started the first course, some kind of exotic fruit, he supposed.

When Jessa cleared away the dishes, her braid trailed across his hand. Their eyes met for one brief moment, and he heard the word, "Jessara." Then she looked away.

He looked back at Delaine. Her jaw was clenched and her eyes brimmed with rage. "If you're going to be my husband, you can't be paying attention to the servants."

Kieran nearly choked; Jessa's face went white.

"Of course, Delaine. I don't know what I was thinking."

Then Delaine laughed. "I'm almost beginning to think Jessa has her eye on you."

Immediately, Jessa's eyes went to the floor and her cheeks turned bright pink. The princess continued. "Although, really, I don't know why Jessa would think she'd catch anyone's eye. She's as plain as dirt."

Once again Kieran was surprised by the sharpness of Delaine's tone. How could such a beautiful woman be so unkind.? He looked over to see Jessa's reaction, but her face was tight and drawn, as if she were determined to not let Delaine's comments bother her.

The meal continued, with Delaine complimenting Kieran on his clothing, his eyes, his physique… Kieran found it more than a little uncomfortable. Then she turned the conversation towards the wedding.

"Father said we can be married in two weeks. He's already sent out the invitations to the nobles."

"In two weeks?"

"I was hoping we could be married the day after the banquet," she said, exhaling a dramatic sigh, "but he insisted there are too many preparations to make, and it will take two weeks to get everything ready." She walked around the table and sat next to him. "Just think, Aiden. Not long from now we'll be married."

She nibbled on his ear and worked her lips to his jaw and then his chin. The greater part of him wanted her to continue, despite his uncertainty about being her betrothed.

A crash brought him back to his senses. He looked down to see Jessa scooping the broken dishes off the floor. "I'm sorry, your Highness," she whispered.

"Get out of here, both of you," Delaine shrieked.

Kieran noted the sudden change. Did he want to marry someone this unpredictable? Suddenly, he didn't want her in the room.

"I'm tired," he said. "Maybe you could come back later."

For a moment, he thought Delaine would fly into a rage right there, but she controlled herself and smiled sweetly at him. "As you wish."

As Jessa and Gilrain moved towards the door, Jessa gave Kieran a quick glance. Kieran motioned for them to come back.

Jessa breathed a sigh of relief. Dropping the dishes had been a desperate act, one that could have resulted in severe punishment. But when Jessa realized that Kieran couldn't resist Delaine's advances, the only thing she could think to do was drop the dishes. Thankfully, the distraction had worked; now Delaine was gone, and Kieran was inviting Jessa and Gilrain to stay.

"Have either of you eaten yet today?" Kieran asked.

"No, sir," they both murmured.

"Then help me finish this. I still can't eat as much as I'd like."

"Then you're not tired?" Jessa asked.

He flashed her a mischievous smile. "I need to talk with both of you, without the princess here."

Jessa had seen that smile before – on her best friend's ten-year-old face. Would that best friend remember her?

While they ate, Kieran continued to look at her. As much as she understood that she had to get his attention, now that she had it, he was making her terribly self-conscious. All she wanted was to disappear.

"Forgive me, sir,' she said, "but will you be needing anything else?"

He rubbed his temples. "Can you do something for this headache?"

Jessa moved behind him and started to move her fingers over his left shoulder, working out the tension in an easy, rhythmic motion. While she did, their song crept into her mind and stirred up dangerous images of a life she would probably never have with him.

He turned around to look at her, and her heart quickened, wondering if he could sense what she felt. She gently pushed his head forward and worked her fingers up and down his neck, trying to still the rising melody. By the time she started massaging his right shoulder, the song escaped from her lips and she found herself humming it.

"What's that song?" he asked. "I think I've heard it before."

"A song I used to dance to."

"I like hearing it," he said, and began to hum with her. Then he turned to Gilrain. "Do I know you?"

Gilrain's brows wrinkled for a moment and then he gave Kieran an odd little grin. "I'm your cousin."

Kieran's shoulders tensed for a moment. "My cousin?"

"We grew up together, first near Ithil, and then in Pent."

Kieran motioned for Jessa to stop. She wasn't sure what to do with herself, then decided it would be best to move away from the men to give them a little more privacy. But rather than leaving, she sat in the chair near the dressing table so she could see Kieran's face.

For the next hour, Gilrain had Kieran's – and Jessa's – rapt attention as he told Kieran the details of his life: Arathor's taking him to Kale and Elisa to raise; the trouble he and Gilrain got into time and time again; the circumstances of how he discovered he was a prince;

his meeting Arathor and accepting that he was the new king; his taking the Hada tattoo and the stone; and how he'd been captured.

Kieran nodded politely through the entire story and asked a few questions, but he showed no sign that the stories were familiar. All Jessa sensed from him was a growing frustration at not remembering, as if he were listening to the details of a stranger's life.

Arathor, what can we do?

Tell him who you are.

What if he doesn't believe me?

Show him the sea shell.

As much as Kieran wanted to hear Gilrain's story, he couldn't help but watch Jessa. When she walked across the room, his eyes followed her, noticing the way her braid swished across her back, the slight swaying of her hips…

And once again, he wondered why he would watch her when he was betrothed to Delaine.

Kieran turned back to Gilrain and tried to concentrate on his tale. The longer he listened, the more frustrated he became. Finally, he dismissed him and promised they would talk later. Now he wanted to know what Jessa was doing in her room. With great effort, he pushed himself up from the sofa and slowly made his way towards her door.

She was sitting on her bed with her back to him, looking at something in her hand. Whatever it was had her full attention, because he had to clear his throat twice before she turned around. She stood so quickly that she dropped the object and let out a cry. Immediately she went to the floor to look for it. Kieran knelt to help her.

"I didn't mean to startle you," he said.

She continued looking around the floor. "I have to find it."

"What?"

She moved closer and bumped into him. And then moved away. "I'm sorry," she whispered.

The two Keldar stones flared, illuminating the room with their blue light. For a moment their eyes locked, and it was as if he was looking past those black pools into her soul. He didn't know her at all, and yet being in her heart stirred up a longing in him to connect more deeply with her.

When she tore her eyes away the connection was gone.

They continued to search – Jessa in one corner and Kieran in another – until his hand came across something small and hard. When he looked at it, he was stunned. It was pink and purple, with silver streaks threaded through it. And he knew that it had once been his.

"Where did you get this?" he asked, still kneeling on the floor.

She tried to snatch it from his hand but he closed his fingers around it. She seemed desperate to have it and with both hands tried to pry his hand open. He was surprised at her strength and had to tighten his grip on it.

"Please, sir, let me have it."

"Tell me where you got it first, Jessa."

She tried to lift one of his fingers, but he was too strong for her and she sighed in resignation. She sat back on her knees and dropped her hands in her lap. "My Eldala gave it to me, when I was eight."

"Your Eldala?"

She looked up at him and he felt the longing in her reach out to the longing in him. "You, Kieran. You gave it to me in Ithil."

Chapter 36

There. She'd said it. Now she had to resist the familiar urge to run away. It was only the surprise in his face that made her stay. He looked at her and then stared at the shell, running his fingers over it. It made her think of a young boy discovering some long buried treasure.

"I remember," he said.

Finally, she thought.

"I remember picking it up on the beach with my father. And I remember giving it to Jessara." He looked up at her and furrowed his brow. "You're Jessara?"

She pressed her fingers to her mouth, feeling the tears well up in her eyes. She couldn't cry now. It would be awful to have him see her show any fondness for him and not have it returned.

She fought her tears and nodded. "Yes, Kieran. I'm Jessara."

"Tell me more."

Her eyes widened at the unexpected request. "Not here," she said.

By the time Jessa and Kieran reached the garden, Kieran was breathing hard and his shirt was drenched with sweat. Still, Jessa was surprised at how much stronger he was only one day after waking up. In her experience, people who had stayed in bed as long as Kieran took days to regain any strength at all.

Kieran leaned against the gate and wiped the sweat from his brow. After a few minutes, Jessa turned the key in the lock, feeling the familiar grating of the tumblers, and the gate's resistance on the stone path behind it. Kieran slowly followed Jessa through the gate and looked around.

"Did you do all this?" he asked.

It had taken all of her courage to bring him to her private retreat and now that she stood here with him, she felt naked and vulnerable. But maybe telling him about the garden would help him see her heart. She had to take the risk.

"Marcus called this 'The Queen's Garden.' He gave me the key when I was ten. I think Alardin's queen planted the first flowers."

"It's beautiful."

Jessa laughed. "It wasn't like this when he brought me here."

"What was it like?"

This was a surprise. Jessa hadn't expected Kieran to show any interest in the garden. Gathering more courage, Jessa took his hand and led him to the tree. Her fingers felt small and safe inside of his. It was just like holding hands with him when they were children.

"No one had taken care of it for years – not since Queen Annalisa, I imagine." And when she said "Annalisa," she looked to see if Kieran remembered the name. All she sensed from him was mild curiosity.

"So Sienna and I started pulling weeds and watering the flowers. It took two years, but it was worth the effort. This is my favorite place."

"You should be proud of your work. It's lovely."

Jessa felt herself blushing. It was the first compliment Kieran had given her. Would he ever see *her* as lovely?

"There's something else I want to show you," she said.

When they reached the oak tree, Kieran had to catch his breath again, giving Jessa the perfect chance to climb up before Kieran could follow. When she sat, she saw him standing there, looking up at her in an amused sort of way, his black eyes flashing in that striking face, the red and gold in his beard highlighted by the sun.

After a moment, he climbed up and sat next to her. And then he saw it – the names she'd carved into the tree. He ran his hand over them and closed his eyes. "I carved something like this once."

Her stomach fluttered.

He looked up at her. "I lost you once, didn't I?"

She fiddled with the end of her braid, debating how much more to tell him. How much did he need to know in order to remember his old life?

"Yes. That's what you saw in your vision."

He tipped his head back against the trunk, exhaling slowly.

"But that doesn't matter now, Kieran. Ciara is trying to keep you here so you can't reclaim your kingdom."

His head came up and he looked at her sourly. "Keep me here? How can she keep me here?"

"If you marry Delaine, Ciara keeps Teleria."

He shook his head. "Maybe I can marry Delaine and get the kingdom back that way."

Jessa couldn't have been any more surprised if he'd pushed her out of the tree. "Are you saying you *want* to marry her?"

"She's beautiful and charming – and I think I'm in love with her."

A cold wave of shock and despair hit Jessa, forcing the breath out of her. Her arms and legs went wobbly and she thought she might fall. Just before she did, Kieran caught her elbow. She wrenched herself free and scrambled down the tree.

As she ran deeper into the garden, she wondered if Delaine had been giving Kieran delendia ever since he'd woken up. It was a powerful aphrodisiac with no antidote. If that were true, it was too late.

Why is that girl always running off? Kieran wondered. He supposed he should go after her, although why, he didn't know. He was going to marry the most charming woman in Teleria. Why would he care about Jessa?

But there had been a brief connection between them in her quarters. And there was something sweet and familiar about holding her hand.

Just as he climbed down to follow her, he heard someone approaching. He turned around and saw Gilrain and Sienna walking down the path. They appeared to be as surprised to see him as he was to see them.

Gilrain called out to him, "How did you get in here?"

"Jessa brought me."

"Where is she?" Sienna asked.

"She just ran off. I don't know where she went." He walked beside them. "Why are you here?"

"Sienna wanted to show me the paintings in the keep."

Having nothing else to do, and not wanting to return to his quarters, Kieran asked if he could join them. Gilrain smiled and nodded.

After entering the keep, they followed Sienna up the winding stairs. When they reached the top, they stood in a round room. The floor was covered in thick, cream-colored carpet, and several portraits adorned the walls. Kieran looked at the first one and froze.

Here was the man who claimed to be his father. He wasn't just familiar because Kieran had seen him in the vision; he was familiar because in this portrait, except for the brown hair, Kieran could have been looking into a mirror.

"That's certainly Arathor," said Gilrain.

Shock and fatigue made Kieran sink into the seat just under the portrait. When Arathor had made his claim, Kieran was hesitant to believe him. The portrait removed the last shreds of doubt.

After a few minutes, he stood and looked at the other portraits, obviously of his ancestors. He moved slowly, looking at each king, moving back in time – Duncan, Aeron, Egron, Jendric, Dalamar, and Alardin.

The names seemed vaguely familiar.

When he looked at Alardin's portrait, he was astonished when he saw Alardin's queen. As much as Arathor was a reflection of Kieran, this queen was a reflection of Jessa.

She was stunningly beautiful and looked down on him with the Jessa's piercing eyes. How could this Jessara be so beautiful and Jessa be so plain?

Sienna drew his attention back to his surroundings. "Sir, I almost forgot. The princess is looking for you. She said she wants you to take your evening meal in her room."

When Kieran reached his quarters, Gilrain was waiting for him. Kieran's legs shook with exhaustion, but he insisted he didn't need Gilrain's help to undress or get into the tub. Gilrain excused himself, and Kieran eased himself into the bathtub, waiting for the scalding water to take the stiffness out of his fatigued muscles.

He put his head back and let his mind drift over what he'd seen in the tower. There was no denying he was Arathor's son. Did that mean he had to give up Delaine and leave Korisan?

According to Jessa, Marcus, and Arathor it did.

He stayed in the bathtub for a few more minutes and then dressed in the newest clothes Marcus had brought – a simple white linen shirt and close-fitting breeches – a vast improvement from what the tailor had first brought him. After pulling on his boots, he made his way to Delaine's apartments.

Two doormen opened double doors that were three times Kieran's height. He stepped into the room, taking note of the stained-glass windows filling one wall, the plush scarlet carpeting, the low blue sofas with their black satin pillows, and the candles in their golden stands, casting a drowsy glow over the room. A flowery scent permeated the air.

A swishing of skirts made him turn around. Again the princess took his breath away. This time a deep purple dress revealed more of a woman than a man should see – unless the man was her husband. But then Kieran practically *was* her husband. Why not let his eyes rove freely over his future bride?

"Good evening, my lady" he said, trying to find his voice.

"You're looking tired," she purred. "Perhaps you should lie down."

He swallowed hard. "I thought we were going to eat."

"The food can wait, don't you think?" she said, grazing her fingertips across his cheek.

Heat sizzled through him and he saw the same fire in her eyes. When he followed her gaze toward the bed in the corner of the room, it roused a host of wild thoughts. Maybe he would follow and let her do what she intended.

Ciara has plans for you, and she must not succeed.

Where had that come from?

She's trying to keep you here so you can't get back your kingdom.

Jessa! What *was* that woman doing in his head? Whatever it was, she'd ruined the moment, and he realized just how exhausted he was. "I'm sorry, Delaine, but you were right. I am tired."

Her face tightened. "Are you saying you don't want me?"

"No, but I should go. It's been a long day."

"Then just have some of this wine, to help you sleep."

Why not? he thought. Maybe it would help him sleep. He took the cup from her, but before he could drink, Jessa's voice was back.

You can't let Ciara win.

Just before he left, Delaine rubbed her thumb over the back of his hand, and a slight tingling raced up his arm.

The fatigue of sending her thoughts to Kieran sent Jessa to her bed. She hoped the effort was worth it. She was just drifting off when she heard his door open and close. She threw off her blanket and peered through her partially open door to see if it was him. Her breath caught in her throat.

If he was magnificent when he was sleeping, it was nothing compared to the way he looked when he was awake and moving. Just the simple motion of lifting his shirt over his head made his muscles ripple. She knew she should look away, but a familiar rush of song tumbled through her, and her eyes wouldn't obey.

When he turned around and looked towards her door, she thought she would die of embarrassment. Instead of the reprimand she expected, he looked pleased to see her watching him. Her stomach fluttered and she quickly closed the door, pressing herself against it, half hoping he would ask to come in. When he knocked, she jumped and opened the door.

He was still half-clothed and stood in her doorway. It was all she could do to breathe and not let her eyes wander over his torso – but again it was impossible. She just wished that looking wouldn't stir up those all-too-easy thoughts about sharing a life with him. She turned away and sank into her bed.

"I'm sorry," she finally managed. "I shouldn't have…"

He moved closer. "Was that you in my thoughts?"

"You can't marry Delaine," she burst out. "You'll never do what you're supposed to do if you stay here."

His expression went from one of annoyance to one of disbelief, as if she were speaking a completely different language. "What are you talking about?"

She crossed her arms and frowned. "Ask Arathor."

Chapter 37

Jessa still didn't know whether she was relieved or angry. On the night when she'd told Kieran to talk to Arathor, he ordered her to go back to the servants' tower. Too shocked to say anything, she quickly gathered her few belongings and hurried back to her own quarters.

It was just as well she had told herself – again and again. Waiting for him to return from his trysts with Delaine would have been torture.

Still, she hadn't seen Kieran for several days, and although it was easier not to see him, she found herself missing him. She tried to convince herself that it was only because she'd spent so much time with him, nursing him back to health. She only half-believed it. In her most desperate moments, she found herself sending thoughts his way.

He never answered.

Whatever she knew of Kieran's actions, she now heard from Gilrain. The reports weren't encouraging: Delaine was making more advances and Kieran was becoming more agreeable to everything she said. Jessa knew it had to be the delendia, but at this point, it was too late. Kieran had made his choice and it would take more than her pleading or sending thoughts to him to change his mind.

Tomorrow the king and queen would hold the betrothal banquet, announcing to Teleria's nobility that Delaine was to wed Prince Aiden of Benalia. And Kieran was doing nothing to stop them. It appeared he had dismissed all the evidence regarding his ties to Arathor, being content to be Delaine's prince.

The soft cooing of doves brought Jessa's night of tossing and turning to an end. On any other morning, she would have enjoyed listening to them, but today they heralded the beginning of a day Jessa would rather not face.

She rolled over and pulled the blanket over her head.

Elath poked at her. "The king wants you."

Can this day get any worse? she wondered. Grumbling under her breath, Jessa went to find the king.

When she reached the throne room, King Rahnak sat on his throne, drumming his fingers on his knees. His mouth curved into a leering smile when he saw Jessa. She started to curtsy, but he grabbed her wrist and pulled her closer.

"Have you considered my request?"

"You flatter me, Majesty. But I cannot be your queen. I value my life too much to take Ciara's place."

His smile turned to a tight line. "Are you implying that I can't protect you from Ciara?"

"Majesty, I…."

Rahnak looked as if he would strike her, but he stopped and stroked her cheek instead. "I have decided to be merciful. I will give you one day to make your choice."

He walked to a side table and took something out of a long, velvet bag.

"You will do three things for me today." He returned and drew a sword from a scabbard. "I will present this sword to Prince Aiden tonight at the banquet. See that Bairn cleans it up." Then he brought her another velvet bag and said, "You will wear this when you serve at the banquet today. And you will sing for my guests."

Try as she might, Jessa couldn't contain the anxiety she felt at his orders and a muffled cry escaped her lips. "Please, Sire. Don't make me do this."

His tone was indignant when he spoke. "You would plead with me? Jessa, this is my command. You will sing for me tonight. And you will wear your hair down."

By the time Jessa found Bairn, she'd subdued her anger enough that she thought no one would notice her frustration. But when she entered the smithy, Bairn looked concerned.

"What is it, Jessa?"

She laid the sword on the table and sat in the chair near the door. "I don't know how this day can get any worse."

Bairn pulled up a chair next to her. Besides Sienna, he was the one person who took the time to listen to her. Putting his hand on her shoulder, he said, "Tell me."

So there in the smithy, she poured out her heart to the man who was most like a father to her. She told him about Arathor and Gilrain's urgent requests to help Kieran remember, her heart connection to Kieran, Rahnak's advances, and his recent request to have her sing, with her hair down.

The last statement seemed to shock Bairn the most. "Jessa, you know our Baraca customs."

How well Jessa did know them. Her mother had drummed into her since early childhood that a Baraca woman only wore her hair down for her husband. If she wore it down tonight, it wouldn't be a simple act of betraying her heritage. It would be considered immoral.

"What choice do I have?" Jessa asked. "If I disobey the king, he could have me beaten… or executed."

And now the prospect of being executed didn't sound so bad. It would be better than watching Kieran marry Delaine and serving the new king and queen.

Bairn looked thoughtful and gave her a thin smile. "You're right. You'll have to go against tradition to stay alive. And perhaps you can use the song to your advantage."

She frowned in confusion.

"Sing to Kieran."

After leaving the sword with Bairn, Jessa returned to her room only to find that Rahnak had arranged for her to take a bath in another of the guest rooms. Now Jessa was submerged up to her neck in steaming water. The liquid heat was enough to calm her mind and make her think about what she had to do tonight.

It was a joy to sing – but only for herself. The more she thought about it Bairn's suggestion, though, the more it made sense. If she had to expose herself by singing, she might as well try to reach Kieran's heart one last time.

Marcus stepped back and stroked his chin. "What do you think?"
Kieran turned and surveyed his reflection. The intricately embroidered white satin coat and knee-length breeches, the white vest with gold buttons, the silk shirt with ruffled cuffs – yes, they were just what Delaine would like.

Three nights in a row, Delaine had invited him to her room, and each night he would come closer to letting her take him to her bed. But each time, something Arathor or Gilrain or Jessa had told him interrupted his thoughts, and despite the way his strength was returning, he would find himself completely exhausted and had to excuse himself.

Tonight he wouldn't let that happen. Delaine had made it clear she had something special planned for him, and it was all he could do to concentrate on Marcus's instructions regarding the banquet.

Kieran stood with Marcus in the courtyard, waiting for the lords and ladies to enter the hall. He tugged at his collar, appreciating Marcus's fine work; he couldn't remember seeing so many overdressed men and women in his life.

A footman called out the names of the guests before they disappeared into a vast room. "Lord Gemlek and Lady Tillia of Agora. Lord Nebron and Lady Seeka of Trevet."

The procession continued, and rather than listen to each name, Kieran let his mind wander – until the herald called out, "Lord Destra and Lady Gelda of Pent."

Kieran turned to see Lord Destra. The man's flaming red hair was loosely tucked under a green satin hat, and his short, stocky figure was stuffed into a blue coat and breeches.

Where have I seen him before? Kieran wondered.

He had no time to think about it. Delaine brushed up against him and held out her hand. Tonight she wore a clinging black dress that drew Kieran's attention to every seductive curve. Taking a deep breath, Kieran put his hand under hers and escorted her into the great hall. As they entered the room, Kieran heard the scraping of chairs across the stone floor as the lords and ladies stood to honor them. Kieran nodded his approval.

Candelabrum, placed every few feet, cast a warm glow over the room. More hung down from the arched ceiling that towered above their heads. Three fireplaces blazed with heat along the wall opposite the door. Yellow and green silk banners, intertwined with ivy garlands, hung from the gray stone walls. A dozen long tables, covered in white linen cloths, draped with more garland and laden with fruit and vegetable topiaries, filled the main floor of the hall.

Delaine steered them towards a table that sat on a raised platform just below the high table.

Trumpets blared, drawing Kieran's attention to the far end of the room. The herald cried out, "King Rahnak and Queen Ciara of Teleria."

A black-haired man of medium build walked towards Kieran and nodded his acknowledgement. His red, fur-lined robe trailed behind him and his gold crown reflected the candle light. The tall, severe-looking woman Rahnak escorted wore her silver hair in tight coils on either side of her head. The train of her black dress brushed against Kieran's boots when she went past him. Delaine lowered her head and Kieran did the same. The queen barely regarded either of them.

When the guests were seated, Kieran's attention turned to Delaine, who was stroking the inside of his thigh under the table. He leaned over to kiss her cheek. "You look ravishing tonight," he whispered.

A servant set the first course of fish pie before him. Kieran picked up the fork and stabbed at it, hardly able to eat.

Delaine laughed. "I can see your mind is somewhere else."

Kieran smiled. "Is it that obvious?"

"You really should eat. You'll need your strength."

And so the evening proceeded. Course after course, Kieran ate foods he was sure he'd never seen before. Between each course, servants brought in tables bearing more food. From time to time, Rahnak or Ciara signaled, and various entertainers made their way to the center of the room to the delight of the guests. Fire eaters, sword swallowers, dancers – Kieran was astonished at how many different forms of entertainment there were. But he found it difficult to enjoy any of it, seeing it only as a way to postpone his night with Delaine.

Every once in awhile, for reasons he couldn't explain, he looked around for Jessa. Once he thought he caught a glimpse of her, but realized it couldn't be her. The woman's hair wasn't in Jessa's customary braid and the dress she wore showed much more skin than Jessa would ever show.

When the stream of food stopped, and the guests had finished sopping up the last drops of gravy from their plates, a footman clapped his hands, and the servants cleared the dishes and swept the floors. Jugglers and acrobats filled the hall with their wild antics and daring moves. Minstrels followed the acrobats, singing tales of love and battle. Kieran drummed his fingers on the table.

"Bored, my love?"

"Distracted."

"Be patient. My father has something to give you before we retire for the evening."

After the entertainers left the floor, the king stood and the room went silent.

"Lords and ladies, honored guests. Welcome to Korisan. It gives me great pleasure to announce the marriage of my daughter Delaine to Prince Aiden of Benalia."

Delaine grabbed Kieran's arm and pulled him up to stand. The room thundered with applause.

"As a wedding gift, I wish to present this sword to Prince Aiden."

A sea of voices murmured approval.

Kieran took a step towards the table, but stopped as he saw a page coming to him. The page bowed and presented the sword. Kieran nodded his thanks to the king. When he drew the sword from its gold scabbard, he was stunned. There was something engraved on it.

"When the line of kings is broken, and an evil ruler takes the throne, a child will arise to end her reign; a child will arise to break her curse."

Kieran dropped into his chair and closed his eyes. A stream of images ran through his head: the letter and the sword, meeting Arathor in Koridoc, being declared the king of Teleria, and the gurithent attack.

"Are you all right?" Delaine asked.

He blinked and looked at her. Suddenly, he sensed the evil pouring out of her. "Yes, Delaine, for the first time in days I'm feeling like myself."

He stood up and looked at the king and queen, raising his goblet in a final toast. "Thank you for your hospitality, but it's time for me to leave."

Then he drained the cup - and realized that he shouldn't have. The room went dark for a moment and everything around him seemed to spin.

Delaine grabbed his hand. "You can't leave yet."

He felt the hair on the back of his neck rise. He meant to tell Delaine "No thank you," but his voice wouldn't obey. The feeling was frighteningly familiar, like it had happened before… in Felonia.

Delaine pushed him into his chair. The king clapped his hands, and a woman entered the hall. Delaine gasped. Kieran would have gasped, but couldn't find any breath left in him.

Jessa stood in the center of the room.

Her unbound hair fell past her hips, held away from her face by a gold head piece. A low-cut purple bodice trimmed with gold fringe was all that covered her chest, leaving her middle bare. The tight-fitting skirt hung well below her navel. A belt of gold coins shimmered on her waist.

She lifted her eyes and let them rest only on him. How could he have not noticed how beautiful she was?

As much as the dress had his attention, her song had him mesmerized. It started softly, and as her courage built, her voice grew strong and clear. It was the most beautiful, soul-stirring song he could remember hearing. It told the story of a people who had long been persecuted by an evil enchantress, and a man named Kieran who left his family and home to search for a hero to save them.

When the song ended, tears streamed down Jessa's face. She bowed her head and silently left the room. Everything in Kieran wanted to follow her, but Delaine took his hand and led him across the courtyard and into her chambers.

Chapter 38

Jessa ran towards the servants' tower, then stopped. If Rahnak was looking for her, this would be the first place he would come. It would be better to hide in Kieran's room. She quietly slipped past the door and threw herself across the bed, lamenting that everything she'd done for the past week had come to nothing.

When she'd held Kieran's gaze during her song, she thought he truly saw her. But instead of following her, he was paralyzed, probably by the delendia. Now she had to endure the knowledge that Kieran and Delaine were...

No. She couldn't think about it.

She rolled over and was pulling the quilt over her shoulders when she heard the door opening, a chair falling over, and someone calling her name. She sat up and turned around. Rahnak was charging towards her, just drunk enough to be dangerous. She jumped up and tried to move towards the door, but he grabbed her arm and threw her to the bed.

"If you struggle, it will just make it harder."

He climbed on top of her. Jessa pushed him away and rolled out from under him. He grabbed her arm and pulled her back. She tried to break free, but his grip was too tight.

"Let me go," she screamed.

"I wanted you to come to me on your own."

"You can't have me."

"I *will* get a Baraca child out of you yet."

"No you won't."

"Most of the women in my castle would consider this a privilege," he said.

"I'm not one of them," she said, still trying to break free.

He tightened his grip. She bit his hand and he let go, screaming with rage. She ran to the other side of the room, stumbling over a footstool. He caught her and picked her up. Turning her around, he ran his hands over her waist. She backed up and tried to find something to hit him with. All she found was a hand mirror. She hit him in the head, but it only made him angry. He pushed her to the ground and got on top of her again, pressing himself closer. While his mouth explored her neck and ears, he held her down with one hand and groped at her breasts with the other.

"So lovely."

She pushed him away just long enough to scream, hoping someone would hear her.

"Only I can help you."

"Let me go!"

"I know you care for Prince Aiden. If you let me do this, I'll stop the wedding."

"I'd rather die," she said, spitting in his face. She screamed again and felt the Keldar stone flare.

While Kieran followed Delaine to her apartments, he felt as if he were in a trance, powerless to stop what he knew would happen. He looked around, vaguely aware of candles and the smell of jasmine. Delaine led him to a chair and left the room for a few moments. When she returned, she stood in front of him, wearing a translucent silk robe that left nothing to his imagination. Her jet black hair fell around her shoulders. The dancing candle light reflected off of the eyes he was trying desperately to avoid.

When she made him stand and caressed his face, his already racing pulse went wild.

"You really are a magnificent man, Aiden," she whispered in his ear. "You'll make a fine consort."

"Why – ?"

"I want you to get a taste before our wedding."

"I can't. I won't."

"You've been hungry for me ever since you woke up."

Delaine untucked his shirt and reached her hands up, slowly moving them over his chest and around to his back. His whole body tensed, trying to ignore her dangerous touch.

She led him over to the bed and pushed him down. He knew what she was going to do and suddenly he wondered if it would just be easier to let her. She sat on top of him and pulled his shirt off over his head. He reached up to touch her, but she pinned his hands to the bed.

As she leaned over him, her hair washed over his neck and chest. It set his whole body on fire.

She kissed him on the neck, moving up to the corner of his jaw. When her lips reached his ear, she whispered, "Why do you keep resisting me?"

Why am *I resisting?*

"Be my lover tonight, Aiden," she said, kissing his chest. "And tomorrow I'll insist we be married."

All kinds of thoughts raced through Kieran's mind. It would bc easy to give in to her advances. Maybe marrying her was how he was supposed to end Ciara's reign. It could be a quiet overthrow, no bloodshed, no resistance. He would have his kingdom and get to partake of the princess, tonight and for a thousand nights after, for the rest of his life.

Then the visions that had come when he'd looked at the sword flashed through his mind. If he slept with her tonight, he would betray Arathor, and himself. He had to break free or he would be under her spell forever. With all of his resolve, he pushed her aside and stood.

"Enough!"

The princess clutched at his arm and her face tightened.

He broke away and moved to the other side of the room. She followed and pressed herself against him. "Come back to my bed and make love to me. Then you can go."

He felt her soft curves and smelled the jasmine in her hair. Her hand was on his back, pulling him closer. She lowered his head and before he could stop himself, he was kissing her. And she was slowly leading him back to the bed.

He knew he shouldn't do this, but couldn't make himself stop. It was as if he'd been offered wine laced with poison and had no choice but to drain the cup. If something didn't happen soon, he knew he would be under Delaine's control forever.

Kieran!

Jessara! He was here to rescue Jessara.

Pushing Delaine aside, he grabbed his shirt and flew out of her room, letting his heart reach out to find his Eldala. He was surprised to hear a woman screaming in his room. When he burst through the door, Rahnak was on top of Jessa.

Despite his fatigue, Kieran felt a surge of adrenaline and bolted across the room. In half a heartbeat, he pulled Rahnak off of Jessa. She looked up at him in surprise.

Kieran was sure the king hadn't expected him to come in, and he used Rahnak's hesitation to his advantage. His first hit to Rahnak's jaw stunned the king, and when Rahnak put up his hands to hit back, Kieran blocked and hit Rahnak in the ribs. Rahnak doubled over, staggering from the blow. The rage was building and Kieran threw him across the room.

Kieran went after him, but the king unexpectedly pulled out a dagger and slashed Kieran across the stomach. It barely registered. Out of the corner of his eye, Rahnak saw Jessa trying to leave the room, but he grabbed her and flung her against the dressing table. She hit with a loud crack and didn't move.

While Rahnak watched Jessa, Kieran saw his opportunity and kicked Rahnak's legs out from under him. The king fell with a thud, but he recovered quickly and stabbed at Kieran. Kieran's heart thundered in his ears and he was breathing hard, but he moved away from the blade just before it connected.

The king lunged. Kieran grabbed Rahnak's knife hand and drove the king to his knees. The knife dropped to the floor and Kieran picked it up and plunged it into Rahnak's side. The king let out a sharp cry and then collapsed on the floor.

Kieran looked around. Jessa lay on the floor, still and quiet. He carried her limp body to the bed. When he put his hand to her head, his fingers were wet with her blood. The healing words came back to him, and when he spoke them, both the wound on her head and the cut on his stomach healed. But Jessa didn't wake up.

What had he done? She'd told him who she was and he had ignored her. He could have taken her away from this place. Instead, he'd remained passive, choosing an easy life with the princess. Now they had to get out of the castle before someone discovered Rahnak's body.

Just as Kieran was catching his breath, several guards burst into his room and surrounded him. Delaine pushed past them. Her hair was disheveled and her face was a mask of hatred.

"Take him to the dungeon," she ordered.

"What's this about?" Kieran asked.

"The princess has accused you of attacking her in her apartments," said one of the guards.

Just as three guards moved to tie his wrists, another motioned for Delaine to look in the corner.

Delaine let out a shriek. "Father! What have you done to him?"

"He was attacking Jessa," said Kieran. "I had to stop him."

"He was the king and she's a slave. Now you'll both pay for your treachery."

"What will you do with Jessa?"

Delaine's eyes glittered with rage. "Enjoy your Baraca whore tonight. Tomorrow you'll both be executed."

Chapter 39

Gilrain and Sienna heard the guards approaching and ducked into a shadowed corner. When Gilrain saw them enter Kieran's quarters, he motioned for Sienna to follow him to Kieran's door. As he heard Delaine pronounce Kieran's sentence, he clenched his fists against his sides. It wouldn't matter that Kieran had been defending Jessa; the execution order would stand.

As the guards dragged Kieran and Jessa away, Sienna muffled a cry.

"What can we do?" she whispered.

There was more pain in her eyes than Gilrain had ever seen in a woman before, and it kept him from answering for a moment. "I have to meet with the others. And you need to get Marcus and Bairn to meet us at Samuel's shop in an hour."

Sienna nodded and went to find Marcus. Gilrain slipped silently towards the castle gate, hoping he could find a way to get Kieran and Jessa out of the castle and through the city unnoticed.

Kieran winced as Jessa hit the floor. He made one last effort to struggle free, but it was useless. The guard untied his hands and threw him against the wall, disorienting him for a moment. When the door closed, he heard the princess's voice through the bars.

"You could have had me for the rest of your life."

"I would have been your mother's puppet. And if I have to choose between you and Jessa, I'll take Jessa."

"You'd choose a slave over a princess?" she said with a coldness he'd never heard from her before.

Kieran slammed his shoulder into the heavy wooden door in a futile attempt to get to her. The princess jumped back.

Rubbing his shoulder, he said, "It's a good thing you're on the other side of that door or you'd be joining your father."

She screamed her frustration, and he heard the echo of her steps as she went up the stone staircase. Now he had to find Jessa.

After a few moments of straining his eyes in the dark and trying to listen for her breathing, he remembered he could use the light from his Keldar stone to find her. He stilled his mind and thought about her. Soon the stone pierced the darkness with its clear blue light. She lay in a far corner, motionless. He picked her up and put her on a stone slab near one wall. As he stroked her hair, he knew that he had to wake her up, but he didn't know the words.

Arathor, please help me, he thought. Then he heard the phrase in his head and spoke it over her. "Teeshka sol Eldala."

In a few minutes, she stirred and rolled onto her side. He slid behind her and spread the quilt over both of them, then wrapped his arm around her waist.

For a few minutes, he listened to her shallow breathing and inhaled the rose scent clinging to her hair. Being this close to her and remembering how she looked at the banquet was stirring up dangerous thoughts. It was all he could do to resist the urge to kiss her. He knew that if he didn't control himself, he would be no better than the king.

Instead, he tucked his arm more tightly around her and closed his eyes, grateful that he'd finally found his Eldala. Before he drifted off, he hoped his cousin could find a way to get them out before the execution.

Jessa stifled a cry when she felt someone lying next to her. Cautiously, she ran her fingers over the arm draped across her waist, working her way to the hand. With much relief, she realized it had to be Kieran; no one had hands like his.

But why was he lying next to her? And where were they?

All she could remember was having Rahnak on top of her and then someone had lifted him off, but she hadn't clearly seen her rescuer's face. Once he started attacking the king, Jessa's only thought was to get out of the room. Before she reached the door, the king threw her against something and she hit her head. Then the room went black.

Now she was in the dark with Kieran next to her.

She sat up, and several things registered at once – the nauseating odor of stale air, human waste, and decaying straw; some kind of small animal scritching in a corner; the plink plunk of water dripping on a stone floor. They must be in the dungeon.

She pulled her knees up to her chest and shivered – and then groaned when she realized she was still in that horrid costume. Once she reached Kieran's room, she'd hoped that Sienna would find her and bring her some clothes, but then the king had come in… The thought made her shiver again.

Unexpectedly, Kieran reached out and touched her hair. She cringed. It wasn't proper for him to see her with her hair down, but he'd seen her this way at the banquet and now she was too tired to braid it.

"Are you all right, Jessara?" he asked softly.

Hearing Kieran say her real name, particularly in the tender way he said it, made her want to cry. She turned around, somewhat relieved that he couldn't see her face. She still wasn't sure how she felt about him or how he felt about her. Just because he knew who she was didn't mean he had any feelings for her.

"My head hurts." She paused. "You came."

Kieran exhaled softly. "You called. I had to come."

He sat up, and by the glow of his Keldar stone started to pull her hair away from her face.

"What are you doing?" she asked.

He laughed softly. "You're a Baraca woman. Only your husband should see you with your hair down."

There was something intimate about having Kieran's hands in her hair – more intimate than having his arm around her waist or sleeping next to him. It made her want to turn around and kiss him. She pushed the ridiculous thought away and laughed nervously as she said, "You saw it this way when I was a girl."

"Yes, I did, but that was different."

Yes that was *different,* she thought. *We were young and free and best friends.* Would she ever have her best friend in her heart again?

When he finished, he lightly tugged at her braid and said, "Not as good as you could have done, but it will do."

She shivered again. He draped the quilt around her shoulders and moved past her to the floor.

"Menan-dai," he said, and suddenly a small flame erupted from the floor. He added some straw and warmed his hands over the fire.

"How did you do that?" she asked.

He walked back to the stone slab. "All descendants of Alardin have some control over nature and the elements."

She was descended from Alardin. Did that mean she had this kind of power? But another question nagged at her now. "What happened to Rahnak?"

Kieran braced himself against the wall and surrounded Jessa with his arms. At first she stiffened, surprised that he would hold her this way, wondering if he would try to take advantage of her. When he just sat there, she pressed closer and let herself take the warmth he offered.

She hadn't realized until now how much she'd longed to rest in the arms of a good man. And now, she wasn't resting in just any man's arms – she was resting in Kieran's arms, feeling the flutter of his breath on her neck and the steady beat of his heart against her back. The song she'd tried to contain for the last few days trickled through her, suggesting new possibilities.

If they weren't in this awful place… if she knew he felt something for her... No, she couldn't let her mind go there. She had to be content with this moment the way it was.

"I had to kill him," he finally said.

"But why am I here?"

Despite his silence, she knew he was holding something back.

"Kieran, tell me."

Before he could speak, she heard Delaine's voice: "*Enjoy your Baraca whore tonight.*"

Jessa pulled away from him, shocked at what Delaine had said. She was tired of being used, but if that was Kieran's intent, she wouldn't be able to stop him.

As if sensing her thoughts, he said, "She was angry when I chose you. But I won't take advantage of you, Jessara. That's not how I see you."

Why did the words "I chose you" send her heart flitting through her body?

"What's going to happen to us?" she asked.

"If Gilrain doesn't get us out of here, we'll be executed tomorrow afternoon."

Chapter 40

Sienna tried to ignore her racing heart. Why wasn't Marcus answering her knock? Maybe he was asleep. She knocked a little louder and waited. When he still didn't answer, she pushed the door open. He wasn't there. She was tempted to panic, but reminded herself that she had to remain calm if she was going to get through this night and the next morning.

She stood there for a moment, thinking of where he could be. Maybe he was with Bairn.

Quickly, but not so as to attract any attention, she made her way past the inner barbican and towards the front of the castle to the smithy. When she went inside, Bairn and Marcus were already deep in conversation. They turned abruptly as she approached.

"Kieran killed Rahnak," she whispered.

"We heard," said Marcus, his face more furrowed than usual. "We were just discussing how to get him out."

"Where's Gilrain?" asked Bairn.

"He went into the city to get the others."

Bairn shook his head. "He won't get past the gate tonight."

"Why not?"

"The guards won't let anyone in or out until after the execution tomorrow."

Again, Sienna pushed down the panic rising up in her. "Then what can we do?"

"My question exactly," said Gilrain, coming up behind them.

Sienna let out a quick sigh of relief – and surprised herself again by feeling a little faint. No man had ever had this effect on her. She'd only known Gilrain for a few days, but in that short time she'd come to look forward to their brief meetings. He was confident and daring. And handsome.

His shoulder-length brown hair, his deep green eyes, and his square, stubbled jaw all gave him a wild, dangerous look she found hard to resist. And when they'd walked together in the garden…

Enough, she thought. This was no time for day-dreaming.

He stood beside her and his eyes flashed briefly to hers.

"I was just telling Bairn we could use the tunnels," said Marcus in reply.

"Tunnels?" Sienna and Gilrain asked at the same time.

"King Alardin and his son built a series of tunnels that go through the castle and under the city. Arathor and Annalisa used one of them to get out of the city before Kieran was born."

"Kieran isn't strong enough to walk that far," said Gilrain.

"Is he still that weak?" asked Bairn.

"I'm afraid so," said Sienna.

"If we had a wagon with a false bottom," Gilrain said, "we could get them out that way."

Bairn frowned. "Even if we did, they won't let anyone in or out tonight."

"They always let the muck wagon go out," said Sienna, "no matter what."

The three men looked at her wide-eyed. "The muck wagon?" Gilrain asked.

"Every day, the groomsmen shovel out the stables and send out the manure in a wagon that goes to the edge of town. If we put Kieran and Jessa under a canvas, and pile the manure on top of them, the guards would never suspect they were there."

Gilrain laughed.

Sienna gave him a playful scowl. "Can you think of anything better?"

The men laughed nervously.

"Now we just have to get them out of the dungeon," said Gilrain.

"The cook will send them a last meal in the morning," said Sienna. "Maybe Marcus could take it and I could distract the guards."

Now Gilrain frowned. "It's too dangerous for you."

"Do you think *you* could distract them?" she asked.

He shook his head. "I don't want anything to happen to you."

His concern made her heart leap into her throat. She hadn't considered that *he* might feel anything for *her*.

"One of the guards has his eye on me already. I'll just stoke the fire a little," she said.

"And then meet us in the stables," said Gilrain. "I'll take the wagon out, but how will the rest of you get out?"

"We'll take Sienna through the tunnel that goes under the city."

"Me? Leave the castle?" Sienna asked.

"Once you help us, you can't stay here," said Gilrain. He took her hand. "And I hoped you would come with us."

Gilrain wanted her to come with him. It was a chance for a life of freedom, something she'd never imagined would happen. And he was right. Once she helped Kieran and Jessa escape, Ciara would have her executed.

A dim gray light crept into the courtyard as Gilrain and Sienna made their way to the servants' tower. When they reached Sienna and Jessa's room, Sienna moved quickly, gathering Jessa's box and a change of clothes for Jessa and herself. She put everything into a canvas bag and looked around one more time, half smiling.

She would never have to sleep here again.

Before Gilrain left, he took her hand. It sent delicious tingles up her arm and into her heart.

"Be careful, Sienna," he said. Then he took the bag and went to the stables to wait for her.

As she descended the stairs to the dungeon, the musty odor from the prison cells almost overwhelmed her. She hadn't been down here for weeks and had forgotten how bad it smelled. She leaned against the rough stone wall and steadied herself as she waited for Marcus.

Soon, she heard his footsteps. "How will you get them to the stables?" she whispered.

"There's another tunnel that leads from here to the keep. Unfortunately, it's on this side of the door, so we'll have to get past the guards."

Sienna had to laugh. Who would have thought the old tailor would be the one to help them?

When they reached the doors to the lowest level of the dungeon, the two guards frowned. "Sienna. Marcus. What are you doing here?"

"Bringing a last meal to the prisoners," said Marcus.

"All right," said one, and unlocked the door to the long corridor.

Marcus followed him to Kieran's cell.

When the guard returned, Sienna took a deep breath and put her hands on his shoulders. "I understand you've been fighting over me," she purred.

Kieran stiffened as he heard the lock turn in the cell door. Surely it couldn't be afternoon yet. Having been on edge all night, he stood and was about to attempt an escape when he saw the tailor come in with a tray of food.

"A last meal?" Kieran asked.

Marcus put his finger to his lips and waited. When the guard's last footsteps faded away, he said, "An escape."

Just then, Jessa stirred. She sat up and wrapped the quilt around her shoulders. Her hair was disheveled and dark circles framed her eyes, but Kieran saw past all that to her true beauty. He still wondered how he'd been blind to it.

"Marcus?" she asked.

"We have to get you out of here now," Marcus whispered.

Her eyes flicked to Kieran and back to Marcus. "How?"

"There's a tunnel. But it's on the other side of the door." He drew a dagger from under the cloth on the tray. "You'll have to kill the guards, sir," he said, looking at Kieran.

Jessa shook her head. "More killing?"

"It's the only way past them," said the tailor.

She walked over to them and stood next to Kieran. "Then let's get this over with."

Marcus tucked some of the rolls from the tray into his pocket and handed Kieran the dagger. When they entered the corridor, Kieran heard someone scuffling on the other side of the door. Marcus went through the door first and Jessa stifled a cry. One of the guards had Sienna pinned to the wall.

Kieran thrust the dagger into Sienna's attacker and he slumped to the floor. Before the other one could shout the alarm, Kieran threw the dagger across the corridor and into his chest. Marcus pulled him off of Sienna and she let out a sigh of relief.

After dragging the guards into the cell and locking the door, Marcus gave Kieran and Jessa each a roll, and led them to the other end of the corridor where he unlocked a small wooden door that led to a low-ceilinged tunnel. They walked for several minutes, the silence interrupted only by their muffled footsteps on the dirt floor and the echoes of their breathing off the stone ceiling.

Presently, the tunnel sloped upward. Marcus led them up a few stairs and opened a door above their heads. Kieran looked around. Jessa gasped. The sun filtered in from a small round window in the first level of the keep. Jessa looked at the stairs with a pained expression. "My window," she murmured, "I'll never see it again."

"There's no time," said Marcus. "We have to go now."

Her shoulders slumped, and she turned to follow Marcus out the door and into the garden. Kieran wanted to assure her that she would see it again if she became queen of Teleria, but it wasn't something he could say now. He couldn't assume she would accept his proposal. Instead he arranged the quilt around her shoulders again. She looked up at him, pale-faced and haggard.

Then her eyes traveled across her garden. For a moment, he felt her sorrow at having to leave her favorite place, and he hoped they would return to it soon. Before they left, she picked a red rose and inhaled its fragrance. Then she dropped it and sighed in resignation.

When they reached the stables, Kieran saw Gilrain and smiled. He frowned when he saw the wagon.

"What's this?" Kieran asked.

"It will take too long to get you out through the tunnel under the city," said Sienna. "So you and Jessa will go in the wagon."

"How will that work?"

Gilrain cleared his throat and pointed to the pile of hay in the corner. "They'll never look for you under that."

"You must be joking," said Jessa.

Gilrain smiled. "It was Sienna's idea."

Jessa wrinkled her nose. "You expect us to go under that?"

"The guards will never suspect you're under there," Sienna said. "We'll put a canvas blanket over you and the muckings over that."

"How are we supposed to breathe?" Jessa asked.

"I can cast a spell for sleep," said Kieran. "Then we won't need as much air."

She looked at him doubtfully. "I'm supposed to go under there with you?"

He frowned. "I'm not Rahnak. Nothing will happen. But I'm afraid you won't smell like roses when we get out."

"And when will that be?" she asked.

"We're meeting Kale and the others in Maquoya," said Gilrain. "That should take half a day. Can you make your sleep last that long?"

"Yes, but you'll have to wake us when we get there."

Just then Sienna emerged from a corner with a dress for Jessa. "Here. Change into this."

Jessa looked relieved for the first time since waking up. "Thank you," she said and excused herself.

When Jessa returned, she wore a simple blue dress. Kieran was surprised at how disappointed he was, but it was probably better this way. Being next to her in the wagon would be difficult enough without her wearing the dress from the banquet.

When their plans were finalized, Kieran and Jessa lay down in the wagon, just an arm's width between them. She turned her back towards him. He put his hand on her head and said the words to give them both a dreamless sleep. Despite her modest clothing, he remembered the kinds of dreams he'd had about her in the past and didn't want to risk her seeing any dream he might have about her now.

Before falling asleep, he whispered, "Sleep well, my Eldala."

Ciara purred with satisfaction. Everything had gone so well.

Having watched Delaine and Kieran in the silver basin, she was satisfied that nothing more would interfere with his complete entrapment.

She called Sharaq from the next room and celebrated her triumph by indulging him with whatever he wanted. She wasn't aware of Rahnak's death or of the escape taking place in other parts of the castle.

Gilrain covered Kieran and Jessa with a canvas blanket. Then he and Marcus piled enough manure on top of them to make the ruse convincing. Before climbing into the seat, Gilrain took Sienna aside. "Be careful," he said.

"I will," she said, and surprised him by kissing his cheek.

As he watched Sienna leave with Marcus and Bairn, he realized how much he'd come to admire and care for her in the past few days. She wasn't like other women he'd met. Most of them fawned and flirted with him. Sienna didn't. What he saw in her face was closer to respect and admiration. She was confident and funny and full of life. And she had the most beautiful smile. He liked all those things about her.

Once Kieran was out of Korisan, he would think about courting her – unless she decided she would rather live with her grandmother in Agora. Just thinking that Sienna might choose to live with Neera made his stomach twist.

Gilrain shook the reins and pulled his hood over his face. When he reached the second barbican, the guards stopped him. Gilrain stiffened and put his hand to his dagger.

"Where's Fulkor?" the guard asked.

Gilrain coughed. "He came down with the croup."

The guard stepped back and waved Gilrain through.

"What about an escape?" yelled the other guard.

"No one could survive under all that crap."

Gilrain smiled. If they only knew.

Chapter 41

Kieran had the horrible feeling they'd been caught. When he realized it was Gilrain waking him up, he let out the breath he'd held in and sat up.

"Where are we?" Kieran asked.

"Aunt Melchiah's cottage in Maquoya."

Kieran had never met his father's sister, but had heard stories about the lively spinster who made her living by selling herbs in the city. "And where are the others?" he asked.

"Everyone is here."

"And Stefan?"

"He's in the barn, fuming over the way we've treated the Malazia." Gilrain did nothing to hide his obvious disgust for Stefan. "What should we do with Jessa?"

Kieran turned to look at her. There was a peace in her face he'd never seen before.

"Let her sleep."

Gilrain nodded. "All right. I'll carry her into the house."

"No," Kieran said, surprising himself at the intensity of his protest. "I'll take her."

Gilrain arched an eyebrow but said nothing as Kieran moved past him and picked Jessa up. It was good to have her in his arms, and he was tempted to bury his face in her neck and breathe in her aroma. But not here and not now.

As he made his way into the house, he noticed his companions conversing in the main room. He gave them a quick nod and caught the eye of an older woman – his aunt he supposed. The woman quickly led him to a back bedroom, smiled, and left. Kieran laid Jessa on the bed and pulled a quilt over her shoulders. Reeling from fatigue, he sat on the edge of the bed and watched her.

Fine wisps of hair had come loose and playfully framed her face. Without thinking, he took one of them and rolled it between his fingers, reliving the moments when he'd braided her hair in the dungeon. It was the softest thing he'd ever felt – except for maybe her hand, or the skin on her waist.

Now he let his eyes wander over her face. She had the most exquisite array of features he'd ever seen – delicate eyebrows, long, dark lashes, high cheekbones, full lips, and a graceful neck. Dreams he'd had before ever meeting her surfaced, making his pulse quicken and stirring a desire in him to explore those features with his lips.

He wrestled the impulse down. She wasn't his – yet. If things worked out the way he hoped, she would be soon. But until then, he would have to keep these kinds of thoughts in check.

Just then, he heard footsteps behind him and turned to see Stefan. Despite knowing that Stefan couldn't possibly have read his thoughts, Kieran felt the heat of embarrassment creeping into his face.

"What are you doing here?" Stefan asked.

Kieran bristled, then stood to leave. "I was making sure Jessa was all right." Their eyes locked for an uncomfortable moment and then Kieran said flatly, "I was just leaving."

Stefan pulled a chair to the side of the bed and looked as if he would say something to her. Kieran stopped.

"Let Jessa sleep. These last few days have been difficult for her." As he left to find his companions, a spark of jealousy ignited a new desire – a desire to make sure Stefan returned home as soon as possible.

When Kieran entered the sitting room, the men stopped their conversation and turned to him. Kale surprised him with a stifling embrace.

"It's good to see you, son."

"And you, Father. It's good to see all of you."

"You had us worried," said Toren.

"How long was I in Korisan?" Kieran asked.

"From the time you were poisoned to today – it's been about two weeks," said Gilrain.

"We *cannot* let that happen again," said Riordan. Toren and Kale nodded in agreement. "You should have a personal escort."

The appeal was unexpected, but Kieran couldn't argue with Riordan. There was too much at stake to lose more time with a second rescue attempt. And now that he'd escaped, Ciara would double her efforts to recapture him.

"Are you volunteering?" he asked.

Riordan's face tightened. "Yes, I am."

"As am I," said Toren.

Kieran sighed. It would take some time to ease back into the role of king. "Your protection will be greatly appreciated."

"And make sure you watch this more carefully," said Bairn, frowning. He pulled Restamar's gold scabbard from behind his back and returned it to Kieran.

"I will," said Kieran, somewhat chagrined. "How did *you* get it?"

"I took it from the table when you left," said Gilrain.

Suddenly Aunt Melchiah interrupted them. "I'm sure you have a lot to discuss," she said, playfully scowling at them, "but I need water from the well." Then she looked at Kieran and Gilrain, and wrinkled her nose. "And you both need a bath."

In all the fuss over Jessa, Kieran hadn't noticed the smell from the wagon until now. He gave his aunt an amused smile, then gestured towards the door. "It seems that the first duty of my new personal guard," said Kieran, "will be to escort me to the creek."

The rustle of straw and a vague awareness of someone standing over her made Jessa think she was still in the castle. And Rahnak was at it again.

No – she and Kieran had escaped. So where was she? When she opened her eyes, she was surprised to see she was on a bed in a small room, and that Stefan stood over her. What was he doing here?

"I was hoping you would wake up soon," he said.

"Where's Kieran?"

Stefan scowled. "After what he subjected you to, why would you want anything to do with him?"

"What do you mean, 'subjected me to'?"

"Putting the Baraca's queen under all that… horse manure. It was undignified."

Jessa rolled her eyes. "They saved my life. And it wasn't Kieran's idea anyway. It was Sienna's."

"Well, you will not have to trouble yourself with that Telerian once we leave here."

Now Jessa remembered why she disliked her cousin so much. Apparently, time had only intensified his arrogance. She smiled to herself, wondering what Stefan would say when he found out Kieran was *Baraca.*

Jessa swung her legs over the edge of the bed and stood. She was just about to ask about Sienna when her friend looked in through the doorway.

"Jessa," she said, smiling.

The two embraced, and then Sienna stepped back. "Kieran was right about you not smelling like roses. Let's get you a bath."

Stefan moved to block their way. "Jessara, you will return to this room as soon as you are finished."

Jessa looked at him sourly. "Are you telling me what to do?"

"You are an unmarried Baraca woman, and I am your only male relative."

"What does that have to do with anything?"

He frowned. "Have you forgotten our customs?"

"All I remember is how you constantly hovered over me. Why do you think I escaped to the forest all the time?"

"You *have* forgotten." His frown deepened into a scowl. "Obviously, living among Telerians has corrupted you – the way you act, the people you associate with" – he glanced at Sienna – "the way you speak. We have a lot of work ahead of us."

Through gritted teeth Jessa said, "I've lived on my own and taken care of myself for ten years. I didn't leave the castle just to have you lord it over me. I'll go where I please and choose my friends – *without* your approval."

Stefan couldn't have looked more shocked if she had knocked him to the ground – which she considered doing for just a moment. Instead, she pushed past him and went to the barn.

An hour later, Jessa was still trying to work up the courage to join the others. But she knew she couldn't stay in the barn all night, so she finished dressing and went into the house.

Heat crept into her face when she walked through the door. Everyone was looking at her, but one person unnerved her when he stared right past her eyes and into her soul. Why did Kieran always have that effect on her? She quickly looked away and buried herself in an overstuffed chair in a far corner.

After a while, Marcus joined her. At the moment, he was the only person besides Sienna, Gilrain, and Kieran that she recognized.

"Where are we?" she asked.

"We're in Maquoya, at the home of Kieran and Gilrain's Aunt Melchiah."

Jessa looked across the room. Sienna and Gilrain sat in an opposite corner, laughing quietly together. Kieran was surrounded by several people, all of whom he seemed to know. Suddenly Jessa felt very alone. And she was at a loss for what to do. It would take time for her to forget the life of servanthood and live a life of freedom – a life she hadn't considered when Gilrain had asked her to help rescue Kieran. But she couldn't go back. Not unless she wanted to be executed.

She exhaled sharply and moved towards the kitchen. A stout woman with graying brown hair and rosy cheeks followed her.

"I'm Aunt Melchiah. Are you Jessa?" Her smile reminded Jessa of Halda.

"Yes, I'm Jessa."

"It must have taken a lot of courage to help Kieran escape."

Jessa nodded and sighed again. Now Kieran was free and he knew who he was – the king of Teleria. He didn't need her anymore. None of them needed her. The thought made Jessa's throat tighten.

"Do you need some help with dinner?" Jessa asked, trying to distract herself.

Melchiah laughed softly. "It's going to be difficult for you to stop being a servant, isn't it?" Melchiah handed her a knife and some potatoes. "If it will make you feel better, you can help me with these."

Jessa gratefully took them and started the mind-numbing chore of peeling and cutting. When she finished with the potatoes, she started on a pile of carrots. Someone put a hand on her arm.

It was Stefan. "Jessara, what are you doing?"

"Helping our hostess."

Stefan took the knife. "This work is beneath you."

"I've been a slave for ten years. How is this beneath me?"

He pulled her aside and his face was grave. "Jessara, you are the queen of all the Baraca. You should not be working in a kitchen."

Melchiah's brows flew up in a question.

"Excuse me, Melchiah," said Jessa.

She pulled Stefan outside and into the barn. "Do you mean to tell me our clan hasn't found another to replace me?"

"No. You are the chosen one and that has not changed."

Jessa hadn't considered that her clan would ask her to step into the role of queen once she'd been freed from slavery. "I'm not sure I want to be the Malazia."

"How can you say that?"

Jessa closed her eyes for a moment, trying to still the anxiety simmering in her stomach. "When I was a girl, I met the previous Malazia. He looked old and tired."

Stefan's face softened for a moment. "At least return home to see your mother. Her heart broke when you were taken." He paused and took her hand. "*My* heart broke when you were taken. I vowed I would find you."

She could almost believe from his face and his voice that he meant it. Then his tone changed.

"Whatever you choose, Jessara, know this: We were betrothed beore you were ever chosen. If you had not been stolen, I would be your Eldala and we would be married by now."

Jessa's anxiety was threatening to explode.

"I don't belong there," she said.

His face darkened. "Of course you belong there. And after I take you home, you *will* marry me."

She stamped her foot and went back into the house. Of all the arrogant, pig headed…

She burst into the room, expecting to help Melchiah. Instead, everyone sat around a large wooden table. When they heard her come in, all the men stood and Kieran pulled out the chair next to Sienna. Jessa frowned and sat down, confused as to why he would do that for her. No one had ever waited on her before. In fact, she didn't think she'd ever sat at a table as a guest.

When Kieran had seated himself directly across from her, Melchiah began to pass the food. Jessa numbly took a warm roll from the basket and before long, her plate was piled high with two different kinds of meat, carrots, potatoes, more bread, apples, and pears. During the meal, Melchiah tried to draw Jessa into the conversation, but it was all Jessa could do to eat and nod and not be overwhelmed by the sudden change in her life.

What was she doing here? She had the uncomfortable feeling that she'd fallen into a very pleasant dream and would soon wake up to find that she was still in the castle and that Rahnak was still alive. And that Kieran had never come.

But he had come. He sat across the table from her, laughing and enjoying the company of his friends and family. He looked so comfortable and at ease.

Occasionally, he would look up and catch her looking at him. Every time he did, her pulse raced and she would turn away and try to think of something to say to Melchiah or Sienna. Then he would return to his conversation and she would find herself staring at him again. Every time she did, little chills danced over her skin, stirring up thoughts she hoped he couldn't read – thoughts about the way he'd draped his arm over her while they slept in the dungeon, the way he held her to keep her warm, the way he whispered "Sleep well, my Eldala." Did any of it mean anything? Or did he feel an obligation to protect her because she had helped him remember?

Sooner than she expected, the meal ended and Kieran stood. Everyone looked at him and stopped their conversation. When he gestured towards her, she swallowed hard.

"I'd like to formally thank the woman who saved my life," he said, holding her gaze.

"As would I," said a tall man with brown hair.

She blinked and nodded.

"This is my father, Kale," said Kieran. "You've met my Aunt Melchiah. Next to her is Riordan, then Toren. And everyone else you know."

When his eyes rested on her, she tried to hold his gaze, but found it impossible. What was he thinking when he looked at her that way?

"Where's Stefan?" Riordan asked.

"I think I insulted him," said Jessa, surprising herself that she'd spoken.

"What did you say to him?" asked Sienna.

"I told him I wouldn't be going home."

Chapter 42

Kieran's fork dropped to his plate with a loud clank, and he nearly choked. It took him a moment to recover. When he did, he saw Jessa had left the room. It took another moment to make himself go after her. When he stood to leave, Riordan and Toren moved to follow, but Kieran put up a hand.

Toren frowned. "Sir – "

"I'll stay close to the house," said Kieran.

"At least take your sword," said Riordan.

Kieran nodded, and after donning Restamar he left the house. A light breeze grazed his face, and he stopped to take a deep breath. An owl hoo-hooted in the distance and a chorus of crickets chirped somewhere in the dark. He quickly glanced at his surroundings, watching for any movement. When he was sure no one else was there, he looked for Jessa.

She sat on a bench in Melchiah's garden, just to his left. When she saw him coming, she drew in a quick breath and stared at him.

"May I sit here?" he asked.

She nodded.

Now that he was here, he wasn't sure what to say. He didn't want to hurt her, but he had to convince her to go home. "Why won't you go back?"

She was silent for a long time, and just when Kieran was going to repeat his question, she rubbed her temple and said, "I've been away for so long – I don't know if I'll fit in with my clan."

Kieran couldn't help but chuckle.

"What?" she asked.

"You might be right. You're not anything like them."

"How would you know that?"

"I was there just a few days before I was captured."

"What made you go *there*?"

Several reasons swirled through Kieran's mind, but he didn't think it was wise to tell her all of them. "To find out if they knew where you were."

She turned to look at him. The breeze ruffled the hair around her face and the moonlight reflected off of her eyes. "Why?"

Kieran listened to her ragged breathing and the sounds of the night. "When the Esgharites took you, I vowed that I'd find you."

"You *wanted* to find me?"

"Jessa, I was your best friend. Of course I wanted to find you."

She stood and started to walk towards the back of the house. Kieran surveyed the area before following, still attentive for any movement. When he caught up to her, he put his hand on her shoulder. "I met your mother while I was there," he said.

She turned and her face softened. "You met Tiana?"

"Yes, and I promised her I'd bring you home."

She turned and continued to walk. Her voice was tart. "Do you know what they'll ask me to do if I go back?"

"They'll want you to be their Malazia."

"You know about that?"

"Yes."

"I won't do it."

Until this moment, Kieran had only been irritated with her. Now something like panic gripped him. "Why not?"

Jessa returned to the bench and sat down. "Kieran, I was seven when I met the last Malazia. He told me that the council would try to control me and that I should fight against them."

Having met Galen, Kieran could believe it was possible. "Maybe you could change that."

"Are you saying you *want* me to go back?"

She was so exasperating! "Jessa, I'm saying you should give it a try."

She stood, and just before going into the house, she said, "I don't want to be queen of anything." The door slammed behind her and she was gone.

If the earth had split open and swallowed Kieran up right there, he wouldn't have felt any more shaken than he did right now. What was he going to do? How was he going to get the support of the hostile clans if Jessa didn't go back and claim her title? And what would it do to his already strained relationship with the Hada? He could just imagine Galen somehow blaming this on him.

A more disturbing thought lurched through him. If Jessa didn't want to be anyone's queen, what would she say when he asked her to be the queen of Teleria?

The next evening, Kieran's aunt handed him a parchment. Her face was grave. "I found this in the town square today," she said.

Kieran scanned the page. His heart felt like it had dropped into his stomach.

"What is it?" asked Gilrain.

Kieran started to read. "By order of Queen Ciara – wanted for attacking Princess Delaine and murdering King Rahnak: Aiden son of Arathor. Reward: 500,000 krona dead or alive. Wanted for aiding in Aiden's escape: Marcus the tailor, Bairn the sword smith, and Sienna the slave. Reward: 10,000 krona apiece."

It sounded as if everyone in the room had stopped breathing. Finally, Sienna said, "What about Jessa?"

Kieran clenched his teeth and looked at Jessa. "Wanted for assisting in Aiden's escape, seducing the king, and aiding in his murder: Jessa, the Baraca slave. Reward: 600,000 krona, dead or alive."

Without a word, Jessa left the room. Kieran was about to follow her when Stefan stood and blocked his way.

"Now you have put her in danger," Stefan said.

Kieran was just barely able to hold his temper. "Do you think I meant for any of this to happen?"

Stefan sneered. "It matters not, Telerian. From now on, Jessara will be under my protection."

Kieran was ready to hit him. Instead he raised his sleeve to reveal the tattoo. "*I* am Hada Baraca."

Stefan drew back, but the surprise in his face quickly changed to contempt. "Wearing the mark does not make you Baraca."

"Jessara, the ancient Malazia, married Alardin. That makes me Baraca. If you refer to me as Telerian again, I swear I'll – "

Melchiah stepped in. "Gentlemen. You have a much larger problem right now. How will you get to Agora without being seen?"

At midnight, Kieran swung astride Fallon. The horse snorted, sending out a plume of white steam. Kieran pulled on his riding gloves and guided the horse to the front of the house where he waited for his aunt. The rest of the company followed – Bairn and Marcus in the wagon, the others on horseback. Sienna rode behind Gilrain, and Jessa rode behind Stefan. With more than a little jealousy, Kieran wished that he'd insisted she come with him. Now it was too late.

Presently, his aunt emerged and handed each person a canvas bag. When Kieran opened his, he wasn't surprised to find an assortment of rolls, cheese, and dried meat. He thanked her, amazed again that his unmarried aunt could afford the abundant food.

Kieran looked over his companions and gave a nod. With his father beside him, he spurred Fallon into a gallop, leading the company through the wilderness and towards Agora.

As the wind whipped past his face, Kieran took a deep breath. It was good to be back in the wild, away from the city. He was still weak from his time in Korisan, but he had noticed that the farther away he was from Ciara, the faster his strength seemed to return.

When he and Kale were some distance ahead, they slowed their mounts and rode in silence for a few moments. Toren and Riordan kept a respectful distance.

When his father spoke, his voice was tight. "I never should have held you back."

"Why did you?"

"My father was a talented smith, but he often went on errands for King Duncan. My mother always said he took too many risks and that he should have stayed closer to home. I begged to go with him. All I wanted was adventure, not the life of a smith."

He looked at Kieran. "I know what it's like to be held back, and I swore I'd never do that to my sons." His voice sounded choked with emotion. This was a side of his father Kieran had never seen before.

"What changed you?"

"After one of my father's errands, the king sent word that my father had been killed. It broke my mother's heart, and she spent the rest of her short life in bed. I was seventeen and took over the smithy. I had to take care of my mother and younger brothers and sisters. Loric helped a little, but he wanted to learn how to make swords. I sent him to apprentice with a blade smith in Maquoya. When our mother died, I moved all of us to Maquoya."

He paused. "When I married Elisa, I vowed I would never put her through that. I'd live a safe life and take care of my family. When you came along, it only strengthened my resolve to stay hidden and bury those childhood desires to fight."

"And now?"

Kale stopped his horse. "I can't hide anymore, Kieran. I swear to you now that I'll do everything I can to help you walk this road and win this battle."

A familiar discomfort squirmed in Kieran's middle at hearing his father give his oath. Kale had sworn fealty in Agora – it seemed like a lifetime ago – and hearing him say it then had been difficult. Now that he knew his father's story, he had a greater understanding of his father's life, and it gave the oath a depth it didn't have before.

They continued in silence and after a few hours of riding, the gray of early dawn broke through the darkness. Presently, Kale led them to an overhanging shelf of rock where they could sleep during the day.

Kieran dismounted and stretched. The rest of the companions did the same. There was very little conversation as they made camp. Most likely they were tired from the long night's travel. The shallow cave was barely large enough to hold them all, and it was with great effort that they didn't get in each other's way.

As the group prepared to sleep, Kieran gestured to Riordan and Marcus. "You can take the first watch. Wake up Bairn and Toren three hours later. Then Gilrain and Stefan. We'll eat and break camp after sunset."

Stefan frowned. "I have sworn to protect Jessara. I will not leave her side."

Jessa scowled at him but said nothing.

"By protecting us," said Kieran, "you *will* be protecting her."

As Kieran opened his bedroll, he looked over at Jessa. Her back was towards him, and he saw the rise and fall of her breathing. When it was time to leave, he would have to insist that she ride with him. There were some things between them that they needed to settle.

Chapter 43

When Jessa realized how close she'd slept to Kieran, a surprisingly pleasant melody fluttered through her. The song deepened as she watched his chest rise and fall with each breath. The dying sun glinted off of his beard, and she forgot for a moment she was still angry with him for telling her to be the Malazia.

Without thinking, she put her hand on his arm and startled when his eyes opened. When he looked at her, the breath caught in her throat and kept her from saying anything. Instead, she turned her back to him and rummaged through her food sack.

She was oddly disappointed when he walked to the front of the cave without speaking to her.

"Any movement?" he asked.

"No one reported anything," said Gilrain.

"Good," said Kieran. "Riordan and Toren can watch while we break camp."

Stefan moved from his post and sat beside Jessa. "We could break off from the others and head north to our home," he whispered.

Jessa shook her head. "I told you yesterday – I'm going to Agora."

He snorted. "To meet Arathor. I still do not understand your reasons."

"And you probably never will." She stood and walked out of the cave. Stefan was close on her heels. She turned and glared at him. "And stop following me."

"If anything happens to you again, I will be disgraced. I will not let you out of my sight."

Jessa threw up her hands in frustration. How could she get rid of him? Before she could stop herself, the words, "I'm riding with Kieran," flew out of her mouth.

In the diminished light, she could just make out the disbelief on Stefan's face. She smiled to herself. And then her stomach knotted. She just made it sound like she *wanted* to ride with Kieran. Maybe some part of her did, but that wasn't the impression she wanted to give Kieran.

Everyone stared at Stefan when he said, "I will not let you ride with that Telerian."

Kieran spun around and hit Stefan in the jaw, sending him to the ground. Stefan wiped the blood from the corner of his mouth and stood toe to toe with Kieran. Kieran towered above him by at least a head. For a moment, the two of them just eyed each other.

After a discomforting silence, Stefan spat out, "It is only my obligation to Jessara that keeps me from leaving this company. Once she has met Arathor, I assure you I will be leaving, and I will be taking Jessara with me."

Not if I have anything to say about it, Jessa thought.

Kieran mounted Fallon and gave Jessa a hand up. When she put her hands around his waist, he told himself it was only because she didn't want to fall off, but it sent an unexpected jolt of longing through him anyway.

For a few moments, he listened to the steady pace of Fallon's hooves on the tough sod. Jessa relaxed her grip and rested her head on his back. It took all of his resolve to keep his mind from imagining the life he could have with her.

"I was surprised when you told Stefan you wanted to ride with me," he said.

She snorted softly. "I thought it would be the best way to get away from him tonight."

"Then I'm just a way to avoid your cousin?"

"No," she said sharply. "I mean, I hope you don't mind."

"Why would I mind?"

"I don't know. Maybe you're tired of my company."

Where did she get these strange ideas? "I don't think I could ever get tired of your company."

They rode along in silence for a while and then she said, "How long will you stay in Agora?"

"Until the war begins."

She went rigid. "War?"

"It's part of my calling. Ciara is amassing a force to invade Teleria. I'm raising an army to stop her."

"To get back your kingdom," she murmured.

She was silent for a long time, and then said, "I need to walk."

Kieran brought Fallon to a stop and dismounted. Kale and the others slowed their pace. When he tried to help her down, she slid past him. Why was she avoiding him?

Instead of remounting, Kieran walked beside Jessa, waiting for her to say something.

"What's my mother like?" she finally asked.

Kieran smiled sadly. "Mara Tiana bears a double burden – losing you and losing your father."

"My father?"

"She told me your father searched for you for a year. His last letter said he thought you were in Korisan. Then the letters ended and she gave him up for lost."

Jessa stopped. "He came looking for me?"

"He gave his life trying to find you."

Apparently overcome with emotion, she leaned into him. He was startled at first, but then he wrapped his arms around her and let her cry, hoping he could absorb her grief and lend her his strength.

Holding her this close, he couldn't help but feel her soft curves pressing into him. But he also noticed that something was missing.

"Where's your Keldar stone?" he asked.

"I took it off."

"Jessa, if anything happens to you, that stone will help me find you. You have to wear it."

She exhaled sharply. "Don't tell me what to do, Kieran. I'm tired of being connected – to you, to Arathor. It's too much."

There it was that stubbornness again. So much for settling things between them.

He remounted Fallon and offered her a hand up, but she refused. Maybe he had spoken too soon when he said he would never get tired of her company. Being with her was becoming more frustrating by the minute.

Why couldn't she be more like the Eldala he'd dreamed about?

From what Sahbél had told him, Kieran knew that Eldala grew together as they matured, and that their marriage was the completion of their childhood bond.

What if they had been apart for so long that there was nothing left between them?

Chapter 44

Kieran stared up at the walls of the Kofar Baraca fortress. The last time he'd been here, he was under Delaine's influence and hadn't cared about anything but sleep. Looking up at it today, he was grateful it was so well protected.

It stood out in the open, but had several layers of defense. A deep ravine, twenty feet deep and twenty feet across encompassed thick stone walls. Along the walls, heavily-manned bow towers were spaced every ten feet. Between each bow tower two guards patrolled the top of the wall. A single hard-packed dirt road led over a series of draw bridges and into three barbicans. Between each barbican were five soldiers.

With the others behind him, Kieran led Fallon through the barbicans and jumped down. Although Jessa protested, Kieran lifted her from the horse. For a moment their eyes met, and he tried to sense something, anything from her. He didn't have to. Her face made it clear she didn't want anything to do with him.

Arathor drew Kieran's attention away with a hearty handshake and an invitation to breakfast in his private dining room. As they walked, Arathor told Kieran that Braeden had been able to secure troops from the Tyman, Linden, Nedebar, and Kendar clans. The southern clans had sent word that warriors would be arriving within the week. When Kieran asked about the Ancala clan, Arathor frowned and shook his head.

"They've made it quite clear they'll only help if you marry the Malazia."

Kieran glanced over at Jessa, hoping she hadn't heard that part of the conversation. He needn't have worried: She appeared to be weary and distracted. He shook his head. As things stood now, there wasn't much chance that she would agree to be his queen.

Upon entering the dining room, he saw his mother, aunt, and uncle. Before Elisa embraced Kale, she rushed across the room and embraced Kieran.

"I was afraid I'd never see you again," she said.

"It's good to be back," he said, kissing her cheek.

As he quickly made introductions, Kieran made sure everyone knew Jessa had helped to rescue him. She must have turned three shades of red when he did, and another shade deeper when Arathor kissed her hand.

Finally, the group sat down to eat a breakfast fare Kieran had seen only once before, when he'd first met Arathor. Platters were piled high with sausages, ham, hard boiled eggs, rolls, twist breads, apples, pears, berries, grapes, and peaches. Several waiters filled their glasses with pear juice.

Kieran looked at the faces of the people seated at the table and realized that if nothing else happened, he was content at this moment. He couldn't be more blessed than he was right now. Then his eyes rested on Jessa. She still looked haggard and didn't join in the conversation. He wondered how she could be so different from the woman he'd imagined. Was there any future with her?

His thoughts were interrupted by Arathor tapping his glass with his knife. Everyone turned to the former king.

"It gives me great pleasure to welcome new friends and old to the Kofar Baraca fortress." He nodded at each person. "And now I'd like you to join me as I raise my glass and drink to the return and good health of my son. Long live Aiden, king of Teleria."

The others raised their glasses. "Long live King Aiden."

It seemed again that Kieran was living another man's life. How could it be that he was the king of Teleria and that the people he cared about most were now toasting his health? It didn't seem real. After a moment, he nodded his thanks and drained his own glass.

When he set it down, Jessa was gone.

Jessa couldn't stand it any longer. The moment they'd toasted to King Aiden's health, she felt a thorny panic and looked for the first opportunity to escape. When Kieran tipped his head back to drain his glass, she exited as quietly as she could.

Now she wandered the fortress, not caring where she went. She was startled when she heard soft footsteps approaching from behind. Turning, she braced herself to deal with Stefan, and was pleasantly surprised to see it was Kieran's mother.

"May I walk with you?" Elisa asked.

Jessa nodded.

Elisa came up beside her and slipped her hand into the crook of Jessa's arm. "No matter how many times I hear them call my son 'King Aiden,' I can't get used to it. He's still just Kieran to me."

"I don't think I'll ever get used to it either," Jessa murmured. Then she felt a wave of dizziness rush over her and her steps faltered.

"You poor dear," said Elisa. "You must be exhausted. Let me take you to your private apartment."

"Private apartment?"

"Of course. The fortress is large enough for everyone to have their own quarters."

As Elisa led Jessa through a maze of corridors, Jessa noted the rich tapestries and woolen carpets that gave the long hallways a friendly feeling. It was a welcome change from the lifeless walls of Rahnak's castle. When they reached the end of the corridor, Elisa pushed open a wooden door, intricately carved with roses and vines. Jessa ran her fingers over the dark wood. It was beautiful. When Elisa led her through the tastefully decorated sitting room and into the bedroom, Jessa stifled a cry.

Spread across the large bed was a white quilt, embroidered with delicate roses, butterflies, and graceful greenery. Jessa was almost afraid to touch it. She was surprised when Elisa sat on the edge of the bed and motioned for Jessa to sit next to her. As Jessa ran her hands over the intricate stitching, she said, "This is lovely. Where did it come from?"

"I made it. It's one of the few things I brought with me from Pent."

Jessa looked into the woman's clear green eyes. They were misty. "What is it?" asked Jessa.

"I was just thinking of our home in Pent. I don't think I'll ever see it again."

"Why did you leave?"

Elisa wiped her eyes with her apron. "A month or two after Kieran found out he was Arathor's son, he killed a soldier who was attacking a woman on the street. After he left, Lord Destra sent soldiers to look for him – three times, in fact. A few months later, Rahnak's agents came and started the search all over. We realized it would be better to leave, so we packed what we could and came here."

Jessa felt a strange connection with Kieran's mother. Here was someone who knew what it was like to be forced from her home. She would have enjoyed talking more with Elisa, but suddenly she didn't have the strength to fight her fatigue and told Elisa she needed to sleep.

Before leaving, Elisa draped a silk nightgown across the bed and pointed out the dresses behind the dressing screen. Jessa thanked her and when Elisa left, Jessa ducked behind the dressing screen, peeled off her traveling clothes, and slipped the nightgown over her head. The slick, cool fabric was refreshing against her skin.

Too tired to let her hair down, Jessa slipped under the rose quilt and closed her eyes, letting sleep overtake her.

Weary from travel, Kieran had almost reached his quarters when he saw his mother approaching.

"Have you seen Jessa?" he asked.

Elisa smiled and pointed to a partially open door. "She's a lovely woman."

Kieran smiled. It was good to know that his mother thought so highly of Jessa.

He gently pushed the door open and looked around. His mother must have picked this room especially for Jessa; there were flowers all throughout the décor – on the sofa, in the trim near the ceiling, in the curtains, and even in the wool carpet.

He called out softly, but Jessa didn't answer. Venturing in a little farther, he saw that she was asleep under his mother's favorite quilt. He sat on her bed so he could look at her. It seemed he was always looking at her when she slept.

Now he watched the way the light from the window above caressed her and held her in its warmth. Suddenly he was jealous of the light. In spite of the knowledge she might never consent to marry him, he wanted to hold her and let her know she was meant to be his.

He let out a heavy sigh. How could he tell her anything when she wanted nothing to do with him?

Chapter 45

Jessa took the sea shell from the boy and they started to play, chasing each other around the trees, splashing each other in the creek, building stick forts, and dancing to the song. Then the ugly men came and snatched her away. She screamed and the boy tried to stop them, but the men knocked him down and threw her over the back of a horse. The next thing she knew, she was in the castle and Rahnak was straddling her. The sound of her screams woke her up.

With no light to tell her where she was, Jessa's heart pounded and she could barely breathe. When the door burst open, she stiffened, afraid it was Rahnak.

"Jessa, are you all right?"

She took a breath. It was Kieran.

"No," she replied, still shaking. "Did you hear me screaming?"

"No, I had your dream."

Of course – it was the Eldala dream connection. She'd thought that once she stopped wearing the Keldar stone, they wouldn't share dreams. Apparently they were still connected by heart.

Kieran lit a candle and she drew in a breath. In his haste, he'd pulled on a blue silk robe, but it was still open to his waist. When he sat next to her on the bed, she hoped he couldn't sense what looking at him did to her.

Everything about him – his face, his body, his movement – stirred up the melody she wanted to ignore. It flooded her with a deep longing to be his forever. But she couldn't let her mind go there. In spite of the longing, she had to remind herself that he was the king of Teleria, and she had no desire to be a queen.

And even if she did want to be queen, what were the chances there could be anything between them? They'd been apart for too long and she couldn't expect that he'd waited all these years for her. Most likely, he was planning to marry someone else.

As she walked across the room, she wrapped her arms around herself to stop her shivering. "I never thanked you for stopping Rahnak," she murmured.

He stood and closed the distance between them. Why did he have to smell so enticing?

"I had to stop him," he said. "My Eldala was in trouble."

"Yes, I think you said that before."

"And I never thanked you for everything you did for me in Korisan." His rich voice was low and tender and made her want to cry. Why did he keep doing that to her? Why did everything about him make her want to cry?

She sniffed and tried to compose herself. "I was afraid it would be too little too late. And on that last night… well, it was what it was."

What could she say about that night? That it was agony to watch him with Delaine. That when she sang to him she'd poured out her heart in the desperate attempt to help him remember who he was, with no hope that he would return her affections.

"I think you should go," she said flatly. "If Stefan found us here, like this… you'd better go."

His brow wrinkled into a question, but he left without protest. She closed the door behind him, at the same time slamming shut the door of her heart.

What was Kieran supposed to do with this woman? She was his Eldala, and he should have been able to catch a glimpse of her heart towards him, but when he tried, the only reward for his trouble was a slammed door.

When he reached the stable, it was early dawn and he was surprised to find a stable boy already there, feeding the horses. The boy's face went white and he gave Kieran a quick bow.

"May I saddle your horse, sir?" he stammered.

Kieran chuckled. He'd forgotten he could have that effect on people. "No, I'll do it myself."

The boy scurried out of the stable and Kieran was blessedly alone. For a few moments, he combed through Fallon's mane and tail, letting the rhythmic motion calm his mind. Then he saddled the horse and climbed onto Fallon's back, thankful that they understood each other perfectly.

On the trail that followed the inside of the fortress wall, Kieran encountered Braeden, also riding. He greeted his friend and they rode in silence. As the sun started to peek over the eastern wall, Braeden spoke.

"Has Arathor informed you of the clans that are sending warriors?"
"Yes, he has. I was hoping for more, though."
"Give them time, sir."
Kieran gritted his teeth. He couldn't get used to being called "sir," "king," or "your Majesty." It always made him think that Arathor was behind him. "We don't have time," he said. "And I need more than four or five clans to send men. I need them all."
"Did you say that the Ancala and others would join you if you married the Malazia?"
"Yes. And that's my other problem. Your Malazia is being very uncooperative."
"What do you mean?"
"Are you aware we share Eldala?"
"It is quite obvious that you do."
"It doesn't seem to matter. I get the sense she's trying to avoid me."
Kieran and Braeden paused their conversation until they were well clear of a pair of guards on the path.
"I'm beginning to think," continued Kieran, "that our joining of hearts was an accident. Certainly there must be someone better suited for me."
Braeden abruptly reined in his horse. "Kieran, the joining of two Baraca hearts, whether by choice of the parents or by chance, is never an accident. To suggest otherwise goes against all Baraca belief."
"What if I want to marry someone else?"
"Why would you want to? You and Jessara are a perfect match."
A perfect match? That was certainly a stretch.
"But what if I did?"
"Eldala must marry. If you choose to marry another, or to remain unmarried, you and your Eldala will spend the rest of your lives with half a heart."
While Kieran and Braeden continued their ride, Kieran's thoughts twisted into a snarled, knotted jumble. When he finally worked through all the tangles, he came back to his original question: What was he supposed to do with Jessa? Now the answer was as clear as a cloudless day. Marrying another woman wasn't a choice at all, not unless he wanted to doom both Jessa and himself to half a life. He *had* to marry her.

~

As Kieran left the stables, he came upon Gilrain and Sienna.

Now there was an unlikely match – Kieran's wild, wolf-like cousin with a dove of a woman. He could see what Gilrain saw in Sienna – he'd sensed it himself. She was confident and poised and graceful. In many ways, she reminded Kieran of Lucia. But what Sienna saw in Gilrain was beyond him.

Kieran cleared his throat, and Gilrain gave Sienna a kiss on the hand. Sienna smiled at Kieran before leaving.

"What are your intentions with her?" Kieran asked abruptly.

He expected Gilrain to react defensively, but his cousin smiled. "I was just going to ask your advice about her."

"My advice?"

"I've already talked with my father, but you know me better than he does."

Kieran supposed that of all the people in Gilrain's life, he was probably the closest. Maybe that explained his concern about Gilrain and Sienna.

"I need a sparring partner this morning," said Kieran. "We can talk in the practice ring."

As the two men faced each other, lunging, parrying, and counter thrusting, Gilrain continued their conversation. "I want to marry Sienna."

"You've always had an eye for women. Why Sienna?"

"She's different."

"How?"

"She's not in awe of me."

"You're obviously in awe of her."

"I suppose."

"But do you love her?"

"Of course I do."

"Then you should marry her."

Gilrain's brows flew up, and he misstepped. "I expected you to say no."

"Why?"

"Well, with the war – "

"Ask her now, but wait until the war is over to marry her."
Gilrain frowned. "Why wait?"
"You might be less inclined to enter the fray if you're married."
"I've never backed down from a fight and you know it."
"Yes, but you've never been married either."
By now, Kieran was breathing hard. Sweat trickled into his eyes and he wiped his face with the back of his hand. "I think I need to work up to these long bouts," he said, halting the match.
The cousins walked to the edge of the arena where a small crowd had gathered to watch them spar. Someone handed Kieran and Gilrain towels.
"What about you?" Gilrain asked.
"What do you mean?"
"When are you going to propose to Jessa?"

Chapter 46

Gilrain stood in Sienna's doorway. It didn't matter how many times she looked at his lean face and green eyes – something wild and free stirred her heart and made her wonder how a man like Gilrain had taken notice of her.

"Lady Sienna, will you join me for a walk?" he asked.

She nodded and took the arm he offered.

They strolled in silence until Gilrain led her to a garden that sloped downward, towards the back wall, she supposed. But if there was a wall, it was hidden by lush evergreens that made a backdrop for hollyhocks, roses, and other plants she didn't recognize. The scene was breathtaking. "Jessa should see this."

"Not yet," he said. He led her farther into the garden and stopped in front of a swan-shaped fountain.

Sienna sat on the edge of the fountain and smoothed her blue linen dress. He sat next to her and took her hand. She liked holding his hand.

"Sienna, I hope I'm not too forward in telling you this," he said.

She tried to breathe.

"We haven't known each other long, but I've come to love you more than my own life."

She blinked and swallowed down her anticipation.

"But there's something I have to tell you first." What could he possibly have to tell her that would cause him to look so concerned?

"Do you remember your family?"

She hadn't thought about her family for years. Once she became a slave, she decided that thinking about them was too painful. "The Esgharites killed my parents when I was young, so I went to live with my grandmother in Barpeta."

"When Kieran and I traveled through Barpeta, we met your grandmother – Neera."

"She's alive?"

"Alive and missing you. She told us all about losing you."

Sienna hadn't cried for a long time. Now she felt her throat constrict and tried to fight back the hot tears that were ready to spill any second.

"I told her I'd try to find you, then bring you back to her."

How many years had it been since she'd seen her grandmother? Ten maybe? As much as she wanted to be reunited with her family, the thought of leaving Jessa and Gilrain now was overwhelming. "I don't have to go back."

"Why wouldn't you?"

"It's been so long. And I don't want to leave you."

He took her hand and pressed his lips to it. "I don't want you to leave either. But I promised I'd take you to Neera. She traveled to A-gora. It's not far."

"Maybe you could bring her here. Then I wouldn't have to go away."

He smiled. "I think I could do that."

She leaned her head against his shoulder. "I love you, Gilrain."

He turned to her and cradled her face in his rough hand. His kiss reached into her heart and made her feel like she was coming alive for the first time. When she stopped to draw a breath, there was a tender look in his eyes.

"Sienna, will you marry me?"

She pressed her fingers to her mouth but couldn't hold back the cry of joy that had to escape. Gilrain silenced it with a hungry kiss.

Later, they strolled arm in arm, slowly walking the length of the garden until they came upon Jessa. She sat on the top of the wall, looking at something. Gilrain gave Sienna a light kiss and excused himself.

Sienna climbed the stairs and settled herself next to Jessa. "So, you've already found the garden."

Jessa took Sienna's hand. "What are you doing here?"

"Gilrain just asked me to marry him." Now there was something Sienna never thought she would say.

"And I suppose you said yes."

"Of course I did."

"You hardly know him."

Sienna ignored the barb. "I feel like I've always known him."

"I'm very happy for you both."

Sienna was surprised at the bitterness in Jessa's voice. "Don't tell me you're jealous?"

Jessa pulled her knees up to her chest and rested her head. "I don't know what I feel."

"You could have this too."

"No I can't. The longer I'm with Kieran, the less I know his heart. I don't think he cares for me at all."

"Have you given him a chance?"

Jessa shook her head. "Sienna, just because you can give your heart away so easily doesn't mean I can."

"You make it sound like I gave it to the first man to come along. I thought you knew me better than that."

"I'm sorry. It's just that… I'm afraid."

"Afraid of what?"

"That there will never be anything between me and Kieran."

Sienna couldn't believe she was hearing this. "How can you be so blind? He hardly takes his eyes off you. And when he's not looking at you, he always knows where you are."

Jessa stared at her, wide-eyed.

"Give the man a chance. And start paying attention."

Jessa sat dumbfounded, listening to her friend's departing footsteps down the stairs and over the stone path. Sienna had accused her of being blind. How could Sienna say such a thing? Jessa wasn't blind. She knew Kieran looked at her practically every moment they were together. She just didn't think it was anything more than looking.

And if it was, she didn't know if she liked it. The guards had looked. Rahnak had looked. Their intentions were never good. Was Kieran any different? Would he use her to satisfy his masculine needs and then cast her aside? Granted, he'd said in the dungeon that he didn't see her that way. If only she knew how he *did* see her.

She sat for a few more minutes and watched the fleecy clouds roll in from the north. A light breeze from the lake danced over her skin and carried a reedy, damp smell. As she stood to descend the stairs, she heard someone approaching.

Arathor was walking along the wall. He stopped and looked at her, almost wistfully. She started to curtsy, but he stopped her. "Jessa, please don't ever think you have to bow to me."

"But sir, you were a king."

He smiled. "Once. Now I'm just a subject of the realm." Then he extended his arm. "Will you join me for a walk, m'lady?"

The arm was more than she'd expected, but the "m'lady" made her stop. "I'm just a servant, my lord."

"You are much more than that, Jessa. And please call me Arathor."

She accepted his offer and they began to stroll around the garden. Bees and hummingbirds zipped among more varieties of plants than she'd ever seen. The two of them walked in silence for several minutes.

She was surprised when he said, "I've heard your story from Dorinda, but I'd like to hear it from you."

"Why would you want to know about my life?"

"Jessa, everyone deserves to have someone hear their story."

It was more than a little disconcerting to think that Dorinda knew so much about her and had shared it with a stranger. At least he was a nice stranger. And he seemed to have a good heart. Despite her discomfort, she put aside her misgivings and began to tell Arathor about meeting Kieran in the forest, being captured and sold, her life in Korisan, and their escape from the castle.

He laughed softly.

She frowned. "What is it?"

"I was just thinking that your circumstances were arranged in such a way to get you to Korisan, so you could save Kieran."

She held her breath. Hadn't she thought the same thing, back in Korisan?

"I'm sorry that your life has been so difficult, said Arathor. "But you have to see you were the only one who *could* have helped him."

They walked for a few more minutes and then he said, "Have you thought about your role as queen of the Baraca?"

"I'm not going back," she said.

"But you were born to be their queen."

She snorted her exasperation. "I don't want to be their queen."

He stopped and looked at her with the same black eyes Kieran had. She wasn't wearing her Keldar stone, but she still felt him boring right into her soul. And she knew she couldn't hide anything from him. Still, she hedged for a moment.

"I don't want the council to control me."

"I think you underestimate yourself. You could change things, make them better for your people."

Jessa's recurring fears threatened to strangle her. How could she admit them to Arathor? But then, how could she hide them? Eventually, he would get the truth out of her. She bowed her head and had to choke out the words. "It's just… I don't … I can't do this."

It was a relief to have finally admitted the truth: She would never be good enough or strong enough to live up to the expectations of others. And it wouldn't matter if she was queen of the Baraca or queen of Teleria. She didn't have it in her to rule.

Chapter 47

The logistics of fighting the Zagorans seemed to fill Kieran's days. He was grateful he had trustworthy men around him who could take up the endless tasks related to war.

All he wanted today was something to help clear his head. If he'd been near the sea, he would have headed straight for it. The lake behind the fortress wouldn't do, and he wasn't in a mood to saddle Fallon. After debating with himself, he finally decided to go to the smithy.

The ringing of hammers reached his ears soon after he left his quarters and he hastened his steps, eager to have a tool in his hand. Upon entering, he noted that Loric and his father were already there, along with Bairn and several Baraca smiths. Kale looked up at Kieran and nodded.

"Getting a head start?" Kieran asked, pulling off his shirt and putting on a sleeveless tunic and leather apron.

"We can't start too soon," said Loric.

Kieran took up a hammer and started working on a half-finished point for a pike. He'd seen very few weapons in one corner of the smithy – half a dozen pikes, a few spears, and halberds with their pick and hammer beaks. But there were no swords. Loric, Toren, and Bairn had a lot of work ahead of them.

With every hammer stroke, it seemed that the weight of being king and fighting a war fell from Kieran like a cloak, and he was able to put his full attention to the piece of metal in front of him. It wasn't long before he was whistling Jessa's song.

Why did his thoughts always lead him back to Jessa?

He let out a heavy sigh and moved on to the next weapon. What was he going to do with her?

Kale put down his hammer and stood next to him. "What is it, son?"

"Jessa." Kieran struck too hard and the spear head flew across the room. The other men stopped their work and stared at him. He took off his apron. This wasn't the place to discuss Jessa.

"Let's go for a walk," suggested Kale.

Kieran agreed.

When they reached the eastern wall, his father said, "She's the girl from the forest, isn't she?"

"Yes. We share a Baraca heart connection."

Kieran expected his father to be surprised by this news, but if he was, he didn't show it.

"So what does that mean for you?"

"Braeden said she's the only woman I can marry."

"And you think that since you share this connection, it should make things easier?"

"Yes."

"But you've been apart for ten years."

"And she's nothing like I expected."

Kale stopped and picked up a gray, fist-sized rock. "Let me show you something."

When they were back in the smithy, Kale placed the plain rock in a vice and tightened it. Then he ran a diamond-edged saw across it. Kieran was curious as to what this had to do with Jessa, but he watched in silence as his father gradually sawed through the rock. When Kale had finished, he released the vice, and both halves of the rock fell to the ground.

Kale picked them up and handed them to Kieran. What he saw stunned him. White and purple crystals caught the light and winked back at him.

"This is Jessa," Kale said. "Inside, she has a beautiful heart. You'll have to look past the rough exterior and get to the treasure inside."

Kieran handed the halves back to Kale, but he closed Kieran's hands around them. "I think you should keep these."

"How am I supposed to get to the inside?"

"Be patient with her and love her. Let her know that no matter what, you'll wait for her as long as it takes."

His father might as well have asked him to fight the whole Zagoran army alone.

Jessa hummed as she walked through the garden. Just this morning, Elisa and Sorina had asked her to help them decorate the great hall for Sienna and Gilrain's betrothal banquet. Jessa had jumped at the chance. Now she took in a deep breath of the green, pungent air, and made note of the various evergreens and flowers she could place on the tables and hang from the walls.

She was just turning down one of the paths when she noticed movement in front of her. She stopped and cautiously moved down the path. A man cloaked in brown was trying to hide behind a large tree. She turned and ran. Just before she reached the citadel, she slammed into someone and looked up.

It was Kieran, just coming out of the smithy, covered in soot and sweat. He grabbed her arms to catch her and emptied her mind of any rational thought.

"What is it?" he asked.

"Someone… in the garden," she panted.

He ran inside the smithy and emerged with his sword. He barked for her to stay with Kale, but she insisted on coming with him. His scowl let her know he wasn't happy with her. By the time they got to the garden, the man was gone.

"What did you see?" he asked.

"A man in a brown cloak."

"What were you doing here alone?"

"Picking out greenery for the banquet."

"Let's go."

Why was he so irritated with her?

Before she could ask, he took her hand and led her to the garrison. It was all she could do to keep up with him. When he stormed into the commanding officer's quarters, the stout Baraca warrior's face turned pale with fright. Despite Kieran's rough appearance, it was obvious he was the king.

"Are you the captain of the guard?" Kieran asked, his eyes flashing.

The man hastily stood and bowed. "Yes, your Majesty."

"I assumed when I entered your fortress that it was well-protected. Was I wrong?"

The captain's face went from gray to red. "What do you mean, Sire?"

"The Lady Jessara found an intruder in the garden. Why are there no guards posted on the northern wall?"

Jessa had never seen him this angry. And why was he calling her "the Lady Jessara"?

The man fumbled with his words. "We have not had an attack here for more than one hundred and fifty years."

"Post guards every ten feet on every section of the wall, night and day. And I want four of your most skilled warriors as an escort for the lady. If anything happens to either of us, I will hold you responsible. Have I made myself clear?"

The man gulped and nodded. "Will there be anything else?"

"Double the guard at the gate."

With that, Kieran turned, and his eyes told Jessa to follow. She blinked and followed without protest. It was more than a little frightening to see how easily he intimidated others. If she'd had any doubts before about his being a king, they had been washed away as if by a flood.

As they entered the smithy, he said, "Stay with me until your guard arrives."

Too stunned to protest, Jessa sat in a chair in the corner and tucked her knees under her chin. As she watched Kieran settle into the rhythm of hammering and heating the metal, she realized that he was a better smith than Bairn – which was saying quite a lot. Bairn had a reputation for being the best sword smith in Teleria. Kieran demonstrated a grace and finesse that Bairn had never shown.

People said that smiths had mystical powers because they could forge the unyielding iron into any form. Bairn had dismissed those stories. He explained that a smith's best tool was his mind, and that it was intelligence, not enchantment, that gave a smith his power.

Kieran might not have been using enchantment to work the iron, but Jessa wondered if he had some kind of mystical power over her. Otherwise she knew she would have been able to stop her eyes from traveling up his forearms, over his biceps, across his shoulders…

No. She shouldn't be looking at him at all. He was the king and she wasn't going to marry him.

She turned around and forced herself to think of anything but him – how to decorate for the banquet, what her mother was like, what had happened to her father. It was pointless; no matter how hard she tried to ignore Kieran, her mind kept wandering back to him. And so did her eyes.

Contentment filled his face as he concentrated on the task in front of him. He was humming under his breath – the song she'd taught him when they were children. An unexpected warmth wrapped around her heart at the thought of Kieran remembering their song. Did that mean he cared for her?

She shook the thought away and let her eyes resume their journey over Kieran's arms. The satisfying memory of having those arms around her slipped in and surprised her. He could have taken advantage of her in the dungeon. Instead he had been tender and protective – and she'd never felt safer or more cherished than she had in his arms. What would it be like to have Kieran's arms around her every night?

Kieran looked up. Jessa froze, embarrassed that he'd caught her staring at him. He smiled, as if he enjoyed it. If she were honest, she would have to admit that she'd enjoyed it, too.

When the four Baraca guards walked into the smithy, Kieran motioned for her to come closer.

"Gentlemen," he said, "you are to stay with Lady Jessara at all times, unless she is in my company or the company of her cousin Stefan. Stand watch outside her apartments and escort her wherever she wishes."

They nodded.

He took her aside and lowered his voice. "Jess, please do as I ask. I don't know what I'd do if anything happened to you." Then he draped her braid over her shoulder, rubbing the loose ends of it between his fingers. "And wear the Keldar stone."

Chapter 48

Kieran looked up at Sienna and nearly choked on his breakfast. "Learn to dance?" he asked.

"Yes, for the betrothal banquet," she said with a sly smile.

Gilrain nodded in agreement.

Kieran grumbled under his breath. He could forge anything, wield a sword to defeat any enemy, fight from the back of a horse, knock a man to the ground in one hit, and give orders as easily as breathing. Why did the thought of learning to dance make him want to run out of the room?

The conversation wouldn't have been so bad, except that everyone he knew was looking at him, as if his answer were the most important thing they'd ever waited to hear.

He ran his finger around the edge of his goblet. "I have more important things to do."

"Such as?" persisted Sienna.

"Training men, forging swords, planning battles."

"If you will not learn to dance," said Bairn, "then I must take your sword."

"What did you say?"

"There is a Baraca proverb that says 'Never give a sword to a man who cannot dance.'"

"And why is that?"

Bairn gave him an amused smile. "There is more to life than battle, sir. You cannot be the warrior you were meant to be if you do not embrace all of life."

Kieran shook his head and exhaled a little more loudly than necessary. "It seems, Lady Sienna, that I have been overruled."

"Good," she said, smiling. "Jessa can teach you today."

Now it was Jessa's turn to choke. "Me?"

"You know all the dances, and you have a perfect sense of rhythm."

Sienna was obviously giving Kieran an excuse to be alone with Jessa. He glanced over at Jessa and knew she was probably thinking the same thing. Her eyes barely met his, and her face was a deep crimson. She dabbed the corners of her mouth with her napkin and stood to leave.

Kieran stood and excused himself. Sienna gave him a look that said she knew why he was leaving. He was surprised when she walked towards him.

"I appreciate your matchmaking attempts, Sienna, but let me do this myself."

She folded her arms across her chest. "If you don't do something soon, you're going to lose her."

"She's not exactly helping me."

"She's learned to hide her feelings."

"What do you mean?"

"She's afraid she has no future with you."

Jessa fumed all the way down the corridor. How could Sienna do this to her? Maybe some part of her wanted to spend more time with Kieran, but she would rather do it on her own terms. And it didn't appear that Kieran wanted to learn to dance. All the way around, it was an awkward situation that Jessa would rather avoid, if at all possible.

She was just opening the door to her quarters when someone put a hand to her shoulder. She jumped and turned around. Kieran had followed her.

"Would you come with me?" he asked.

Before Jessa could refuse, he took her hand and led her to his room.

He motioned for her to sit, and she waited as he left to get something. When he returned, he handed her a small velvet bag. Whatever was in it was quite heavy. When she pulled it out, her breath caught in her throat.

It was an iron rose.

"You made this yesterday – for me?"

He nodded. "Not everything I forge has to be for war."

She traced the surprisingly delicate petals and leaves, and wondered how he could have made something this fragile from a rod of iron. "Kieran, I don't know what to say."

"Tell me you like it."

"Of course I like it. It's lovely."

As if she'd just given him the best news of his life, a dazzling smile spread across his handsome face. It was the kind of smile that could make her forget her fears about being queen, or of never having a future with him. And she couldn't help but return it.

"I know it won't replace the roses in your garden," he said, "but maybe you'll think of me every time you look at it."

How could she tell him that she didn't need anything to remind her of him? He was practically *all* she thought about, night and day.

"I didn't thank you for coming to my rescue yesterday," she said softly.

He put his hand over hers, like it was something fragile. She was surprised at how gentle he could be, and more surprised at how much she enjoyed having his hand cover hers. It was almost as enjoyable as being in his arms.

"I will always come to your rescue. Always."

"Really?" Her question surprised her as much as it appeared to surprise Kieran.

His face hardened, and his answer had an edge of frustration to it. "When I say I'll always come for you, I mean it. It's up to you to believe me."

Hot tears filled her eyes and constricted her throat. "Kieran… I'm sorry. I know you wanted to come for me. And you told me my father came for me. But believing no one would come was… well, it was easier than hoping."

When he looked at her, his iron features softened. "You've had a hard life, Jessa. But that life is over. You have to start hoping and trusting again."

"Kieran, I do want to trust you."

He reached for her Keldar stone. As he rolled it between his fingers, the back of his hand lightly brushed across her neck. She sighed under her breath.

"I'll wait as long as it takes until you do," he said. Then he tugged at her braid. "Now, I have orders from Sienna to learn how to dance. When do my lessons start?"

Kieran impatiently spent the next few hours listening to reports of incoming troops from Braeden and Riordan, forging weapons and horseshoes with Kale, and sparring with Gilrain, who, he noted, was unusually distracted.

When he could wait no longer, Kieran raced to the garden. His path eventually led him to a willow hut with two windows woven into it. He sat in one of the chairs just outside of it and closed his eyes, recalling how pleased Jessa had looked when he gave her the rose.

Despite his skills, it was the most difficult thing he'd ever made. It had taken all of the previous day to forge the rose, and he'd only finished just before midnight.

He was nodding off when he heard someone whistling a familiar tune. When he opened his eyes, Jessa stood in front of him with a tangle of fir branches in her arms. He waved a hand to dismiss her escort. "What's all this?" he asked, taking her burden from her.

"For the banquet."

"The whole fortress is being turned upside-down for this banquet."

She gave him a teasing scowl. "We can't spend all of our time preparing for war. There's more to life than that."

He laid the branches down on the chair. Jessa motioned towards the willow hut.

"Are you ready?" she asked.

He nodded.

"Let's hope it won't take as long to teach you this time as it did ten years ago," she teased.

He arched an amused brow. "What are you going to teach me today, Miss Jessa?"

Jessa put her hands on her hips and her eyes flashed her annoyance.

Kieran smiled. "That's just how you looked when I first met you."

He expected her to look away as she usually did, but when she held his gaze, the look in her eyes made him hot all over and he could hardly breathe. When she moved closer, his hand seemed to have a mind of its own, and he tucked a strand of hair behind her ear. He thought she would pull away, but she stood there still as a statue, her eyes never leaving his.

Then she wrenched her eyes away and cleared her throat. "Shall we begin?"

Jessa swallowed hard and watched Kieran put his hand under her palm. When he placed his other hand on her upper back, she wished she could still her racing heart. She put her hand on his shoulder, counted out the beat, and hummed a waltz she'd heard in Korisan.

As she predicted, Kieran fumbled in his footsteps, and she had to step quickly to avoid his feet. She stopped and looked up at him. No wonder he was misstepping. He was staring at her.

"You have to watch your feet until you learn the steps," she said, hoping he could hear the exasperation in her voice.

He blinked. "I'm sorry, Jessa. I was distracted."

Why did he stare at her so much? She was as plain as dirt.

He surprised her when he said, "You're a beautiful woman."

She let out a breath that said, "You don't know what you're talking about," and counted out the beat again. This time, Kieran dutifully watched his feet, and after a few moments he was doing better – not perfect, but better.

When they stopped, he gave her a sheepish grin. "Being Alardin's descendant helps me with everything else. You'd think it would help me learn to dance."

"Not unless there are enchantments for making your feet cooperate," she said, somewhat amused. And then she remembered the question she'd had when he made the fire in the dungeon. "I'm a descendant of Alardin. Do I have powers like yours?"

"Melchiah said you were known as the best healer in Korisan. Maybe it was because of Alardin."

A crash of thunder jolted Jessa out of her thoughts. She went to the door just in time to see blackened clouds pouring out a cascade of rain. Without thinking, she rushed to pick up the branches on the willow chair. Feeling as unhappy as a wet cat, she put the branches in a corner and wrapped her arms around herself.

Kieran was staring at her again.

"Do you know how uncomfortable that makes me?" she asked.

"What?"

"You – looking at me all the time."

He gave her a boyish grin. "You're nice to look at."

"I think you must be blind. Look at me. I'm drenched."

He moved closer and brushed away the wet strands of hair clinging to her eyelids and cheeks. "It doesn't matter, Jessa. I thought you were beautiful the first day I met you."

"I was eight, Kieran, and I was plain then."

He frowned and trailed his finger along her jaw. She stiffened, remembering how Rahnak had told her she was beautiful and then tried to get whatever he could out of her.

"Never plain," he said and tilted his head.

She held her breath. If he was going to kiss her, was she going to let him?

Another clap of thunder made her jump, and she moved towards the door to escape.

She shivered and took a deep breath, taking in the smells of rain and wet plants and damp earth. When she heard a crackling sound, she turned around, grateful to see that Kieran had started a small fire on the dirt floor.

She crouched and put her hands near the flames. "I didn't know how much I would miss my garden."

Kieran crouched next to her. "What do you miss about it?"

"Digging in the dirt and watching the butterflies do their zigzagging dances." She glanced over at Kieran. He was watching her intently again.

She ignored how uncomfortable it made her feel and looked back to the flames. "It was the one place in Korisan that was mine. I knew I could get away from Rahnak and Delaine there." She shuddered, thinking again of the look on Rahnak's face when he'd attacked her.

Jessa's knees started to ache and she stood. "Are you ready for more waltzing?"

Chapter 49

Kieran whispered the words to stop the rain and helped Jessa carry the greenery back to the dining hall.

When he'd started the rain, he was trying to keep Jessa from leaving after the first lesson. He just hadn't been sure what she would do. She was the kind of woman who would be as likely to run through the rain or stay. When she stayed, he knew he'd done the right thing.

He'd planned to learn the dances and talk with her. When he leaned down to kiss her, he wasn't surprised; he'd been dreaming about kissing her for the last few nights and always woke up with the horrible feeling that she'd shared his dreams. Part of him was glad that the thunder had stopped him, and part of him was disappointed.

Now, as they walked side by side in silence, Jessa held her hands behind her back. She glanced up at him every once in a while and each time she did, the curious looks she gave him made him wonder what she was thinking. He could have used the stone to reach out to her mind to find the answers, but he didn't want to intrude. Arathor had never used the Keldar stone to violate Kieran's privacy, and Kieran wouldn't do that to Jessa. The only clue he had was her face, and Sienna's revelation earlier in the day: "*She's afraid she has no future with you.*"

After they reached the dining hall, Kieran set the branches on a bench. Jessa thanked him and assured him that she could take care of the rest. He wanted to stay and help her, but she made it quite clear she wanted to be alone. Just before leaving, he asked, "Will I see you before the banquet tomorrow afternoon?"

She just arched an amused brow. He kissed her hand and left before he could see her response.

When Kieran entered his quarters. Dorinda was waiting for him. She wore her customary dark cloak, and her wrinkled face was furrowed. "I must speak with you," she said, standing to greet him.

He nodded and motioned for her to sit. "What is it?"

"Have you asked Jessara to marry you?"

The question made him flinch. "I'm trying to court her, but she doesn't seem interested."

The mystic frowned. "You must get her to say yes soon."

"Why?"

"I know you will not have the support of many of the clans unless they hear you are going to marry the Malazia."

"Yes, but I thought I'd have plenty of time."

"I have had visions of the Zagoran army entering Teleria, perhaps in three or four months. You will need every available Telerian and Baraca warrior you can find in order to defeat them."

He stood and paced back and forth between the fireplace and the sofa. "I won't rush her, Dorinda."

"I could give her a nudge."

"No. I don't want anything you say to influence her. She has to make up her mind without knowing anything about the alliance."

Dorinda sighed and stood. "Kieran, there are difficult things I must show her, related to her fulfilling her position as Malazia. If she asks about you or an alliance, I will not hide the truth from her."

Kieran growled under his breath. It pained him to think Jessa would have to see the same kinds of visions that Dorinda had shown him.

Jessa rubbed the fir branches between her fingers and savored the spicy smell. She should be eating right now, but she wanted to finish hanging the branches from the walls and decorating the linen-covered tables before going to bed. She had too much to do tomorrow to let this wait. And she was less likely to run into Kieran if she stayed here.

Frankly, after spending the afternoon with Kieran, she was glad to be alone. It had been very suspicious that the storm had cleared just as they finished the last dance. If she hadn't known better, she would have thought he conjured the rainstorm just to keep her there.

Fiery notes ran up her spine when she remembered the way he'd leaned in to kiss her. At the time, she was afraid he *would* kiss her. Now she almost wished that she'd let him. For the last few nights, she'd dreamed of more than just kissing him and hoped he hadn't shared any of those dreams.

Her cautious side still wondered what his intentions were. His concern for her safety, the gift of the iron rose, and the attempted kiss could have been indications that he cared for her, but it would take more than that to convince her that his feelings went any deeper than casual infatuation. And would it matter anyway? As she kept reminding herself, he was the king, and she didn't want to be a queen.

Just as she placed the last branch on the last table, she was startled when someone entered the room. She turned around and drew in a quick breath.

A short, cloaked figure was coming toward her. At first, Jessa thought it was the intruder from the garden, but as the figure came closer, the hood dropped and Jessa saw an older woman before her. Something about her ancient face was familiar.

"Kieran said I would find you here," the woman said.

"Do I know you?"

"I am Dorinda, the Hada mystic."

Jessa motioned for her to sit at the closest table.

"I have a message from your mother," Dorinda said.

"My mother?"

"When I told her I had seen you coming here, she said to tell you that she is anxiously awaiting your return."

Jessa groaned. "If I go back, they'll ask me to be their queen."

"And that is the very thing you must do."

"Did the council put you up to this?"

The woman looked mildly amused. "I am independent of the council and answer to no one but myself."

Dorinda motioned for Jessa to walk with her. After a few moments, they arrived at Jessa's room. As they sat on the flowered sofa, Dorinda put her gnarled hand on Jessa's. "I am from a long line of mystics. It is a heavy burden we bear. But we also have the privilege of choosing the Malazia in every generation. I am the mystic who chose you."

"*You* chose me? Why?"

"I saw pieces of your life before you were born."

Jessa felt her throat constrict. "What pieces?"

Dorinda left her hand on Jessa's, closed her eyes, and a series of images passed through Jessa's mind.

Jessa's mother and father standing over a cradle, smiling; Jessa playing at her mother's feet; Kieran giving Jessa the sea shell; the slave traders taking her away; the slave market in Korisan; Jessa sitting next to Kieran's bed, drawing out the poison; Jessa sleeping in the dungeon; Jessa sitting on a throne with a crown on her head.

Jessa cried out in frustration. “You could have stopped me from going to meet Kieran or being captured. I’d still be with my family.”

“It was not my place to interfere at the time. You were destined to meet Kieran. And you were destined to save him.”

Not this again. “Why are you here?”

“Because I know you are having trouble making up your mind.”

“About what?”

“About many things, but particularly about being the Malazia.”

Jessa stood. Dorinda was starting to sound like Stefan, Kieran, and Arathor. And Jessa was tired of people telling her what to do. “My choice won’t make any difference to anyone. And I won’t be governed by your visions. The council can find another Malazia.”

She walked toward the door, but the mystic caught her arm and another series of visions flooded her head.

Jessa’s mother lying in bed, dying of a broken heart; Baraca fighting Baraca; Baraca fighting Telerians; Kieran’s army falling to the Zagorans; Ciara enslaving Baraca and Telerians.

Jessa looked back at the mystic. “What… was that?”

Dorinda looked haggard. “It is what will happen if you refuse to be the Malazia.”

“How can you be sure?”

“In my seventy years, I have never been wrong.”

A nauseating feeling hit Jessa dead center. “No. I can’t do it.”

“There is one more thing I must tell you.”

Jessa didn’t want to hear anymore.

“Before I chose you, your parents named you Jessara. When they did, they were not aware of the name’s true meaning.”

“I’m named after the first female Malazia. Why would that matter?”

“The name Jessara means ‘Valiant Queen.’”

Chapter 50

Kieran knew he should have been more optimistic as he watched warriors from the Tyman, Nedebar, Linden, and Kumai clans file into the barracks. He should have been grateful that anyone had shown up. But there were so few of them. And if he couldn't get Jessa to agree to marry him… He shook his head in frustration.

A voice from behind startled him. "You're too young to be carrying such heavy burdens."

It was Sahbél. His arrival was the one bright spot in Kieran's day. Then he saw the concern on Sahbél's face.

"What is it?" Kieran asked.

"Ciara is spreading disease and famine out from Korisan into surrounding areas of Teleria."

Kieran swore out loud. "The sooner we end her curse, the better."

"Has there been any word on that subject?" Sahbél asked.

"Arathor and Dorinda aren't sure. All they can give me is speculation." He shook his head. "But I have more pressing matters to attend to."

"Such as?"

Kieran smiled. "I'm glad you asked. I'm forming a war council, and I want you to be part of it."

He led Sahbél to a room furnished with a large, rectangular table and several chairs. Arathor and Kieran's other companions were already there, debating the best strategy for building Kieran's forces. Sahbél sat to Arathor's right and Kieran sat to Arathor's left. While the debate grew louder, Kieran's mind kept wandering back to his dancing lessons with Jessa, and his conversation with Dorinda.

What had Dorinda told Jessa? And what could *he* say to her? His present relationship with Jessa was difficult enough. Broaching the subject of a Baraca-Telerian alliance with her could be like putting a spark to a pile of dry brush.

A question from Gilrain pulled Kieran back to his present task. He blinked and asked Gilrain to repeat himself.

"How soon did Dorinda expect the Zagorans to be here?"

Kieran answered with a blank stare.

Gilrain frowned. "You're distracted again. Send Dorinda to the council so we can ask her ourselves."

The other men did a poor job of hiding their knowing smiles. It was quite obvious they knew who was distracting him. Kieran shook his head.

"It won't happen again," he growled.

"At the moment," said Arathor, "you should take care of that other matter."

Sahbél raised a questioning brow.

"I'm still trying to court the Malazia."

"You found her? Where was she?"

"I found her in Korisan, by accident."

"I'd very much like to hear *that* story," said Sahbél.

"Another time, my friend. Arathor's right. Until things are settled with Jessa, my mind will not be on war."

Kieran excused himself and went to find Dorinda. As he walked by the kitchen, the familiar smell of apple pie curled itself around his nose. When he entered the kitchen, he was surprised to see Jessa standing behind a pile of peeled apples.

"What are you ladies up to?" he asked.

"We're cooking for the banquet," said Sorina, keeping her eyes on her rolling pin.

When Jessa brought her head up, her black eyes captured him all over again. He wished they were alone so he could talk to her. When she looked down and started cutting apples, he smiled. If she did become queen, he could imagine her working in the kitchen beside the cook, or digging in the garden, up to her elbows in mud.

He moved closer, took one of the apples out of the pile, and started tossing it from one hand to the other.

Jessa let out a mock cry. "You scoundrel." As quick as lightning, she caught the apple in mid-toss. "These are for the pies. If you're hungry, get one from the cellar."

He gave her a bow and tugged at her braid. She yanked it out of his hand. "Either help or get out of the kitchen."

Just before he left, he snatched the apple she'd taken back and took a bite before she could stop him.

When Kieran found Dorinda, she was putting her cloak in her satchel. "Leaving so soon?" he asked.

"The other mystics will be meeting in the Ancala camp. We have much to discuss."

"May I ask what?"

She looked up at him, and her face was filled with sorrow. "Our chief concern is how you are to end the curse."

Kieran's stomach did a flip. "I'm assuming it involves killing Ciara."

Dorinda shook her head. "It involves death, but I do not know if it will be Ciara's death."

Kieran was silent for a moment as he contemplated what that could mean. Then he said, "Before you leave, I'd like you to meet with my war council."

She looked somewhat amused. "I was wondering when you were going to invite me."

When Kieran entered the banquet hall later that day, he noted that all of his friends and family were there, including Sahbél. He also noted that Stefan was absent, but he wasn't surprised. He'd only seen Stefan once since arriving at the fortress.

Realizing he was overdressed, Kieran left to change into something more suited to the occasion. As he returned to the corridor, he saw Jessa and Sienna walking just ahead of him. He moved between them and offered both arms.

"Such fine ladies need an escort."

Sienna laughed and Jessa blushed. Each woman took an arm and when Kieran glanced at Jessa, he could hardly swallow. She wore a purple brocade dress with a scooping lace-edged neckline and a tightly cinched bodice that accentuated her perfect figure. Instead of a single braid, her hair was in several braids, each embellished with golden threads and intricately looped around her head. A delicate fringe of hair framed her face, and she looked more beautiful than ever.

When they reached the banquet hall, Sienna curtsied her thanks and immediately went to Gilrain's side. Jessa continued to hold Kieran's arm as he escorted her to a table.

"The décor is lovely," he said. She looked up at him and smiled. "As are you," he added.

She sat and took a sip from her goblet.

He sat next to her and soon the other guests were seated. Before the meal started, Uncle Loric stood beside Gilrain, and Neera stood next to Sienna.

Gilrain had brought Neera to the fortress just a few days ago. She had offered a reward to Gilrain and Kieran for finding Sienna, but they had agreed that seeing the family reunited was reward enough.

Neera raised her goblet and said, "We are here to honor this man and this woman."

Applause filled the room. Loric raised his hand to quiet the guests and Neera said, "Have you, Gilrain, son of Loric, pledged your troth to this woman?"

"Yes, I have."

Then Loric said, "And have you, Sienna, grand-daughter of Neera, pledged your troth to this man?"

"Yes, I have," she answered.

"Then," said Loric, "raise your glasses and join me in a toast to this couple's health and future."

"Aye," said everyone in the room.

"Aye," said Kieran, all the while wondering when he would be standing in Gilrain's place as his father raised a toast to Jessa and himself. He drained the cup and a young Baraca girl filled it.

Presently, more Baraca youth brought in platters of food – quite simple compared to the food in Korisan, but certainly more familiar: roast pheasant and duck, grapes and apples, a variety of breads and cheeses, and Sorina's apple pies. Soon the guests were enjoying the food, laughing, talking, and raising various toasts to Gilrain and Sienna. Kieran was soon caught up in a conversation with Sahbél.

His friend was asking him how he'd found Jessara. When Kieran finished recounting all that had happened since leaving the Nedebar fortress, Sahbél shook his head. "You're a very lucky man. You'd be in Korisan still if it weren't for your Eldala."

Kieran took a bite of pheasant. "I know. Now I have to find a way to marry her."

When the dancing finally began, Kieran's mother had to encourage him to join in the celebration, but after one dance, Kieran began to enjoy himself and stopped worrying about all the mistakes he was making. Jessa, he noted, danced with every other man in the room. He wondered again if she was trying to avoid him.

After the final line dance, Kieran slumped in his chair and stared into his wine goblet. Sahbél moved his chair closer.

"I can see why you're having trouble," said Sahbél.

Kieran flicked a glance at Sahbél and then stared into his wine again.

"I don't know if you've noticed, but her eyes hardly leave you," said Sahbél. "I just think she's afraid. Have you told her how you feel?"

"I made an iron rose for her, said things to her – "

"But have you *told* her?"

Kieran shook his head.

"You should tell her tonight – before you lose her for good."

Kieran would rather fight a gurithent than face Jessa's uncertainty. But Sahbél was right.

Kieran drained his goblet and strode towards Jessa before he could change his mind. Just as he reached her, Marcus stepped to the front of the room.

"This next waltz is at the request of the newly betrothed couple, in honor of their Baraca friends."

When Marcus drew out a wooden flute and started to play, Kieran froze. It was the dance of the Eldalafar. He extended his hand to Jessa and said, "May I have this dance?"

Shyly, as if he were a stranger, she took Kieran's hand, and they began the waltz, moving in time to the playful melody of their song. Kieran's feet knew exactly where to go, leaving his mind free to concentrate on Jessa's face. When she looked at him without flinching, waves of molten heat spread through him.

Over the course of the dance, he closed the space between them and waltzed her through the double doors leading to the flagstone courtyard. As they continued to dance, her scent wrapped itself around his heart until he could think of nothing but her. Their Keldar stones flared in a sparkling blue light and her breath came in quick gasps. When she looked up at him with widening eyes, he did the only thing he could.

His lips captured hers.

They were softer than he'd imagined. Her breathless sigh encouraged him to continue, but he knew there was something he had to say first.

"I love you."

He tilted his head to kiss her again, but she stepped back, and there was a question in her eyes.

"What is it?"

"There's something I have to know."

"Go on."

"Dorinda showed me what would happen if I don't become the Malazia."

Kieran's shoulders tensed.

"I saw your army fall. Why would that happen?"

Why this question now? He still hadn't decided how to approach this subject with her. Anything he said could push her away. But to remain silent would be worse.

He led her to a bench in the shadows and sat beside her. Before speaking, he took a deep breath. "When I traveled through Teleria, I met Sahjahn, leader of the Ancala Baraca. He told me that many of the outlying clans and the Baraca gangs would never fight the Zagorans unless I married the Malazia."

Immediately, Kieran felt a wall rise up between them. This was going about as badly as he'd expected.

When Jessa spoke, she couldn't hide her disappointment. "Then you need me to help build your army."

He stood and started to pace. "Jessara, I've never loved anyone but you. I didn't know you were the Malazia until I spoke with your mother."

Jessa opened her mouth to speak but someone interrupted her.

"I knew it was you."

Kieran jerked his head around to see Stefan walking across the courtyard.

Chapter 51

Still reeling from Kieran's revelation, Jessa drew in a sharp breath and felt Kieran's arm come protectively around her shoulder.

"Is it your habit to eavesdrop on private conversations?" Kieran asked.

"It is my habit, Telerian, to watch over my cousin."

Jessa stiffened. "What did you mean, 'I knew it was you'?"

She couldn't see Stefan's face, but she knew he was glaring at both of them. "Kieran is the boy you went to meet every day, is he not?"

"Yes, not that it's any concern of yours."

"Jessara, I am sorry to have to tell you this, but on the day you were stolen, I swore I would kill him."

Jessa felt all the blood drain from her face.

Kieran stepped between them. "If that's the only way to settle this, then so be it."

Stefan pushed his finger into Kieran's chest. "I will meet you at dawn in the arena. Swords and shields, no armor."

Stefan turned to Jessa. "When he is dead, I will take you home."

Jessa's knees felt like water and she leaned against Kieran. "Is there any other way?"

Kieran stroked the top of her head. "Jessa, I can't ignore this challenge. I'll do what I can to not kill him, but I *will* defend myself."

Lying in her bed, Jessa still couldn't believe Kieran had kissed her. Only the memories of the softness of his beard brushing across her cheek and the song flooding her heart when his lips met hers told her it had really happened. And it was better than she ever could have imagined. Why had she let that nagging question stop him?

His answer had shocked and angered her, and it had planted another seed of doubt about his intentions. But then he had said that he'd never loved anyone else. The thought almost made her cry. When she remembered that she didn't want to be anyone's queen – not even Kieran's queen – she *did* cry.

Jessa brushed away her tears and turned her thoughts to the duel between Kieran and Stefan. As much as she disliked Stefan, she didn't want to see him die. But if she had to choose between them, she would rather lose Stefan. She didn't know what she would do if Kieran died.

And then the thought of losing Kieran made her realize that something in her heart had changed. Like a new rose opening its petals at the first touch of spring, Jessa knew that her heart was beginning to open to Kieran.

Jessa couldn't contain her anxiety as she entered the practice arena to watch Kieran's duel. Despite his promise that he would try to spare Stefan, she had the awful feeling that in just a few minutes, one of the men would be dead.

Stefan stood in one corner, angrily thrusting into the air. Kieran stood in the other corner, calmly working through his practice forms. She knew that under Kieran's calm exterior was a man who could kill in one stroke.

After a few moments, Toren called the combatants to the center of the arena and announced the start of the contest. Jessa watched with hardly a breath. Stefan picked up his shield and held his head high as he strode to the center of the ring. When Kieran walked from his corner, his lack of emotion startled her. And why didn't he have a shield?

Kieran made the first strike. Stefan blocked the blow with his wooden shield. The shield's bottom quarter dropped off as it shuddered and cracked. Stefan yelled, surprised at the ferocity of Kieran's blow. Kieran struck again, and Stefan blocked the second blow with his sword. After each attack, Stefan retaliated with a wild series of high and low strokes, growling his frustration as Kieran deftly blocked each one.

When Stefan made a downward stroke, Kieran's sword came up, but it left his midsection open. Stefan used the opportunity to slash at Kieran's stomach. Kieran clenched his jaw while staggering backwards from the force of the blow, ignoring the blood coming through his leather jerkin.

Charging at Stefan with a fierce yell, Kieran used a series of high and low slashing cuts, followed by a head butt. With blood flowing freely from his brow, Kieran's next stroke shattered Stefan's shield. Stefan yelled in frustration and hurled the shield at Kieran. Kieran used his sword to block it.

Jessa felt light headed and had to remind herself to breathe. Elisa put a sympathetic arm around her.

"I'm sure Kieran will be fine," Elisa whispered. The tremble in her voice wasn't convincing.

Stefan charged ahead like a raging bull. Kieran sidestepped and blocked Stefan's stroke. Stefan staggered forward, regained his footing, and grabbed a double headed axe from the stash of weapons in the corner. The move took Kieran by surprise, and the crowd let out a collective gasp at Stefan's desperate move.

Kieran ducked and rolled to avoid the axe. When he came up, he quickened his pace and blocked the blows from both weapons. Finally, a slashing blow from Kieran dislodged the axe from Stefan's hand.

Through a series of high and low serpentine cuts, Kieran threw Stefan off balance. Kieran used the opportunity to slam his shoulder into Stefan's chest, momentarily stunning him. Stefan retaliated wildly, but misjudged the distance, and Kieran easily sidestepped the thrust. Kieran moved in and hit the space between Stefan's thumb and hand with his sword's pommel. The sword fell from Stefan's hand and he rolled onto his back. Kieran stood over him, his sword poised to kill.

Jessa let out a cry and Kieran looked up at her. She couldn't speak, but her heart reached out and said, "Spare him."

As if he were coming out of a trance, Kieran shook his head and sheathed the blade.

Jessa's heart raced like a thousand horses and she took a deep breath. Kieran offered Stefan a hand up, but Stefan glared at him and spat on Kieran's hand. Picking up his sword with his good hand, Stefan ran from the arena, cursing all the way out the door.

In a heartbeat, Jessa was at Kieran's side. He threw off his jerkin, revealing a shirt drenched with sweat and blood. Jessa didn't care. She leaned into him and wrapped her arms around him. He was alive and that was all that mattered. Another petal in her heart opened up.

He pulled off his shirt and she stepped back, trying to avert her eyes. And then wondered why. He was nice to look at.

When he said, "Jedza mar kaavah," the cuts on his stomach and eyebrow healed. Toren gave him a new shirt, and after he'd pulled it over his head, he tugged at her braid and said, "So you do care."

She batted her eyes at him. "I didn't want to see all my hard work go to waste." Then she put her hand in his and they left the arena. As they walked toward the stable, her voice barely came out in a whisper. "I thought you were going to kill him."

Kieran's jaw tightened. "I spared him for you."

Inside the stable, Jessa breathed in the familiar odors of hay and horses. A flock of doves cooed in the rafters. Jessa walked past the stalls and stopped when she came to Kieran's horse. She scooped up a handful of oats and let Fallon nibble them out of her hand.

"I'm just glad it's over," she said.

When she turned to look at him, her breath caught in her throat. He was leaning against the doorframe, arms crossed, staring at her so intently she could feel it.

"You're doing it again," she murmured.

"I know. You'll just have to get used to it."

She looked away and stroked Fallon's nose, trying frantically to figure out how to change the subject. "How do you live with the burden of being the king?" she asked.

He walked towards her and began to curry a buckskin mare in the next stall. "At first, I didn't want to believe it. I was happy with my life as a blacksmith. To be honest, I didn't go to find Arathor until I ran away."

"When you killed that soldier?"

"Yes. How did you know about that?"

"Elisa told me."

"It forced me to find Arathor. And it led me to Dorinda."

"She came to you too?"

Kieran laughed softly. "You weren't the only one to see what could happen if you don't walk in your destiny."

Jessa shuddered at the memory of Dorinda's visions. "Then you had a choice?"

"I did then and I do now, every day."

"Dorinda told me she chose me because of the circumstances of my life. Even my name means 'Valiant Queen.' But I don't think I have the courage to do this."

"I think you've shown incredible courage already."

"What are you talking about?"

"Living as a slave and staying alive, helping me, singing in Kori-san."

Jessa shook her head.

"Courage is not the lack of fear," Kieran said, "but instead is the decision that something else is more important than your fear."

"That sounds like something Arathor would say."

"It is."

They laughed together.

"At least you've had your family and friends to help you walk through this," she said. "I feel so alone."

He put down the curry comb and moved close enough that she felt his breath on her face. "You're not alone."

"What do you mean?"

His hand came over hers. She bit her lip and noticed again how the song in her sensed the fire in him. Then he smiled and said, "You have me."

"Why would you do that for me?"

He ran the back of his fingers along her cheek and tipped her face up to his. The song grew louder. "Because I love you, Jess."

She closed her eyes and yielded to him, letting his strong arms surround her. There was nowhere else she would rather be than right here, in Kieran's embrace. "This feels like a dream," she said. "I'm afraid I'll wake up and you'll be gone."

"How can I make you understand that I will *never* leave you?"

She looked up and the desperation in his eyes dissolved her fears. She felt another petal in her heart unfurl.

"Kieran..."

He pulled her close, but not so close that she couldn't see his passion for her. She folded into him, and her whole body trembled with anticipation. His hands came up and he buried his fingers in her hair. His kiss was heady and intoxicating, and made her feel like she was flying.

Her arms came up around his neck and he pulled her closer. She was exquisitely aware of his earthy scent, the soft tickle of his beard on her face, and the way his lips danced with hers. When she pulled away for a breath, she felt more alive than ever before.

Chapter 52

Ciara cursed out loud. Kieran's powers were increasing. It was the only explanation for why she couldn't use her silver basin to find him. As much as she hated to admit it, she had only herself to blame. If she'd been paying closer attention to him and that wretch of a slave, he'd be dead. It had been foolish to celebrate her victory prematurely.

The only clue she had to Kieran's whereabouts came from one of the castle guards. He'd reported that he sent the muck wagon through the castle gate on the morning of the execution, and that it had traveled north, towards Maquoya. As soon as she heard the news, she sent Sharaq to find Kieran. After waiting several days, and hearing nothing, she was now preparing to leave the castle to find him herself – which reminded her just how desperate she was. She hadn't been outside the castle for more than twenty years – not since first entering Korisan in her quest to retake the throne.

A knock at her door startled her.

"What is it?"

A page wordlessly entered her room and laid a scroll on her dressing table. When he left, she picked up the scroll, noting it bore Sharaq's seal. As she read the contents, she let out the first sigh of relief she'd breathed in days.

One of Sharaq's spies had infiltrated the Kofar Baraca fortress. Jessa was there. It was unfortunate that Jessa had raised the alarm before the spy could search for Kieran. She would have to tell Sharaq to have him executed for his blunder.

Then Ciara smiled. She couldn't get to Jessa yet. But at the first sign of her leaving the fortress, Ciara would have her guriths waiting. And once she had Jessa, Kieran was sure to follow. Men always came to the rescue of their "one true love."

Jessa sat across from Arathor, sipping cascabel tea. He'd called her to his chambers after breakfast. So far, their conversation had been unremarkable. She waited somewhat impatiently for him to explain why he'd invited her. She knew from experience that he never made idle conversation.

He put down his cup. "Have you made a decision?"

Jessa wanted to feign ignorance, but she knew it wouldn't do any good. "I'm closer to going home than I was the last time I spoke with you."

"May I ask why?"

Jessa took another sip and then stared into her tea cup. "Dorinda came to see me."

Arathor chuckled. "She can be very persuasive."

Jessa looked up. "You've had the benefit of her revelations?"

"She came to me before Kieran's birth and told me that my son would be the one to fulfill the prophecy." He paused. "Are there any other reasons?"

She felt her face flush, remembering her last encounter with Kieran in the stable, particularly the way he'd kissed her. "Your son thinks I have the courage to be the Malazia. I'm still not sure."

Arathor excused himself and when he returned, he carried a long wooden box. He set it on the table in front of her. "I agree with him. And because I do, it's time to give you this."

Jessa put down her cup and leaned forward to lift the lid.

She drew in a breath. A short gold scabbard lay among the velvety folds of the box.

She lifted the scabbard and drew out the double-edged weapon. The grip fit her hand perfectly. She sliced through the air as Bairn had taught her. Then she took it to the window and held it up to the light. An intricate pattern of swirls and spirals ran the length of the blade. When she turned it over, she saw the words "Bear Shed'ar well, Queen Jessara."

When she was a child, her parents had told her the story of Jessara, queen of the Baraca, and her sword "Shed'ar" – "Brave-hearted." It had stirred a desire in her to have her own sword and to be a part of some grand adventure.

The sword fell from her hand and hit the carpet with a dull thud. She spun around to look at Arathor. "Why are you giving me Queen Jessara's sword?"

"It's time for you to take up your ancestor's mantle."

Before she could argue, there was a knock at the open door. Arathor bid the page to enter.

"They just finished this, sir," he said as he brought in a wooden trunk and set it down.

When Arathor pulled out the contents, a thorny knot grew in Jessa's stomach. It was armor for a woman.

"More of Jessara's things?" she asked.

There was a mischievous twinkle in Arathor's eye. "No, I had the armorers make this for *you*."

Jessa sat in her quarters, staring at the trunk and the sword. Sienna came into the room and sat next to her.

"What's all this?" Sienna asked.

"Gifts from Arathor."

Sienna stood and opened the trunk. "Jessa, did you see this? It's beautiful." She pulled out the breastplate and laid it on the bed. It was gold, with a silver rose emblazoned on the front. Next to the breastplate, she set down gold vambraces and greaves.

Jessa sighed. "What am I supposed to do with all this?"

There was Sienna's quirky little smile. "I think you're supposed to wear it."

A knock at the door made Jessa look up. Marcus stood there with a bundle of clothing. "My lady," he said. "You'll need these first, I believe."

Jessa sighed. Apparently, she wasn't going to get out of this easily.

Marcus laid the clothing on a chair. "Riding clothes for your journey home, a new woolen cloak, a belt for your sword, and a gambeson to wear under the armor."

Then he gave Jessa a wink and left.

"May I?" Sienna asked with a curtsy.

As Jessa pulled on the pieces of clothing, she recognized Marcus's fine attention to detail. Everything fit perfectly – the silk undergarments and blouse, the blue split woolen riding skirt, and the black riding boots. When she looked in the mirror, she drew in a breath.

Despite what Kieran had said about her beauty, she'd never believed him. Now she thought twice about it. She let her eyes slowly travel up from her skirt to her face. She did have a nice figure – not as thin as Sienna's and not as full as Halda's. Her heart skipped a beat when she saw Kieran's reflection.

Kieran was sorry Jessa had seen him. He could look at her all day and never get tired of it. "My pardon for intruding," he said as she twirled to face him.

"How long have you been standing there?" she asked.

"Not long enough."

Sienna smiled and excused herself.

Jessa scrunched up her face and gave him a kiss on the cheek. "Now that you're here, you can help me with this armor."

"Armor?"

"Arathor gave it to me, along with Queen Jessara's sword. I still don't know why."

Kieran would have to ask Arathor about this later. He would never allow Jessa to go into battle. Still, Jessa had asked for his help and he wasn't going to miss this chance to be alone with her.

"First the gambeson," he said, lifting the heavily padded tunic over her head.

"Is this necessary? It's so hot."

Kieran smiled. "It will absorb the force of a blow. You'll be glad you have it if you ever get hit." *Which will never happen,* he thought.

"Have you decided to go home?" he asked as he buckled the vambraces onto her wrists.

She adjusted one of them. "Yes."

After he buckled the breastplate to the back piece, his hands lingered on her waist. "Have you really thought this through?"

"Kieran, *you* told me I should go. Are you telling me to stay now?"

"I know you have to go home. I just don't know if I can let you go."

She leaned into him and rested her head on his chest. "You'll have to," she said. "I'm leaving tomorrow, before I change my mind."

"I wondered when you would make that decision," said Stefan.

Kieran looked up and his jaw clenched. For a moment, he wished he'd ignored Jessa's plea to spare Stefan's life.

"I will prepare for travel," Stefan continued.

"As will I," said Kieran.

"I assure you, Telerian, I can take care of my cousin quite well."

"But I was the one who promised to bring her home," said Kieran. "And she's my responsibility now, not yours."

"As you wish," he said and then left.

"You shouldn't come," said Jessa. "You could be captured or killed."

He tucked a strand of hair behind her ear and left his hand on her cheek. "Jessa, I'd risk death to see you safely home."

It took him by surprise when she stood on tiptoe to kiss him. He looked into her eyes, and soon he was conscious of nothing but the sweetness of her soft lips on his.

"Absolutely not!" said Toren. "You can't put yourself at risk like this."

When Kieran had broached the subject of escorting Jessa to the Hada fortress, he'd anticipated some resistance from his companions, but not quite this much. Toren's protest opened up a round of objections from the others.

Only Kale remained silent. It wasn't until the debate died down that he spoke. "Don't you see? He has to go."

Gilrain looked at Kale like he'd just sprouted two heads. "Have you lost your mind, uncle?"

"You of all men should understand," said Kale with a wry smile.

"Me?"

"If Sienna were leaving, you'd do the same thing."

Kieran thought Gilrain might spring like a wolf right there. "But Kieran is the king," said Gilrain. "And after what happened the last time – no, he shouldn't go."

"He lost her once," said Kale, "and now she's his responsibility."

Kieran put up a hand to silence more protests. "I planned to take Riordan and Toren with me, along with a small contingent of Kofar warriors, and Jessa's personal guard. If it will make you feel better, you can come too."

Gilrain glared at him. It was amusing to see Gilrain this upset.

"It's madness," said Riordan.

"I promised her mother and the council that I'd return her."

"What about your preparations for war?" asked Braeden.

"I'll give orders before I leave. And you each have your tasks that I trust will be completed."

"Is that a command, Sire?" Riordan asked.

"No, but you swore to protect me and I expect you to keep your word."

Kieran found Arathor in the practice arena. Toren twisted the three parts of the wooden practice dummy. Arathor deftly avoided the spinning swords and shields. Kieran stepped in and continued to turn the urchin. Toren nodded and left.

"Why did you send armor for Jessa?" Kieran asked.

Arathor blocked the wooden sword. "Because she may have a part to play in this battle."

"She's not a warrior."

Arathor smiled. "In some ways, I think women can be much more fierce than men when they have to be."

"Surely you're not asking her to put herself in danger?"

"Have you forgotten that you're both already in danger?"

"Well, of course. The minute we left Korisan we were in danger. But Jessa is *not* going to be anywhere near the battle."

Arathor wiped his brow with his sleeve and stared at Kieran. "Do you suddenly have the wisdom of the mystics? Have you seen her future?"

"No, but I can't imagine she'd have to fight."

"Whether she does or not, you'd be wise to teach her the way of the sword."

Chapter 53

The wet, dreary morning greeting Jessa matched her dismal mood. All night she'd gone over the arguments for going home, weighing them against what she already knew about her clan. She had the feeling she was walking into another kind of slavery, and she had had enough of slavery to last three lifetimes.

The doubts were magnified by the fact that she didn't know how long she would have to stay. For all she knew, it could be months before they would let her leave to see Kieran – if they let her leave at all. On the other hand, if they did let her leave, she wouldn't be able to spend very much time with Kieran anyway: He had a war to wage, and he wouldn't have time for her until the war was over. Either way, she didn't want to leave him.

Now as she climbed onto Kieran's horse, a whistling breeze penetrated her many layers of clothing and armor, and the cold seeped into her bones. It wouldn't have mattered if the day had been sunny and warm. Nothing could take the edge off of her misery.

As the travelers gathered near the front gate of the fortress, Elisa and Sorina came to bid them farewell. Jessa regretted that she hadn't spent much time with either of them, especially Elisa. The woman's company had been a bright spot in her visit here. Jessa knew she would miss her terribly.

The only comforting thought was that Sienna was coming with her.

Jessa knew from years of friendship that Sienna could be stubborn, but yesterday morning, she'd seen a whole new side of her friend and it was a little frightening. When Jessa broke the news of her departure to Sienna, Jessa expected Sienna to stay with Neera.

Instead, Sienna insisted on coming with her. Nothing would convince her to stay, not even Jessa's argument that the Hada would never accept her, and would most likely look down on her. Sienna crossed her arms and said, "You're going to need me more than ever."

Jessa shifted her armor and put her arms loosely around Kieran's waist. Kieran kicked Fallon's flanks and the horse bolted forward so quickly that Jessa had to tighten her hold on Kieran to keep from falling off. If only she were as eager as the horse to be on the road.

Jessa sighed and looked at the companions. Just in front of Kieran were Toren and Riordan, Kieran's self-appointed escort. Behind Kieran rode Stefan, Jessa's four guards, two more guards for Kieran, and Gilrain, with Sienna. Gilrain's horse led Jessa's horse, Brielle.

Before they left the fortress, Kieran had taken Jessa to the stable and given her the buckskin mare. When she asked him why *that* horse, he'd smiled and said Fallon had grown attached to her. Then Kieran promised he would teach Jessa to ride while they traveled.

But not today. Today, she was glad she was riding with Kieran.

She pulled her cloak tighter around her shoulders and slid as close to him as she could. He looked over his shoulder, as if he were watching for someone following them. Jessa doubted anyone would. They were staying off the roads and traveling cross-country. She pressed her face against his back to hide from the wind. It was going to be a long, melancholy journey.

By late afternoon, the group dismounted by the banks of a wide river. Riordan went ahead to find a shallow place to ford. Jessa looked up at the sky and stretched, stiff from the day's ride. At least the rain had stopped, and the afternoon sun was burning away the clouds. She took off her cloak and climbed a large boulder to soak in the warmth of the sun. Soon Stefan was beside her.

Jessa rolled her eyes. Ever since Stefan had learned of her decision to go home, he'd been peppering her with matters of Baraca etiquette. It always left her head spinning. Now she clenched her jaw, hoping he wasn't here to give her more instruction.

Unexpectedly, he took her hand. "Jessara, once we are home, perhaps you will forget this infatuation with Kieran."

She gave him a sideways look. "And marry you?"

"Surely you are not thinking of marrying him?"

Jessa jumped from the boulder and turned to face Stefan. "He's my Eldala and whether I marry him or not, I won't join my heart to yours. If you care for me at all, don't ask me about it again."

Jessa walked over to Sienna, relieved that Stefan didn't follow. She took an apple from the food purse in Sienna's hand.

"Where's Gilrain?" Jessa asked between bites.

"He went to help Riordan."

"I still can't believe he's letting you come with me."

Sienna tossed her head. "I can be very persuasive when I need to be."

"Yes, I can just imagine you persuading Gilrain. It could be months before he sees you again."

"It's good for them to not have us for a while. They can be miserable together."

"With this war they're planning, they won't have time to be miserable."

By the time Gilrain and Riordon found a crossing, it was late, and the group decided to set up camp. After a meal of cheese, bread, and dried fish, Kieran began instructing Jessa on using the sword. She remembered some of what Bairn had taught her, but it had been several years since she'd used a sword. Now she wished she'd paid more attention. Still, Kieran was very patient with her. While Sienna and Toren watched, Kieran showed her the fundamentals, slowly leading her through a series of parries and blocks.

When they stopped, every muscle in her body ached. As Toren helped her remove the armor, she winced. Kieran put his hand on her and said, "Nashka mar havalat." A gentle warmth flowed from his hand into her entire body and relieved the pain.

"I'm the healer, remember?" she said.

He flipped her braid off her shoulder. "Sometimes the healer needs a healer," he said, smiling. Oh, that smile. It still had the power to make her melt if she let it.

"It's too bad I can't keep you around longer," she said as she removed her vambraces and set them next to her satchel.

He picked up her sword and breastplate, and laid them next to the vambraces. "You should take off your clothes." And then his face turned red.

She laughed.

"That's not what I meant," he said. "You won't get to sleep if you're cold and wet."

She ducked behind some bushes and changed into dry clothing. "Do you have any spells for keeping me warm?"

Kieran's voice faltered. "Just me."

Jessa's heart jumped into her throat. It was playful teasing, that was all. She hadn't expected him to offer himself. She hoped no one else had heard him.

"What kind of Eldala would I be if I let you get cold tonight?"

"Well, if you put it that way…"

They each spread out their bed rolls, and Jessa snuggled underneath a woolen blanket Elisa had given her. She expected Kieran to put his back to hers, but instead, he put his chest to her back, moved her braid over her shoulder, and put his arm around her waist. Lusty chills danced up and down her arms and legs, sending the melody crashing through her head. How was she ever going to get to sleep?

When the melody quieted, she relaxed and pressed herself as close to him as she could. She felt his slow, steady breathing on her neck, his strong arm tucked around her, and the warmth of his body soaking into hers. Familiar thoughts of having Kieran hold her every night flitted through her head.

Jessa had to admit that she'd wished for this very thing for as long as she could remember. But her wish wasn't for just anyone to hold her; she wanted *Kieran* hold her – for the rest of her life. Another petal loosened its grip, and she knew that if things kept going like they were, it wouldn't be long until her heart was in full bloom.

A twig cracked and Kieran startled awake. He looked around in the gray light. Jessa hadn't moved all night and neither had he. His arm was still around her. Regretting that he couldn't enjoy the moment a little longer, he sat up and saw one of the six Baraca guards approaching. The other travelers were still asleep.

"Sir, we saw two horsemen on the western ridge."

After belting on his sword, Kieran leaned over Jessa and kissed her cheek. "Sorry to wake you, love. We have to go."

Within the hour, the travelers had forded the river and were threading their way through the hills leading to Arath. Despite making good time, Kieran was uneasy. He'd hoped that by staying off the main roads they could avoid Ciara's spies for at least two days. The news this morning had confirmed a fear he'd kept to himself – the cloaked figure Jessa had discovered in the garden was one of Ciara's spies, and he'd gotten word back to Ciara about Jessa's whereabouts, if not Kieran's. He knew that if Ciara caught Jessa, he would have to go after her. That was probably why Ciara had put such a high price on her head.

Now he tried to overcome those fears. They would only distract him. And if Jessa sensed his apprehension, she would be alarmed. It was difficult enough for her to be going home. She didn't need to share his anxiety.

After several hours of mostly wordless travel, Kieran abruptly reined in Fallon and looked out over a harsh landscape.

How could this be? From the stories he'd heard, the hills leading to Arath were some of the most fertile in Teleria. Now it looked like the landscape in the south – brown and dead. Obviously this was Ciara's work.

He couldn't hold in his frustration any longer. He dismounted and shouted his anger to the sky, not caring if Ciara's entire army knew where he was. When he'd spent himself, he went to his knees and placed his hands on the ground. He was surprised to see a patch of green grass coming to life beneath him. If only he could make it spread to the rest of the land. He stood and swore to himself he would end the curse, no matter what.

Chapter 54

Jessa was relieved when Kieran called a halt late that afternoon. In the midst of a grove of stunted, scrubby trees, the travelers dismounted and led the horses to a small creek – the only other sign of life in the area. Kieran sent the Kofar guards into the thicket to search for spies while Toren and Riordan stayed close to him.

After the group settled, Kieran called Jessa over to Brielle and handed her a bridle. She took it, and with Kieran's hand over hers, she put the tack over the mare's ears and nose, trying to concentrate on the horse and not on Kieran's hand. Then, with some difficulty, she managed to lift the saddle and cinch it down as tight as possible.

Kieran made a step with his hands to help her into the saddle. He put her feet in the stirrups and she took the reins.

"Just tap your heels and turn the reins in the direction you want to go," he said.

"You mean like this?"

Before Kieran could hold her back, Jessa clapped her heels to Brielle's flanks and the horse raced away from the camp. Jessa had never dreamed she would have a horse of her own, and here she was, going faster than she'd ever ridden before. It was invigorating to feel the wind on her face and to be in control of this powerful horse.

Suddenly, Kieran was beside her, yanking Brielle to a stop. "What do you think you're doing?" he asked.

She scowled. "Riding my horse."

"You have no guard and no armor. You can't put yourself in danger like this."

She took the reins and followed him in sullen silence. At her first chance to let Brielle run, Kieran had accused her of putting herself in danger. They were in the middle of nowhere. What could happen? And why was he being such an ass about it?

When they reached camp, Kieran dismounted and offered to help Jessa down. She jumped to the ground and pushed past him. Before she could get away, he grabbed her by the shoulders and pulled her back. She tried to break free, but he tightened his hold on her and made her look at him. His beard fairly bristled on his clenched jaw. The last time she'd seen this look on his face was at the Kofar fortress, when she told him about the intruder in the garden.

"I swore to your mother I'd bring you back," he said.
"Well, I wouldn't want to ruin your reputation."
His hands dug into her shoulders. "Jessa, if anything happens to you – "
She wrenched free and took Brielle's reins. As she removed the saddle and started to brush the horse, Sienna came up beside her.
"What was that all about?" Sienna asked.
"Kieran thinks I'm being reckless."
Sienna started to braid Brielle's mane. "You can't fault him for that. He's worried about you."
"He's worried about his honor."
"Have you noticed the only time he gets angry with you is when you're in danger?"
"So now I'm not paying attention again?"
Sienna just laughed.
Jessa growled. Sienna was right. If Kieran didn't care, he would have let her be as reckless as she wanted. Now she had to admit to him she was wrong.

It was dark before Jessa finally went to apologize. Kieran was just opening his bedroll under a tree near the edge of the camp, away from everyone else. She sat on the ground next to him and unrolled her blankets. Kieran said nothing.
"I'm sorry," she said as she arranged her bedding.
"Please be more careful next time."
She turned to him, and although she couldn't see his face, she could have sensed his frustration without the Keldar stone. "I will."
He knelt in front of her and took her hands. "Jessa, I'd rather die than lose you." When his lips met hers, she felt a rush of warmth and leaned into him, savoring the fervent song he always seemed to stir up in her.

Kieran didn't know what had woken him first – a crash of thunder or Jessa's shriek. He bolted to his feet and scanned the darkness.

"What is it?" he whispered.

"There's something out there, watching us," Jessa replied.

A sudden gust of wind carried a familiar stench. Before Kieran could decide what it was, a flash of lightning revealed a black feathered creature coming towards them.

"Gurithents," he and Jessa said at the same time.

Stefan and Gilrain were next to Kieran in an instant, swords drawn. Riordan and Toren lit torches. Kieran barked for the Kofar guards to get Jessa and Sienna to safety.

The men stood in the center, watching the gurithents approach. The beasts paced back and forth in front of the men, systematically charging, looking for weaknesses. One gurithent rushed towards Kieran, and he quickly sidestepped, bringing his sword down across the creature's beak. The beast staggered and kicked at Kieran, tearing his shirt with its talons.

As if they had one mind, the gurithents continued with the same pattern of attack: pacing, watching, rushing forward. Then they disappeared into the darkness. Kieran stood poised for their next attack. A flash of lightning gave the men a split-second warning as the gurithents emerged from the dark with their next assault. Each man countered the attack with equal intensity.

One gurithent leaped over the top of Gilrain. With a sweeping blow, Gilrain cut off both of its legs. As the creature tried to right itself, Gilrain stabbed at its body. The gurithent shrieked and fell limp on the rain-soaked ground. The rain blinded Riordan for a moment, and he struggled to fend off his attacker. Gilrain went to his aid and pierced the creature's tough, feathery armor. Stefan misjudged the speed of his gurithent and it kicked him to the ground. With Stefan down, the beast attempted to jump on him. While it was in mid-air, Stefan plunged his sword into the gurithent's belly, disemboweling it in the process. Gray blood sprayed everywhere.

The gurithent attacking Kieran charged headlong into him, knocking him to the ground. As it rushed past him towards Jessa, Kieran cut off its wing. It screeched in pain and turned on him. One low cut severed the creature's leg. As Kieran rolled out of the way, he jumped to his feet and sensed the creature's intent: Capture the Baraca woman. Kieran yelled in rage and cut off its head.

As quickly as it had begun, the skirmish was over. Five dead gurithents littered the camp. Kieran was breathing heavily and sweat mixed with rain trickled down his face and neck. Gilrain and the others looked as weary he felt.

"I thought they were solitary creatures," said Gilrain.

"They are," said Stefan. "Why would there be five of them?"

"Ciara must have sent them to get you," said Gilrain.

"No, they were after Jessa."

"She wants Jessara so she can get you," said Stefan.

Kieran wiped his brow and spit out gurithent blood.

"Why?" asked Gilrain.

"She knows that if she captures Jessa, I'll go after her," said Kieran.

"So once again, you have put my cousin in danger," growled Stefan.

"And I will need your help to keep her safe."

"What do you mean?"

"When I leave her with the Hada, you'll have to protect her."

For once, Stefan had nothing to say. When he finally spoke, his voice was strained. "I will protect her, but not because it is your wish."

Kieran couldn't ask for more than that and nodded his thanks. As Stefan walked away, Kieran heard him say, "You are not the only one who loves her."

Chapter 55

After a night of tossing and turning, Jessa woke up and nearly choked when she saw Kieran's blood-spattered face. She swallowed down her nausea – until she saw a smoldering pile of gurithent bodies. Farther away were five gurithent heads, impaled on staffs. She covered her mouth and ran to the creek, just barely reaching it before she threw up.

In a few minutes, Sienna stooped next to her and started washing her face. Jessa dipped the cool water and rinsed out her mouth.

"Those gurithents were after you," Sienna said.

"I thought they wanted Kieran."

"They kept coming towards you. Ciara must have sent them to capture you."

Jessa's gut clenched and she bent over the creek again.

As much as Jessa wanted to ride Brielle, when the time came to leave camp, she decided she would be safer riding with Kieran. While they rode in silence, she looked at her surroundings.

The roads should have been flanked by grass and fields of flowers, but the ground lay desolate and bleak. Half-shorn sheep foraged for a paltry meal. In the distance, farms that should have been surrounded by bountiful crops were barren. The farmhouses weren't any better. The few she saw looked worn out and lonely with their fallen thatched roofs and their empty windows.

With such a bleak landscape in front of her, Jessa let her mind wander over the events of the last few weeks. So much had happened it made her head spin: finding her Eldala and learning he was the king of Teleria; escaping from Korisan; discovering that many Baraca clans would fight only if she were to marry Kieran; learning that her name meant "Valiant Queen"; and hearing Kieran say, "I love you."

It wasn't only her life that had changed; something inside of her had changed. She didn't think of herself as a slave, but she hadn't started thinking of herself as a queen. Dorinda, Arathor, and Kieran believed she could take up her ancestor's mantle. She still didn't quite believe it. Yet here she was, on her way home to claim her title.

As for the possibility of being the queen of Teleria… she was sure Kieran would propose. She was surprised that he hadn't asked her already. What was she going to say when he did?

The sight of Gedelar made Kieran want to cry. The town had never been very prosperous while he'd lived here, but the people never went hungry and most paid their taxes. Now hollow-eyed children dressed in rags stared at him before scurrying into their sagging cottages. The few garden plots he saw were tangled messes of withered plants and vines. Rubbish fires smoldered in many corners, sending a greasy, foul-smelling smoke into the air.

When he came upon his father's smithy, he couldn't hold back the tears. The building where he'd first learned how to make a knife had fallen in on itself and was now a pile of rubble.

Whether this was Ciara's doing or just the result of hard times, Kieran didn't know. When his initial shock and grief had passed, all that was left was a fiery anger he hadn't felt in a long time. When he was finally on the throne in Korisan, he would restore the blessing of Alardin over Teleria to ensure that this never happened again.

But first Ciara had to be defeated. And for that, he needed the help of every able-bodied man in Teleria, including those less inclined to help. It made proposing to Jessa all the more urgent.

He had hoped to ask her while they traveled. The opportunity just never seemed to come up. If he didn't do it before they reached the Hada fortress, he might never get another chance.

As they passed through Gedelar and entered the fringes of Ithil, he had an idea. Yes, the forest would be the perfect place to propose. But was she ready to say yes?

Just after dawn, Kieran and Jessa rode deep into the Forest of Ithil, followed by Toren, Riordan, and the Kofar warriors. The men dismounted first, forming a wide perimeter around them. Kieran guided Fallon deeper into the forest so he and Jessa could be alone.

When he dismounted and helped her down from Brielle, she looked around and smiled. “Is this where I think it is?”

“It’s where we first met.”

She took his hand and they walked to the Old Man of the Forest. She put her other hand on the trunk and leaned into it. “I used to come here every day, even before I met you.”

“So did I.”

For the next few hours, they walked in the places where they’d played together as children. It was the first time they’d really been alone with each other since being in Korisan. When they came to someplace familiar, one of them would say, “Do you remember building a fort here?” or “This is where you showed me how to whistle,” or “This is where we fell into the creek.” Kieran was pleased to see that Jessa seemed happier than he’d ever seen her.

When they reached a wide clearing, Jessa stopped. “This is where I taught you to dance.”

Kieran started to hum their song and extended a hand. “Shall we?”

Her eyes widened, and she gave him a smile that only magnified her beauty. She took his hand, laid her head on his chest, and they started to dance to the song of the Eldalafar, waltzing through the forest as if it were their private ballroom. Soon, he felt the song in her reaching out to the fire in him, and he knew something in her had changed. Her heart had opened up to him in a way it never had before.

In time, they were under the tree again, and he gave her a hand up so she could climb to the lower branches. He followed and sat next to her. After a few moments of silence, Jessa took in a quick breath.

Her hand was on the names “Kieran and Jessara.”

“When did you do this?” she asked.

“I carved that just before you were taken.”

When she looked at him, he felt the anguish she’d carried for ten years. It mingled with his own, and for a time he held her as they wept for all the years they’d lost.

“I’m sorry I wasn’t able to save you that day,” he whispered into her hair.

She put her hand on his face. “Kieran, I know you tried.”

He wiped the tears from her eyes and then said, "Marposa nish tehai." In a matter of minutes, Kieran was pleased to see that hundreds of butterflies had landed on or around the tree. Many were on Jessa and some were on Kieran.

Jessa's eyes widened in astonishment. "Did you do this?"

"Just for you, Jess."

If there had been any doubt in Jessa's mind about Kieran's love, this moment had erased it.

She couldn't believe how many butterflies were here, and she recognized only a few – Monarchs, swallowtails, skippers, fritillaries. They seemed to wear every color of the rainbow. She wished she had time to look at each fluttering jewel.

And then she felt Kieran slow time so she could.

After what seemed like hours, she jumped from the tree and Kieran followed. She leaned into him and put her arms around his waist, feeling his heart nestled beside hers.

"Thank you for bringing me here," she murmured, "and for the butterflies."

Kieran tipped her chin up and held her eyes with his. "I hoped you would like this."

"I do."

She still didn't understand why or how Kieran loved her, but it didn't matter. All that mattered was that he *did* love her.

When he moved in to kiss her, his scent was wild and inviting. As she reached up to kiss him back, she felt the last petal of her heart open and realized the truth. It was time to tell him.

"Kieran, I love you."

He dropped to one knee and tried to speak, but his voice faltered. She took his hand to encourage him.

"Jessara, my Eldala, will you marry me?"

She pulled him up and looked into his stunning eyes. Her heart was beating a rapid staccato, but her voice was steady and sure. "Yes, Kieran, I'll marry you."

He wrapped his arms around her, and she drew his head down and kissed him, all the while looking into his eyes. He pulled her closer and kissed her mouth and eyes and neck with a fierce passion he'd never shown before, as if he'd been waiting until now to show her how much he adored her.

Chapter 56

Jessa smiled. "You were right, Sienna."

The two women sat near the fire, preparing an evening meal for the group.

"About what?" asked Sienna.

"When you said everything was different after Gilrain proposed – I understand now what you meant."

"As I recall, you laughed in my face."

"Yes, and I'm sorry. I couldn't have imagined how loving Kieran would change the way I see things."

Sienna nudged Jessa with her shoulder and dropped some dried beef into the iron kettle. "I'm glad you said 'yes.' I was worried you'd turn him down."

Jessa added some dried mushrooms. "I can't believe I ever doubted him."

Sienna stirred the stew and sprinkled fresh wild scallions over the top of it. "You know what this means?"

"What?"

"You're going to be the queen of Teleria."

Jessa stopped what she was doing. Caught up in the emotion of Kieran's proposal, she had forgotten that agreeing to marry him meant she was also agreeing to be his queen. Sienna's reminder brought it careening to the front of her mind.

When she looked up, she saw Kieran, just a few paces away, going through his sword forms with great precision. His intense black eyes and hardened jaw were filled with a stern confidence. That, added to his commanding stature, reminded her once again that he was the king.

And she'd agreed to be his queen. There was no getting out of it now.

With thoughts of being queen still dancing crazily in her head, Jessa wandered the camp under a starry sky. When she found Kieran sitting against a tree, she sat down and rested her back against his chest. He pulled her closer and tucked his arms around her.

She tipped her head back towards his chin, feeling his beard on her cheek as he said, "I love you."

She put her fingers over his and explored the backs of his strong hands. It still surprised her how large they were compared to hers. "I'm going to miss you, Kieran," she whispered.

They wove their fingers together, and when he kissed the tender skin behind her ear, she let out a soft sigh, listening to the melody that curled itself around her insides. "I wish I knew how long I have to stay with my clan."

His kisses moved down her neck and the song grew louder. "I wish I knew, too," he said. "But if you leave, I want you and Sienna to go to Morigon."

"Why Morigon?"

"That's where my mother and aunt will be going. And it's about as far away from the fighting as possible."

"But not Ciara."

"You'll have to be careful no matter where you go. But Ciara will have less chance of finding you if you go to Morigon."

Kieran's lips found her shoulder. Now the melody was all she could think about – that and how to spend more time with Kieran before they reached the Hada fortress

"Isn't the sea near here?" she asked.

He sounded cautious when he answered. "Yes."

"Take me to see it. Then we could have at least one more day."

"I really should get you home."

"Please Kieran. When we get to the fortress, you know they won't let me spend much time with you. It's the last time we'll get to be a-lone."

He laughed softly and tugged at her braid. "You can be very per-suasive, m'lady."

It hadn't taken much for Jessa to convince Kieran to go to the sea-shore. As Kieran saddled Fallon, Gilrain tried to talk him out of it.

"I still don't like the idea of you traveling with us now," Gilrain said, "but to expose yourself by traveling to Kolachel – it's madness."

"I was going to take Toren, Riordan, and the Kofar guards. But if it will make you feel better, you can come too."

"I won't leave Sienna."

Kieran laughed. "That's what I thought. You and Sienna can go with Stefan to announce our arrival in two days."

"You're taking too many risks."

That was about the most ironic thing Kieran had ever heard his cousin say. He took the reins and swung astride his horse. "I'll be careful."

Something in Gilrain's eyes said he had his doubts.

Kieran moved alongside Brielle, gave Jessa a hand up, and waited for Toren, Riordan, and the Kofar guards to surround them. Stefan gave him a cursory nod before he, Gilrain, and Sienna left for the Hada camp.

Kieran gave Jessa a nod, and the two of them spurred their horses forward, just far enough ahead of the guard so they could have some privacy. "In all the years you lived here, no one ever took you to the sea?" he asked.

"My parents made sure I lived a sheltered life."

"My father took me there every chance he got."

"Is that where you found the shell you gave me?"

"Yes, it is. I found two of them – a matched pair. I still have the other one. It was the only part of you I had besides the Eldala dreams."

She smiled. "I suppose becoming Eldala was just an accident."

"Braeden said that it's never an accident when a Baraca boy and girl become Eldala."

There was an odd look on her face when she stopped to take his hand. Then she smiled. "I guess that makes us a matched set."

A stiff afternoon breeze brought a tangy smell to Jessa's nose. Kieran breathed deeply.

"It's like coming home," he said as he sent his guards ahead to secure the beach.

When they signaled that it was safe, he led Jessa down a steep trail flanked on either side by short, tough grasses. Upon reaching the sand, they left the horses with one of the Kofar guards. Jessa took off her boots and stockings, tied up her riding skirt, and ran towards the water so she could drink in the vast expanse of sapphire blue.

She'd heard her mother speak of the sea when she was a child and had always longed to visit it. When Kieran gave her the shell, she pleaded with her father to take her to the shore. He refused, saying it was too dangerous for her to leave the fortress.

Now she smiled as her feet sank into the warm sand and the wind played with the hair around her face. Then Kieran was beside her, removing his boots and rolling up his trousers. He took her hand and they stepped into the water together. The icy water danced around her legs, and Jessa laughed as she felt her feet sinking deeper into the sand with each wave that washed over them.

She waded in up to her knees. Raising her arms to the sky, she spun around in a giddy dance. This was what it was like to be completely alive, and it was the most satisfying thing she'd ever felt – except maybe for one of Kieran's kisses.

One of the horses whinnied, and Jessa looked behind her. When she'd said she wanted to be alone with Kieran on the beach, she forgot that the guards would have to come with them. She sighed. Being married to the king meant having less privacy than she'd had as a slave. She would just have to get used to it. For today, she would enjoy his company.

Jessa left the water and stooped to pick up a pink shell. "Thank you for bringing me here. It's better than I could have imagined."

Kieran knelt with her and started to scoop up small, white shells from under a piece of driftwood. "I'm glad I could share it with you. And I needed to come here."

"Why?"

"This is where I come when I need to think."

She took a deep breath again and listened to the waves pounding against the shore. A flock of raucous sea birds played on the wind. Then she stood, dusted the sand off of her hands, and waded into the water again. A splash of frigid water from behind stole her breath. When she turned around, Kieran was grinning like a little boy.

"Why you…"

Jessa splashed him back. Kieran laughed and drenched her with a second splash. She ran after him and pushed him into the waves. He pulled her down and a wave washed over her head. When she caught her breath, she got up and walked back to the shore to find a dry patch of sand.

As she sat down to soak in the warm sun, Kieran lay next to her and closed his eyes. His wet shirt clung to his skin, and it reminded Jessa of the times she'd seen him in Korisan, half-clothed and sleeping. Back in the castle, she thought he was the most handsome man she'd ever seen. Knowing she was going to marry him made him even more handsome.

She leaned over and trailed her fingers across his beard, along his neck, and down to the Keldar stone over his heart. He caught her hand and kissed it, then opened his eyes and rolled on top of her.

"Beautiful Jessara."

She felt a warm melody run through her when he said it. The ardor in his eyes only deepened the song. It echoed inside her like a loud chorus, filling her head with dangerous thoughts.

He grasped her shoulders and pulled her closer. His heart was thundering as much as hers. She smiled – until he covered her mouth with his and traced her lips with his tongue. She let out a rough moan and pulled his taste into her. The song in her reached out to the fire in him, and their hearts mingled in a fiery dance.

This was where she should be, where she *wanted* to be, never parted from him. When she laid her head back to catch her breath, it was as natural as could be to ask the question that had rolled around in her head all day: "When can we get married?"

All Kieran wanted right now was to make one of his dreams come true. Jessa's question was like a splash of cold water.

What could he tell her?

After what had just happened between them, and the way her dress accentuated her beautiful curves … The thought of marrying her now was more than tempting.

He stood and tried to gather his thoughts. “Let’s walk,” he said, giving her a hand up. When his guards followed, he was glad her question had stopped him from letting his desires get the best of him.

He wove his fingers into hers. “We have to wait until after the war.”

“How long will that take?”

“I don’t know. A few months, a year – I really can’t say.”

“Why can’t we marry now?”

As much as he didn’t want to leave Jessa with her clan, it would be much better for him if she weren’t around right now. He had a war to plan, and she would be a distraction.

“Ending Ciara’s reign has to come first. Right now that means driving out the Zagorans.” He looked into her eyes. “This hasn’t been an easy decision, Jess, but it’s the only one I can make. I don’t have the luxury of getting married anytime I want.”

“Then Teleria comes first?”

“You knew all of this before I proposed.”

He could feel the disappointment in her, and it seared his soul to think Teleria would always come first.

“This is what I was born to do,” he said. “It’s the one thing that drives me to the battlefield. I have to lay everything else down.”

She stopped and looked up at him. “If anything happens to you Kieran, I don’t know what I’ll do.”

He put his arm around her and they continued down the shore. In a few moments, they reached a place in the bluff where his father had brought him many years ago. A narrow waterfall spilled from the top of the cliff and came down in ribbons over moss-covered boulders. Ferns and grasses lined each side of the grotto. Jessa drew in a breath and was about to climb one of the rocks. Kieran put his hand on her shoulder to stop her.

“Heart of my heart, I love you more than my own life. If I could marry you now, I would.”

She put her hand to his face. He ran his hands down her arms and she closed her eyes, her chest rising and falling erratically at his touch. As he moved his hands past her waist to the small of her back, she pressed into him and dug her fingers into his shoulders. Every soft curve molded against him.

With the taste of her last kisses still on his lips, his heightened senses took her in – her enticing rose scent, her rapid pulse, and her shallow gasps for breath. His heart was hammering in his chest, and his whole body ached for her, wishing he could become one with her in every way.

It didn't help when she said, "Servants who coupled in the castle were pronounced married the next day."

He let out a sigh. "I've wanted you for as long as I can remember, but that custom is for common people."

"We're just a man and woman who love each other."

"No, Jess. I'm the king of Teleria and you're going to be my queen."

Her face fell in disappointment. She tried to break free of his embrace, but he wrapped his arms more tightly around her waist. "Even if we were common, I want to promise to love and honor you in front of our friends and family with a clear conscience. How can I do that if I take something only a husband should have?" He tipped her chin to look in her eyes. "We have to wait."

He let her go and she sat on one of the rocks. "You're right," she said. "I just can't bear the thought of being away from you."

He sat on the ground next to her and twirled a piece of grass in his fingers. "I don't want to leave you either. But whether we were married or not, you'd still have to go back. Your mother and the council need to know you're all right." He frowned. "And I don't think Calafar Galen would accept you as the Malazia if you were already married to me."

"Why not?"

Kieran sighed at the memory of splitting the table in half. "He barely tolerated me when I was there. When I told him I was your Eldala, and that I intended to propose to you, I thought he might kill me in front of the council. If we were married, he'd say that I corrupted you. Then he'd throw both of us out, and you'd never get a chance to change things."

"But you have corrupted me."

He laughed and ran his fingers over the back of her hand. "There is something you can do so we can be together even when I leave."

Her eyes widened. "Tell me. I'll do whatever I can."

He would be taking a risk by joining his heart to hers. She might see memories and dreams that he would rather not share. But it would also deepen the connection they already had. "You can let the Keldar stone become part of you."

"Like yours?"

"Yes, but once you take it, it can't be removed. You'll be connected to me and to Arathor in ways you never have been before."

She pulled the chain from her neck. "What do I have to do?"

He moved to take the stone and then hesitated. His stone was over his heart. In his present state of mind, it wouldn't be good for his hand to be anywhere near Jessa's heart.

"What is it?" she asked.

"Maybe you should do this."

She slid the stone off of its chain and caressed his face with her stunning eyes. "I want you to do it." Then she put the stone in his palm and placed his hand just above her left breast. He waited, letting himself enjoy her skin against his palm.

It was softer than her hair, or her lips, and he wasn't sure he could keep his hand from drifting a little lower. But then the stone went into her skin and Kieran felt his Keldar stone burning in his chest. Fighting the urge to collapse, he caught Jessa just before she dropped to the ground.

Chapter 57

A deep throbbing in Jessa's chest brought her out of her twilight sleep. She absently put her hand over the source of the pain and felt something warm and smooth embedded in her skin. She opened her eyes and looked down. Then she remembered the exquisite pleasure of having Kieran's hand on her, followed almost immediately by the searing pain as the Keldar stone worked its way into her skin.

And she remembered the strange dreams she'd had. Or strange memories. She wasn't sure. She'd felt intense rage at watching a soldier attack a woman, doubt when meeting Arathor, pride at being declared king, and grief over losing a best friend. Those were Kieran's memories. Did that mean he saw hers?

She turned on her side and wondered how long she'd been asleep. The grotto was mostly in shadow, but thin rays of morning light filtered through the mist and cast dancing rainbows on the walls. She rolled towards the opening of the cleft and saw Kieran's silhouette. He sat with his back to her.

She thought to call to him, but waited so she could watch him. He held himself straight and tall, arms resting on his knees, head held high. The breeze ruffled his hair and his shirt. Even from the back, he seemed calm and self-assured as he looked out over the sea. She was amazed again at the turn her life had taken. How could it be that this good man loved her?

When he suddenly got up and walked towards her, the breath caught in her throat.

"You called?" he asked.

She blinked. "No, but I was thinking about you."

He gave her a crooked smile. "You'll have to learn to control your thoughts."

"I saw some of your memories when I was asleep."

"I wondered if you would."

"Will it always be that way?"

"I know that with Arathor, the farther apart we are, the fewer thoughts we share." He tucked a strand of hair behind her ear. "But he's not my Eldala. It might be that distance won't make any difference."

As they walked along the beach, taking in the smell of the sea and drinking in the warm sun, Jessa noticed that their spoken conversation flowed more naturally, as if they were anticipating what the other would say. But when they were silent, she noticed something deeper – an affectionate, unspoken exchange that made her aware of just how difficult it would be to tear herself away from her Eldala.

By late afternoon of the next day, Jessa was tired and hungry – and her patience with the Hada guards was almost to the breaking point.

"We have orders to keep out Telerians," one of them said.

"I am *not* Telerian. I am Jessara, your Malazia."

She had said it at least a dozen times already, and each time it was met with the same doubtful look and the same ridiculous answer: "You are dressed like a Telerian and you speak like a Telerian."

Jessa growled her frustration and looked at Kieran. "Is this what you had to deal with when you were here?"

He crossed his arms and smiled. "We had help from Dorinda."

Jessa turned back to the guard. "Look in my black eyes and tell me I am not Baraca."

The guard climbed down the stairs, opened a small side gate, and stood in front of her. He stared for the longest time, as if he half expected her eyes to change color. After an exasperating pause, he motioned for her to come inside.

"What about King Aiden and his guards?" she asked.

"The king and the Baraca guards may enter, but the others must stay here."

Jessa was just about ready to draw her sword when Stefan came through the gate. "I have orders from Calafar Galen to let them all come in. We must not let it be said that we denied hospitality to the king and his companions."

This wasn't like Stefan at all. As Jessa led Brielle through the gate, she tried to sense Stefan's intent. Kieran's presence kept her from sensing anything.

Stefan came along side her and took the horse's reins. "Now that you are here," he said, "you must behave like the queen you are."

"I can take care of my horse."

"Queens do not lead horses, nor do they ride them."

If Jessa hadn't been so tired, she would have argued with him. Instead she kept her protests to herself. Then she looked around and let out a gasp.

There was the round tiled courtyard where she'd played. And the swan fountain still bubbled. She laughed out loud.

"What is it, Jessa?" Kieran asked.

She pointed to the fountain. "I must have fallen into that thing a hundred times when I tried to walk the edge."

By now, a crowd had gathered, and men and women in simple but elegant clothing pointed and whispered. Jessa felt as if their eyes were boring right through her. When she stared at one of them, the woman shook her head. Jessa looked down at her clothes. She'd worn them on the entire journey and now they were dusty and travel-stained. She hadn't felt this self-conscious since wearing that awful dress at Delaine's banquet.

When Kieran put his hand in hers, several gasps escaped the onlookers' lips. She supposed that they had never seen a Telerian man, let alone a king, holding hands with a Baraca woman. Good. Now they had something more disturbing than her clothing to gossip about.

More gasps erupted when Sienna walked beside her. Sienna ignored them and took her other hand. "I've missed you, Jessa."

"How have they been treating you?"

"Well, at first they wouldn't let us in, but then Stefan insisted. Since then, Gilrain and I have kept to ourselves."

When they reached the main keep of the fortress, Stefan stopped and handed Brielle over to a boy. Kieran and his men did the same.

"Now," Stefan said, "before the banquet, you must see your mother."

"Banquet?"

"Celebrating your return. Calafar Galen wanted to make sure you were really the Malazia, but your mother and I convinced him that his inquiries could wait until tomorrow."

Why didn't Jessa like the sound of that?

While the others waited outside, Stefan led Jessa and Kieran down a long hallway to a small room with plain furnishings. Jessa's stomach fluttered. She'd been looking forward to meeting her mother, but now she wasn't so sure. She gave Kieran a quick glance and felt his reassurances holding her up. She was grateful again for their connection, and was sure she would need more of Kieran's mental strength before the night was over.

While they waited, Kieran took her hand again. Stefan gave her a disapproving look, but she ignored him. He could stew all he wanted. There was nothing he or anyone else could do to separate her from Kieran now that she had the stone.

When her mother finally entered the room, Kieran and Stefan stood. Kieran had said that when he'd met Tiana, she was wearing black and looked weary. Now her face beamed and she wore blue silk. It made Jessa self-conscious all over again. She quickly smoothed her hair in place and stood to embrace the mother she'd missed for so many years.

Finally, Jessa's mother stepped back and there were tears in her eyes that matched Jessa's. "My daughter Jessara," she said. "King Aiden told me you were alive, but I could not make myself believe it." She turned to Kieran. "You are a most honorable man, sir, and I thank you from the bottom of my heart for returning my daughter to me."

"It was my pleasure, Mara Tiana."

Tiana stopped for a moment and scanned Kieran's face. Her eyes widened. "I did not see the resemblance before."

"Excuse me?" Kieran asked.

"You look just like him." She stared into space, as if reliving a painful memory. Then she looked at Kieran again. "I suppose we will see you at the banquet tonight?"

"Of course." He kissed Jessa's hand. "Until tonight, my lady."

"Until tonight."

When he left, Stefan remarked, "I told you he was forward with her, Aunt Tiana."

Jessa had had just about enough of her cousin.

"He is a good man," Tiana said, shaking her head. "It is such a shame."

"What?" Jessa asked.

Tiana clucked her tongue. "We will speak of this later." She looked at Stefan. "Please leave us. We will see you at the banquet."

Stefan bowed and left. Jessa's mother motioned for her to sit at a table in another part of the room. She poured tea into a delicate cup and handed it to Jessa. Jessa wrestled down her frustration and slowly sipped the mint tea.

After a few moments of almost unbearable scrutiny, Jessa spoke up. "What did you mean about it being such a shame?"

Her mother put down her cup and stared at the tea. "I could not speak in front of your cousin. When I first met King Aiden, he told me of sharing Eldala with you, and of his intention to marry you."

Jessa started to speak, but her mother raised a hand to stop her.

"You must know by now that before you were chosen, we had intended to join your heart to Stefan's."

Jessa nodded and tried to still the panic at the thought of where this conversation might lead.

"I have seen your cousin change from an overbearing child to an arrogant man," Tiana said. "I know that he is not the best choice for you."

"Then let me marry Kieran."

"Sometimes, daughter, we do not always get what our heart desires."

"How can you say that? He's my Eldala, and I love him."

"I cannot go against tradition or the council's wishes. You must sever all ties with the king and marry Stefan."

Jessa just about spit out her tea. "I already told him I'd marry him."

Tiana walked to the fireplace and leaned against the mantle. "Jessara, you must go through the separation ceremony so you can join with Stefan."

"Separation ceremony?"

"It is rare, but there have been times when children… have accidentally become Eldala. It will be painful, but you must do this so you can be the Malazia."

Jessa walked to her mother's side. "A Tyman Baraca told Kieran that the Eldalafar is never an accident. Kieran and I were meant to marry."

Tiana turned to look at her. "No," she whispered. "I will not go against the council."

Jessa couldn't believe she was hearing any of this. Everything in her wanted to leave the fortress and never come back. But it wouldn't help Kieran's cause, and it would only hurt Tiana.

The Keldar stone started to throb and Jessa rubbed her chest.

"What is that?" her mother asked.

"One of Alardin's Keldar stones. I took it two days ago."

Tiana sat on the sofa and looked as if she might faint. Jessa sat beside her.

"What's wrong?" Jessa asked.

"The Keldar stone will prevent you from being separated from the king. You will have to marry Stefan without being his Eldala."

Chapter 58

Sienna had that annoyed look on her face again. "I can't believe they're telling you to marry Stefan. You think they'd be pleased that a Baraca is going to be queen of Teleria."

"I told you they were arrogant," said Jessa. "I'm still surprised they're going to let you be my companion."

Sienna laughed.

Suddenly, three women entered Jessa's room and filled a bathtub with steaming water. When Jessa dismissed them so she could undress, the women stayed.

"We are here to prepare you for the banquet, mistress."

"I can take care of myself."

When an older woman entered, her commanding presence filled the room. The other women lowered their heads.

"I am Cala Elena, wife of the calafar. I am here to oversee your training as the Malazia. You will submit to my authority in all things until you take your place as the queen."

Something about Elena reminded Jessa of Ciara. That alone made Jessa's hackles rise, but she kept her thoughts to herself.

"These women will bathe and dress you every morning." Elena said. "In time, you will get used to it. If they do not treat you well, please tell me and I will have them dismissed."

Jessa swallowed hard. Elena left, and Jessa stared at the wall as the women began to remove her traveling clothes. *I will never get used to this,* she thought.

"Please step into the tub, my lady," one of the women said.

Too tired to protest, Jessa slipped into the bathtub, tipping her head back as she tried to relax. The hot water eased the pain of the Keldar stone and almost made her forget her embarrassment.

Kieran tugged at his collar as he entered the banquet hall. The council members nodded curtly at him. Tiana gave him a smile. Stefan waited at the door. When Kieran reached his place, everyone stood as a herald clapped his hands and announced, "The Malazia."

It took only a few seconds for Kieran's eyes to drink her in.

The torch lights danced in her black eyes. Her satin hair was looped in intricate braids all around her head. She wore a cream-colored dress with gold brocade on the tightly-cinched bodice. The bell sleeves rested just below her shoulders, and the neckline revealed an ivory expanse of neck and bosom, making his pulse quicken. The Keldar stone glinted, and the pleasant memory of putting it there raced through him.

The memory was quickly replaced by jealousy when Kieran saw Stefan escort Jessa to her place. She exchanged glances with Kieran as she walked past him. Her smile couldn't hide the fact that she was simmering on the inside. He would have to ask her about it later.

Calafar Galen raised his glass and said, "We publicly wish to thank Stefan for returning our Malazia to us." He gestured towards Kieran without looking at him. "And we thank King Aiden of Teleria for helping him."

Had Stefan taken credit himself, or had the council insulted Kieran on purpose? He could imagine either one being true.

Everyone sat and the meal began. Kieran hardly noticed what was set in front of him. How could he eat when all he could think about was Jessa?

Kieran stood outside the council chambers, hoping this meeting wouldn't last long. A servant opened the door and led him to a chair. He sat down and waited for the council to allow him to speak.

He looked at the council's table. It had been temporarily repaired, but it was still obvious where his sword had the split the marble.

"Aiden, king of Teleria," Galen said through tight lips. "We owe you our thanks for aiding in the return of the Malazia."

Kieran stood. "I did more than aid in her return. I was the one who found her."

Galen smiled. "Quite by accident, we have been told."

Obviously Stefan had spoken with them already. "Yes. Ciara's guards captured me and brought me to Korisan. Jessara helped in my recovery, and our friends arranged our escape."

"Then your work is finished."

"When I was here last, I promised to restore your Malazia. I have kept my word. Will you join the battle?"

Galen ran his hand over the split in the table. "How could we forget, after the way you disrupted our last meeting? But our answer is the same. This is not a Hada fight."

Kieran walked towards the table. "The Zagorans will not distinguish between Telerians and the Baraca. By refusing to join the fight, you doom your kinsmen and yourselves."

Galen waved a hand to dismiss him, but Kieran stayed. "There is another matter to discuss," he said.

"And what would that be?"

"Jessara has consented to marry me."

Galen's pale brow glistened. "Our Malazia would never consent to marry a Telerian. What hold do you have over her?"

"Only the love a man has for a woman."

"Is she carrying your child?"

In two strides, Kieran was over the table. With one hit, he knocked Galen out of his chair and into the wall. "Jessara is the most honorable woman I have ever met. How dare you insult her."

Galen sat up and wiped the blood from the corner of his mouth. Several council members came to Galen's side. He pushed them away and picked up his chair. "You will leave this fortress before dawn. You will sever your connection with the Malazia, and you will not set foot in this place again."

Two men came to escort Kieran out of the room, but he wrenched free of their hold. "You have sealed the Hada's fate. When the Zagorans come, your clan will not be protected."

It was well after midnight when Kieran met Jessa near the swan fountain. The moonlight reflected off of a pale green dress that clung to every appealing curve, and he tried to ignore the familiar desire to become one with her. She took his hand and led him past the gate and into the forest. When they reached a clearing, she stopped and leaned into him.

"What did Galen say about the marriage?"

"He accused you of carrying my child."

"What did you do?"

"I knocked him to the ground."

She laughed softly. "I can see you doing that. Then what happened?"

"He told me to sever our connection and then he banished me from the fortress. I have to leave before dawn."

"So soon…"

"I know."

"My mother said that our connection can't be broken because of the Keldar stone."

She reached underneath his shirt and covered his stone with her hand. Her palm was hot and trembling, and it sent another wave of desire through him.

"I can't be without you," she said. The desperation in her voice made his heart break.

His arms surrounded her and he stroked the top of her head. "Jessa, I thought I could give you up, but now I don't know if *I* can be without you either. These last few weeks have been the best of my life."

He buried his face between her neck and shoulder and started to kiss her velvet-soft skin. She trembled and pressed herself into him so that almost every part of her was touching him. Eventually, she let go and began to unbraid her hair.

"No, Jessa. Not until we're married."

"Kieran, if… if something happens to you…"

He put his fingers to her lips to silence her. "I'll come back."

"You can't make that promise. This is our last night together, and I know we can't spend it as husband and wife, but I want you to see me this way."

"I did once, in Korisan."

She frowned. "I didn't have a choice then. But I do now."

There was something sweet and sensual about the way she slowly loosened the braid, as if she were offering him the deepest part of herself before they were separated. When she finished, she took his hands and brought them to her head so he could run his fingers through the soft, cinnamon curtain falling over her shoulders and back. Then she pulled his head down and put her mouth to his. Her kiss made him think he might burst into flames right there.

As their tears and kisses mingled, Kieran spoke the words to slow time. The Keldar stones flared, and Kieran and Jessa were keenly aware of the bond growing between them. With no effort at all, every dream or thought they'd had about the other passed from one heart to the other. It was alarming and exhilarating to know and be known in such an intimate way.

When they parted, they knew beyond any doubt that their hearts had been forged into one heart.

Chapter 59

Jessa rested her arms on the window sill and watched a cardinal flitting from tree to tree. When the scarlet bird whistled and flew off with his mate, Jessa wished she could fly off to be with Kieran.

She scolded herself. Self-pity wasn't the answer. It hadn't helped her in Rahnak's castle, and it wouldn't help her now. She had a job to do: claim her title as Malazia and try to convince the council to send Hada warriors to Agora. How she would do that she didn't know, but Kieran was counting on her, and she wasn't planning on letting him down.

Her handmaiden Shula knocked on her open door. The smell of bacon made Jessa's mouth water. She took the breakfast tray from Shula and noted there were also scrambled eggs, sausages, biscuits with gravy, fresh strawberries and grapes, and two kinds of juice. She laid the tray on the table and invited Shula to eat with her. The girl stared at her wide-eyed.

"M'lady, it would not be proper for me to eat with you."

"As I told you before, Shula, you're not my servant. Besides, I could never eat all of this."

Shyly, the girl sat across from Jessa and started to nibble at one of the sausages. In a few minutes, Sienna joined them and started picking grapes off the stem and popping them into her mouth. Jessa took a bite of egg and biscuit, and washed it down with some apple juice.

While Sienna chattered away, Jessa looked at her friend. She was glad Sienna had insisted on coming with her. She could have stayed with Gilrain. Jessa knew that Sienna missed Gilrain, but she hid it well; she was her usual bubbly self.

When they finished eating, Jessa walked behind the dressing screen. She picked up the green dress from last night and stopped. It still carried Kieran's earthy scent. She brought the dress up to her face and breathed him in. A wave of grief threatened to drown her. She steadied her heart and pushed the pain away. She didn't have time for this.

When she walked from behind the screen, the three women from before had returned to give her a bath.

"My lady-in-waiting can take care of me," said Jessa.

"But m'lady, we have orders from Elena."

"I'll speak with Elena."

The women nodded and backed out of the room. Sienna gave Jessa a teasing smile. "I wondered when you would put an end to that nonsense."

Jessa sighed. "Elena won't be so easily dismissed."

Before Sienna had a chance to brush through Jessa's hair, Tiana entered and motioned for Sienna and Shula to leave. Jessa sat in front of the mirror and started to unfasten her braid. She smiled as she thought of the way Kieran had watched her when she let her hair down last night. He had been as still as a statue – until she lifted his hands so he could run his fingers through it…

Jessa tried to steer her mind away from another painful memory and watched in the mirror as her mother picked up a silver brush and pulled it through her hair.

"I think you have the longest hair of any woman in our clan," said Tiana. "This alone will bring you great honor." Tears were forming in her mother's eyes. "When you were taken, I did not think I would ever get to do this again."

Jessa's voice caught in her throat. "If I'd known what was going to happen, I would have stayed home."

"You were a free spirit, Jessara. And as King Aiden pointed out to me, I could not have kept you here."

Jessa turned to face Tiana. "I'm sorry for the heartache I brought to you and Father. If I could go back and change it – "

Tiana wiped away her tears. "Daughter, let us not speak of the past. You are home now and can finally lead our people." She resumed brushing Jessa's hair. Her voice sounded cheerful and held none of its former regret.

"You have a full day. First, you will meet with Cala Elena. Later today, you will speak with Calafar Galen and the council, and tonight you will receive your mark." Then she leaned over and whispered, "But the most important ceremony begins tomorrow night."

"What's that?"

"You will begin the purification rites."

Before Jessa could ask what the rites were, her mother finished braiding her hair. Someone knocked on her door and entered without waiting for permission.

Before Jessa could protest, Elena escorted her out of the room and across the compound to a glass-enclosed building. Short wooden tables held piles of dusty scrolls and books. More books than Jessa had ever seen filled numerous shelves, and light streamed in from the blue glazed windows.

Elena motioned for Jessa to sit down. "For the next few months, I will instruct you in matters of Baraca history, custom, dress, deportment, and leadership."

"First I have a question for you."

"What?"

"My mother mentioned the purification rites."

"We will begin the rites tomorrow."

"I know. But what are they?"

Elena pursed her lips and spoke to Jessa as if she were a child. "It is the process whereby we cleanse your mind of unwanted memories and desires so that you will be able to properly lead the Baraca."

This didn't sound good at all. Who were they to say which memories and desires were unwanted?

"We usually begin the process when the Malazia is thirteen," Elena continued, "but since you are older and have spent so much time among Telerians, it will take longer than usual."

What have I gotten myself into? Jessa wondered. Maybe she should have gone with Kieran.

Before the thought went any further, Elena began to fill Jessa's head with the intricacies of Baraca custom, most of which Stefan had already explained. When Elena led Jessa through a detailed history of the Baraca, Jessa noticed that Elena left out some details.

"What about Alardin defeating Leandra?" Jessa asked.

Elena's eyes narrowed. "Who told you about that?"

"I heard it from… someone." Jessa thought it would be better not to mention she'd heard it from Arathor.

"The Hada clan is the oldest Baraca clan, and we keep the history of our people. Whoever told you that was misinformed."

Jessa frowned, but decided it was best to keep her arguments to herself.

When the lesson ended, Stefan escorted Jessa to her meeting with the council. Her mind was reeling from all she'd learned today, and she hardly noticed when Stefan started to speak. She blinked and asked him to repeat himself.

"I am sorry," he said.

These were not words Jessa had ever expected to hear from her cousin, and she reached out with her heart to see if he was being truthful. "For what?"

"For many things, Jessara, but most of all for trying to stop you from marrying Kieran. I will not interfere again."

She stopped and put her hand on his arm, looking into his intense black eyes as she did. There was something there beyond contrition. She sensed that he really did love her. "Stefan, I'm grateful for this. But why the change of heart?"

He knit his brows together. "I spoke with your mother last night. I see now that Kieran is a good man and that he truly loves you."

"The council won't let me become the Malazia unless I marry you."

"I know. I will tell them that I cannot marry you."

"Why?"

"Because I know you will always love Kieran. I could not live in a loveless marriage."

When they entered the council chambers, Jessa immediately noticed the black marble table. It had been split in half and was held up by wooden supports.

What could have split marble like that? she wondered. Then she remembered what Kieran had said about Galen wanting to kill him. She shuddered at the thought of Kieran raising Restamar above his head and splitting the marble with the force of his blow.

After a few moments, the council members silently entered the chamber. Calafar Galen was the last to enter. He held his head high, even when seating himself between the other members. It was obvious he relished his role as leader of the Hada. Jessa wondered if he had taken her place in leading all of the Baraca.

He nodded to her and began to speak. "We are pleased to have our Malazia in our midst. But we must confirm that you are indeed the Chosen One."

"How will you...?"

Galen raised a hand to silence her. "You do not yet have permission to speak."

Jessa growled inwardly. More control. If she did become Malazia, this was one thing she would change.

Over the next two hours, Galen and the other council members questioned her about every detail of her young life. Jessa had to reach into the deepest corners of her mind to find the answers, but in the end, Galen and the others acknowledged that she was the Malazia. Jessa was exhausted.

"And now," said Galen, "the matter of the marriage."

Jessa clenched her jaw. Stefan stood and waited for permission to speak. Galen nodded.

"Most honored calafar," Stefan began, and then glanced at Jessa.

She gave him a tight smile and hoped he would be far more eloquent and diplomatic than she in this matter.

"After much thought and observation, I have come to the conclusion that King Aiden would be a better choice for my cousin."

Several members slapped their hands on the table. Galen stood to silence them. "We have already told the king to sever his ties with the Malazia. She will marry you."

Stefan's eyes flashed. "I will not be part of a forced marriage."

Galen drummed his fingers on the table and gave Jessa a suspicious smile. "Perhaps after your purification rites you will be more agreeable to the idea of marrying Stefan."

Jessa's meeting with the council had left her head pounding. Now as she sank into her bed, all she wanted was to be alone. Unfortunately, her mother found her before she could fall asleep.

"There will be a celebration of your womanhood tonight. Then you will take the Hada mark."

Jessa thought of the first time she'd seen Kieran's tattoo. It was her first clue as to his true identity. She should have taken her own mark when she was thirteen, the year that her clan would have declared that she was a woman. Now, the thought of having someone stick needles into her arm was abhorrent. But if she were to prove to other clans that she was the Malazia, she would have to take the mark.

After Jessa had bathed, Tiana slipped the traditional white dress of the marking ceremony over Jessa's head. Jessa shivered. The translucent fabric clung to every curve. For all that it revealed, she might as well have been wearing nothing. Then her mother brushed through her hair and deftly pulled it out of her face with two gold combs. Jessa frowned.

"Yes, daughter," said her mother, "only your husband will see your hair unbraided, but it is part of the ceremony."

He's already seen it, Jessa thought with a smile. And when he'd run his hands through her hair, it had been almost as intimate as the last kiss they had shared.

When Tiana finished, she escorted Jessa to a large room, occupied by what must have been every woman from the clan. Jessa tried to ignore the churning in her gut as the women stared at her figure, nodding their heads and whispering comments.

Jessa and Tiana sat at a large rectangular table, and the other women moved to their places. When they were all seated, her mother stood. "Ladies, you honor me with your presence. We were not able to celebrate my daughter's coming of age at the proper time, but she has returned, and we celebrate it now."

Another woman stood and looked Jessa over as if she were breeding stock. "I will be the first to declare that the daughter of Tiana and Devan has come into her full womanhood."

Jessa felt her face flush. She hadn't felt this exposed since being inspected at the slave market. What made this worse was that these were her people, and she would have to look these women in the eye every day.

One by one, the rest of the women walked past Jessa, bringing gifts related to her crossing the threshold of womanhood: a dark, tasteless liquid "from the lobelia flower, so you may give your husband many children"; honeyed milk "to enhance your beauty"; a gilded hand mirror and brush; on and on it went. In between gifts, Tiana made her drink something called "melosa." All Jessa knew was that it dulled her senses. She gladly kept drinking, hoping it would take the edge off of her embarrassment and the pain of what was to come.

Chapter 60

Sienna sat next to Jessa, rubbing a salve into the tattoo. Jessa tossed and turned, calling out Kieran's name. Sienna put her hand over Jessa's heart. "If only I could have Kieran or Arathor heal her," she murmured.

Just at the moment she said it, the stone glowed and she heard Kieran in her mind. Or maybe he was in Jessa's mind.

When Sienna took her hand away, the tattoo had completely healed and Jessa's fever was gone. A peaceful smile came over Jessa's face.

Sienna let out a relieved sigh and moved through the room, hanging up Jessa's clothes, straightening pillows, dusting – anything to keep herself busy. She couldn't let her mind dwell on being away from Gilrain. But no matter what she did, she couldn't keep her mind from wandering back to their last moments together.

Saying goodbye to him had been the most difficult thing she'd ever done. She sniffed back the tears as she remembered the breathless way he'd covered her face and neck with kisses. When she looked into his eyes, they held more pain than she'd ever seen in them. Now she almost wished that she and Gilrain had the same kind of heart connection that Kieran and Jessa shared.

Jessa stirred and Sienna went to her side. Her eyes fluttered open and she smiled.

"How are you?" Sienna asked.

Jessa put her hand to her head. "I think I had too much melosa. How long have I been asleep?"

"The ceremony was last night. Now it's evening again."

Sienna smoothed the quilt over Jessa. "You can thank Kieran for your recovery. Somehow he healed the tattoo and brought down your fever."

Jessa managed a weak smile. "I thought I dreamed that." Then she rolled over and went back to sleep.

Sienna went to get something to eat. When she returned, Cala Elena was standing next to Jessa's bed.

Sienna curtsied. "She's doing much better, but she's still weak."

"Make sure she has something to eat before she comes to my chambers tonight. And make sure she wears the dress from last night's ceremony."

Jessa was right – Elena was very much like Ciara – arrogant, demanding, and threatening. "Please, m'lady. I don't think she'll be strong enough for the ceremony tonight."

Elena's angry eyes flashed. "She will be there, regardless of her condition."

Tiana led Jessa to a chair in the center of Cala Elena's chambers. As five women formed a circle around her, a feeling of dread engulfed her. Being here was worse than having all those women "declare" her womanhood. At least Jessa had chosen something a little more decent to wear this time.

Cala Elena entered the room and scowled. "I told your Telerian servant to have you wear the dress from the marking ceremony."

"I decided – "

"You are not the Malazia yet. You still answer to me."

Jessa gritted her teeth. "I decided to wear *this* dress."

Elena glared at her, but said nothing more. After closing the curtains, she extinguished all of the candles save one, and set it in a stand near the center of the room. When she had seated herself next to Jessa, the women began to chant in a language Jessa had never heard before.

Elena poured a clear liquid into a goblet. She put it in Jessa's hand and told her to drink.

"What is it?" Jessa asked, hesitant to take any.

"An ancient drink to help you begin your rite of passage."

Jessa sniffed and pushed it away. It smelled like something from a chamber pot.

"Jessara, you cannot go against the ancient ways," Elena said, pushing the drink back into her hand. "It is the first step in the purification rite."

All Jessa wanted to do was escape. "Why do I have to do this?"

"Every Malazia participates in this. It will help to clear your mind of anything that would hinder you in your role as the Chosen One. You must forget everything if you are to be a servant of your people."

"You were among Telerians for so many years," another woman added. "I am sure you have many painful memories."

"Actually, I don't."

"You have no choice," Elena persisted.

Jessa looked to Tiana for help but her mother's eyes were closed. "What if I just take a sip?"

"No. You must drink it all."

I hope Kieran appreciates this, Jessa thought.

She held her breath and drained the cup. As soon as she swallowed, a strange sensation came over her. She was aware of the people in the room, but they seemed far away, like they were enshrouded in mist. The chanting became more like a hum and the smell of incense was heavy in the air.

What had Elena given her that would make her feel this way?

It was early morning when Jessa woke up. Her dress had been replaced by a linen shift. The thought of someone else dressing her made her cringe again. She sat up, looking for Shula. The girl slept on a sheepskin pallet. Sienna was curled up on a straw mattress in the corner.

Jessa lit a candle and put on a cloak and sandals before she walked to the mirror. The shadows cupped her eyes and gave her a ghostly appearance. She brought the candle closer and looked at the stone in her chest. The puffiness was gone, and now a silvery blue circle rested on top of her skin. She ran her hand over it, remembering the shock on Kieran's face when she'd put his hand there, and the acute pain of her body absorbing the stone.

She lifted her sleeve and looked at the tattoo on her left arm. Most Baraca took the mark on their wrists, but she'd wanted hers in the same place as Kieran's – and just like Kieran's it was the Tree of Life, with a crown just above the tree.

She blew out the candle and went outside. When she reached the swan fountain, pink and gray light greeted her. Of all the places in the fortress, this had been her favorite place to come. She loved listening to the water shooting out of the swans' mouths and splashing in the pool below. Now she realized how much she had missed it. If she ever returned to Korisan, she would put a fountain in the garden.

She sat on the edge of the fountain and rearranged her cloak around her shoulders. She was startled when a young woman approached.

"Begging your pardon, my lady. May I join you?"

"Of course. I was just trying to wake up."

"Is it true that you have spent the last ten years among Telerians?"

Jessa nodded.

"Did they torture you?"

"Torture me? Why would you think that?"

The girl looked around and then drew closer to whisper. "Calafar Galen says that all Telerians are murderers and thieves. They will torture any Baraca they find."

Jessa laughed. "There are Telerians who believe the same things about us."

The girl's eyes widened. "But they do not know us."

"And Calafar Galen doesn't know Telerians. They're really no different from the Baraca."

"But we have heard that they made you a slave."

"The Esgharites made me a slave, and yes, a Telerian king bought me. But most Telerians are good."

The girl looked surprised.

Jessa pulled her cloak more tightly around her shoulders and began to tell the girl about Arathor, Kieran, and Elisa.

"I have many friends who are curious about Telerians," said the girl. "Would you tell them what you have told me?"

Jessa smiled and nodded.

Sienna found Jessa sitting under a chestnut tree. Dark circles framed her eyes. Sienna joined her and tucked her knees under her skirt.

"What did they do to you last night?" Sienna asked.

"They gave me some kind of drink. I felt like I was floating."

"What are they trying to do to you?"

"Make me forget my life. And Elena kept trying to convince me that Kieran is just using me."

"I don't like it, Jessa. I think we should get out of here."

Jessa rubbed her temple. "If I can find out what Elena put in that drink, maybe I can take something to keep it from working."

Sienna unfolded her legs and stretched. "Why would you want to stay?"

"I think I've found a way to get the Hada to help Kieran."

Sienna's brow wrinkled.

"I just spoke with a young woman who wants to know more about Telerians. And she has friends who might be persuaded to fight."

When had Jessa become so determined? "Galen and Elena won't like it."

"The younger Hada have to know the truth. Galen tells them horrible things about Telerians. It's no wonder they're suspicious."

Obviously, there was no persuading her. "All right, but first we should find out what's in that drink."

Sienna stood outside the Hada archives, wishing again that Jessa were here. Only the Malazia and the record keepers were allowed in this building. If Sienna were caught, she could be banished from the fortress. But with all that Elena had Jessa doing, Jessa never had a moment to herself.

Now it was midnight, and while Shula stood watch, Sienna opened the door to the glass building, hoping that no one would see her. The stacks of scrolls and books made her stomach turn. It could take her days to read through all of these. Not knowing where to start, she set down her lantern and unrolled the first scroll she found.

Two hours later, she yawned as she reached for a large book on a high shelf. She blew the dust off and sneezed. As she laid it on the table, she saw that the title had worn away from the wooden cover. She leafed through it and was about to put it away when something caught her eye.

Jessa wasn't going to believe this.

Chapter 61

"You're distracted again."

Kieran looked up at his uncle. Everyone on his war council nodded in agreement.

"Am I?"

"You've been staring at the table since you got here."

Kieran rubbed his temple. Loric was right – he *had* been staring at it. But it was difficult to concentrate. His mind kept going over the details of the dream that had haunted him every night for the last two weeks.

It always ended the same way – just as he leaned in to kiss Jessa, a pack of gurithents ripped her from his arms and dragged her to the dungeon in Korisan. Kieran was never able to stop them. Every morning, his heart raced and his clothes were drenched in sweat.

He knew she was safe; she was with her people and in far less danger than she would be with him. So why did he have this overwhelming sense that something was wrong?

"What were you discussing?" he asked apologetically.

"Dorinda was telling us she had another vision," said Arathor.

Dorinda had arrived last night. She'd come from the Ancala camp with news of Sahjahn's promise to add his warriors – and those of the other hostile clans – to Kieran's army.

Now the mystic was speaking with his war council.

She pressed her fingers together. "I saw the Zagorans arriving in large sailing vessels. They had horses and siege weapons."

"How many ships were there?" asked Kale.

"The harbor was full."

The room went silent as the weight of her words hit them all.

"So many," Riordan murmured.

Arathor was strangely calm. "They'll have to come through Lenkar. Then they'll take Felonia and march on to Korisan."

"That divides the country in half," said Kieran.

Riordan shook his head. "How can we hope to defeat them?"

Each man looked to Arathor for the answer.

"What did Alardin do when he faced them?" asked Gilrain.

"Alardin's advantage," said Arathor, "was that Leandra wasn't expecting him."

"She has had had many years to build an army," said Bairn, "and I am sure she will expect resistance this time."

"If every man in Teleria came to our aid, we still wouldn't match their numbers," said Kale.

Arathor folded his arms. "Kale is right. We can't hope to win this war with strength of arms alone."

"What do we know about them?" Kieran asked.

"The history books say that they're ruthless and barbaric. They destroy everything and everyone in their path."

"Then what can we do?" asked Loric.

"We must fight them with cunning and guile," said Arathor. "We can use our knowledge of Teleria to our advantage."

"How?" asked Gilrain.

"The Zagorans move as one army. If we can split them into smaller groups and lead them to places where they are vulnerable – valleys, river crossings, marshes – we might be able to pick them off like sparows."

"What else can we do?" asked Riordan.

All this time, Sahbél had been silent. He looked up and cleared his throat. "We take small groups at night and we sabotage their supplies – break their wagons, cut loose their horses, steal their food and weapons."

"Will that work?" asked Toren.

"It's how we fight the Esgharites on the border," said Sahbél. "After a while they give up from discouragement."

Gilrain's green eyes blazed. "That sounds like my kind of war."

Kieran flashed him a smile. "I was just thinking that. You can work with Sahjahn."

"Sahjahn?"

"The Baraca are swift and silent. Who better to get into the Zagoran camps and disrupt things? And Sahjahn needs a challenge. I'll send a message for him to meet you here."

"How many Baraca can we expect?" asked Toren.

"If all of us fight, two thousand," said Braeden. "That includes some of our women."

"Women?" asked Kieran.

"Baraca women are known for their fierceness in battle," said Arathor. "Before Jessara married Alardin, she played an important role in the battle against Leandra."

Kieran shot Arathor an angry glance. He would never allow *his* Jessara to participate in the battle. Her life was in enough danger without entering the fray.

"What are your orders, sir?" asked Toren.

Kieran blinked and turned his attention to the smith. He'd been distracted again. "Orders." He paused. "Send messengers to Brecken of Pomora, Adamar of Kelefar, and Bonifar the peddler. Tell them 'The time is now,' and have them come here immediately, with as many men as they can find. I want word to go out to every cartographer, carpenter, smith, cooper, potter, weaver, and any other craftsmen you think we can use. We'll need their skills. We'll also need herbalists, healers, and cooks."

Kieran was surprised again by how easily he gave orders. He continued. "Have every Telerian who's willing to fight report here. They should bring farm tools and anything else we can convert into weapons. Those who can't fight can give us food and supplies."

"And what of those who won't help?" asked Toren.

Toren had touched on a problem Kieran had tried to solve since he'd started traveling in the spring. From what he'd observed, many Telerians were either afraid of Ciara or saw no advantage in trying to overthrow her. Until now, he hadn't found a solution to this dilemma. Distasteful as it was, now he had one.

"They may change their minds when they lose everything they have to the Zagorans."

Kieran stood and dismissed his council. He needed to clear his head, and riding Fallon was the only way to do that.

As he cantered his horse along the inside wall of the fortress, he found his mind drifting back to Jessa. He had hoped that once he returned to the fortress and had immersed himself in planning the war he would stop thinking about her. He was wrong.

When he worked in the smithy, she sat in a corner, watching him. When he trained his men, she was in front of him, practicing her forms. When he rode Fallon, she rode beside him, atop Brielle. Once, he walked through the garden, and he could have almost touched her as she sat in the willow chair. And when he dreamed, she shared more than a heart connection with him.

Now he almost wished he'd never suggested that she take the stone. How could he concentrate on the tasks at hand if she was always in his mind?

When he returned to the stable, Dorinda was waiting for him. He greeted her as he dismounted and led Fallon into the barn. She folowed and stood watching while he removed the saddle and started to curry his horse.

"Did the mystics discover how to break the curse?" he asked.

Dorinda pulled some oats from a bucket and let Fallon take them from her hand. "No, I am afraid not."

Kieran swore under his breath. Another puzzle.

"I was pleased to hear that Jessara accepted your proposal."

He smiled at the memory of that day – covered in butterflies, looking into her jet-black eyes.

"Did you tell her about the alliance?"

Kieran nodded.

"And she is with the Hada now?"

"She's been there for two weeks. I haven't had a chance to speak with her yet."

"She should not stay long."

Kieran arched a brow. "Why not?"

"She is disrupting Galen's carefully laid plans. He will do anything to stop her."

Jessa hardly had time to miss Kieran. Between spending time with her mother and Elena and the young people, she didn't have a moment to herself. She was quite surprised when Kieran woke her up in the middle of the night.

At first, she had only a vague awareness of his presence, and she let herself take pleasure from the mingling of their hearts. But then he said her name, and there was an unexpected urgency in his voice. When she sat up in bed, she saw him sitting next to her. His face hadn't been this stormy since the night of the gurithent attack.

"Dorinda said you're in danger."

"If she's talking about the purification rites, I'll be fine. I've been taking cascabel before Elena gives me the drink."

The clouds in his face darkened. "What are you talking about?"

"Galen's wife is leading me through some kind of process so the council can control me. She gives me small doses of gurithent poison every night. But I take cascabel to counteract it."

"Gurithent poison? Where did they get that?"

"Sienna said that the Hada captured a gurithent two hundred years ago and extracted some of its poison. In small doses, it removes certain memories without the side effects."

"They're erasing your memories?"

"No, they're not. I'm taking cascabel."

"That alone should make you want to leave now."

"Kieran, I can't leave now."

"Why not?"

"I've been teaching the younger Hada about Teleria and the curse. I think I can get them to help."

He gave her a strained laugh. "No wonder Galen is upset with you."

"Galen?"

"Dorinda said you're disrupting his plans."

"He can be as angry with me as he wants."

"She said he'll try to stop you."

"Stefan is here. Galen can't touch me."

Kieran exhaled his impatience. "Don't underestimate him, Jess. He wields great power and will do anything to keep it."

She knew Galen enjoyed having power, but she'd never considered him a threat. "Just another week, Kieran. They're so close to wanting to leave."

"It's not worth it. I want you to get out of there."

"It *is* worth it. You need their help, and I'm the only one who can convince them."

The storm broke and his anger hit her like a surging wave. It took all of her courage to withstand it. "Kieran, you know I'm right."

"Go to Morigon as soon as you can."

Chapter 62

"Sneaking out again?" asked Sienna.

Jessa stamped her foot into her boot and pulled on her riding gloves. "I'm too angry to sleep."

"What's wrong?"

"Kieran – he ordered me to leave."

"Well, there must be a reason. He only gets angry with you –"

"When I'm in danger. I know. He thinks Galen will try to stop me from talking to Jerrec and his friends."

"You've mentioned Jerrec before. Who is he?"

Jessa pulled a cloak around her shoulders. "The self-appointed leader of the younger Baraca. He's on the verge of helping Kieran. He just needs a little push." She looked at Sienna. "Do you want to come with me?"

Sienna gave her a sleepy smile. "No, I'll stay here and tell Elena you're in bed."

Jessa frowned. She would have preferred not to ride alone, but Sienna was right. If Elena discovered that Jessa was gone, she would go into one of her lengthy tirades about how a Malazia was supposed to behave. Jessa had heard it from her more times than she could count, and it was something she would rather not face.

After avoiding the groomsmen and saddling Brielle, Jessa urged the mare forward, ducking under low branches. This was the fourth time in two weeks she'd been able to ride. She knew she was taking a risk every time she did, but it was the only taste of freedom she had. From the moment she arrived, the nightmares she'd had about living a new form of slavery were slowly coming true.

But Galen and Elena hadn't won yet.

Jessa approached a stream and slowed Brielle to a walk, recalling last night's ceremony. Once again, Elena had tried to get Jessa to agree that Kieran was using her. When Jessa refused – again – she sensed that it was taking all of Elena's resolve not to explode in anger in front of everyone. For the rest of the evening, Jessa maintained the upper hand, and after two hours, Elena left the room, muttering under her breath.

At the time it was maddening, but now Jessa laughed. There was something satisfying about standing up to Elena and Galen. It was a test of wills, and Jessa was winning. Among other things, Jessa still refused to marry Stefan, told everyone her name, and wouldn't use formal Baraca speech. She could hardly wait to see the look on Galen's face when he found out she was inciting the younger Baraca to rebel.

Unless Kieran was right. What had he said? *"He wields great power and will do anything to keep it."*

If only she knew what the "anything" was.

It didn't matter. She was having an effect on the younger Hada, and she wasn't going to let Galen stop her. She just wished she knew what to tell them to get them to leave the fortress. She couldn't ask Kieran. She knew he was still angry with her, and she didn't want to talk with him anytime soon. The only person who might be able to help was Arathor.

Feeling more like herself after her morning ride, Jessa sat across the table from her mother, sharing a late breakfast. Tiana sipped mint tea and took a bite of raspberry scone.

"How did you know about the Keldar stone?" Jessa asked.

Tiana's eyes went wide and she almost choked.

"I'm sorry," said Jessa. "I was just curious because you mentioned it the first day I was here."

Before Jessa could say anything more, her mother pulled down the collar of her dress to reveal a faded blue stone. Jessa put down her cup.

"You…?"

"I joined my heart to another's heart, against my parents' wishes." Tiana paused, and her face was tight. "We took the Keldar stones anyway. When my parents found out, they forbid me to ever see him again. Then they betrothed me to Devan."

"Then Father wasn't your Eldala?"

Tiana shook her head. "In time, I learned to love your father."

"How did Father feel, knowing you'd already joined your heart to someone else's?"

"Devan was too kind to ever speak of it."

This news was shocking to say the least. Jessa couldn't help but wonder who her mother's Eldala was, but Tiana looked so distressed that Jessa decided to leave the question unasked.

After an uncomfortable silence, Tiana set something in front of Jessa.

"What's this?" Jessa asked.

"I thought you might like to have it."

Jessa looked down at a charcoal drawing of a man with dark hair and kind eyes.

"Father," she whispered.

"Devan adored you. It broke his heart when the Esgharites took you away."

"Then you knew they weren't Telerians?"

"I know that Galen *accused* Telerians, but I never believed him. Telerians would never steal a child from her family. But Galen does whatever he can to control people. He has tried to control me ever since you were chosen."

"How?"

Tiana poured more tea and slowly stirred in some sugar. "He told us how to educate you and dress you, and wanted us to restrict you in every way. Your father always refused. When Devan left to find you, Galen blamed me for your abduction."

Jessa's throat tightened. "Every day I wished that Father would rescue me. But when he didn't come, I gave up hoping."

Her mother wiped a tear from her cheek. "He was determined to find you, Jessara. I should have gone with him. But I was afraid to leave the fortress."

Jessa picked up the portrait and traced her father's features. The weight of his death hit her like a flash flood. "Tell me more about Father. I've forgotten."

"He was a good man – patient and kind, never cross or harsh with anyone."

"I can still see his smile."

"He used to hold you in his lap and tell you the most wonderful stories."

"I don't remember the stories, but I do remember his beard tickling my face, and the smell of pipe smoke."

Tiana looked down and drew something from her pocket. "I carry this with me all the time. It is all I have left of him."

When Tiana laid the object on the table, Jessa was stunned. It was her father's pipe.

Jessa picked it up and let her fingers explore the intricately carved bowl and the smooth mouth piece. When she held it up to her face and inhaled, she could see her father's kind face. Waves of grief she'd held in flooded her heart, and she began to sob. Tiana pulled her close and held her as they both shed tears.

Jessa had forgotten how much she missed having a father. Marcus and Bairn had tried to watch over her, but they'd never been able to replace him. She was her father's little princess and he was her strong tower – the one person she could count on to make everything better.

When Jessa's tears stopped, Tiana stroked her face. "I miss him, too."

Her mother stood to leave, but Jessa took her hand. "Thank you for telling me about your Eldala. I know it was difficult for you to share."

"I know you believe you cannot marry anyone other than King Aiden. But it is possible to love another."

"Mother… you may have learned to love Father, but I've given Kieran my answer. I won't – "

"Jessara, for the sake of our clan, for the sake of all Baraca, you must marry Stefan."

"Stefan already told the council he refuses to marry me. He won't live in a loveless marriage."

Tiana looked as if Jessa had slapped her.

"I'm sorry… I'm not saying you and Father had a loveless marriage. But I won't sacrifice my heart for any reason, not even for our clan."

Tiana shook her head and left the room. Jessa sighed. Maybe her mother could live without her Eldala, but Jessa would never walk away from Kieran, especially after what had happened between them on their last night together.

She pushed the painful memory away and put her nose to the pipe to inhale her father's scent again – which only brought more unwanted tears.

Her father was gone. Who could give her the protection and wisdom she needed now? Was there anyone who could make everything better?

Without thinking, she let her mind call out to Arathor. Just as it had been with Kieran, she felt him sitting right next to her.

"You're thinking about your father."

"I didn't realize until today that I missed him."

She didn't know how it was possible – Arathor was miles away – but she felt him surround her with his strong arms. She melted into him and sobbed again as he stroked her head.

"Devan was a good father," he said. "He must have loved you very much to go looking for you."

"But he died because of me."

Arathor loosened his hold and drew back to look at her. "How long are you going to blame yourself for your father's death?"

"But it *is* my fault. If I hadn't run away all the time, I never would have met Kieran and then the Esgharites wouldn't have taken me – "

"And my son would still be in Korisan, under Ciara's control – or dead."

She looked down and absently fingered the end of her braid, thinking of all the times Kieran had twisted it between his fingers.

"Jessara, it's time for you to put aside your guilt. It prevents you from walking in your destiny."

It was just what her father would have said. And now that Jessa thought about it, Arathor reminded her of her father in many ways. He would have the answer she needed.

She explained how she'd met with the younger Hada, and how they were on the verge of helping Kieran.

"What will sway them?" she asked.

"Tell them Ciara hates the Baraca as much as she hates Alardin's descendants. When the Zagorans come, they'll spare no one."

Jessa and Stefan, along with several younger Baraca, stood before Galen and the council. The calafar stared at Jessa. She sensed in him the same struggle for self-control she had felt from Elena. When he spoke, his voice was tight. "This is your fault."

Jessa held his stare and returned it. After a long pause, she said, "Did you think I'd stand by and let you fill their heads with lies?"

"We have taken great pains to protect our clan from the Telerians. We will use whatever means necessary to do that – even if we have to bend the facts."

"I'd say you've done more than bend the facts. You've made it sound like the Telerians are as bad as the Esgharites."

Galen started to speak, but Jessa cut him off. "I've lived among them. They're nothing like you've painted them."

"You were corrupted by them. Or by one of them anyway."

Jessa fingered Shed'ar. If Kieran hadn't already split their table, she would have done it now. Instead, she said, "If sharing Eldala with the King of Teleria and agreeing to be his queen means I've been corrupted, then I'll gladly admit it."

Red splotches covered Galen's pale face. Jessa smiled. The power was slipping from his grasp, and he knew he couldn't do anything to stop it. "I will not allow this to continue," he said.

Jerrec had been silent since telling Galen of their plans to leave. Now he stood just in front of the calafar. "There are one hundred of us. You cannot stop us from leaving."

Galen stood and leaned over the table so his nose almost touched Jerrec's. His face was a mask of rage. "If you and the others leave, you will not be allowed to return."

Jerrec clenched his fists and tightened his jaw. "So be it." Then he turned, followed by his friend Faran and the young people who had come with them.

Galen turned to Jessa. He did nothing to hide his contempt for her. "You have insulted the council and our people for the last time. You and your family are hereby banished from the Hada fortress. If you attempt to return, it will be under pain of death."

Chapter 63

Kieran dropped his hammer and stared at his cousin. "What did you say?"

"Sienna and Jessa are here."

"I told Jessa to go to Morigon."

"Apparently she ignored you."

Kieran picked up the hammer and laid it on the anvil. What was he supposed to do with this stubborn woman?

It was bad enough that Elisa and Sorina hadn't listened to him. They argued that he needed every woman he could get to roll bandages and cook and tend to the wounded. Then, a few days ago, Aunt Dena and Aunt Melchiah had arrived. They brought their entire collection of herbs and volunteered to help.

How could he argue with them? He had sent out a call for the very help they could provide. But having his mother and aunts this close to the battle only weighed him down with fear for their safety, giving him one more thing to worry about.

Having Jessa here was worse. It not only put her closer to the battle, but it gave Ciara a better chance of finding her. If Jessa were captured now, Kieran would have to choose between rescuing her and fighting for his kingdom. It wasn't a choice he wanted to make.

And now she would be more of a distraction than ever. It was bad enough that he was dreaming about her every night. Having her here meant he would have to keep his thoughts under more control than usual.

Gilrain moved to the bellows and started to pump as Kieran picked up the spearhead and thrust it into the fire. Gilrain cleared his throat. "Sienna and I have decided to get married this week."

"I thought you were going to wait."

"I want to have at least one night with Sienna before I put my life in danger."

Kieran picked up the tongs and pulled the metal from the fire. Was he the only one in the family who was thinking clearly? Everything in him wanted to tell Gilrain what a fool he was for not waiting. But he knew there was no convincing Gilrain once he'd made up his mind. And if Kieran wasn't the king, he might want the same thing.

"Fine," Kieran growled. "Just don't let it affect your fighting."

Gilrain's voice was strained. "I told you before, when I fight, nothing is going to distract me."

Kieran wanted to say more, but Braeden interrupted.

"Sir, a group of Hada Baraca would like to meet with you. They are in the great hall."

"Who?"

"Hada Baraca. They came with Jessara."

"Tell them I'll meet with them in a few minutes."

Gilrain arched an amused brow. "You'll have to thank Jessa when you see her."

Kieran threw down his hammer and left.

Kieran was expecting Baraca warriors. It didn't look like anyone in the room was older than fourteen. They all stared at him with an awe that bordered on worship. When they dropped to their knees, Kieran ignored the familiar urge to stop them. He appreciated their loyalty, but how could he ask them to fight? They were children. The thought of sending them into battle was almost as distasteful as sending Jessa.

Finally, one of them stood and clasped his hand.

"I am Jerrec of the Hada Baraca. We have come to help."

Kieran looked the young man over. He was the oldest in the group, maybe seventeen. His blond hair fell past his shoulders and his eyes flashed with an intense pride. He gestured to another young man with black hair and a thin moustache. "This is Faran. Jessara told us you needed help. When she left, we came with her."

"Are you here to fight?"

"Of course."

Kieran rubbed the back of his neck. Then he motioned for Braeden. "Please find quarters for our guests." He would have to think long and hard before letting them join in combat.

Kieran waited in the doorway of the practice hall to watch Jessa. Everything about her was beautiful. Even now, she moved through her sword forms as if they were an intricate dance. He was tempted to freeze time so his eyes could drink in her movements – the way she held the sword, the way her graceful body glided through the forms, and the way her braid swished back and forth as she stepped from side to side.

Then he remembered why she was here – and why he was here. He cleared his throat and walked towards her. "I told you to go to Morigon."

"You haven't seen me for three weeks, and that's all you can say?"

She brushed her hair out of her eyes and moved to the practice urchin. Kieran took the handles and started to spin the three parts. She jumped to dodge a flying mace. "What about 'Jessa, I missed you' or 'It's so good to see you'?" she asked.

"What happened?"

"You were right about Galen." She blocked an incoming sword and struck at a wooden shield. Kieran was surprised at her agility.

"But why did you come *here*?"

She stared up at him. "You have to ask?"

Her dark eyes flashed with a fire that stirred his blood. If he hadn't been so angry with her, he would have kissed her right there. "You shouldn't be here," he said.

"I'm one of the best healers in Teleria. You'll need me."

Her refusal to yield reminded him of the first time he'd met her, when she insisted that the tree belonged to her. Back then it was amusing. Now it was like a slap across the face.

What was he supposed to do with this stubborn woman?

After a long day of trying – and failing – to make spearheads, Kieran was tired and frustrated. All he wanted was to be alone. Before he could take a hot bath, Stefan knocked on his open door and entered.

"What can I do for you?" Kieran asked as he took off his shirt.

Stefan fidgeted with the grip of his sword. Kieran was too tired to read Stefan's intent and hoped he wouldn't have to defend himself.

He was stunned when Stefan said, "I have come to join your fight."

Kieran raised an eyebrow.

"I was wrong about you – about Telerians in general. And I do not want to see the Zagorans destroy my clan."

The unexpected good news was overshadowed by a question that had gnawed at Kieran all day.

"Why did you let Jessa come here?"

Stefan's face darkened. "When Galen banished us – "

"Banished?"

"Galen blamed Jessara for corrupting the younger Hada, so he banished Jessara's entire family. We cannot return."

"That sounds like Galen."

"Jessara was determined to come here. I tried to stop her."

"You swore to protect her. Letting her come here was a mistake."

Stefan gave him an amused smile. "You know how stubborn she can be."

The morning sun gilded the leaves and flowers, and a light breeze blew in from the lake, ruffling Kieran's hair. If there hadn't been a war to prepare for, it would have been a perfect day. But as far as Kieran was concerned, Gilrain and Sienna's wedding was just one more distraction.

As king of Teleria, it was within his power to preside over weddings. Now he stood just to the right of his cousin, waiting for the bride to arrive. Gilrain was nervously tugging at his sleeves. Uncle Loric and Aunt Sorina stood next to Gilrain with hands clasped. Loric looked about as proud as Kieran had ever seen him. Next to them, Neera wiped a tear from her cheek. Kieran's parents, along with other family and friends, made up the crowd of witnesses. Arathor had consented to escort Sienna when she arrived.

Suddenly, Gilrain drew in a quick breath. Sienna was walking up the path. She wore a flattering light blue dress with gold trim. She took Arathor's arm and walked towards Gilrain. Jessa walked just behind her, wearing the pale green dress from the night when they'd said goodbye outside the Hada fortress.

How was he supposed to conduct a wedding with Jessa here, looking as radiant as the sun? Her eyes caught his and Kieran barely remembered the words to join Gilrain and Sienna as man and wife. When Gilrain and Sienna exchanged vows, Kieran couldn't help thinking that one day he would be saying the same words to Jessa.

One day… who knew when that would be? For a moment he envied his cousin and the night he would have with his bride.

Before Kieran knew it, Gilrain was kissing Sienna and the crowd erupted in cheers. When they adjourned to the banquet hall, Jessa stayed as far away from Kieran as possible. All he could sense was her simmering irritation with him. It was just as well. He was still angry with her and had too much to do anyway.

After making the obligatory toasts to the bride and groom, Kieran was about to leave when Sienna took his hand and asked if he would have the first dance. All he wanted was to return to the mountain of tasks ahead of him. He was thankful when he saw Dorinda standing in the doorway. He excused himself and escorted Dorinda outside.

"Have you noticed the weather?" she asked.

Kieran looked up at a cloudless sky. "Should I be concerned?"

"It is late summer. The rainy season should have started already, but there has been no rain for two weeks."

Kieran crossed his arms. He didn't have time for riddles.

"This may be Ciara's work," she said. "If the Zagorans are bringing siege engines, they will need dry roads. We cannot give them that."

"I can sustain a storm for a only few hours."

"This is beyond your skill alone."

"Then what can I do?"

"It will take you, Arathor, and Jessara *together* to conjure weeks of rain."

"Jessa?"

"She is a descendant of Alardin and bears a Keldar stone."

Kieran felt like a dozen hammers were forging swords on the inside of his skull. "Can she help from a distance?"

Dorinda shook her head. "It will not work if you are apart. She will have to go with you wherever you go."

Chapter 64

Jessa walked into her room and was stunned. From one wall to the other, it was filled with roses and wild flowers. She rushed in and moved from flower to flower, inhaling their perfume. When Kieran had had time to do this, she didn't know.

Sienna had told her that Kieran was working night and day, forging weapons, training men, and meeting with his war council. When he wasn't doing any of those things, he was riding his horse or sparring with Gilrain or Arathor.

Jessa missed him.

Not that she had any free time of her own. For weeks now, she'd been helping Elisa – rolling bandages, cutting and drying herbs, and cooking. Any free time she had, she spent with Elisa and her mother.

When Jessa had first arrived, she was concerned that her mother wouldn't get along with Elisa. She needn't have worried. Elisa immediately ushered the travelers into her room and served all of them tea and scones. It took no time at all for Tiana to warm up to her. Now when Jessa wanted to find her mother, all she had to do was look for Elisa.

If only Kieran had welcomed her as warmly as his mother.

The memory of their argument in the practice hall still troubled her. She hadn't meant to be so harsh with him. But the way he'd spoken to her reminded her of Galen and Elena, and she wasn't about to take orders anymore. He could have at least acknowledged that he was glad to see her. When he stormed out of the hall, part of her wanted to go after him and apologize. But the other part of her felt justified for coming, and she was afraid she would regret anything she said to him.

Since that time, she had sensed that he wasn't angry with her, and she was ready to apologize for ignoring him. If only she had the time.

Something lying on her dressing table caught her eye. It was a letter, sealed with blue wax and imprinted with the eagle from Kieran's ring. She broke the seal and inhaled his fiery scent.

Heart of my heart,

For the last few weeks, we have walked the same corridors, breathed the same air, and watched the same sunrises and sunsets. But I have not lived. I would rather be lame than walk without you. I would rather breathe in your fragrance than take in my life breath. I would rather be blind than watch the sun rise and set without you.

I have missed your beautiful heart next to mine, and for your absence, I have no one to blame but myself. You offered help in Teleria's time of need and I pushed you away. If I had the power to turn back time and prevent myself from causing you pain, I would.

Dear, sweet Jessa, I want you to know that I love you more deeply than I ever thought was possible. But as Teleria's king, I must lay down everything – even a future with you – in order to defeat the Zagorans and secure Teleria's freedom.

The only thing that sustains me is hope – the hope that when the last battle has been fought, we will be married and will fall asleep and awaken in each other's arms for the rest of our lives.

There was more, but Jessa's tears kept her from reading. She knew she had to find him.

She looked in the smithy. He wasn't there. She checked the stable. Fallon was in his stall. She ran to the practice arena. It was empty. No one had seen him in the barracks. Not knowing where else to look, she called out to him with her heart.

Eldala, where are you?

In her mind, she saw the lake. She ran to the garden and climbed to the top of the wall.

Kieran stood on the shore, looking out over the water. When he turned and looked at her, the ache of missing him hit her dead center and her knees went weak. For a moment she let herself drink him in – his reddish-blond hair, his playful black eyes, his broad shoulders, his commanding stature. It was like seeing him for the first time in Korisan, and the same fluttery melody danced through her.

When she finally mustered the courage to climb down the stairs, he waited for her. She looked at him and smiled. "Thank you for the flowers. They were lovely." He moved closer. "And your letter –"

"Was eloquent," he said.

"Made me cry." He closed the space between them, and it was all she could do to stay on her feet. "I'm sorry, Kieran. I should have gone to Morigon, but all I could think about was being with you."

He put his arm around her. "No, Jessa. I'm the one who should be apologizing."

"You already did, in your letter." She kissed his knuckles. "You certainly have a way with words."

They climbed the stairs together. When they reached the top of the wall, she looked over the water. A flock of black ducks erupted from the lake, and a blue heron stalked fish among the cat tails. Kieran tugged at her braid.

Jessa gave him a teasing scowl. "Elisa told me it's your birthday."

"My birthday?"

"She said she's planned a celebration for tonight."

"I don't have time for celebrations."

"You can't spend every minute working."

He started to protest, but she spoke before he could. "You're tired, Kieran. I can see it in your face." She put her hand over his heart. "And I can feel it here." He covered her hand with his. "You have to live life."

He brought her hand up and kissed her palm. She closed her eyes and took a slow, deep breath. Then he put his other hand on her cheek and gently kissed her.

"I love you," he whispered.

She ran her fingers over his mouth and beard, down his neck, and back to his chest. "And I love you, Kieran." When she reached up to kiss him again, the melody turned into a soul-stirring symphony.

As much as Kieran had thought he didn't have time for celebrations, he was glad his mother had planned this, and that Jessa had persuaded him to come. It was a relief to put aside the burden of war and live life, as Jessa had put it. And he recalled what Bairn had said about not giving a sword to a man who couldn't dance.

Now he sat at the head of the table, surrounded by the people he loved most. His mother and father looked pleased that he had taken the time to come. Arathor looked lost in thought, occasionally glancing up at Tiana. Uncle Loric and Aunt Sorina sat next to Gilrain and Sienna. Marriage seemed to have taken the hard edge off of his cousin. Kieran didn't know if that was good or bad, but Gilrain certainly seemed more content than ever.

Neera was laughing with Dena. Melchiah and Tiana were chatting like old friends, and Jessa was just to his right, looking more enticing than usual in the candlelight

As Kieran listened to the conversation, he thought about how much his life had changed in a year. Until now, he had hardly had time to think about it.

A year ago, he had stood outside his parents' home, angry that they had kept the truth from him. Now he understood their reasons and had forgiven them. A year ago, he had denied his heritage and had hoped to disprove it. Now he was living it. A year ago, he had been a cautious blacksmith from Pent. Now he was the king of Teleria.

A year ago, he had wondered if he would ever find his Jessara. Now she was practically his wife.

He took her hand and kissed it. The look in her shining eyes made him hot all over.

After a meal of Kieran's favorite foods, including Aunt Sorina's apple pie, Arathor stood and raised a glass. "My son Aiden is twenty-one. This was the year I had intended to tell him of his heritage. But fate took a hand, and now Aiden stands poised to defeat the Zagorans."

Kieran glanced over at his cousin. Gilrain gave him a wry smile. Whether it had been fate or Gilrain's slip of the tongue, Kieran didn't know, but he was glad either way. If he'd discovered the truth this year, there would be no one to stand against Ciara.

"Let us drink to his success, and to the freedom of Teleria."

Everyone raised their glasses in a resounding, "To the freedom of Teleria."

Kale was the next to stand. He caught Kieran's eye, and for a moment there was an unspoken exchange between them. Kieran sensed Kale's pride and confidence in him. It took Kale a moment to compose himself.

"When Arathor first brought Kieran to us, I wondered how I'd be able to raise a king. It seems that despite my mistakes, he's become a better king and warrior than I could have imagined. Now the time has come for him to take his place as the rightful ruler of Teleria. May his kingdom always prosper."

"To prosperity," they all said.

Kieran was surprised when Gilrain stood. It wasn't like his cousin to make a speech. "I've seen Kieran walk the difficult road from blacksmith to king. There were moments when I didn't think he would stay the course" – Kieran frowned – "but I was wrong. He's far surpassed my expectations and hopes. I have no doubt he will succeed in whatever he does. Long live King Aiden."

"Long live King Aiden."

Kieran's throat was tight and his eyes were misty. He stood, and before raising a toast of his own, he looked at each person here. Who knew when they would all be together again? The grief from uncertainty threatened to overshadow the joy of being with family, and for a moment, he couldn't speak.

"I wouldn't be where I am or who I am without the help of everyone here," said Kieran.

Elisa and Sorina were on the verge of tears.

"Arathor my father, it took great courage to give up your only son to be raised by a blacksmith from Maquoya. Thank you for taking that risk. Thank you for having the confidence in me to be king and for your patience when I came to you, hoping to prove you a fraud.

"Mother and Father, thank you for having the courage to take me in as your son. You risked everything, and I wouldn't be who I am today without your love and guidance.

"Uncle Loric, thank you for the years of sword training. They served me well. Aunt Sorina, thank you for giving up your only son to walk with me on my journey to be king."

Sorina wiped a tear from her cheek.

"Gilrain, thank you for giving me the push I needed, and for the confidence you've shown in me."

Gilrain nodded and gave him an amused smile.

Kieran raised his glass and everyone joined him in a silent toast. Then his eyes rested on Jessa. Their eyes locked and it seemed as if everyone else in the room had vanished. "Most of all, I want to thank the woman who saved my life in Korisan, my long lost Eldala."

Heart of my heart, he heard.

Then he caught Tiana's eye. "And a heart-felt thanks to her mother."

Before the others could answer Kieran's toast, Tiana stood. When she glanced at Arathor, a blue light flashed across the table. She shook her head as if coming out of a trance and then looked at Kieran and Jessa.

"When I first met King Aiden, he told of the Eldala he shared with my daughter. It broke my heart, because I knew he was meant to be the heart of her heart. But I also knew that the council would never allow the marriage. At the time, I did not dare to go against the council's wishes. Now I heartily give my consent and my blessing to the joining of these two hearts."

Unexpectedly, Arathor left the table. Tiana sat and stared at her lap. Had something happened between them?

Whatever it was, Kieran would have to ask about it later. There was something else on his mind.

He turned to Jessa. She was the most stunning woman in Teleria.

"For so long, I was afraid I'd never find you. Now here we are, surrounded by our families. In their presence, I pledge my troth to you, Jessara. When the battle is over, we shall be husband and wife."

He tipped his goblet and drained it.

If someone had told Jessa she would be celebrating her Eldala's twenty-first birthday, surrounded by loved ones, she wouldn't have believed them. But she *was* here, and it took her a moment to swallow down the lump in her throat. Then she stood and faced the man who had pledged to marry her.

"Heart of my heart, from the moment I met you, I dreamed of the day when we'd be married. Despite overwhelming odds, we are toether at last. I now pledge my troth to you, King Aiden. I wait expectantly for the day when I will call you husband."

When Jessa sat, the joy in her heart mingled with the joy in Kieran's heart, and it was all she could do to contain it. But there was something else in him – an uncertainty and sadness that hung on him like heavy armor. She wished she could take it on herself so he would be free of it when he went to battle.

She glanced at him again, and before she could discern what was causing the pain, he offered to escort her to the garden. She took his arm, noting her mother's smile.

When they were alone, she asked, "What's wrong?"

Kieran let out a heavy sigh. "Something you don't need to carry."

"Why not?"

"Because it's *mine* to carry, Jess. And this isn't the time to talk about it." He gave her a smile and tugged at her braid. "Today is my birthday and I'm not finished celebrating."

She shivered – not from the cold, but from the intent she saw in his wide eyes and felt in his heart.

She tucked her hand in his and they walked through the garden, exchanging glances and thoughts. She tried again to find the source of his grief, but he'd buried it, and she knew better than to explore any further. When they reached the willow hut, he led her inside and offered his hand.

She felt him slow time as they danced to the exquisite song flowing between them. He pulled her closer and she rested her cheek against his chest.

"Your beautiful heart next to mine," she whispered.

He tipped her face up and grazed the backs of his fingers along her cheek, down to her jaw and neck. She caught his hand and brought it up to her face so she could breathe in his scent of soot and earth. Then his mouth was on hers, desperate and feverish and hungry. With each kiss, his essence filled her soul, and she was acutely aware of just how intertwined their hearts had become. If either of them were to die…

She pushed the thought away. She had to believe that they would both survive. If she let that hope slip away, she wouldn't be able to face what was to come.

Chapter 65

Ciara looked at her reflection from across the room and flinched. Who was this stranger? The sunken eyes, the wrinkled cheeks and brow, the pursed lips, the sagging jowls – they couldn't possibly belong to her.

In a fit, she knocked the mirror to the ground.

If this was the price she paid for bringing the drought *and* maintaining the curse then maybe the cost was too high. After all, she had a reputation to maintain. Cursing under her breath, she spun around and started to pace the room.

She had created the drought so her Zagoran soldiers could easily move their battering rams and catapults from Lenkar to the major cities. The war machines weren't really necessary. They were more a show of force than anything, one more way to intimidate the people and crush the rag-tag group of Telerians Kieran called an army. They would lose all hope of expelling her once they saw the siege engines and the size of her army.

My army. She hadn't commanded an army for more than a hundred years, and the soldiers who had just entered the sea port included some of the most brutal mercenaries in Zagora. Of course, employing them had come at a high price. She wouldn't have had to use quite as much Telerian tax money if she'd recruited disgruntled Telerians, but then Ciara didn't trust Telerians. She never had. They were weak and undisciplined.

No, bringing in the Zagorans had solved many problems. They lived for conquest and didn't mind killing women and children.

Once they swept across Teleria like an iron flood, the land would be hers – not because she wanted a country, but because she had promised to exact her revenge on Alardin's descendants.

Having studied the kings of Teleria over the years, she knew they had a weakness for their people and their country. The best way to punish Alardin's progeny was to enslave the inhabitants and ravage their beloved Teleria.

Ciara threw a robe around her shoulders and flew down the stairs to her private chamber. She poured water from the pitcher into the silver basin and waited for the liquid to still. When an image appeared it was clouded. It had never been clouded before. Was she losing her power to control the visions?

She drummed her fingers on the edge of the basin and waited.

Two men and two women sat at a round table. The older woman had a deeply etched face and was dressed in black. She was instructing the other three to join hands. Then she walked behind them, speaking in an ancient tongue that was vaguely familiar. When they were finished, Ciara sensed the powerful connection among them. It seemed that their combined strength was more than the sum of their separate minds.

The old woman led them outside where they raised their hands and looked up at the blue sky. As they spoke the word, "Ishkalar," the wind blew purplish-gray clouds across the sun, and rain started to pour by the barrel from the heavens.

When they turned to go back inside, Ciara finally saw their faces. A string of curses flew out of her mouth.

She understood how Kieran and Arathor could join minds; they were descendants of Alardin. But how could that Baraca slave link with them?

Ciara looked more closely at Jessa's face and panic began to claw at the back of her throat. The girl bore an uncanny resemblance to an ancient Baraca queen, the woman Alardin had clearly had his eye on when he'd first entered Teleria. Ciara fell back, just catching the edge of a chair.

If the three of them were conjuring rain, Ciara wouldn't be able to stand against them. She paced the room, upsetting the basin and splashing water all over herself. In her present state, she was too distracted to care. What could she do? Breaking the link was impossible; they had to do that themselves.

She would have to eliminate one of them.

It was time to redouble her efforts to capture the Baraca woman.

A disturbing anxiety stirred in Kieran's middle. Listening to the drip, drip, drip of water falling from his tent into the puddles only magnified it.

Just last night, his troops had set up camp outside of Maquoya, near the marshes surrounding the Iligan River. Tomorrow they would have their first encounter with the Zagorans. Up until now, everything had gone smoothly.

The Baraca youth, now numbering at least two hundred, were using their newly acquired mapping skills to make detailed reports of troop movement and size. None of them had been caught, thanks in part to Gilrain and Stefan's instruction in killing quietly, and in part to an innate Baraca talent for stealth.

The youth had also intercepted dispatches meant for Ciara. Kieran had smiled as he read each one. Gilrain and Sahjahn were doing just what Kieran had hoped they would do. The Zagoran commanders complained of broken axles, missing horses, and stolen weapons and food.

As for the remainder of Kieran's troops, Braeden and Loric were leading one fourth of them to Nosora. The desert would provide the perfect environment for setting sand traps to stop the advancing Zagorans. Bairn and Sahbél were leading another fourth to the outskirts of Toboso, south of Korisan. If they arrived before the Zagorans, the Telerian warriors could hide among the boulders that littered the landscape and ambush the enemy.

In spite of their careful preparations, Kieran couldn't shake the feeling that something would go wrong and that their planning would be for nothing. Worse than that were the gnawing doubts that threatened to steal the very life out of him. When it came to actually fighting, would these men follow him?

Kieran shivered and walked to the brazier to put in more charcoal. As he warmed his hands, Arathor entered the tent.

"Do you want to tell me what's wrong?" Arathor asked.

Kieran gritted his teeth and stirred the coals. Arathor waited in silence. When Kieran spoke, his voice was strained. "I know I was born for this moment – to defeat Ciara and save Teleria. But every time I measure myself, I come up short."

Arathor's face darkened. "The only one who underestimates your importance is you. You must decide now to set your face like iron and persevere. If you do, no force in Teleria can stop you."

Kieran snorted softly. "You told me that once before."

"And it's still true."

"I'm asking these men to give their lives for a hopeless cause."

"Hopeless cause?"

"The Zagorans number in the thousands. We stand very little chance of defeating them – or Ciara. Good men will die for no reason."

"Do you think it will be your fault if they die?"

"That thought's crossed my mind more than once."

"This battle started with Ciara, more than a hundred years ago. She promised to have her revenge on us and on the Baraca. The blood that's shed will be on her hands."

Kieran ran his hand across his newly shaven face. "If I knew how to break the curse, maybe the Zagorans would leave."

"It sounds like you're running from this fight."

"I won that battle a long time ago."

"Then what's this about?"

"I'm the king of Teleria and I've given countless orders. But the thought of ordering men to their death – "

"These men know the price they'll have to pay."

"Yes, but will they lay down their lives for a man who's never gone to battle? Do they see me as their king?"

Arathor half smiled. "Walk among their campfires tonight and listen. I think it will answer your question."

Jessa let out a weary sigh. This was the first moment she'd had to breathe all day. When she wasn't rolling bandages or labeling jars of herbs, she and the few healers who had come were teaching the other women how to treat battle wounds. But in the moments when she could snatch some rest, the gloom in her soul threatened to consume her. Not even Sienna could cheer her up.

Part of her dark mood came from the rain. It had been coming down for two weeks, and the gray skies only magnified her fears that she would lose Kieran. The other part came from carrying some of Kieran's burden.

She hadn't intended to, not since the night of his birthday. But when she and Kieran and Arathor had forged the bond to start the rain, it was almost impossible to ignore Kieran's grief and doubt. So without asking him, she'd decided to bear some of it to give him the clarity he needed for the tasks ahead. That had been several days ago and now she wondered if taking his burden had been a mistake.

As she sat in front of a small campfire, sopping up the last drops of soup from her bowl, the men around her didn't give her a second look. She wasn't surprised. With so many women coming to help, she looked like just another kitchen maid. After all she'd been through, it was nice to return to the anonymous life of a servant – and it gave her a chance to hear what the men were saying about Kieran.

The few words they spoke here centered on the coming battle and the man who would lead them.

"I heard he's never seen battle," said one.

"Yes, but I've heard he bested five opponents with his sword," said another.

The first man slapped him on the back and laughed. "You'd believe anything, Jared."

"All I know," said another, "is that I'd rather follow him and fight against Ciara than put up with her taxes."

Several others nodded their heads, and the men grew silent again, lost in their thoughts.

A few moments later, Jessa sensed Kieran's approach before he reached their fire. The men around her shifted uncomfortably, and most wouldn't look at him. Kieran crouched down to warm his hands, giving no indication that he recognized Jessa.

"Is there something you need, Sire?" one of them asked nervously.

"I was just going to ask you the same thing."

"Sir, why would you do that?"

Kieran took his time, looking each man in the eye with that commanding gaze. The men returned to staring at the fire. Jessa flicked a glance at him and wished she could keep her eyes on him a little longer. With everything she had to do, she'd hardly had a chance to see him and she missed looking at him. However, if she risked staring at him now, his men might think some kitchen maid had an eye for the king.

When Kieran spoke, he sounded more confident than he had in days. "The moment you volunteered to fight, you became my responsibility."

The fire popped and someone added another log. After a respectful silence, Jared worked up the courage to speak. "If you could do something about this rain…"

Some of the others laughed and pointed at him. "Don't listen to Jared, sir. He has wild ideas."

Kieran stood and smiled. "I'll see what I can do."

Almost as soon as Kieran left, Jessa's mental connection with him ended and the rain stopped. The men looked up in surprise and saw the clouds drift away to reveal a full moon. Jessa just smiled to herself and continued to watch Kieran move from campfire to campfire, talking with his men and spreading confidence. When he walked towards his tent, Jessa followed at a distance.

She parted the opening of his tent just enough to see him with one eye. His back was turned to her, and he'd just taken off his wet shirt to change into a silk robe. Every inch of him was breathtaking, and a warm melody settled in her stomach. No matter how many times she saw him this way, she could never get used to it.

Before she could go into his tent, someone grabbed her arm. It was Riordan. "What business does a kitchen maid have here?"

Jessa never had a chance to explain. Kieran opened the tent flap and looked at them. "What's the trouble?"

"I caught this woman spying on you. Should I have her punished?"

"No, I'll take care of her."

Riordan gave him a puzzled look and let her go. Jessa rubbed her arm and followed Kieran into the tent. He poured himself something to drink and leaned over a table to look at a map. She grew tired of waiting and sat on a chair behind him.

When he finally spoke, his voice was sharp and he didn't look at her. "These men haven't had a wife's company for weeks. If they hear that a woman came to my tent, they'll think the king was having a night of pleasure with a harlot."

"I made sure no one saw me."

"Riordan saw you."

"I forgot about him – but he's supposed to be watching."

He frowned at her. Then his face softened. "Why did you come?"

She let her eyes scan his face before she answered. There was something different about him, but she wasn't sure what it was. "I thought you needed some encouragement, but after watching you walk among your men tonight – "

"Then it was you I saw. You shouldn't be outside."

"Let me finish."

"I'm sorry, m'lady. Please continue."

She ignored his sarcasm. "I was going to say that the men have found their captain."

"How do you know that?"

"Before you came to their fire, I sensed they were full of doubts. When you left, they were ready to follow you anywhere."

Kieran moved closer, and when she caressed his face, she realized he'd shaved off his beard. Now there was nothing to hide his square jaw, and it gave him a more determined appearance.

"Jessa, you have to stay inside."

"I can't stay inside forever."

He captured her hand. "I still wish you didn't have to be here." His rough fingers traveled over hers, slowly tracing each one. When he turned her hand over and let his fingers dance across her palm and over her wrist, the melody moved from her middle and spread to her arms and legs. "It's not safe for you," he said.

"At the moment, I don't think either one of us is safe," she whispered.

His brows drew together in a question.

"If you keep this up, I'll have to insist on spending a night with the king."

The look in his eyes said that if she asked, he might say "yes." It was with some regret that she stepped back from him. He frowned, and when he spoke, his tone was grave. "Ciara could capture you at any time. You have to be careful."

She looked up at him, feeling traces of the anxiety he'd carried before. And then she realized that in the midst of preparing for battle, he was worried about her. For a moment, she wished that she *had* gone to Morigon. At least she would have been safe there. But then Dorinda or Arathor would have called her to Agora so she could help bring the rain.

Once again, it seemed that fate was taking a hand in her life. And once again, she was powerless to stop it.

"If Ciara does capture me," she said, "you have to promise me that you *won't* follow."

Kieran pulled her close again and rolled the end of her braid between his fingers. "Jess, you know I can't make that promise."

"I'm just one Telerian. You have a whole country to save."

The painful look in his eyes only emphasized what she already knew to be true. "Eldala," he whispered, "if anything happens, I *will* come for you."

His arms came up around her and she stifled a sob. Part of her wanted to argue with him and give him all the reasons why he shouldn't follow her, but the other part knew his heart towards her. If Ciara captured her, Kieran would do whatever was necessary to find her and rescue her, even if it meant facing the queen. And if he faced Ciara…

She pressed herself into him and listened to the song humming between them. As much as she tried to cling to hope, she couldn't see how any of this could end well.

Chapter 66

Kieran had anticipated it would be difficult to sleep on the eve of battle, but this was absurd. Every time he started to drift off, his mind went back to his last moments with Jessa. He had wanted to ask her to stay so he could spend the night holding her. When he realized that just holding her wouldn't be enough, he did the only thing he could: He sent her away.

He rolled onto his back and stared at the tent ceiling. Jessa's encouragement last night had helped him tremendously. But she'd done more than that. Soon after the three descendants of Alardin had joined minds to bring the rain, Kieran knew that Jessa was carrying part of his burden so he could concentrate on the coming battle. Now he wished he had thanked her. It could be days before he saw her again.

He sat up and ran his hand over his stubbled face. The flap to his tent parted and a woman stepped inside. She wore a white nightgown, and a single braid hung over her shoulder. What was Jessa doing here again?

He threw on his robe and moved next to her. She bit her lip and handed him a piece of cloth. "I made this for you to wear."

He took it from her and fingered the delicate roses she'd stitched along the length of the smooth fabric. Although the embroidery wasn't as intricate as anything his mother had made, she'd obviously spent many hours making it. "It's beautiful, Jess."

He expected her to smile; the sorrow in her eyes was like a dagger to his heart. "What is it?"

She turned her face away.

Kieran cupped her face and stared into her velvet-black eyes. He had always been careful to stay out of her thoughts, but she had been hiding this for a long time, and he wanted to know why she was so miserable.

They stood for a moment, eyes locked, but she wouldn't let him into her mind and he finally let her go.

Jessa took the cloth from him and draped it over her shoulder. She couldn't hide the quiver in her voice when she said, "May I gird you for battle?"

The request was unexpected and it took him a moment to answer. "I would be honored."

He watched her walk across the room to open his iron-bound trunk. Her braid swished over her back and her hips swayed slightly as she moved the armor to his bed. How was it that everything she did looked like a dance? It took all of his will to not sweep her into his arms for one last waltz. Instead, he planted himself and kept his eyes on her. After moving every piece of armor, she turned and motioned for him to come closer.

When she untied his robe and slid it off his shoulders, her gentle touch sent sparks of desire through him. She fanned them into a flame as she let her hands travel slowly up his arms, down to his heart, and across each scar on his chest. As difficult as it was, he stamped his desires down to ashes and waited.

She took the embroidered favor and carefully wrapped it around his waist, smoothing the cloth into place. The shadows hid most of her face, but he thought he saw a tear rolling down her cheek. Why was she so sad?

Satisfied with her work, she tied the cloth once and tucked it into his breeches. Then she moved behind him and held up a simple white shirt. He slid his arms into it, and she smoothed it across his shoulders. He felt her lean into him and rest her hands and cheek against his back. If only he knew what was troubling her, maybe he could ease her pain. When he reached out his heart to her again, the barrier was still there, resisting him.

She walked around to face him. Starting at the bottom of his shirt, she slowly fastened each button, keeping her eyes off of his. Just as she finished with the top button, he lowered his head to kiss her. She avoided his lips and reached for the gambeson. He slid it over his shirt and she tied the front and back halves together. Her face was tight, as if she were mustering all of her courage to prepare him for battle.

And then Kieran understood.

No wonder she was miserable. She was afraid she was never going to see him again. If he hadn't been so distracted with planning for the war, he would have seen it. He should have seen it. She was the heart of his heart, and while she was lending him her strength, he looked right past her. Now she was doing the only thing she could to protect him, and it was killing her.

He tipped her chin up so she had to look at him. "It will be all right, Jess."

She shook her head and wrapped her arms around his waist. The tears she'd tried to hold in finally burst, and she sobbed with such anguish that her whole body quivered. He pulled her closer, sliding his fingers over the top of her head.

She was right. He couldn't predict the future, and any assurances he might give her would be empty. There was only one thing he could do for her.

He enveloped her in his arms, absorbing her grief, offering what he could to calm her fears. At first he thought she was opening up to him, but then he felt her heart clench into a tight ball. Why wouldn't she take what he was trying to give?

In a few moments, she composed herself enough to give him the breastplate. He held it in place while she picked up the back plate and joined the two halves. After buckling on his greaves and vambraces, she handed him his sword. He leaned down to kiss her again and this time she let him.

It was the most sorrowful kiss they'd ever shared.

Overlooking the field of battle, Kieran felt his whole body knot up with anticipation. According to his spies, the Zagorans would arrive at any moment. Surveying the ground below him, he could have touched the anticipation in the air; his men were eager to fight. He couldn't blame them. They'd been waiting for weeks to drive out the Zagorans. But no one was more eager to fight than Kieran.

Ever since the night Arathor had placed the ring on his finger, Kieran knew he would have to go to war. That had been almost a year ago. Now he felt an odd mixture of impatience and fear drawing him as taut as a bowstring.

He shifted in his saddle. Fallon pawed at the ground and shook his head, as if he understood the importance of what was to come. Kieran reined him in. "The battle will be here soon enough, my friend."

Then Kieran heard it – the steady cadence of heavy boots on the road. A moment later, an iron river of Zagorans poured over the hill.

Their numbers hit Kieran like a crashing wave. He steadied himself as he watched them move towards the bridge. Leading them was a heavily-built warrior dressed in silver armor. His arms were bare, and his hands were larger than Kieran's. His black hair was tied in a warrior's knot and his face was as cold as stone. Underneath him, his black horse pranced and snorted, sending out a plume of white steam.

The warrior looked vaguely familiar. Before Kieran could remember where he'd seen him, he heard the word ***Sharaq*** in his mind.

Of course. This was Ciara's bodyguard and consort. Jessa had mentioned him. But how could Jessa know that Sharaq was leading the army? The possibility that she could see any of this through his eyes made him cringe.

His thoughts returned to the field when he saw the Zagoran standard: A giant snake held an eagle in its coils, its massive fangs poised above the eagle's head, ready to strike. Kieran glanced at his breastplate and then at the Telerian standard waving to his right. Ciara had taken Alardin's crest and recreated it to taunt him.

She was wasting her time.

The eagle had prevailed once; it would prevail again. And this time, the snake would die.

As the Zagorans approached the bridge, Sharaq moved to one side. First to cross was a large company of horsemen, their faces as stern as Sharaq's. Five teams of oxen followed, straining at the weight of the catapults behind them. The bridge quivered, but its weakened supports held. Kieran raised his hand and signaled his men at the bridge to pull the supports. He watched the bridge collapse, plummeting horsemen, catapults, oxen, and infantry into the churning water.

Warriors on both sides of the bridge shouted as their comrades tried desperately to find a way to escape, but their armor weighed them down and they were lost. Sharaq's face tightened and he shouted for his men to hold the lines. As soon as they'd reassembled, Kieran signaled for his archers to release their arrows.

A barrage of arrows flew over the Zagorans, blotting out the sun. Most of the missiles found their marks, but not as many Zagorans fell as Kieran had hoped. Again Sharaq shouted for his men to re-form their ranks. Kale motioned for Telerian cavalry to show themselves at the front edge of the marsh.

When Kieran was sure that Sharaq had seen his horsemen standing on solid ground, he had Kale signal for them to retreat. Just as the Zagoran cavalry and archers entered the marshes, Kieran stretched out his hand and said, "Ishkalat."

A gray mist began to rise from the brackish water and creep over the ground, engulfing the Zagorans in a thick fog. Many of the horses faltered on the treacherous ground. Riders and archers alike screamed and swore out loud as the black bog sucked them in. Still, about half of Sharaq's soldiers made it through before Toren signaled for his men to come in behind them. Sixty pikemen held the solid ground and divided Sharaq's forces, blocking those who had entered, and preventing the remainder of the cavalry from joining their comrades.

As the pikemen turned them aside, the Zagoran cavalry retreated, only to be assaulted by Kieran's reserve forces, waiting just behind them. Kieran watched the two armies come together to form one confusing whirlpool of swords and spears. On the other side of the river, Gilrain's forces were already routing the Zagorans who had come across the bridge.

Despite the disruption in their lines, the Zagoran cavalry moved forward, slowly picking their way across the soft ground. In a matter of minutes, they reached Kieran's position on the hill. Kieran drew his sword. Memories from his travels flashed through his mind – Brecken and Muriel's struggles on the frontier, Adamar's rescue, the Hada Baraca's suspicion of Telerians, and his own captivity in Korisan.

Like a river being released from a dam, Kieran's suppressed rage surged, and he let out a war cry that seemed to shatter the sky. The ground trembled, and a piercing light shone from Restamar. Fallon surged forward, moving Kieran towards the battle. Kieran raised his sword and plunged into the tossing sea of warriors.

The faces of friends and foes swirled around him. To his right, Kale charged forward, yelling at the top of his lungs, his blade clashing against the enemy's blade. To his left, Arathor had already felled three horsemen and was galloping towards a fourth.

In the midst of the fray, Kieran was aware of nothing beyond the ring of steel on steel, the cries of battle and death, and Fallon's powerful body, propelling him forward. With hardly a moment to breathe, he found himself locked in battle with one Zagoran after another, pressing the attack and returning their blows.

When one Zagoran fell, another took his place. There seemed to be an endless stream of them. Kieran was vaguely aware of his Telerian warriors, but knew they were facing the same overwhelming numbers. If any of them survived, let alone defeated the Zagorans, it would be a miracle.

Jessa shivered, partly from the cold, partly from the memory of Kieran's war-cry, and partly from the apprehension stirring inside her. She watched the battle from the hillside and wondered again why she was here when she could be in a warm tent, helping with the wounded. It was a question Sienna had asked her this morning, and at the time, Jessa's answer made sense. Now she wasn't so sure.

All night long, she'd dreamed of Kieran's death. When she woke up, nothing could purge the dreams or the panic from her mind. Talking with Sienna hadn't helped. Girding Kieran for battle hadn't helped. By the time she returned to her tent, the fear had grown into an indescribable terror, and it was then she decided to defend Kieran on the field.

She'd asked Sienna to help with her armor, and in spite of her friend's protests of "You can do more good helping the wounded," and "I know Kieran won't want you there," Jessa convinced her there was no other way, so Sienna had consented to help her.

After wrapping a cloak over her armor and finding a different horse to ride, Jessa hoped she would look like just another female Baraca warrior. When Kieran passed by the ranks of horsemen, he hadn't noticed her.

Now she was on a hill, straining her eyes to keep track of Kieran and Fallon in the sea of warriors below her. She watched with morbid fascination as Kieran moved from one fray to another. How could the man who was so gentle with her be such a fierce warrior? From the time he'd let out his first ear-piercing cry until now, no one who challenged him remained standing. He was quick and efficient, usually killing in one or two strokes with a single-minded purpose.

It was that single-mindedness that made Jessa's heart stop. Sharaq was riding straight for Kieran, and Kieran was oblivious to Sharaq's approach.

Jessa spurred her horse forward, trying to dodge flying blades and falling men. Only her agonizing need to get to Kieran kept her from being overwhelmed by the death around her. Occasionally, a Zagoran horse drove its flank into Jessa's mount, and she had to tighten her grip on the reins to keep from falling off.

If she didn't reach Kieran before Sharaq did…

Then she was just a few paces away from both of them.

The fighting around Kieran and Sharaq paused, as if everyone knew that they were meant to face each other alone. Jessa could hardly breathe. This was worse than her nightmares.

Sharaq's face was hard and free of any sweat. His bare arm bulged as he withdrew his sword and pointed it at Kieran in a silent challenge. Kieran was breathing hard, his legs were shaking, and his head was drenched in sweat, but he never took his eyes off of the Zagoran commander.

Almost as soon as Kieran and Sharaq dismounted, Kieran's sword came up and the two swords shuddered against each other. In just a few strokes, Kieran had taken charge of the fight and the Zagoran warrior had to move back to absorb the force of the blows. The look on Sharaq's face said that he hadn't expected Kieran to attack with such intensity.

Then Sharaq went on the attack, bringing his sword up, around, and down. Kieran matched his blows. Sharaq charged ahead, missed, and his forward momentum forced him down on one knee. Kieran took advantage of the misstep and put the edge of his sword along the back of Sharaq's neck. The Zagoran was surprisingly quick and swung his sword around, knocking Kieran's sword back.

As Kieran continued to block Sharaq's attacks, he faltered, and a heavy blow knocked him backwards. Jessa couldn't see Sharaq's face, but she had the feeling he was giving Kieran one of his ghastly grins. He pointed his sword at Kieran's neck and said, "It is time for you to yield, Pretender."

Kieran charged forward with a yell, but Sharaq took advantage of Kieran's weakness and spun his sword around to knock Restamar out of Kieran's hand. In half a heartbeat, Sharaq plunged the tip of his sword into Kieran's right shoulder. Kieran blinked at the shock and pain of the injury.

Sharaq only laughed as he pulled his sword out of Kieran's arm. While he stood there gloating over his victory, Jessa approached him from behind. Before Sharaq could deliver the final blow, Jessa drove her sword into a gap between Sharaq's pieces of armor. The Zagoran faltered and Kieran used the opportunity to retrieve his sword and cut off Sharaq's head.

Jessa's arms were shaking and she dropped her sword. Waves of dizziness swirled around her. Before she fell from her horse, one of Kieran's soldiers caught her and helped her to her feet. Kieran stared at her long and hard. His eyes seethed with silent fury.

She wanted to say something – anything – to make him understand why she'd come to the field. But something told her he wouldn't listen.

After healing his wound, Kieran spoke to the soldier who had caught Jessa. "Take her back to her tent – and make sure she stays there." Then he looked at her and his black eyes pierced her heart. "Pack your things. Tomorrow you're going to Morigon."

Chapter 67

Jessa let out a long, heavy sigh as she packed the last of her few possessions into her trunk and closed the lid. She knew why Kieran was sending her away. The look on his face had said it all. It broke her heart to think he might never understand why she'd risked her life.

If she had to leave, she wouldn't go to Morigon. It was too much like going into exile. She would go back to the Kofar fortress and help Elisa and Tiana. If Kieran got angry with her for not following his orders, she didn't care. He was so unhappy with her now it really wouldn't matter what else she did.

She sat on her bed, removed her boots and stockings, and lay down on the feather mattress. Just after drifting off, she heard someone stirring outside her tent. Most likely it was one of her Kofar guards. They followed her everywhere, and she'd almost learned to ignore them. She rolled onto her side and closed her eyes again.

In her dreams, she felt someone put a rag over her face and heard herself cry out. Then someone bound her hands and hoisted her over a knotted shoulder. When she woke up, she realized it hadn't been a dream.

"Have you lost your mind?" Riordan shouted. "You can't go looking for Jessa now."

"And how can you be sure that Ciara has her?" asked Toren. "Maybe she left for Morigon."

"If you'd been there," Kieran said, "you wouldn't be asking that."

Kieran had gone to see Jessa before she left. He'd wanted to apologize for being so harsh with her on the battlefield. But after he entered her tent, a cold terror raced through him when he saw her empty bed. A quick sweep of the room told him someone had taken her.

Her boots were at her bedside, her trunk was still there, and when he went to check the stable, Brielle was in her stall. His first impulse was to saddle Fallon and ride after her, but his better judgment reminded him that he had a duty to inform his council.

So here he was, half listening to their arguments, all the while berating himself for letting this happen again. Why had he let her stay? He could have sent her away at any time, and he and Arathor could have conjured the rain without her. Had some selfish part of himself wanted her to stay? Or was this some sick twist of fate, sending the two Eldala down a road they had no choice but to follow?

Suddenly Stefan entered the tent and the men fell silent. Kieran hoped Stefan hadn't heard their discussion. It wouldn't do any good for him to find out that Jessa was missing.

"What is it?" Kieran asked.

"I have learned that the Hada are under attack."

Hadn't Kieran warned Galen of this very thing? After the way the calafar had denied his request and banished not only Kieran, but Jessa and her family, Kieran felt he owed the Hada nothing.

"What do you want *me* to do about it?"

"I would like your permission to take Baraca warriors to defend them."

Sending Baraca warriors to Ithil would severely deplete Kieran's already meager army, but Stefan had been loyal and almost contrite since returning to the Kofar fortress. If he wanted to defend the Hada, Kieran wouldn't stop him. "Take as many as are willing to defend your clan."

Stefan's jaw nearly dropped open, as if he had expected Kieran to deny his request. Before he spoke, he inclined his head in respect. "Thank you…your Majesty."

Kieran nodded and watched Stefan leave the tent. Then he let his eyes rest on each man there: Arathor, the most confident person Kieran had ever had the privilege of knowing; Kale and Gilrain, the men who knew him better than anyone else; and Riordan and Toren, the companions who'd had hardly left his side since that night in Maquoya. Would he ever see any of them again?

The question was irrelevant. He had to put his misgivings aside and give his orders.

"Gilrain and Arathor will lead the remainder of my army."

Gilrain looked like he would protest, but Kieran didn't give him the chance. "You'll have to move quickly so you can get ahead of the Zagorans and stop them from entering Korisan." He paused, looking Arathor in the eye. How would he take this next bit of news?

"If I don't return, I've signed a decree stating that Arathor will take my place as king."

A collective gasp spread through the group. Toren was the first to break the silence. "Then you really mean to go after her?"

"Of course I do."

"You'd throw it all away for a woman?" asked Riordan.

This wasn't the time for Riordan to question his judgment. Kieran shot him a warning glance and said, "She's not just a woman. She's my *heart.* I have to go."

Arathor cleared his throat. "How do you propose to get into the castle?"

"I hadn't thought that far ahead," said Kieran. "Do you have a suggestion?"

As Kieran approached the edge of the city, he looked around, trying to master the dread surging through him. His attempt to rescue Jessa would probably end in death – his death. But it didn't matter. None of it mattered anymore. If she died, he was as good as dead anyway. What point would there be to living if he had to live with half a heart?

A small cave suddenly appeared in front of him. Just before Kieran had left Maquoya, Arathor had sketched a map of the tunnel system beneath Korisan for him. According to Arathor, the tunnel in front of him would bring Kieran up into the castle's stable. As he crouched to enter the tunnel, he was glad he'd left Fallon with Gilrain. This was no place for his horse.

An hour later, he pushed his way through a trap door and inhaled the familiar smell of horse and straw. Despite the pungent odor, the stable air was refreshing after the close, musty air of the tunnel. He hoisted himself up, brushed the straw off of his cloak, and pulled up his hood.

Walking towards the main part of the castle, Kieran's hand went to the Restamar's hilt, and his eyes flew back and forth, watching for guards or anyone else who might stop him. He was tempted to call out to Jessa, but decided against it. If she knew he was here, she would tell him all the reasons he should leave, chief among them that this was a trap. Of course it was a trap, one he was walking into with both eyes open.

When he ducked through the door leading to the courtyard, he noticed a line of people wending its way towards one of the rooms off of the courtyard. Each person carried a heavy leather bag.

Tributes. They were paying tributes. Kieran clenched his empty fist until his hand ached. The thought of his people giving *anything* to Ciara was more than he could stand.

Still hidden by his cloak, Kieran found the servants' entrance to the throne room. As he entered, he noted that only six men guarded the queen. His heart was beating wildly, and he tried not to breathe as he approached the back of the throne.

There was a sudden commotion, and the six guards surrounded him. They seized his sword and made him bow in front of Ciara. The people bringing tributes began to murmur and Ciara motioned for them to come closer.

"This man has attempted to take my life. He mistakenly believes that the throne of Teleria belongs to him."

Many in the crowd wagged their heads. How had Ciara blinded so many to her true nature? Or were they content with things the way they were?

"Where is Jessa?" he asked.

One of the guards struck him across the face. "You do not have permission to speak."

Kieran licked the blood from the corner of his mouth and surged forward to break the guards' hold. The queen stood and spoke words Kieran had never heard before. The spell paralyzed him. Ciara brought her face close to his and stared at him.

Now he could see how fatigued she really was. Her eyes were sunken in, her skin was taut across her high cheekbones, and deeply etched wrinkles surrounded her thin lips. Still, the pride in her face hadn't completely vanished, and her cold eyes glittered in a haughty, amused sort of way.

"Did you really think I wouldn't know you were here?" she asked. She took his face in one hand. Kieran winced as her sharp nails dug into his cheek.

"Where's Jessa?"

"You're not in a position to ask that."

Kieran forced himself to look into her eyes. "Tell me where she is!"

The guards moved in, and the last thing Kieran felt was something hard coming down on the back of his head.

When Kieran woke up, he lay on a cold stone floor, chained to the wall by his wrists and ankles. His head felt like someone was hammering from the inside. He forced himself to a sitting position and tipped his head back to the wall, shivering from the cold. From somewhere deep inside, he was able to muster the words "Men-an-dai." Tiny flames erupted from the floor and he moved as close as his chains would allow to soak up their feeble warmth.

His stomach grumbled from lack of food and his head protested being in this position. He lay back down and tried to call to Jessa. Nothing. He tried again. After a few minutes, a faint voice stirred in his head.

You shouldn't have come.

Where are you?

It doesn't matter. You can't save me now.

I'll find a way.

The grating of the cell door opening interrupted them. Kieran untangled his thoughts from Jessa's and stood, kicking the flames out. A dim torch revealed that the visitor was Delaine. As she approached, all he wanted to do was break her neck.

"Where's Jessa?"

"Not that old song," she purred.

She ran her spidery fingers across his chin. Her cold touch did nothing to him. He met her green eyes but remained silent. She walked her fingers down to his neck. "I've missed you," she said, brushing her lips against his ear.

Kieran surged forward to try to grab her, but she stepped back before he could.

"Tell me you've missed me, Aiden."

"Where's Jessa?!"

She rolled her eyes. “Why would it matter? I can make you forget your Baraca whore.”

“You’re the whore, Delaine – prostituting yourself for your mother.”

It was the second time he’d seen this kind of shock on her face. When she finally spoke, her voice was shaking. “If you’ll agree to marry me, my mother will spare your life. And you can still have your kingdom.”

“She can’t give me what’s already mine.”

The door flew open and Ciara’s shrill voice raked over Kieran’s ears. “Leave him alone.”

Delaine’s face fell. “But you said…”

“Never mind what I said.” She flicked her hand at her daughter. “Leave us.”

The princess started to protest.

“Now!”

Kieran listened to Delaine’s footsteps clicking across the floor and echoing up the staircase. Then he turned his attention to Ciara. She was standing in front of him, tapping a frail finger against her cheek, looking him over, just far enough away that he couldn’t reach her.

“Where’s Jessa?”

“We’ve had this discussion already.”

“You obviously used her to get me here. I think I deserve to know where she is.”

“That’s not as important as where she’ll end up if you don’t cooperate with me.”

“Then you intend to kill her?”

She snorted loudly. “Death is too good for her.”

“What do you mean?”

“She must be punished for what she did to Sharaq.” Ciara laughed. “Don’t look so surprised. Very little escapes my notice.” She started to pace in front of him. “My soldiers were very fond of their commander. They need a woman’s company to ease their pain.”

Of all the things to do to his Eldala… Kieran lunged at Ciara, but jerked back when he reached the end of his chains.

“If you’ll agree to fight my harakan, I’ll let her go.”

Just the name made Kieran’s flesh crawl. “Harakan?”

"A beast I created especially for you. It has all of the endearing qualities of the gurithents, including their poison. And it has the amazing ability to come back to life."

"How do I know you'll keep your word?"

"You'll just have to trust me."

Kieran couldn't help but laugh. "I'd rather trust a snake."

Ciara stepped closer. For a moment, her features contorted and she took on the appearance of a wild animal.

"Will you fight my harakan or not?"

Chapter 68

Jessa would have preferred living in one of her nightmares. Anything would have been better than having to endure the last three days. Today would be no different.

A guard roused Jessa from her prison cell and pushed her to the public square. When she reached the arena, Kieran was already there, bound in chains, and surrounded by a dozen guards. When Ciara and Delaine took their places, the guards forced Kieran to his knees.

With great ceremony, the queen introduced Kieran to the ever-increasing crowd of onlookers. "For threatening my life, the Pretender to the throne will fight my harakan. Such will be the fate of any who choose to stand against me."

Some in the crowd hid their faces, but most jeered and threw rotten food at him. The guards removed Kieran's chains and released the harakan. Every time Jessa looked at the creature, she wanted to run and hide.

It stood upright, like a gurithent, but it was at least three heads taller than Kieran. Its cracked, black skin seemed to ooze with a thick, fiery substance. Sharp spikes lined its arms and legs, and its clawed hands held a flaming sword. Each time it charged at Kieran, it let out an ear-shattering shriek that nearly made Jessa double over in pain.

While Kieran struggled against the creature, Jessa worked her hands back and forth to distract herself from the nerve-wracking battle in front of her. Today was the worst of all. It was taking longer than usual for Kieran to defeat it, and the wounds Jessa had healed for him just last night were replaced with new ones.

As Kieran and the harakan circled, Jessa felt Kieran's exhaustion and frustration. She slammed her hand on the balcony railing and cursed fate again for bringing them together just so Ciara could tear them apart.

"Arathor, do something," she whispered. "Help us."

No, Jess. Don't call for him.

Jessa drew in a breath, partly because she hadn't expected Kieran to hear her and partly because Kieran's momentary lapse in concentration nearly earned him a harakan bite in the neck. He swept his sword just under the creature's torso and took off its legs. It groaned in agony and its fiery sword fell to the ground. Kieran took off its head before it could defend itself.

Some in the crowd cheered, but most railed against him for ending the spectacle. Ciara held up her hand. It took a moment for the crowd to settle down. When they did, Ciara spoke. Her voice carried across the square.

"Congratulations Pretender. You have finally defeated my harakan." The queen stopped and smiled with cruel anticipation before speaking again. "Tomorrow, a new fate awaits you."

Sometime in the night, the screeching of the cell door hinges woke Jessa. A guard grabbed her and dragged her into a lower section of the dungeon.

"What are you doing?" she asked, risking a hit across the face for her question.

The guard just smirked. "Her Majesty has special plans for you."

Jessa swallowed hard as she stumbled along, still trying to wake up. When they reached the lowest level of the dungeon, the guard stopped and opened a door at the end of the corridor. He pushed her in and chained her to a wall by her wrists.

Someone in the room groaned.

"Where am I?" she asked.

The guard chuckled. "The queen thought it would bring you comfort to share a cell with the Pretender tonight."

Jessa lit her Keldar stone and strained her eyes in the pale light. Kieran looked up at her weakly. Jessa brought her hand to her mouth to stifle a sob. Obviously, the guards had had their sport with him after the fight in the arena. His stubbled face was so swollen from cuts and bruises that she hardly recognized him. Her eyes traveled down his body, noting every wound on his neck, arms, and chest. His wrists were bleeding from where he'd fought against the manacles, and his breathing was ragged and labored.

As she had for the last few nights, she said, "Jedzah mar kaavah."

Nothing happened. She repeated the words, louder this time.

Kieran shook his head. His voice was hoarse and every word took great effort. "It won't work anymore. I've already tried."

"You can't just give up."

"There's nothing more we can do."

"Why won't you call for help? It would just take a few men – Arathor, Gilrain, Kale… We have to do something."

Kieran slid down the wall and rested his arms and head on his knees. "I won't risk their lives for mine. It's over."

"Over? You can't mean that."

While she waited for him to answer, her mind wandered into his and she felt the hopelessness and self-disgust churning inside of him.

He laughed bitterly. "Here sits the mighty hero of Teleria, chained to a wall in Ciara's dungeon. And all I can do is wait for her to execute me in the morning."

Jessa couldn't help but shudder. This must have been Ciara's plan all along – to publicly humiliate him, wear him down to nothing, and finally end his life, most likely in full view of all the citizens of Korisan. How could it have come to this? Jessa wanted to scream her frustration to the dark, but she knew it wouldn't do either of them any good. If this was their last night together, she didn't want to spend it wallowing in fear and despair.

Kieran hissed through his teeth. "The worst part…I've failed everyone – my countrymen, my family…" He looked up at her, and even in the dim light, she saw that his eyes were laced with sorrow. "Most of all I failed you… again."

She moved closer. If only she could touch him, comfort him. She closed her eyes and let her heart reach out to his. He refused to let her in.

Fine. She would make him listen. "Kieran, I love you. Nothing will change that."

"Even knowing how this ends?"

"I'd go through it again, just to love you and have you love me."

"You wouldn't say that if you knew – "

"If I knew what?"

He said nothing more. Normally, Jessa wouldn't have pushed him for answers, but she had to know. She forced herself into his mind, past the barriers he'd erected, and into his deepest thoughts. Once she was there, a series of rambling images swirled around her, disorienting her for a moment. It took all of her will to fight against them and find the memories she wanted.

Ciara was pacing in front of him, and at first her words were garbled. When Jessa focused her mind, she heard it: *"My soldiers were very fond of their commander. They need a woman's company to ease their pain."*

"A woman's company." Sudden understanding made Jessa's gut clench and she threw up what little food was in her stomach. She wiped her mouth and watched as Kieran crawled across the stone floor. With both of them straining the limits of their chains, they were inches apart.

There were tears in his eyes when he spoke. "She said that if I fought the harakan, she would let you go."

"And you believed her?"

"I had to take the chance."

"Kieran…"

"Jess, promise me you'll try to get away."

"How? I'll be chained here…"

"No, she'll take you to watch the execution."

A sea of nausea threatened to drown her. She couldn't bear to think of it.

"That will be your chance," he said. "The guards won't be watching you."

"Do you think I can keep my mind on escaping while Ciara kills you?"

He leaned forward, stretching himself to be as close to her as possible, all the while wincing as the manacles dug into his wrists. His lips barely brushed against her cheek.

"Please try. One of us has to survive."

By now, she was practically choking on her tears. "No! Living without you won't be surviving. You know that. It's why you came for me. It's why I went to the battlefield to protect you. I won't live with half a heart."

He closed his eyes and his Keldar stone grew brighter. For one brief moment, it felt as if he was engulfing her heart in his. But instead of comforting her, it only made her share the despair and guilt racking him from head to toe. The thought of failing her and all of Teleria was killing him.

"Promise me, Jess. Please try to get away."

A few hours later, the guards entered the cell and unchained Jessa and Kieran. After tying their hands, the guards marched them through the corridor, up the spiral stairs, and into the public square. Jessa expected the guards to put her in the usual spot on the front row, just to the right of Ciara's box, but they kept her near Kieran.

A lifeless sun shone down on them, and Jessa shivered against the wind that whipped her hair into her mouth and eyes. Despite the chill hanging in the air, there seemed to be three times as many people today, and almost everyone in the crowd appeared pleased to watch Kieran die.

Jessa hung her head and hoped it would be over quickly.

Suddenly, Jessa felt Ciara behind her. Her hateful intentions were directed at both of them. She put her hands on their heads and leaned in to whisper something. Jessa had to strain to hear it.

"I know you share a special bond" – Jessa stiffened – "so I thought you'd appreciate sharing more than just each other's thoughts in your last moments together."

Ciara raised her hands and spoke words that sounded like gibberish. Jessa expected nothing more than the strong connection she'd shared with Kieran when they brought the rain. But this was something new.

When Kieran looked at her, she saw herself through his eyes, but she also saw him through her own eyes. This was worse than she could have imagined. Wasn't it bad enough that she had to watch Kieran die without sharing the pain of his death?

After moving Jessa to one side, the guards prodded Kieran towards a wooden platform that had seen more than its share of executions. Iron hooks protruded from the four corners, and caked blood covered the top and sides. The sight of it made Kieran and Jessa shudder.

The guards untied Kieran's hands and made him lie down on the platform. When they slid him across the top of it, large splinters dug into his back, and Jessa cried out from the pain. They drew his body as taut as possible, and *Jessa's* arms and legs ached. As the guards tied Kieran's wrists and ankles to the hooks, it felt like the ropes were digging into Jessa's wrists and ankles.

And then his thoughts became her own.

How could all these people want me to die? Maybe it's better that I won't be their king.

No, Kieran. Ciara has poisoned their minds.

What will happen to the others – the people who gave up everything for freedom? All of their sacrifices have come to nothing.

Don't say that.

What good am I to anyone now? I'm just a weak blacksmith who can't even save himself.

Jessa lurched towards him, but the guards held her back.

With great ceremony, Ciara approached the platform. Restamar caught the light and glinted menacingly in her hands. Kieran and Jessa's hearts beat a frantic rhythm. They convulsed as they felt her place the cold blade against Kieran's chest. When she leaned down to say something, her face was a mask of pleasure and eagerness.

"How fitting that the sword that once drove me out of Teleria will be the instrument of your death. When you're dead, Teleria will be mine forever."

Tears rolled down their cheeks, and the anguish and fear became so great they could hardly breathe. When their eyes locked, they shared their final words: ***Eldala, I love you.***

With a feral scream, Ciara drove Restamar through Kieran's heart. His body went rigid; Jessa broke free of her guard and threw herself across him. Their cries of agony merged, filling the arena and traveling outwards, until a blanket of pain covered the entire city.

Just outside Korisan, Arathor dropped his sword and clutched at his chest. Gilrain was immediately at his side, fighting off the Zagorans who threatened to take advantage of his weakness. The former king was vaguely aware of Gilrain and Kale carrying him to his tent, where he fell into a fitful sleep.

Chapter 69

A light breeze danced over Jessa's skin and teased her hair as she stood on the bluff overlooking the sea. The day of her wedding had finally come. She looked up into Kieran's dark eyes and recited her vows to love and cherish him for the rest of her life.

Just as Kieran tilted his head to kiss her, Restamar erupted from the ground between them and flew into Jessa's hands. Kieran's face went white. Arathor stepped in to defend him. Before Jessa could stop herself, she had thrust Restamar through Kieran's heart. His blood splattered across her wedding dress and into her face.

Her screams woke her up.

She opened one eye and looked around. She was back in Kieran's cell. If she looked hard enough, she could still see him chained to the wall.

She ran her hand across the dull ache in her chest and cried out again. Dried blood covered the front of her dress. She looked at her hands. There was blood on her skin and underneath her fingernails, and she thought she tasted some at the corners of her mouth. It was true. She *had* killed Kieran.

No. Ciara had killed him, and Jessa had thrown herself across him just before he died.

Before Jessa had taken the Keldar stone, she wouldn't have believed that one person could become so entwined with another. After sharing thoughts and dreams and emotions, it was almost impossible to tell where one of them ended and the other one began.

Now Kieran was silent.

When he'd taken his last breath, it felt as though the queen had taken Jessa's heart out of her chest, torn it in half, and put the other half back inside her, broken and empty. By the act of killing Kieran, Ciara might as well have killed Jessa.

It would have been better if she had.

From now on, Jessa would live with half a heart – if it could be called living. He was gone and there was nothing she could do to bring him back. There were no words of enchantment to reverse death.

Kieran...heart of my heart...forgive me.

Wasted words. He wasn't there, and it was too late to beg forgiveness … from anyone. Kieran was dead and it was her fault.

She could have gone to Morigon. She could have stayed away from the battle. One more healer on the battlefield wouldn't have made any difference. Had it been some hidden desire to be near him that made her throw caution away? If she had been more careful, she would be safe and Kieran would be alive.

And why had he come to rescue her? Hadn't she told him countless times to save his country and not her? He was just as stubborn as she was. He'd chosen her instead of Teleria and she took no comfort in it. By choosing her, he had sacrificed his life and his country. Their reckless choices had condemned the people they loved to live under Ciara's curse.

If Jessa ever saw them again, how could she face them? How could she face anyone, knowing what she had done? What would Kale and Elisa say when they found out that their only son was dead? What would Arathor say?

If she called out to Arathor, maybe he could rescue her. But then she would have to tell him everything, and the thought of facing Arathor, even in a vision, was too much to bear. He'd depended on her for so much. And in the end, she'd let him down.

She'd let them all down.

No, despite her promises to Kieran that she would try to get away, it would be better if Ciara took her to the Zagoran soldiers. Better to die in obscurity than to have to face Kieran's family.

Waves of nausea and grief rolled over her, plummeting her into a whirlpool of despair. If only she could sleep without dreaming.

Hadn't Kieran once given her a dreamless sleep? Somehow the words came to her mind, and she whispered them to the dark, hoping she wouldn't wake up for a very long time.

A somber, almost lifeless Korisan met Arathor as he passed through the city gates. The streets should have been bustling with people, merchants should have had their doors open for business, and traders should have been shouting in the streets. Instead, doors were closed, booths were empty, and the few people they saw on the street looked angry or distressed.

"I've never seen the city like this," said Kale.

"What do you think happened?" Gilrain asked.

Arathor had his suspicions. Ever since waking from his unexpected collapse on the battlefield, a nameless dread had been gnawing at the back of his mind. He'd only felt pain that severe a few times before – when he had taken the Keldar stone, when Kieran had taken it, and when his Eldala had taken it. There could be only one other reason for feeling it now, and it wasn't a possibility he wanted to consider. Until he was certain, there was no point in sharing his thoughts with his companions.

He still wasn't sure he wanted Kale and Gilrain with him. They should have been helping with the battle outside the city. The Telerians could use all the help they could get. They were doing their best to keep the Zagorans out of Korisan, but it would only be a matter of time before the enemy broke through their defenses. Arathor shuddered to think what the Zagorans would do once they entered the city.

Before they reached the public square, the three men stopped in front of one of the shops and went inside. The afternoon sun reflected off the odd-shaped bottles lining shelf after shelf. Arathor breathed in an aroma he hadn't smelled for years – various herbs and dried plants mixing together in a scent like no other.

Soon a short, balding man came from another room. His eyes grew wide with surprise. "King Arathor?"

"Yes, Samuel. It's good to see you."

"How did you know?"

"Know what?"

"Please come with me."

An uncomfortable feeling twisted in Arathor's stomach as he followed his friend into the back room. Samuel led them to a bed in the corner. Arathor closed his eyes, pushing down the rage and grief thundering just under the surface.

Kieran was stretched out in front of them. Dozens of cuts and bruises covered his face. Rope burns dug into his wrists, and countless scars criss-crossed his arms. Kale flinched when he saw the wound in Kieran's chest.

Just below the Keldar stone was a gaping hole. Someone had put a sword through Kieran's heart.

"What happened to him?" Kale finally choked out.

"For the last few days," Samuel said, "Ciara made him fight a creature she called the harakan. She said it was punishment for standing against her. This morning she executed him in the public square." Samuel stopped and a shadow of sorrow passed over his face. "When it was over, the most agonizing cry of grief covered the city. I've never heard anything like it. It's been quiet ever since."

"How did you get him?" Gilrain asked.

"Someone said the queen was going to keep him on display today, as a warning to anyone else who might try to take her throne. I couldn't stand the thought of it so I bribed one of the guards to let me bring him here."

"We should get him back to camp," said Kale.

"I don't think that's wise," said Samuel. "If the soldiers at the gate saw you, they might start asking questions."

"We'll take him through the tunnels," said Arathor.

When they arrived at camp, Kale laid Kieran on Arathor's bed and started to wash the blood from Kieran's chest and arms. Gilrain paced the tent like a caged wolf. Arathor bowed his head and finally let the tears come.

After a few minutes, he looked at Kale. A track of tears ran down Kale's tightened jaw as he took care of Kieran's body. This was the man who'd raised Kieran from boy to blacksmith. If anyone in this room had a right to grieve, it was Kale.

Arathor let his mind drift back to the night he'd delivered Kieran to Kale and Elisa. He still remembered the look on Kale's face when he asked him to take the boy into his home. Kale was so reluctant to believe he was capable of being Kieran's father, but he'd overcome his fears and had done everything he could to raise up a king. Now he was doing the last thing he could for his son.

My son is dead. Arathor could hardly believe it. If it weren't for the body in front of him and the dull ache in his chest, he wouldn't have believed it. Arathor had sacrificed everything – his throne, his fatherhood, and the life of his beloved Annalisa – just to ensure that Kieran would fulfill his destiny and end the curse. Kieran's one impulsive act had brought it all to nothing. By putting his life in jeopardy for one person, Kieran had put the whole kingdom in jeopardy.

Arathor stopped himself. It wouldn't do any good to blame Kieran now. What was done was done. This was the time for action. The thought of letting his country suffer one more day under Ciara's curse was excruciating. She couldn't be allowed to stay on the throne.

Arathor couldn't lift the curse; that was Kieran's destiny. But he could end Ciara's reign. And at the same time, Arathor would avenge Kieran's death.

Without a word, Arathor belted on his sword and walked towards the tent door. Gilrain stopped him.

"Where are you going?"

"To put things right."

"Then you mean to kill Ciara," said Kale.

"I should have ended this a long time ago."

"Why you?" asked Gilrain.

"Alardin should have killed Leandra when he had the chance. No one knows why he didn't. Maybe he'd seen enough killing. I don't know. I should have listened to my father when he warned me about Rahnak, but I didn't."

"So you're going to charge in without a plan?" asked Kale.

Arathor let out an exasperated hiss. This wasn't the time for arguments or caution.

"Aren't we forgetting someone?" asked Gilrain.

"Who?" asked Kale.

"Kieran went to save Jessa. We can't leave her with Ciara."

"How do we know she's still alive?" asked Kale.

"How do we know she's *not* alive?" asked Gilrain.

Kale looked at Arathor. "You have that stone. Can't you call to her or something?"

Arathor closed his eyes and concentrated on finding Jessa. After a few minutes, he still couldn't hear her, but he did sense something – the deep agony of loss and…guilt.

"Yes, she's alive."

Gilrain's eyes flashed in his lean face. "When do we leave?"

A knock at the door woke Ciara from a nightmare. Her bed clothes were drenched with sweat, her heart was beating a frantic rhythm, and her legs were shaking. She hadn't been this afraid since… since learning that Arathor and Annalisa would have a child.

The knock came again, louder this time. What was she doing in bed? She required very little sleep and never slept during the day. And why wasn't her servant there to open the door? She pushed herself out of bed but had to sit down before she could put on a robe.

Elath called out to see if she was in the room.

"Come in," she said. Her voice barely came out in a whisper.

"I have a message and a parcel from your army near Korisan."

"Leave them on my bed."

As she watched Elath leave the room, Ciara tried to make sense of the images still swirling in her head. She'd had this dream before and blamed it on the fatigue of maintaining the curse and strengthening her army. Perhaps having it again meant it was significant. She closed her eyes and pushed away her fears as she put herself back into the dream.

She stood on the highest peak in Teleria, surveying all of her troops. The snake and eagle standard fluttered lazily in the breeze. All of a sudden, the wind ripped the flag from its pole and carried it to her feet. When she reached for it, the eagle flew from the cloth and into her face, clutching the snake in its talons. She let out a silent scream as she watched the great bird land in front of her and tear the snake apart before eating it.

She shuddered and opened her eyes.

When she stood to retrieve the scroll from her bed, her legs felt like gelatin and drops of sweat formed on her brow. What was happening to her – first sleeping until late afternoon and now acting like an invalid? She mustered her strength and made it to the bed before collapsing.

Ciara started to open the scroll, but stopped to look at her hands. She'd always thought they were her best feature, second only to her face. Now every vein showed through thinning, wrinkled skin. This was impossible. Now that Kieran was dead and his army as good as defeated, keeping up her youthful appearance should have been easy. She spoke the words to renew herself and watched her hands return to their former beauty.

When she read the message, she swore out loud.

The Telerians were keeping her troops out of the city. This was ludicrous. Her forces were far superior and should have been able to break the Telerians' defenses with little trouble. She took a deep breath. Whoever wrote the message was panicking for no reason. By the end of the day, the Telerians would learn that their pathetic leader was dead and they would run away like whipped dogs.

Ciara was about to open the parcel when Delaine burst into her room.

"What do you want?" Ciara asked.

"I came to see if you were all right."

"Why wouldn't I be?"

"Don't you remember?"

"No."

"When you drew the sword out of Aiden's – out of the Pretender's body, you fainted. I ordered the guards to bring you here."

Fainted? Ciara remembered the delicious sensation flowing through her when she thrust the sword into his body. She remembered the way he writhed in pain. She even remembered the pathetic cries of the Baraca slave. But she couldn't remember fainting.

"It must have been the excitement of knowing I had killed my enemy." Ciara rubbed her throbbing temple. "Was there anything else ?"

"My lady-in-waiting said the body's disappeared."

"What did you say?"

"The most recent rumor is that someone took it."

"Why didn't you tell me this sooner?"

"I didn't think it was important."

"Important? My enemy's body disappears, and you didn't think it was important? What kind of fool have I raised?"

Delaine opened her mouth to say something, but Ciara interrupted her. "If someone took him, it means there are still people in Korisan loyal to him. I'll find out who they are and – " A sudden stab of pain in her chest made her stop. It took a moment before she could continue. "Send word to my soldiers that they are to search every inch of Teleria until they find him."

"Will there be anything else, your *Majesty*?" Delaine asked.

Ciara ignored Delaine's tone. "That will be all."

Delaine turned and knocked the parcel to the floor. She picked it up and started to unwrap it. "What's this?"

"Something from one of my captains."

Delaine held up a large piece of cloth, and Ciara's heart began to race.

This was Ciara's standard; there was no mistaking the field of red, and the gold embroidery around the edges. But something had changed. Instead of a snake holding an eagle in its coils, the standard showed an eagle devouring a snake.

Ciara clutched at her chest and could hardly draw a breath. The last thing she heard was Delaine's shriek. Then everything went black.

It was after midnight when Ciara woke in a cold sweat. She'd had the dream about the standard again, but there was another dream, something far worse than watching an eagle feast on a snake.

The public square overflowed with Telerians and Baraca. Every face was filled with accusation and hatred. The guards shoved Ciara forward and bound her hands and feet to the execution block. Delaine and Rahnak stood to one side, joining the crowd in their jeers and taunts. The crowd grew quiet as someone approached the table.

Ciara's throat tightened. When the man looked down at her, there was no mistaking him.

It was Alardin.

"What are you doing?" she asked through clenched teeth.

"Correcting a mistake I made long ago."

She was about to let out a string of curses when his face changed. Now Kieran stood over her.

She fought the compulsion to wince as he drew the cold blade a-cross her skin. She tried to turn her face away, but he managed to whisper into her ear, "Your time is over. We end this now."

Before she could say anything more, the blade came down. She woke up just before he pierced her heart.

Ciara drew back her covers and lit a candle at her bedside. Just that simple effort made her short of breath. She closed her eyes, willing herself to remain calm. When she'd mustered the strength to rise, she heard footsteps padding across the thick rug.

She held up the candle and almost choked.

"Arathor."

The deposed king came closer.

"So you've come to avenge your son."

He said nothing.

Something was wrong. He was Arathor, but not Arathor.

Ciara's heart started to race again. When he put the sword tip under her chin, the room started spinning and her gut clenched.

"Kieran. No! I watched you die in the square."

Kieran remained silent, holding the sword to her neck.

"Parfavia monakot," she said.

Her spell should have pinned his arms to his sides. Instead, he dug the blade in a little more.

She grabbed the dagger she kept under her pillow and yelled for help. A dozen guards burst into her room.

Kieran gave her an amused smile and whispered, "Kel-lema men-an-dai kah-gish tehai."

A wall of flames erupted from the floor and engulfed some of the guards. The others ran from the room.

Ciara wiped the sweat from her brow and stood, trying to master the fear that was choking her. It was all she could do to think. Whatever she did, she had to distract him, stall him – anything to gain the advantage. "What will you do with me, Pretender?"

"Your time is over. We end this now."

She screamed and threw the dagger. Kieran batted it away with his hand. She lunged at him and he drove the sword into her chest. Her fury kept her from noticing the blood flowing out of her body and onto the rug. With one last effort, she heaved herself forward. He stepped aside and she stumbled to the floor. She was able to let out one last shriek as she watched Restamar coming down to take off her head.

Chapter 70

Kieran sat at Jessa's bedside and watched Sienna draw a cool cloth across Jessa's forehead. Sienna hadn't left Jessa's side since Kieran had brought Jessa to Maquoya. Now he was glad Gilrain had allowed her to stay at the front.

Sienna flicked a glance at Kieran. "I still don't understand why you can't wake her up," she said.

It wasn't the first time he'd noted frustration in Sienna's voice. Jessa's condition was beginning to wear on all of them.

He shook his head, and despite his attempt to hide his irritation, his words were strained. "I've told you before – it's an enchanted sleep."

"Didn't Gilrain wake you up from an enchanted sleep?"

"That was different," he said as he stroked Jessa's cheek. "I wanted to wake up. I don't think Jessa does."

Sienna dipped the cloth in cold water again and wrung it out. Her voice was as tight as Kieran's. "It's been three days, Kieran." She stopped and looked at him. Her eyes were red. "I'm worried about her."

Kieran covered Sienna's hand and his voice softened. "We're all worried about her." To be honest, he'd been worried about her since he'd found her.

After he'd killed Ciara and watched her body melt into the floor, Kieran rejoined Arathor, Kale, and Gilrain, and the four of them cautiously made their way from Ciara's tower to the dungeon. Kieran had called out for Jessa, but she didn't answer. His heart was thundering like the hoof beats of a hundred horses by the time they found her in the lowest level of the prison.

Nothing woke her up – not the crashing of the cell door onto the stone floor, not hoisting her over his shoulder, not fighting their way out of the castle, not even the arduous retreat through the tunnel. When they reached camp and she hadn't woken, Kieran realized that she'd put herself to sleep.

Kieran and Sienna had kept a constant vigil over her, but nothing they did seemed to help. He was beginning to wonder if she would ever wake up.

Sienna sat on the other side of the bed and yawned.

"Why don't you go get some sleep?" he said. "I'll watch her for a while."

Sienna gave him a tight smile and nodded. When she left, Kieran moved closer to Jessa. Her braid came over her shoulder and he started to roll the end of the braid between his fingers, watching the erratic rise and fall of her chest and the faint flutter of a pulse in her graceful neck. How many times had he watched her while she slept? And how many of those times had he wondered if she would ever find it in her heart to love him, all the while fearing that she wouldn't?

He rubbed his eyes and fought the sleep that called to him. At least he didn't have to worry about winning her heart. There was no doubt in his mind that she loved him with a passion and devotion as fiery as his own. That was small comfort now; it would mean nothing if she didn't wake up.

Her eyes fluttered and he hoped this was the moment. She groaned, but remained asleep. Kieran let out a slow breath and murmured the words to wake her up, words he'd spoken countless times already: "Teeshka sol Eldala." They hadn't worked before. Why did he think they would work now?

He tried reaching out to her heart again. Nothing he did could scale the wall she'd put up to protect herself from more pain. He could understand that. If he had watched her die, he would have done the same thing. Still, it grieved him to think that her beautiful heart lay bruised and battered in the dust. Was there nothing he could do to bring it back to life?

With one final effort, he desperately tried to put his mind into hers. All he found was the memory he'd seen before: Ciara thrusting the sword into his heart, and Jessa feeling his last breath.

He caressed her cheek and fingered the wisps of hair that always seemed to frame her face. For the hundredth time, he let his eyes linger on the long, dark lashes, the delicate cheekbones, the exquisite lips. She was truly the most glorious woman in Teleria. He didn't deserve her.

He leaned down and kissed her cheek. "Come back to me, Jess."

Kieran stood to stretch, and someone startled him by entering the tent. He turned and saw Dorinda, bearing a tray of fruit and bread. She set the tray on his map table and gave him a motherly scowl.

"When was the last time you ate?" she asked.

Kieran couldn't remember the last time he'd eaten. He rubbed the back of his knotted neck and took a pear from the tray. "What brings you to our camp?" he asked before taking a bite.

She drew up a chair next to the table. "I came as soon as I knew."

"Knew what?"

"The curse has ended."

Kieran almost choked. "What are you talking about?"

"Can you not see it around you?"

He took another bite and tried to think. He'd been so intent on taking care of Jessa that he hadn't paid any attention to his surroundings. "Please tell me."

"In my visions, I saw the Zagorans laying down their weapons and leaving Teleria. And there is something in the air, something I have not felt in twenty years." She smiled, deepening the wrinkles around her eyes. "It is peace, Kieran – peace among the Baraca clans, peace between Baraca and Telerians" – she put her hand over her heart – "peace inside of me."

"Peace? Is that your only evidence?"

"Is that not the greatest gift you could give your country?"

"I suppose I've been so determined to get rid of Ciara and the Zagorans that I forgot about peace. When I imagined the end of the curse, I thought we'd have solid evidence – an end to poverty, restored crops, a better life for Telerians."

"The land will not truly be restored until you give the blessing."

He cocked a brow as he finished the pear.

"I will explain more about that later."

He reached for a roll and tore it in half. "I still don't understand how this can be happening. The mystics never told me how to end the curse."

"Do you remember that I told you it would involve death?"

"Yes, but at the time, you couldn't tell me *whose* death."

"It was *your* death."

Kieran felt as if someone had tightened iron bands around his chest, forcing all the air out of his lungs. Before his legs collapsed underneath him, he sat on the edge of Jessa's bed. When he finally found his voice, all he could say was, "What?"

Dorinda moved her chair closer and ran her gnarled fingers over the back of his hand. Her wise eyes twinkled, as if she held some secret and couldn't wait to share it with him. The excitement softened her wrinkles, and Kieran could almost imagine what she'd looked like as a girl.

"When you left to rescue Jessara, I found an ancient prophecy in one of my scrolls." She paused and smiled. "It said, 'In Teleria's darkest hour, the chosen one must walk away from his kingdom and lay down his life for the one he loves most.'"

Kieran's throat tightened as he stroked Jessa's cheek. There was no denying she was the one he loved most. She would always be first in his heart, above his family, above his country, above himself.

He thought back to his last moments, stretched out on the execution block. He'd been consumed with guilt for leaving his country in Ciara's hands. To learn now that laying down his life for Jessa had won his country's freedom was almost more than he could comprehend. Following his heart had led him to the very thing that was necessary.

Dorinda put her hand on Jessa's head. The joy on her face quickly changed to concern.

"What is it?" he asked.

"Death is calling to her. She is losing her will to live."

Kieran looked down at Jessa and his heart froze. She was barely breathing and he couldn't see her pulse. "I've already tried to wake her. I don't know what else to do."

"You have to go into her heart."

He raked his fingers through his disheveled hair. "I tried. She won't let me in."

"As her Eldala, you must find a way, or she will not live past the night."

Jessa looked into the dark. She lay in a soft bed, covered with quilts. Something heavy was wrapped around her waist, and someone with a familiar earthy scent lay behind her. Most likely, it was part of her recent dreams.

How long would it take for her to stop dreaming about Kieran? And why was she dreaming at all? Hadn't she cast a dreamless sleep over herself? There must have been some part of her that wouldn't let him go. If she were lucky, she would forget him. She couldn't imagine going through the rest of her life with Kieran wandering in and out of her thoughts – if she did go on living.

He was gone, and death would be a welcome escape. She'd felt it speaking to her in her dreams, urging to let go of him and drift off into nothingness.

And then another dream would come. Kieran would call to her and tell her she had to wake up and come back to him. It was all a trick of her mind, wishful thinking. He was dead, and there was no Kieran to come back to.

But this last dream was different. This time he'd stood in front of her and held something in his hand. It was a withered rose bud. The color had faded to a dusty brown, and its fragile, wrinkled petals were falling to the ground. As he breathed on it, the rose started to come to life. And then it started to beat, as if it were a heart.

When he held it in front of her, he said, "Please take it."

"Why?"

"I need you."

"No, Kieran. You're gone, and there's no reason to live."

"But I *am* alive, Jess. I'm alive and I'm here waiting for you."

The pleading look on his face made her take the rose and put it in her chest – not that it would do any good. It couldn't be possible that Kieran was alive. More desperate thinking. But when it hid itself inside of her, she felt the pull back to life.

She strained against the darkness to see where she was. Whatever was on her waist was wrapped so tightly around her that she could hardly move, let alone breathe. Cautiously, she let her fingers travel across it – a rough hand, a thick forearm, a well-muscled bicep…

Panic gripped her throat and strangled off any rational thought. She tried to push the fear away so she could think.

She had to be in the Zagoran camp – probably in the tent of a high-ranking officer – and while she'd slept, this man had forced himself on her. She choked down the bile rising into her mouth and tried to roll off of the bed as quietly as she could.

The man tightened his hold and pulled her closer. She groaned, using all of her strength to free herself. The force of escaping threw her to the floor, and she winced as her shoulder slammed into a chair.

The man woke up, and before she could scream for help, a blue light pierced the darkness.

Then he said, "Jessara."

What was Arathor doing here? And why would he be sleeping next to her?

In a heartbeat, he drew her into his arms. The light from the stone illuminated the space between them, and she let her eyes travel over his face, noting the level brows, the square, stubbled jaw, and the black eyes. When a relieved smile spread across his handsome face, it felt as if all the air had been forced out of her lungs.

Kieran!

Before she could say his name, he hugged her so tightly against his chest that she could hardly catch a breath. She sat there stunned, listening to the thundering of their hearts.

When he finally broke the silence, his rich voice flowed over her like honey and stilled her racing mind. "Heart of my heart, I didn't think you'd wake up."

She drew back and stared at him. All she could manage to say was, "You're alive."

"Yes, alive and here with you."

"But how, when…?"

He brushed his thumb over her lips. "I don't know. All that matters now is that you've come back to me." He leaned in and kissed her. The way his lips gently danced with hers and the familiar song he evoked erased any doubt that this was her Eldala. Suddenly, it felt like all the fallen petals of her life were coming back together.

When she kissed him back, she savored the sweet song of reunion flowing between them. It didn't matter why he was alive; it just mattered that he *was* alive, tucked safely in her heart.

Chapter 71

A lazy morning breeze ruffled the tent flaps, and Jessa's eyes fluttered open. When she looked around, she knew she wasn't dreaming. This was Kieran's tent, and he was alive. Her heart skipped a few beats when she saw him just a few steps away from her, bare-backed, pouring water into a ceramic basin.

Her breath caught in her throat, and an aching melody wrapped itself around her whole body. She'd seen him this way before, so why was her body acting as if this were the first time?

Without a sound, she turned on her side and watched him.

She'd never thought that a man could be beautiful – until she'd met Kieran. She saw it in the way he wielded a sword, in the way he rode Fallon – in the way he looked at her when their eyes locked. Now she saw it in the way the muscles of his back moved as he scooped the water up and splashed it over his face and hair. The drops caught in the sharp whiskers on his serious jaw, then trickled down his neck and onto his broad shoulders.

He ran a towel over his face and surveyed himself in the fragment of mirror hanging in front of him, running the back of his hand over his jaw line, as if trying to decide what to do with a few days of growth. He turned to reach for the razor and stopped when he saw her.

In a heartbeat, he was at her side. His intoxicating masculine scent pushed its way into her brain until she could hardly think. When she looked at him, she saw a new fierceness in his eyes that was frightening and wonderful all at once. How could he be any more handsome than he already was?

Without thinking, she reached up to trail her fingers over his face and down his neck to the scar over his heart. "I still can't believe you're real."

"Then believe this." He caught her hand and kissed each finger. When she let out the familiar soft sigh, his eyes widened and he took her in his arms to capture her lips. She winced when his stubbled jaw grazed her chin.

He laughed and kissed her cheek. "I should do something about this."

"I once told you I preferred you with a beard," she said, remembering the day when he'd asked for her opinion.

And then the bizarre changes in her life startled her all over again. In Korisan, she was a slave. Now she was almost the queen of Teleria.

He gave her a crooked, boyish smile. "What about now?"

"The beard is better. Just don't kiss me while it's growing out."

Almost immediately, he scooped her into his lap and started to caress her neck with his lips. "Do you think you could stop me?"

She pretended to push him away. "I suppose I could try."

When he pulled her closer and playfully nibbled at her earlobe, she couldn't help but giggle. "Why would you *want* to stop me?" he whispered.

He was right. Why *would* she want to stop him?

A few hours later, Jessa sat up in bed, watching in wonder as one person after another made their way into Kieran's tent. After receiving Kale and Elisa, Gilrain and Sienna, and finally Arathor and Tiana, Jessa had lost track of how many people had come to give reports of the battle or to bend their knee to the new king. Despite the stream of visitors, Jessa knew that Kieran was constantly aware of her, and that it took great effort for him to concentrate on anyone else.

Now the most surprising group of visitors pushed their way into the tent.

Riordan and Toren stood protectively in front of their king as a dozen of Ciara's soldiers knelt before him. Jessa sensed that Kieran couldn't decide whether to be angry or amused with them. Whatever his mood, his tone was gruff.

"Why are you here?" he asked.

The soldiers gave each other quick, frightened glances. One finally worked up the courage to speak. "Sir, we've come to give fealty."

Kieran's brows knit together and he rubbed his newly shaved chin. Jessa smiled. He'd decided that giving his visitors a good first impression was more important than her desire to have a bearded Eldala.

"How do I know Delaine didn't send you to spy on us?" Kieran asked.

The spokesman's eyes widened in apparent astonishment. "The princess fled from Korisan. No one knows where she is."

Kieran motioned to one of his men. "Send someone to find out if this man is telling the truth." Kieran motioned to another man to escort Ciara's soldiers from the tent. Before they left, Kieran said, "If I find out you're lying, I'll have your heads."

When they were gone, he turned to Gilrain. "What do you think?"

"You spent more time with Delaine than I did…"

Kieran scowled and then looked at Jessa. "And what do you think, Jess?"

Jessa thought she was just a spectator, and so it took her a moment to realize he was seriously asking for her opinion. "Delaine is a vain, selfish woman, but I don't think she has a head for planning revenge."

"Something Ciara never had a chance to teach her," Kieran said.

"You shouldn't underestimate her. I sensed almost as much evil in her as in Ciara." Jessa narrowed her eyes. "And from the way she used delendia on you… it's clear she knows something about enchantments."

Kieran's face darkened, and Jessa felt the irritation surging through him. It was obviously still a sore subject for him.

When his annoyance had passed, he said, "Jess is right. I want someone to find Delaine and watch her. She won't plan anything yet, but she might in the future."

A contingency of Baraca warriors interrupted their conversation. Jessa nearly fell off the bed when she saw Stefan in their midst. Several Hada council members followed. They all bowed low at the waist, and Kieran stood to greet them. Stefan gave Jessa a quick glance and then turned his attention back to Kieran.

"I have news from Ithil. We expelled the Zagorans from the Hada fortress, and have come to give fealty to the true king of Teleria."

Kieran hid his surprise from Stefan, but Jessa felt it. He was almost as shocked as she was.

"What brought this about?" Kieran asked.

Stefan gave him a crafty smile. "The council members were as contrite as scolded children when I told them you had allowed me to come."

"And Galen?"

One of the council members frowned. "Galen left the council chambers, swearing like a madman. We expelled him from the clan, along with his wife, Elena."

Jessa was surprised by how much that news pleased her.

"Who is the new calafar?" Kieran asked.

Stefan's face flushed. "I am."

Kieran chuckled and extended his hand to Stefan in a traditional Baraca greeting. "Congratulations, Calafar Stefan. May this be the beginning of a new alliance between the Hada clan and Telerians."

Kieran felt Jessa's amusement mirroring his own and laughed quietly to himself. Stefan's news was certainly unexpected, but greatly appreciated.

Now Sahbél was standing in front of him. The two friends embraced, but when Kieran scanned Sahbél's grave features, his amusement vanished.

"What is it?" Kieran asked.

"I'm afraid I bring difficult news."

After all the encouraging news today, Kieran had almost started to believe there wouldn't be any bad news. He let out a heavy sigh. Of course there would be bad news; it was inevitable in war.

Sahbél continued. "We lost three hundred men, including Bairn and Brecken."

Kieran returned to his chair, feeling the enormous weight of commanding men to their death. He bowed his head, wishing he could give in to the grief. As king, he didn't have that luxury. Grieving would have to wait.

But his throat constricted at the memory of Brecken's hearty laugh and Mariel's tight features. Now Kieran wondered if the price of freedom had been too high.

He looked up at Sahbél. "I promised triple pay for the surviving families. Would you please deliver my personal condolences to Brecken's wife in Pomora, and make sure she gets double compensation?"

Sahbél put a hand to Kieran's shoulder and nodded. "It would be an honor to speak for my king."

When Sahbél left, Kieran turned to look at Jessa.

He'd taken great pleasure in having her in his mind all morning, and treasured the thoughts they shared. Feeling her absorb his grief now – and adding to it with her own – was almost more than he could bear. He was about to go to her when his uncle burst into the tent.

"You won't believe this," Loric said, hardly able to contain his excitement. "One minute the Zagorans had the upper hand, and the next, they were stumbling around the field. When they realized something was wrong, most of them fled. We killed the rest." He gave Kieran a curious look. "Can you explain it?"

Kieran let out a long, slow breath. "A lot's happened in the last few days. But trust me when I tell you that the curse is broken."

Loric's eyes widened. "How?"

"I'll be glad to tell you, but not today."

"I also have difficult news," said Loric.

Kieran braced himself.

"I'm sorry to report that we lost more than two hundred."

"And Braeden?"

"He fell in battle," Loric said.

First Brecken and Bairn, now Braeden. Kieran couldn't think of anyone – outside of his family and Jessa – whom he would miss more, except perhaps Sahbél. Braeden had been a cherished friend, a faithful companion, and a trusted advisor.

Kieran closed his eyes against the grief threatening to drown him. Loric left, and Kieran motioned for Toren. "How many more are waiting to see me?"

"At least a dozen, sir."

"Please give them my apologies and tell them to come back tomorrow."

Toren nodded. "What should I tell Dorinda?"

All Kieran wanted was to be alone with Jessa, and he was tempted to send Dorinda away, but he knew that if she was here, she had something important to say. And he had something important to ask her.

"Tell her I'll see her in a few minutes."

Toren nodded and left.

Kieran looked up at Jessa. Tears streamed down her face. Watching her only magnified his sorrow. He sat next to her on the bed and put his arms around her. "What is it, Jess?"

She gulped in a few breaths before speaking. "I can't believe Bairn is gone."

Kieran put his forehead to hers and closed his eyes. Of course. She'd told him that Bairn had been like a father to her. "I'm so sorry," Kieran said.

Suddenly, her grief engulfed him, and unlike the morning when she girded him for battlc, there were no barriers between them. His heart slid easily into hers, and for a time, their shared sorrow seemed to fill the tent like a fog. As the faces of lost loved ones drifted into his mind, Kieran finally let himself feel the anguish of loss.

His throat tightened at the thought of Mariel and her unborn child. How would she survive without her husband? No amount of gold could take away the sting of Brecken's death.

Jessa put her hand to Kieran's heart and continued to weep. He stroked the top of her head.

"I'm sorry you lost Braeden," she said through her tears. "I know you were close."

"He taught me about being Baraca, and he convinced me I had to marry you."

She wiped away a tear and gave him a puzzled look. "Convinced?"

Kieran tugged at her braid. "Well, you didn't make it easy for me, did you?"

"No, but all that matters is that I'm here now." Her voice faltered. "And we're together." Then she started to cry again.

He tilted her chin up. "What is it?"

"I should have gone to Morigon. Then you wouldn't have had to…"

Her face wrinkled in misery and she pressed herself into him. His arms surrounded her, and he let her sob into his chest. Then he felt something new. Just underneath her sorrow was an overwhelming sense of guilt.

"What's this about?" he asked.

She gripped his shirt, and when she spoke, her voice was muffled. He heard her more with his heart than with his ears. "It's my fault Ciara killed you."

"*Your* fault?"

"If she hadn't captured me… if you hadn't come after me… I almost lost you because of my stupid pride." She took a few gasping breaths. "I felt you die. I wanted to die with you."

He pulled her closer and felt her deep anguish. Watching him die had almost killed her. Maybe knowing the truth would ease the guilt she still felt.

"When I died, the curse ended."

She pulled back and stared at him, wide-eyed.

"Dorinda found a prophecy that said, 'In Teleria's darkest hour, the chosen one must walk away from his kingdom and lay down his life for the one he loves most.'"

"Then…"

"My love for you saved Teleria."

Dorinda gratefully took the cup of tea Kieran offered and settled herself in a chair. Kieran thought she looked more like a queen than an ancient mystic.

"You are a sad one, son of Arathor," she said.

"The burdens of war," he replied.

He sat on the floor just in front of Jessa's bed. Jessa moved closer and rested her hands on his shoulders. He took one of her hands and kissed her palm.

"Can you tell me how I came back to life?" he asked.

Dorinda smiled and sipped from her cup. "I have an inkling, but I want to hear your story first. What do you remember?"

Kieran shuddered and took a deep breath. "I remember Ciara plunging Restamar into my heart and Jessa throwing herself across me."

"And after that?" Dorinda asked.

"I don't remember dying. It was more like floating away on a raft at sea. I smelled the clean air and heard the cries of the gulls overhead. I don't know how long I was there, but I remember thinking it was incomplete – *I* was incomplete without Jessa."

"Did you hear her calling to you?"

Kieran placed Jessa's hand over his heart. "No, but I sensed her grief."

Dorinda looked at Jessa. "Did you call to him?"

"I didn't think he could hear me." Jessa let out a long, slow breath. "Wait. I do remember. I did call out to him."

"And then you came back?" Dorinda asked.

"It wasn't that difficult," Kieran said. "I knew Jessa needed me, so I willed my mind to return to my body and my heart started beating again."

Jessa ran her fingers through Kieran's hair, and he had to stop to regain his concentration. "I woke up in Arathor's tent. Gilrain, Kale, and Arathor were there, talking. I can still remember the shock on their faces when I sat up. We went through the tunnels to get to the castle, I killed Ciara, and we went to find Jessa."

Dorinda took another sip of tea. "That matches the legends I have heard."

"Legends?" Jessa asked.

Dorinda had that secretive look on her face again. What did this woman *not* know?

"More than two hundred years ago, a mystic spoke words of prophecy over two Eldala. He said that their connection would be so strong that death would not separate them. Most people thought it meant when one died, the other would die, or that they would be able to speak to each other across the chasm of death. Many years later, the man died in battle. The woman was so distraught that her tears of grief were strong enough to bring him back to life."

Kieran turned to face Jessa, who by now was very still and very quiet. Their eyes locked, and when Jessa finally spoke, it was in a whisper.

"Are you saying that my grief called Kieran back from death?"

"Yes. The two of you share a connection so strong that death will not separate you."

Dorinda rose from her chair and set her tea cup on the table. "You will find that connection very helpful when you restore King Alardin's blessing."

"You mentioned that before," said Kieran. "Please explain."

"The blessing came from Alardin, but it will take both of you, as completed Eldala, to restore the blessing."

"Completed Eldala?" Kieran asked.

"She means married Eldala," Jessa murmured.

Dorinda's eyes twinkled. She smiled and thanked Kieran for the tea. "Now I must go. I have other matters to attend to."

Kieran watched her leave, certain this wasn't the last time they would see Dorinda.

He turned to Jessa and pulled her to her feet. His beautiful Eldala had called him back from death. He looked into her soft black eyes, sensing all of her admiration and passion for him. Her lips were trembling – until he covered them with his mouth and let himself feel the familiar torment of wanting all of her and not being able to have her yet.

Chapter 72

Jessa breathed in the fragrant sea air. It couldn't have been a more beautiful day. The sun shone out of a turquoise sky and sparkled on the water stretched out before her. Beneath her feet, pink and yellow flowers poked their heads through an emerald carpet of grass.

It felt like spring, so it was hard to believe that it was really the first month of winter. Now that Ciara was dead and the curse had been lifted, it took very little effort for Arathor to eliminate the winter and provide several weeks of spring for Kieran and Jessa's wedding celebrations.

When Kieran had suggested that they marry near the sea, Jessa couldn't have been happier. And when he led the wedding party to Kolachel, she couldn't have been more surprised. How appropriate that they would exchange vows overlooking the beach where he'd found the shells – and where she'd asked him when they would be married.

She still remembered the hunger they both felt when he'd kissed her in the sand.

In a few hours, their cravings would be satisfied.

She pushed the thought away. If she dwelt on what the end of this day held for her and Kieran, she would be a wreck before she ever spoke her vows. It was one thing to live with the anticipation of desire, and quite another to know that it would soon be fulfilled. Better to not think about it.

If only her mind would cooperate. It kept returning to earlier in the day. While Sienna, Tiana, and Elisa had arranged her hair into intricate braids, their knowing glances and beaming smiles only added to Jessa's nervous excitement.

Jessa stood in the tent's doorway and tried to focus again on the expanse of blue sea that seemed to go on forever. The breeze tugged at her dress and she smiled. Elisa had made this dress just for her, and now Jessa ran her hands over the white satin, accented with silver and gold threads that matched the cords in her hair. The cool fabric reminded her of rose petals, and it flowed over her body like cream. Full-length sleeves dripped off of her wrists, and a wide v-neckline rested on her shoulders.

She let out a slow breath and watched Stefan walk towards her. When she took his arm so he could escort her to Kieran, she felt every part of herself tremble. How was she going to make it through this day?

As they walked through the crowd, Jessa tried to concentrate on the people who turned to watch her. She recognized only a few – Kale and Elisa, Sorina and Loric, her mother, Dorinda, Marcus, Neera, and some of Kieran's companions. A tear rolled down her cheek as she wished that Bairn, Braeden, and her father could be there to see her wedding.

Then her eyes were drawn to the edge of the bluff.

Arathor faced her, ready to oversee the wedding vows. Gilrain stood to Arathor's left, and Sienna waited at his right. And just in front of Arathor was her Eldala.

The wind played with Kieran's sun-lightened hair, and the smile on his impossibly handsome face couldn't have been any wider. Just underneath a white silk shirt that accentuated his broad shoulders, she saw his Keldar stone, glowing bright blue. She felt her own stone glow in response.

When she finally reached him, her heart was dancing to a wild rhythm, and she could hardly get a breath. She took his arm, feeling her body hum with such anticipation that she had to steady herself against his side.

Arathor, looking as proud as Jessa had ever seen him, cleared his throat, and the crowd quieted. "We are here today to witness the exchange of vows between Aiden and Jessara."

Kieran clasped her hands and took a deep breath. She looked up into his eyes and tried to concentrate on his words. She barely heard them for the heartbeat pounding in her ears.

"Jessara, my Eldala, heart of my own heart. In front of our family and friends, I gladly pledge my eternal love and devotion to you alone. I owe you my very life, and it is that life I now give to you, without reservation."

Jessa's chin trembled as he slipped a delicate gold band onto her finger and kissed her hand.

She looked up and let her eyes caress his level brows, his sparkling black eyes, and his strong, bearded jaw. Was this really happening? When she first saw him, asleep in Korisan, she hadn't dared to hope that his heart would ever be hers, or that she would be standing in front of him, working up the courage to recite her vows.

"Kieran, my Eldala, heart of my own heart. I promise to love you and no other for the rest of my days, honoring and cherishing you as my husband. To you and no other do I give myself, without reservation." Then she placed a matching gold band on his finger.

Arathor beamed as he said, "You may now kiss your bride."

Kieran put his arms around Jessa's waist, lifted her off the ground, and gave her a slow, deep kiss that left her breathless and light-headed.

When they came apart, Arathor turned them to face the crowd and said, "I now present Aiden and Jessara, husband and wife, king and queen of Teleria."

Still recovering from Kieran's intoxicating kiss, Jessa was only dimly aware of the applause coming from their friends and family.

The rest of the day was a blur of feasting, dancing, toasting, and more than a few ravenous glances and unabashed kisses from Kieran. When evening finally came, Elisa, Sienna, and Tiana helped Jessa prepare for her first night with her husband.

Kieran waited impatiently outside Jessa's tent, listening to the women fuss over his bride. When she finally emerged, he almost stopped breathing. A blue silk robe clung to every delicious curve, and her satin hair was pulled back into a single braid. That delicate fringe of hair framed her already exquisite face, and everything in him wanted to partake of her right now. He was almost sorry he'd arranged a special tent for them on the shore.

She lightly kissed his cheek, and his already thundering heart galloped wildly in his chest. He scooped her up in his arms and lifted her to Fallon's saddle. Sitting in front of her, he clapped his heels to the horse's flanks, and aching desire surged through him as she put her arms around his waist and rested her cheek on his back. By the time they reached the tent, he could hardly think, and it took a moment before he could survey the area.

The moon dancing on the water and the soft lapping of the waves against the shore only enhanced this already perfect night.

Kieran dismounted and lifted Jessa from the saddle. She took his arm and he pushed the tent flap aside for her, hoping she would appreciate his preparations. Fur pelts strewn with rose petals covered the feather bed and spilled onto the floor. A dozen candles burned all around them, and the heat from a coal brazier drifted into the air.

He came up behind her and wrapped his arms around her waist before whispering into her rose-scented hair. “Do you like it?”

His efforts were rewarded when she turned to him and smiled. Then her brows drew together in a question when she saw the trays of food on the table.

“Provisions for two weeks, m’lady.”

“Two weeks?”

He led her to the fruit tray. “For the Eldala-rasta.”

“Eldala-rasta?”

“Dorinda said that Eldala cannot be truly completed until they’ve spent two weeks together… alone.”

Her dark eyes widened in understanding and she gave him a sultry smile.

“So are you hungry?” he asked.

She untucked his shirt and slid her fiery hands up his sides and onto his chest. “Yes,” she whispered, “but not for food.”

He reached for the belt of her robe, but before he could untie it, she put the end of her braid in his hand.

“First this, Eldala.”

With trembling fingers, he slowly worked the braid out of her hair. When he was done, his hands danced through the silken waterfall flowing over her back. His lips nuzzled the soft skin just under her ear, then traveled down her neck, and onto her shoulder.

She let out a rough moan and dug her fingers into his hair. Her slow, searching kiss made his heart beat out a frantic rhythm. He pulled her closer to deepen the kiss, achingly aware of her soft, tantalizing curves, her enticing scent, and the sizzling melody her touch aroused. When he could deny his cravings no longer, he swept her up and carried her to the fur-covered bed.

Despite the intimate heart connection they already shared, nothing could have prepared them for the fiery symphony that exploded between them when they came together as one flesh. Their rapturous cries split the silence of the night, and a playful sea breeze sent the blessing of Alardin dancing across Teleria.

Acknowledgements

I would like to express my heart-felt appreciation to the many people who were part of my writing journey. Thank you…

Jody C. ~ for giving me a voice on your homeschool message board, and for mentioning the *Brave Writer* program for homeschooling moms.

Teresa W. ~ for encouraging me to buy *The Writer's Jungle*, and for helping me with my first attempts at writing poetry.

Julie B. ~ for pouring your writing knowledge into *The Writer's Jungle*, and for encouraging homeschool moms to be brave writers.

Cindy in Texas and Richelle in Minnesota ~ for cheering me on while I hammered out my 53,000 words in 2005.

Donetta J. ~ for being my NaNoWriMo partner and for cheer-ing me on. I'm looking forward to reading your works-in-progress.

Trisha M. ~ for encouraging me to start over, for talking me down from my "depressed writer" ledges, and for your excellent photographic skills.

Karen H. ~ for being my writing mentor through your blog and your *Legend of the Guardian King* books.

Julie C. and Heather M. ~ for your fine editing. I'm a better writer because of it.

Brenda Z. ~ for knowing just where to put your knuckles and elbows in my knotted neck and shoulders.

Rochelle L. ~ for dolling me up for my author photo-shoot. You're an extraordinary make-up artist and a Beautiful Soul.

Kristal S. ~ for being my writing partner. It helped to have someone who understood exactly what I was going through.

Countless cheerleaders, including ~ Judy G., Laurie F., my "Captivating" group, Michelle P., Nancy D., Joe's "Wild at Heart" group, Kimberly and Doug G., and the ladies from the "Homemade Coffee Shoppe."

My parents and grandparents ~ for having the courage to write, and for instilling in me a love of writing and reading.

My dear family ~ for believing in me when I didn't believe in myself, and for encouraging me to continue when it seemed like the writing would never end.

Anna ~ for being as patient as a five-year-old could be when she wanted to spend time with her mom and all her mom wanted to do was finish the next chapter. I hope you understand some day why I had to do this.

Joshua ~ for names like "Korisan" and "Rahnak," and for asking me to get off the computer to spend time with you. You're a great kid.

Brandon ~ for helping me imagine Teleria (I wouldn't have had Arathor, gurithents, or the harakan without you), and for your encouraging words: "This is the first childish thing you've ever done" and "I'd watch a movie of your book."

Joe ~ for your loving support, for answering all those "guy" questions, for describing fight scenes, for reading over countless drafts, and for assuring me that everything would turn out okay. I couldn't have written this story without you.

Photo by Trisha Mason © 2007

Michelle Gregory grew up in Tucson, Arizona. From an early age, she loved reading and writing. She received a Bachelor's degree in Elementary Education from Oklahoma Baptist University in 1987. Feeling a call from God to pursue her love for writing, she began her first literary venture in 2005, and will soon be working on her second novel.

Michelle and her husband of twenty years reside in Mesa, Arizona, and enjoy homeschooling their three children, as well as indulging in frequent getaways. When Michelle isn't writing, she also enjoys blogging, playing with her kids, watching chick movies, working on her scrapbooks, and reading a good book.

You can read her blog at michellegregory.blogspot.com, or contact her at MichelleDGregory@gmail.com.